Mission in the East

Path of the Ranger, Book 14

Pedro Urvi

COMMUNITY:
Mail: pedrourvi@hotmail.com
Facebook: https://www.facebook.com/PedroUrviAuthor/
My Website: http://pedrourvi.com
Twitter: https://twitter.com/PedroUrvi

Translation by:
Christy Cox

Edited by:
Mallory Brandon Bingham

DEDICATION

To my good friend Guiller.

Thank you for all your support since day one.

Content

MAP

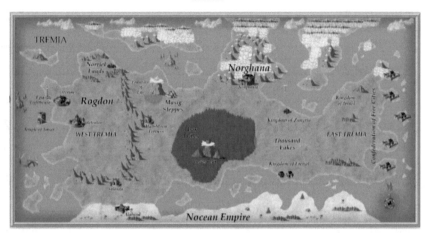

Chapter 1

Lasgol sat with his eyes closed at the bow of the Norghanian war ship as it eagerly sailed the northern seas heading east. He could feel the cool sea breeze on his face and was grateful for it. He had been concentrating for a good while, working on repairing the fragile bridge between his mind and his inner pool of power. The task was arduous and tedious, so he had ended up sitting beside the half lion, half eagle figurehead. There, the breeze and spattering from the waves cooled him off, which made the task easier to bear.

As usual, he had begun by calling upon his *Aura Presence* skill and using it on himself—to identify his own mind, body, and power auras—and then focusing on the first one. Going through his mind and finding the tiny white spot where the bridge began was a long, hard process Lasgol wanted to improve on. He found it frustrating having to look for the bridge every time. He did not understand why he could not immediately identify it after having looked for it so many times.

"If you want anything in life, you have to work hard and with determination in order to get it," he murmured to himself.

He let the frustration pass and focused on repairing the bridge. For this he used his *Ranger Healing* skill, which was not even remotely as efficient or powerful as Lasgol wanted it to be. But at least it worked, which is what really mattered. Changing one step of the bridge from white to green took him an eternity of time and effort. But he was beginning to see progress, and the entrance was no longer Izotza's icy white but the strong green of Lasgol's magic.

"Secure that rope!" Captain Ulmendren shouted to his sailors from the ship's stern.

The officers' shouts and the sailors running at his back nearly broke his concentration, but Lasgol managed to remain focused on the bridge and continued applying his energy to repairing it. It might take him his whole life, but he was going to get to the other end of the bridge, to his pool of inner energy. He was intent on it and he was not going to give up.

He now worked on it rigorously every morning, if possible. He made himself do it because he knew it was important. He could not let the fragile link break. If for some reason—and there were usually several—he could not do it in the morning, he worked on the link in the evening before going to bed. Being consistent and working every day on the repair was the only way of achieving it: he was well aware of that.

Helping Healer Edwina find the rupture spots to heal Engla's and Gerd's minds had strengthened his wish to develop his magic power. And for this to happen, he first had to heal himself. It was really more like repairing himself, but when he thought of it that way, he felt a little weird. Regardless, he was proud of himself for helping his friend and the Elder, and that was why he was determined to complete the process of repairing his link, no matter how hard it might be. He was aware that at the pace he was going it might take forever, but even so he would continue and enjoy every little success, no matter how small it might appear.

He focused on checking his mind's aura. He was not sure whether it was wishful thinking or reality, but he felt that with the passing of time he was beginning to find it less difficult to locate his bridge, and this gave him the strength to keep trying. He wished Gerd could recover soon and join them in their next mission—he missed the gentle giant and regretted leaving him at the Shelter—but Edwina had not finished healing him.

He heard footsteps behind his back, and by the sound they were not his friends but the heavier footsteps of large, muscular men: Norghanian soldiers, members of the ship's crew. He heard the sound of the war axes hanging from their belts banging against their scale armor and knew they were not doing sailor tasks but warrior work, otherwise they would not be wearing their armor and weapons. Even though they were moving behind him and his eyes were shut he could almost see them—it was amazing how his Ranger training had sharpened his senses.

The Panthers were resting, minding their own business under the sails with Ona.

"There's the weirdo meditating about life again," Viggo commented with a face that clearly meant he found it was ridiculous.

"He's not meditating," Astrid corrected him. "He's working on repairing his link like Izotza, the Lady of the Glaciers, told him to," she explained while she cleaned her Assassin's knives. She was sitting on the deck beside the main mast.

"Some scholars believe meditation is good for the person," Egil added. He was sitting a little to one side, reading the compendium tome Sylvia had given him at the Camp. "It's a way to relax the body, calm the nerves, and pacify the mind. It's something I've always wanted to learn but haven't had the time so far; some day I hope to do it, I find it a most fascinating discipline."

"How strange you should find anything fascinating... but if it's good for the nerves you know who we can test it on," Viggo said with a nod toward Nilsa, who was listening but was also alert to what the captain and the nobleman who was accompanying them were doing.

"Very funny," she replied without sparing a glance in his direction. "My nerves are much better," she assured him.

"Well it's barely noticeable," Viggo said sarcastically.

"I don't know why you had to make him an anti-sickness potion," Nilsa said reproachfully to Egil. "He looks a lot better, but the journey is a lot more pleasant when this numbskull spends it dizzy and throwing up into the sea."

"You know, she's not wrong," Ingrid said with a grin as she checked her bows. They had been at sea for two weeks now and the sea salt and air were not good for weapons, particularly precision ones.

"I took pity on his poor, dizzy soul," Egil said, looking saintly. "Besides, the remedy is in Sylvia's book. I can't not make it if I know how. That would be bad, and I'm not a bad person."

Nilsa turned to Egil with a look that said, "I don't see why not."

"You're too good to him," she said accusingly.

"I'm a Healer Guard: it's my duty to help you if you're not feeling well, get sick, or are wounded," Egil said, raising his arms as if he had no choice but to intervene.

"Well, by healing him you make the rest of us sick," Nilsa said with a feigned face of horror.

"She's right there too," Ingrid said, chuckling.

"My sweet love, are you in a bad mood today that you feel the need to mess with me so much?" Viggo asked her in a false lovesick voice.

Ingrid looked up from her bows and glared at him reproachfully.

"Don't use that foolish nonsense with me unless you want me to get really angry."

"Of course, my lovely Blondie."

Ingrid made a fist and threatened him.

"You're going to get what for..."

"I'd better go and see what the sailors have to say. I might get myself some beer. There's no self-respecting Norghanian ship that doesn't carry the odd barrel of beer."

"Don't get into trouble," Astrid warned him, raising an eyebrow.

"Trouble? Me? Never," Viggo replied with a roguish smile, and went off to chat up a couple of soldiers who were resting beside the starboard rowing benches.

Lasgol went back to the group, and Ona welcomed him by rubbing her head against his thigh.

"How did it go? You look tired," Astrid asked him with concern.

"It went well," Lasgol replied, sitting beside her on the deck. "Well, as well as it can go. I'll keep trying tomorrow."

"It sounds like torture," Nilsa commented as she watched him with a frown.

"It is, kind of... I won't lie to you," he admitted with a grin.

"Do you want me to make you a tonic to clear up your head from the aches and heaviness?" Egil asked in an attempt to be helpful.

"There's no need," Lasgol replied, waving the matter aside. "I appreciate it, but I have to learn to bear it. I can't depend on medicine every time I get a headache for something self-induced."

"Ugh, such a twisted statement gives me a headache," Nilsa laughed.

Astrid joined her, "Yes, that was twisted."

"Don't be cruel... what I mean is that because this is something I have to do every day, I'd better get used to it."

"That's a wise thought," Egil nodded. "Medicine should be saved for ailments that really require them. We can't just give our bodies concoctions for every minor discomfort we experience. Medicines have secondary effects on our system and we should use them carefully. A healthy lifestyle and good nourishment are what's recommended to reach old age."

"Well, that's perfect, because we spend our life traveling from one place to the next, eating cured meat and salted foods," said Nilsa.

"Today they're preparing smoked herring for lunch," Ingrid said. "The cook has already started, I'm beginning to smell it …"

"Well, let's try to eat as healthy as we can, within our special circumstances," Egil replied with a grin.

Nilsa turned and wrinkled her nose.

"I'm not sure I like this mission we've been charged with in the east," she commented, scanning the immense dark-blue sea in that direction.

"It's probably because we barely know anything about it," Ingrid said.

Nilsa nodded.

Egil looked up at the clouded sky.

"Important missions are usually shrouded with secrecy," he told them.

"I guess it's so they don't get thwarted before they even begin," said Astrid.

"Irrefutable, my dear Assassin," Egil smiled at her. "The less we know about a delicate mission, the more chance of success."

"Dolbarar already told us it was delicate and of the utmost importance," Lasgol said. "He has the details," he added with a nod toward the nobleman beside the captain. "And I hope he reveals them to us soon. I don't like going on a mission blindly."

"You're not the only one. I'm quite uneasy myself," Ingrid admitted. "Traveling abroad, to the far east of the continent, on a mission we know nothing about and which in all probability will be complicated, isn't something I like at all."

"So has our beloved King Thoran requested, and so we must comply," Egil said sarcastically.

"Well, at least you take it with humor," Nilsa said, looking unhappy.

"I don't fully trust this Malthe Larsen. He looks too friendly for a Norghanian nobleman," said Ingrid, looking at him out of the corner of her eye. He was a man in his early fifties with Norghanian features—tall and thin, with refined looks. His hair was blond with silver streaks and he wore it well trimmed, as well as his goatee. Every time a breath of air ruffled his hair he would pass his hand over it to smooth it back into place. He was dressed in quality clothing and he carried a light sword and dagger at his waist—both exquisite weapons not from the north, but he did not look like a great fighter.

"Not all Norghanian nobles are unpleasant," Egil replied with a smile.

"You know what I mean," Ingrid said. "He sounds too sugary when he speaks."

"That's because he's an Ambassador of the King, and they tend to be overly kind and vague, as well as secretive and highly intelligent," Egil explained. "That's what they teach them in diplomacy, a difficult art and certainly quite fascinating."

"Yeah, he has a reputation at court for being clever and a good diplomat," Nilsa said. "I'd already heard about him. He spends a lot of time away from the kingdom on official missions: treaties, dealings with other kingdoms, that kind of stuff."

"Well, he's been put in charge," Astrid said.

"That gives us the assumption that this must be a diplomatic mission then," Egil commented.

"It would be a change..." said Nilsa, ironically.

"Look," Lasgol said with a nod toward the stern.

Captain Ulmendren and Ambassador Malthe Larsen were coming toward them with Viggo walking beside them.

"They're coming to speak to us," said Nilsa.

"What can my darling dumbass have done now?" Ingrid said with a snort as she watched him approach with the captain and the ambassador.

"We'll soon find out," Astrid said as she watched the three men approach, her keen gaze not missing a detail.

Captain Ulmendren and the nobleman stopped before them. Viggo sat down beside Ingrid with his legs crossed. She gave him a look filled with doubt. Viggo smiled at her like a good boy.

"Royal Eagles," the Captain greeted them respectfully.

"Captain Ulmendren," Ingrid replied, standing up to return the greeting.

"I must announce that drinking and gambling are forbidden on board my ship," the Captain said. "These are two activities that always end up in brawls and disorder. I will not allow that on my ship. Whoever I find breaking that rule will be thrown overboard," he added, eying Viggo.

"It's allowed on other ships," Viggo said.

"Not on mine," the Captain replied sternly.

"Well, that makes the journey boring..." Viggo protested.

"There will be no drinking or gambling," Ingrid promised the Captain as she glared at Viggo, who simply shrugged and made a face.

"We've left behind the coast of the Kingdom of Zangria and are passing the lower area of the Island of Fish," Captain Ulmendren informed them. "Once we're clear of it we'll be off the coasts of the Kingdom of Irinel."

"Wow, is that where we're headed?" Nilsa asked, unable to hold back.

"That is correct," the captain confirmed. "We'll dock at the coastal city of Kensale. You'll disembark there, and I will wait for you at port until you've completed your mission for the return journey."

"What are we supposed to do there?" Ingrid asked directly. Her tone revealed she was not pleased with the lack of information.

"My orders are to bring you to this city and wait for your return," the Captain said, looking at the nobleman.

"I will explain the mission to them, thank you very much, Captain Ulmendren," the Ambassador dismissed him with a slight nod.

The Captain nodded as well and left them.

"Well, I believe I owe the famous Royal Eagles an explanation," he said in a pleasant voice and with a smile.

"Yes, I believe it is time for an explanation, Malthe Larsen," Ingrid said.

"You see, I have specific orders from his Majesty Thoran which I must follow to the letter," he explained. "If it were up to me I would tell you all about the mission, but I can't."

"Dolbarar told us to follow your instructions, and we'll do that, but we'd appreciate any information you can give us," Ingrid said.

"I'll do what I can to inform you," the Ambassador smiled at her. "For now all I can say is that, after we dock, we'll head to the capital of Irinel. I must deal with their monarch over important matters."

"Is that our mission? To escort you to the King of Irinel?" Ingrid asked blankly.

Malthe gave her a big smile.

"That is part of the mission. The rest you will know in due time," he replied, and with a deep bow the Ambassador turned back toward the stern of the ship.

Ingrid watched him leave with a frown.

"I tell you, I don't trust this diplomat at all..."

"Well, let's complete this mission as soon as we can and go back home," Astrid said.

"Are you in a hurry? Don't you want to enjoy the ship's voyage and discover the kingdom of Irinel?" Viggo asked with irony.

"I want to have a talk with my uncle—an intense one," said Astrid, and her eyes shone with lethal gleam. "There are many things he needs to explain and which I want to understand. Especially the attack on Lasgol and everything related to his strange 'quest.'"

"And the theft of the Orb," added Nilsa.

"Yeah, I'd also like to know who that warlock with the dragon-pommel swords, that Drugan Volskerian, is," said Egil. "And what he's up to. I'm afraid it might be important and unsettling."

"Camu's worried and wants to know what happened to the Orb," Lasgol said. "I also want to know what all this mess is about and why we're in the middle of it," he finished, putting his hand to his head where he had received the blow.

Ona growled once and showed her fangs.

"Why, it's easy to understand. It's because the weirdo and the know-it-all are always getting into trouble, and if not them it's the bug. That's why we're in this mess," Viggo said, entirely convinced of it.

"It appears we have a lot to investigate and learn when we get back from this mission," said Astrid.

"Yes we do, and we will. We have to find out everything—find the culprits and discover their motives," Ingrid said.

"Well, once again we're going to have a whale of a time," Viggo stated in an acid tone.

Lasgol had a feeling his friend was right. Solving the various mysteries was going to be complicated and very dangerous.

Chapter 2

"Can anyone tell me why this is called Fish Island?" Viggo asked as he looked at the island from the port side of the ship.

Egil stood beside him and looked at the island in the distance. It was not clear, but they could make out some high cliffs.

"I can answer that question," he said gaily.

"Well, I'm shocked you would have the answer to any question," Viggo replied, feigning astonishment.

Egil laughed at his mocking statement.

"I'll show you so you can better understand," Egil said and ran back to the foot of the mast to search among his things. He stroked Ona, who greeted him with a mournful moan, and went back to Viggo with a wood-and-leather cylinder.

"What do you have in there? A bunch of gold coins piled one on top of another?"

Egil shook his head.

"Something a lot better," Egil said excitedly.

"Surprise me," Viggo said, crossing his arms over his chest with a look that anticipated he was not going to like whatever it was.

Egil took off one of the wooden stoppers and pulled out a rolled-up map from inside the long container.

"It's a map!" he told Viggo excitedly as he unfurled it.

"I was afraid of that…" Viggo replied, shaking his head and snorting like a horse.

"A map is a great treasure," Egil nodded.

"Only in your head, wise-guy. Treasure is gold, jewels, and precious gems," Viggo retorted, and at that moment Ingrid walked by carrying two water-skins for the group and she nodded at them. "Well… and my Ingrid is a treasure too," he admitted to his friend.

Egil looked at him in surprise.

"I see that you've fallen prey to the gentle winds of love."

"I just feel funny from that potion you gave me," Viggo grunted.

"Would you rather I didn't make it for you and be dizzy?"

"Almost… but no. I'd rather feel funny than dizzy and vomiting."

"I figured as much…" Egil smiled. "Look here on the map," he told Viggo as he pointed at the island with his finger.

"Looks like you're right… it does resemble a fish—a hungry fish, because its mouth is open and it has a funny tail."

"Big mouth? Are you talking about yourself?" Nilsa asked as she came toward them.

"Ha, ha. Isn't Freckles funny!" Viggo replied, making a face.

"I am pretty charming," Nilsa replied.

"Yeah, as much as the sea," Viggo moaned.

"What are you doing with that map?"

"I was showing Viggo Fish Island so he would understand why it's called that," Egil explained, showing the map to Nilsa.

The redhead studied the map for a moment.

"Well yes, it does look like a fish with its mouth open," she admitted. "Does the island belong to the Kingdom of Zangria? I seem to recall that being the case. Is that right, Egil?"

"Yes, it belongs to the kingdom of Zangria. The inhabitants are indigenous and ethnically similar to the Zangrians but ultimately different. They're called the Zantos."

"I hope they're taller and slimmer," Viggo commented ironically.

"Don't be mean," Nilsa said, elbowing him.

"I'm not being mean. I'm just stating things as they are. Zangrians are short and wide, not to mention they're also hairy and ugly. You can't argue with that," Viggo said.

"Well… they certainly are… although I've always heard that beauty is in the eye of the beholder. So there's no need to speak ill of them either…" Nilsa said to Viggo.

"Why not? Are they listening?" Viggo raised his arms.

"The island's inhabitants are even shorter and wider at the shoulders than the Zangrians," Egil told them.

"Who would've known!" Viggo cried, beaming.

"Really? That's hard to imagine," Nilsa said. "I've never seen one, I think…"

"That's only natural. Very few have. They don't leave their island. They consider it holy and live their entire lives there. In fact, it's believed the Zangrians are actually descendants of the few who left the island in olden times. They don't anymore."

"That's odd," Nilsa said, surprised.

"They believe that if they leave their island the great monster will come out of the sea and destroy them," Egil explained.

"What a bunch of superstitious dwarves," Viggo said, looking toward the island.

"Well, they miss out on all of Tremia—that's a pity if you think about it," Nilsa said, looking sad.

"There are countless ethnicities and cultures in Tremia, each with its own peculiarities. Many of these cultures are fascinating, very different from ours."

"Yeah, don't you try selling that to us after meeting those strangers of the deserts with eyes like rubies," Viggo said.

"They're a most unusual and fascinating culture. I must go back and visit them," Egil said dreamily.

"And what are the people of the Kingdom of Irinel we're going to, like?" Viggo asked. "By the way, at first I thought we were going to the Kingdom of Erenal."

"Don't be silly, they're two very different kingdoms. Erenal is in Central Tremia, south of Zangria. Irinel is on the northeastern coast," Nilsa said, unable to believe he had mixed them up.

"They might be as different as you say, but the names are very similar," Viggo replied.

"Yeah, they're identical. I-R-I-N-E-L and E-R-E-N-A-L," Nilsa spelled slowly and loudly, pronouncing each letter and drawing out each word.

"I'm not stupid!" Viggo protested. "They sound similar if you mention them separately!"

"Your brain is separated!" Nilsa mocked.

Egil could not hold back a guffaw.

"Yeah, great, side with her, wise-guy," Viggo said reproachfully to Egil, who could barely keep from laughing.

"The people of Irinel look quite a lot like me," Nilsa informed Viggo, running her hands along her figure.

"Clumsy and impossible!" Viggo said, seizing the chance to counter.

Egil kept laughing—he was having a ball.

"You're worse than silly—you're a total numskull," Nilsa snapped.

"Keep calling me names, I don't care," Viggo replied.

Egil tried to smooth things over. "What Nilsa means is that the people of the Kingdom of Irinel share the same physical characteristics as her."

"Redheads?" Viggo asked.

"That's right. Pale skin and freckles," Egil explained. "Very different from the inhabitants of the Kingdom of Erenal who, as you know, have dark hair and sun-tanned skin."

"Are the people of Irinel like the Norghanians? Tall and strong?" Viggo wanted to know. "I'm just asking in case we have trouble."

Egil shook his head.

"Only the Norghanians are tall and strong, as are the Norriel in Tremia, as far as I know."

"Who are these Norriel? I don't remember ever hearing of them."

"They're a tribe of warriors who live north of Rogdon, in western Tremia," Egil told them. "They're said to be a tribe of stubborn warriors. The Kingdom of Rogdon has tried to conquer them on several occasions and hasn't had any luck."

"Wow, Rogdon has a strong and disciplined army," Nilsa said. "King Thoran and his brother hate them, so they must be formidable rivals."

"They are," Egil nodded. "The Kingdom of Rogdon is a military power. Their Lancers are unequaled in open land battle."

"So they have cavalry," Viggo guessed.

"The best in all Tremia. It destroys the infantry in direct confrontation," Egil said.

"Then why can't they overpower a simple tribe in their own territory? They can't be that good then," Viggo said a little disdainfully.

"The Norriel live in high mountains difficult to access. The cavalry can't go up there. The Norriel destroy whoever tries to take their mountains, they always have," Egil continued. "Their warriors are fearful with the sword. They use longer-than-usual swords that they make themselves and wield them with either one or both hands. They fight with barely any armor and they're very aggressive, almost like wildlings when they fight."

"I like these Norriel already!" Viggo said. "Maybe I'll meet one someday. Yeah, I'd like that."

"If you do, don't make him or her angry," Nilsa warned him.

"No matter how good they might be with the sword, they won't be a match for the best Assassin in Norghana," Viggo replied confidently.

"One day your cockiness is going to cost you dearly," Nilsa warned him again.

"Not at all."

"Listen to Nilsa," Ingrid said as she walked by and overheard the redhead.

"Your friend does nothing but mess with me," Viggo replied. "You might tell her to be kinder."

Ingrid stopped and turned her head to glare at him.

"You don't need me to fight your battles, do you?"

Viggo threw his head back.

"It's not that, and you know it. You're always covering for one another, especially when it's about me."

"That's because you deserve it," Ingrid replied with a smile at Nilsa, who chuckled.

Viggo shook his head and muttered under his breath.

Ingrid winked at Nilsa and left them with a smile.

"So, we're going to the Kingdom of Irinel and from there to who knows where," Nilsa said.

"It's going to be fantastic! I haven't had the good fortune to travel to Irinel, and the kingdoms of the East are entirely unknown to me. I've always wanted to visit them and find out what their people and culture are like," said Egil. "I bet we'll encounter fascinating things."

"I'm sure…" Viggo grumbled with his arms crossed.

A cry of alarm was heard.

"Ships ahead!" one of the soldiers shouted from the bow.

"From Irinel?" the Captain asked.

"They're two sail ships!"

"Zangrians, sir!" warned another soldier.

"Look what you've done!" Nilsa said to Viggo accusingly.

"Me? What have I done?" he said, waving his arms.

"Spoken ill of them!" Nilsa raised her arms to the sky.

"They couldn't have heard me! It's a coincidence!"

"It's not a coincidence, it's the universe punishing you for your bad thoughts!" Nilsa accused him.

"Yeah, the universe, the stars, and the heavens," Viggo replied, rolling his eyes.

Ingrid and Lasgol went to the bow with the rest of the Panthers following behind them.

"How many ships?" Ingrid asked.

"Three large war ships without the Zangrian flag," Lasgol told them using his *Hawk's Eye* skill to better assess the threat.

"They're not going to attack us, are they?" Nilsa asked.

"They're not flying the Zangrian flag..." Astrid commented with a frown.

"And what does that mean?"

"I'd say they're not Zangrian soldiers if they're not flying the kingdom's flag," Ingrid said.

"Those ships do not belong to the Zangrian fleet," Egil confirmed.

"Seeing as we're in Zangrian's sea zone, if they're not part of their fleet, then who are they?"

"They're pirates," Astrid said.

"Indeed they are," Egil nodded.

"Well, this is going to be fun," Viggo said, smiling. "I was beginning to get tired of this quiet journey. A little action will be great."

"Yeah, sure. Disregarding that we might die," Ingrid retorted.

"Or the Ambassador," said Lasgol.

"Well, if the ambassador dies, there goes our mission," Viggo smiled broadly. "We should look on the bright side."

"We're not going to let the Ambassador die, you scatterbrain," Ingrid snapped reproachfully. "We have to fulfill our mission, and that includes the Ambassador returning safe and sound with us."

"Yeah, but that's a detail we might overlook..." Viggo suggested with a look at the Ambassador.

"We're not going to overlook the Ambassador's life!" Ingrid said menacingly.

"They might not attack us," said Nilsa wistfully.

They all watched the three ships coming straight toward them, riding the waves propelled by their two sails.

"Tack to port!" came the Captain's order.

The ship started to veer and the waves made it sway abruptly.

"They're following course, sir!" one of the soldiers shouted from the crow's nest.

"Trim that sail!" the Captain ordered.

The soldiers went from one side of the ship to the other, concern visible on their faces.

"They keep coming!" cried another watch.

"They're coming for us! They're pirates!" cried the Captain.

The Panthers exchanged uncertain looks.

"Just like I said, don't know why you're always doubting my instincts," Viggo said.

"To arms, everyone!" Astrid urged.

They ran to fetch their weapons. If the pirates caught up with them there would be fighting. In the blink of an eye the Panthers had their weapons ready to face the enemy. Ingrid ran to starboard.

"I want to see what speed the enemy's approaching at," she cried.

Lasgol and Astrid joined her.

"They're coming in fast," Lasgol commented.

"How many pirates do you make out?" Astrid asked him.

"I can see three dozen," Lasgol replied.

"Wow, those are quite a few pirates!"

"We're only two dozen," Nilsa said, arming her bow.

"Two dozen Norghanian soldiers besides us, who are worth a hundred," Viggo said as he poured poison on his knives.

"It's one thing to be good, and a very different thing to be worth a hundred soldiers," Ingrid said to dampen his sails.

"I alone am worth at least thirty pirates," Viggo said, sure of himself. "Even the know-it-all is worth ten!"

"Not sure I'm worth ten…" Egil said, checking his arrows. "I find your statement optimistically exaggerated. But I appreciate the vote of confidence from the best Assassin in all Norghana."

"Thank goodness you know how to recognize talent," Viggo said, puffing out his chest and smiling.

"You'd better stop talking nonsense and get ready," Ingrid said cautiously, "things are about to get difficult."

Lasgol, who was watching the pirate ships intensely, pointed at them.

"They're picking up the pace—they're coming for us. We'd better get ready to repel their attack."

"Ready! Everyone to their post!" the Captain shouted.

Part of the soldiers in the crew started gearing up. They grasped their scaled armor and put it on, then they grabbed their helmets and shields and finally their axes and spears. Meanwhile the rest of the soldiers retrieved the long oars and prepared to row.

"To the oars!" the Captain shouted, "We have to lose them!"

"It looks like the Captain wants to leave them behind," said Nilsa. "You think we'll make it?"

"No idea, but we'd better get in position to release," Ingrid replied back.

"They're too far away," Viggo said, watching the pirate ships.

"Let's wait until they're in range and teach them what's waiting for them if they try to board us," Ingrid ordered.

"If they try to board us they'll end up as fish food," Viggo said as he squinted at the enemy with a lethal gleam in his eyes.

Lasgol called upon his *Hawk's Eye* skill to watch what the pirates were doing.

"Be prepared. They have archers and are taking up positions at the bow," he warned.

"They'll be the first to fall," Astrid said beside him with lethal confidence.

The Panthers nocked their bows and aimed at the starboard board, calculating the ship's sway on the waves in order to release accurately. Releasing at high sea, from a ship riding the waves, was not ideal to say the least.

"At my signal!" Ingrid told them, and they stood aiming in the midst of a tense silence.

Chapter 3

The three enemy ships were coming in fast to intercept them. Everyone was aware the pirates were going to try to board them and take the ship. Lasgol was watching the bow of the first ship where several archers were aiming their bows. They were Zangrian, no doubt, and he did not understand why they would attack a Norghanian war ship. Pirates generally sought easier prey, like merchant ships loaded with goods, weapons, even gold and silver. It was uncommon for pirates to attack war ships since there was a lot to lose and little to gain, which made it bad business. The only valuable assets in this case were the ship itself and the soldiers' weapons—not a bad plunder if there was no resistance, but if there was, which was the most obvious outcome being a ship full of soldiers, it was bad business. This made Lasgol suspect there had to be another reason for it, one they did not know.

What is it? Camu messaged him.

In the haste of preparing for the attack, he had completely forgotten his friend.

We're being attacked. Three pirate ships. Stay where you are.

I help.

Not now, let us deal with it. If we need you I'll let you know.

You tell, I come up to help.

Don't worry, I will.

Where Ona?

Lasgol turned his head and saw the snow panther beside the mast of the ship.

Ona is at the foot of the mast. You'd better go below with Camu, Lasgol transmitted.

Ona growled twice; she did not want to go below.

"Ambassador Larsen, get under cover!" Captain Ulmendren shouted.

The Ambassador looked at the Captain, then at the pirate ships getting closer, and finally at the Panthers who were waiting to release.

"Royal Eagles, defend the ship! It must not be taken!" he ordered in a voice bordering on hysteria.

Lasgol looked at him in surprise. Ingrid and Astrid exchanged a blank look.

"Look here, the brave noble! You'd think he was having a panic attack," Viggo commented mockingly.

"We know our duty," Ingrid replied in a dry tone.

"Defend the ship!" the ambassador cried and ran to hide in the hull.

"Wow, he's more nervous than me at my worst," Nilsa commented, looking surprised.

"We'd better repel the attack, or else the Ambassador is going to poop in his pants," Viggo laughed

"If they board us, Norghanian blood will run," Astrid said, watching the crew with a look of concern.

"We could use our long bows to keep them at bay," Nilsa suggested.

Ingrid and Astrid thought for a moment.

"On firm land perhaps, but here, with the waves and the ship going up and down, the long bow isn't the most suitable choice," Ingrid said.

"This strong wind also doesn't help matters," Astrid added, pinning back her jet-black hair which was flying about her face.

Ingrid leaned on the ship's rail and watched the enemy as she calculated the swaying of the ship on the waves.

"We'll use the composite bows," she decided. "The long one's no good in these conditions, and the short one, which would be ideal, would let the pirates get too close."

Astrid nodded in agreement.

"Composite bows, everyone," Ingrid commanded.

Lasgol, Egil, and Viggo were already arming and slinging their quivers over their shoulders.

Captain Ulmendren was following a northern course parallel to the eastern coast of the island, trying to flee from their pursuers. The huge cliffs were crowned with seagulls that seemed to watch the maritime pursuit taking place below. The pirate ships were coming at them from the east and the Captain was trying to leave them behind by running north. It was a complicated maneuver. He had managed to prevent the ships' courses from crossing but now he was having trouble escaping. If the pirates caught up with them and rammed them from the starboard side they would be in serious trouble.

"All hands to the oars!" he ordered. "We have to put distance between us!"

The soldiers left their weapons on the deck and started rowing to propel the ship with the strength of their arms and bodies.

Egil was holding the corner of a scarf with his arm raised. The wind was sending the scarf to the west.

"The wind is in their favor…. With two sails on their ships, I'm afraid they will catch up with us," he concluded.

"We won't be able to outrun them?" Nilsa asked.

"Not without fighting," Egil replied.

"Well then, we'll have to fight," said Astrid.

"This is going to be fun," Viggo smiled.

"Get ready to clear the bow of the first ship—everyone release on my signal," Ingrid said.

They all nodded.

They nocked their arrows and prepared to release.

The Norghanian soldiers were rowing as hard as their strong bodies would allow. The cliffs to the left of the ship seemed to fly by, but the three other ships with their two sails swollen full cut through the waves at tremendous speed. The rowers' efforts could not defeat the wind, which was more powerful.

"Release now!" Ingrid ordered.

The Panthers released and their arrows flew swift and straight to the prow of the first pirate ship. The distance between them was barely four hundred and fifty paces. Six enemy archers who were aiming at them fell before they could release.

"Release again!" Ingrid cried.

The six comrades nocked a new arrow almost in synchrony, although Ingrid and Nilsa did so an instant before the others and Egil and Viggo an instant after the rest.

The arrows flew fast in a straight course from one ship to the other. Six more pirates fell backward with arrows in their bodies. The bow was left without a pirate standing, but the ship kept coming.

"Wow, even the wise-guy hit the target!" Viggo laughed.

"My shots were a little low, but since they're short… I got my man," Egil said with a shrug.

"What's surprising is that *you* hit your target," Nilsa said to Viggo.

"I'm getting better every day, even with the composite bow," he replied.

Several arrows from the enemy ship tried to reach them but fell short.

"Those Zangrian blockheads—besides being ugly dwarves, they're bad shots."

"They're not bad shots, they're just not as good as we are," Ingrid corrected him. "Don't be too confident."

"Me, too confident? Never," he smiled.

Ingrid gave him a warning look.

"They're not sending more archers to the bow," Nilsa said.

"They either don't have any more, or the Pirate Captain has realized he's facing skilled archers and doesn't want to suffer more casualties," Lasgol said.

"Probably both," said Egil. "Still, he's keeping her collision course. They're intent on boarding us."

"We have to slow them down," said Ingrid. "Release at will and try to hit the pirates."

The arrows flew swiftly from the Norghanian ship and hit several of the pirates.

"Keep releasing!" Ingrid cried.

The pirates sheltered behind the oar benches and in the ship's hull. Ingrid, Nilsa, and Astrid hit three other pirates, but Lasgol, Egil, and Viggo hit only wood.

"They're covering themselves, we don't have a shot," said Lasgol.

"Let's destroy their sails, without them they won't catch us," Egil told them.

"Fire Arrows?" Ingrid asked.

"Fire is our ally," Egil responded.

"Fire Arrows, everyone!" Ingrid ordered.

They picked the arrows marked "fire" and nocked them carefully. Elemental Arrows had to be manipulated with care, and even more so in unfavorable conditions like fierce wind and unpredictable movement.

"At my signal!" Ingrid cried. "Aim at the sails and mast."

"We definitely won't miss the sail," Viggo told Egil with a wink.

"Let's hope the fire takes," Egil replied.

"Shoot with strength," Lasgol advised him. "The greater the impact, the more likely the tips of the arrows will break and combust."

Egil nodded.

Ingrid gave the order.

The Fire Arrows left their bows, seeking the enemy sails and masts. Ingrid's arrow hit the mast right above the sail. The head of the arrow broke and there was a small explosion of fire. The upper part of the sail began to burn. Nilsa hit the lower part of a second mast and the fire started up the wood. Viggo's and Egil's arrows hit the two sails, but the impact was not good and there was not the expected fiery explosion.

Viggo cursed out loud.

"That wasn't good," Egil complained, disappointed by his shot.

Lasgol's arrow did explode and part of the main sail began to burn. Astrid hit the secondary sail which also caught fire.

The Pirate Captain started giving orders to his people amid loud cries to put the fires out.

"We have to keep shooting, they're bringing water," said Nilsa.

"Release, fast!" Ingrid ordered.

Six other Fire Arrows descended on the ship, three hitting the main sail and three striking the secondary one. Only four managed to explode and start a fire, but it was enough for the pirate crew to panic. They ran from one side to the other, looking for water to put out the fires devouring the sails.

"Nilsa, come with me, we'll bring down the pirates trying to put out the fire while the rest keep releasing Fire Arrows."

"I'll switch to common arrows," said Nilsa.

The two archers hit a pair of pirates running with buckets of water, while Astrid, Lasgol, Viggo, and Egil continued trying to burn down the sails.

Captain Ulmendren's voice reached them loud and clear.

"We're almost past the east coast! Keep rowing with all your might!"

Lasgol looked to the port side and saw that indeed they were close to clearing the cliffs as they headed north. He turned his head to starboard and saw the second ship almost upon them. It was passing the first one, which had both sails aflame.

"Beware! The second ship is closing in!" he warned as his comrades continued attacking the first ship.

"We have to stop it!" Ingrid yelled.

"Same tactic?" Nilsa asked.

Ingrid nodded. "We have to burn down those sails!"

Lasgol noticed that the first ship was hanging back, her sails in flames. The effect was that the second one rapidly overtook it and headed toward them at great speed.

"Release! They're coming at full tilt!"

The Fire Arrows flew across the sea, seeking the sails of the second ship. They hit the mast and the sail and the fire exploded. But this time the pirates were prepared. They had witnessed what had happened to the other ship and they had buckets of water ready. As soon as the arrows exploded, the fire was put out.

"They were expecting it!" Nilsa cried.

"Release again!" Ingrid ordered.

The pirates, foreseeing more fire, started soaking the sails with sea water to keep them from burning. Half the crew was rowing and the other half poured water amid their captain's orders, who was pointing at the sails and shouting in Zangrian.

"We're not damaging the sails this time, we'll have to change our strategy," Astrid said.

"Earth Arrows at the crew," Egil suggested. "That will confuse them."

Ingrid gave the order to change arrows.

"Release at those pouring the water!" Astrid said.

The Earth Arrows flew at the pirates who were pouring water on the mast, sails, and deck. They hit their targets, and with every explosion of earth a few pirates were blinded and stunned, unable to do anything. They dropped buckets and barrels of water and wandered the deck in a daze as their captain shouted out orders they could not carry out.

"It's working! Release!" Ingrid cheered.

They continued releasing Earth Arrows which exploded with each impact, spreading a cloud of smoke, earth, and stunning and blinding substances which managed to knock down the pirates they hit and whoever was near. When they did not hit a person but the mast or the rowing benches, the effect was lessened but it also caused damage.

The Pirate Captain was ordering his men to take cover with much gesturing and shouting.

"They're hiding!" cried Nilsa.

"And they're still coming! They're going to ram into us!" Astrid warned.

"What do we do now?" Viggo asked. "They're hiding like rats!"

"Egil? What do we do? They're already upon us!" Ingrid cried.

Egil was watching the attack with his eyes half closed, thinking of a way out.

"We have to delay them…. Lasgol, can you see their captain clearly? I can't between the distance and the smoke and chaos we're generating," he asked his friend.

"With my *Hawk's Eye* skill I can see him clearly," Lasgol confirmed. "He's hiding behind some barrels and is directing operations from there."

"Is he at the ship's helm?"

Lasgol shook his head. "An older sailor is at the helm, a little more to the captain's right."

"Okay. I have a plan," Egil told them. "We release Earth Arrows at the rowing benches so they'll have to take cover and stop rowing."

"But they'll keep going if the sails are intact," said Ingrid.

"We'll deal with that," Egil smiled. "Astrid, Lasgol, I need you." He waved them over to one side to confer with them.

"You heard Egil. We'll release against the rowers with Earth Arrows!" Ingrid told Nilsa and Viggo.

"I'm not sure I'll hit anything," Viggo muttered, wrinkling his nose.

"As long as arrows keep falling on the rowing benches, we'll create chaos," said Nilsa, who had caught Egil's intention.

Viggo shrugged.

Nilsa nudged him. "Come on!"

The three started releasing without aiming at people but in an arch so the arrows would fall on the men as they rowed crouching, following their captain's orders. The enemy ship was closing in fast and was going to ram into them, on the port side, right under the railing where the Panthers were standing to repel the attack.

Astrid ran to the mast to rummage in her bags and brought out a new bow and a quiver full of arrows before she ran back to the others.

Egil looked at her questioningly.

"I always carry it ready just in case," Astrid said, showing them the elaborate bow.

Lasgol glanced at it and nodded.

"Nice bow."

"It's my Forest Sniper bow—it's special and one I'm very fond of," Astrid replied.

"Let's put it to good use," Egil said, pointing at the enemy ship.

Astrid nodded and nocked a long-range arrow. She got down on one knee on the deck and pulled the string back to her cheek, aiming carefully.

"I can't see the Captain, there's too much smoke and dirt. It's obscuring my vision," she said.

"Please help her, Lasgol," Egil said.

Lasgol got down beside Astrid as she aimed. Following the swaying movement of the ship and scanning the enemy ship, he was able to distinguish the head of the enemy captain.

"Two barrels on the stern, right in the center at the back, can you see them?" Lasgol said with his head at Astrid's same level.

"I can see part of a barrel, yes, in the middle."

"The one you see is the barrel on the left. The right one is also shrouded in smoke and there are two pirates beside it. You have to aim there, clearing the top of the left barrel but aiming to its right. The captain is hiding between the two barrels."

"I get it," Astrid said, and she began to slowly reposition her arm a little more to the right.

"I can see his head and a raised arm. He hasn't moved and is yelling orders to his crew," Lasgol told her.

"As soon as the ship initiates its upward movement, I'll release," Astrid said as she counted the time in between waves.

While she was aiming for an accurate shot, her comrades were releasing everywhere and creating a cloud of dust with Earth Arrows, which was beginning to affect the rowers. They were throwing themselves on the deck and crawling, seeking clean air and abandoning the oars.

"Three, two, one," Astrid counted the waves.

"You can do it," Lasgol encouraged her.

Astrid released her arrow.

Lasgol followed its flight as it flew over the sea between the two ships at great speed, heading straight at the pirate ship's stern, to the very center, slicing through the smoke and clearing the top of the barrels as it buried itself on the right side of the captain's forehead. His head whipped back and he fell dead.

"You got him! What a shot!" Lasgol cried.

"Did I? I can't see a thing," Astrid said.

"He's not getting back up. He's dead," Lasgol confirmed.

"Fantastic," Egil said. "Now the helmsman: you have to bring him down. Without the captain and helmsman the ship will drift."

"Where's the helmsman?" Astrid asked Lasgol.

"Two paces to the right of the Captain. He's hiding behind two crew members. Since he can't let go of the helm, he won't be moving."

"I can't see them at all. I'll have to shoot blindly."

"Take it easy, I'll guide you."

The enemy ship was losing momentum without rowers or a captain to give orders. It was slowing down but still following a collision course.

Astrid released, following Lasgol's instructions.

"You've hit one of the pirates guarding the helmsman. Correct two hand-spans to the right and a tad higher because you've hit him in the leg, left thigh."

Astrid nodded and moved the bow slightly to the right and up.

"You've got it," Lasgol told her.

Astrid waited, concentrating on the ship's movement, and when the time came she released. The arrow brushed the arm of the second pirate and went on straight into the helmsman's stomach.

"You got him!" Lasgol cried happily.

"We've run out of Earth and Fire Arrows," Ingrid warned.

Egil strained his neck.

"We won't need them, the pirate ship is changing course. It's veering to starboard," Egil said smugly.

"Are they retreating?" Nilsa asked.

"Nope, they're drifting. They have no captain, no helmsman, or rowers at the oars," Egil beamed.

"Great job!" he congratulated Ingrid.

"You were amazing!" Lasgol praised Astrid.

"Thanks, but I'm afraid we're not in the clear yet," she said, pointing east.

Lasgol turned to look and saw the third ship heading toward them.

"It's going to ram into us!" Nilsa cried.

Chapter 4

The enemy ship rushed past the vessel the Panthers had just sabotaged and left it behind in the blink of an eye. She headed straight to ram into them, and instinctively the Panthers released against the pirate ship, although it was too late to stop her.

"Tack to port!" they heard Captain Ulmendren shout.

Lasgol looked to port and noticed they had already passed the eastern side of the island. They were tacking away from the coast.

"He's trying to keep them from boarding us!" Ingrid said as she released at the pirates while they took cover on the deck or hid behind the barrels and cargo by the two masts.

"It's a good maneuver, but I doubt we'll prevent the crash," Egil calculated as he watched the incoming speed of the remaining pirate ship.

"Release!" Nilsa cried, nocking arrow after arrow.

"Row with all your might! We have to avoid them ramming into us!" Ulmendren shouted.

Lasgol was releasing at the pirates who, armed and crouching, were preparing to board. Like Egil, he could not stop thinking they would not manage to turn the ship in time to avoid the crash. They were tacking to port in order to be parallel with the northern coast of the island, which also had cliffs. The pirate ship was coming in fast to ram her figurehead, shaped like a great spear tip, into their starboard side from where they were shooting. They were never going to tack in time.

"Prepare for impact!" he warned his comrades.

"They're already upon us!" Ingrid cried.

"Hold on tight, the crash will be hard!" Egil urged them.

They stopped shooting and ran to grab ropes anchored to the deck.

"Attack! Draw the starboard oars in!" Captain Ulmendren yelled.

The Norghanian crew drew the oars back before the imminent crash.

"Hold tight!" Ingrid called.

"Hold fast!" the Captain cried to his crew.

There was a tremendous crash toward the stern on the starboard side. The spear tip figurehead of the pirate ship rammed into the Norghanian vessel, shattering the hull's wood. The sound of splintering wood against steel was strident and menacing, and several rowers and some Norghanian soldiers who were arming themselves to repel the attack were thrown toward the ship's bow like ragdolls. The pirate figurehead destroyed part of the stern, and with it the rudder. It remained wedged into the hull, accompanied by the ominous sounds of wood breaking wood.

"Defend the ship!" the Captain shouted. "They're boarding the stern from starboard!" he pointed at the first pirates, who were already jumping on board the Norghanian ship armed with spears and knives.

Ingrid reacted immediately and managed to keep her balance after the impact and released. She hit the first pirate who reached the deck and her arrow buried itself in his heart and he fell forward on the deck. While she nocked again Nilsa was already releasing and caught another pirate who was running toward the Captain. Ulmendren was trying to retreat aft, but the crash had injured him and he was limping ostensibly.

"Protect the Captain!" Ingrid shouted.

"I'll get him out of here," Lasgol replied, realizing the Captain was too close to where the pirates were pouring in from their ship. He started to run, and as he did he called upon his *Improved Agility* and *Cat-like Reflexes* skill. He reached the captain, who was being defended by several Norghanian soldiers delivering axe strokes and covering behind their round wooden shields.

"Captain, with me!" Lasgol urged him as he grabbed Ulmendren's arm and pulled him back.

"Crew! All to arms! Repel the assault!" the Captain ordered as he withdrew dragging his injured leg, pulled by Lasgol.

The pirates lunged into a full attack. They poured in through two points in small groups, some swinging on ropes and others along planks they had placed between the two ships. The Norghanian soldiers hastened to reject them with their characteristic brutality, delivering such fierce axe and shield blows that the pirates were either knocked down or thrown overboard. The cries of battle turned into a din as the pirates boarding the ship yelled and the Norghanian soldiers did the same as they fought them back. The fight became frantic as the Norghanian axes and the Zangrian spears sought the death of the enemy.

The Norghanian soldiers had the advantage of being much taller—with their axes they could split their assailants in two with one blow. The pirates, mostly Zangrian, were much shorter, but they were also strong and broad and had the advantage of carrying spears which they used to launch stinging attacks at the defenders. If the Norghanians were not alert they found the tip of a spear buried into their hearts.

All the soldiers and members of the crew lunged into attack since they had to repel the assault. When the attackers crashed against the defenders the Norghanians formed a defensive wall. The pirates had taken the stern fast and the defenders were trying to push back the attack and regain control. The assailants, on the other hand, were trying to advance to the middle of the ship and were pushing the Norghanians back with their spears. They delivered strong, penetrating blows to force the defenders to retreat.

Ingrid and Nilsa had trouble aiming and releasing, since if they were not careful they might unwillingly hit their own people. Since the Norghanians were so much taller and were forming a barrier before the archers, it was difficult for the Rangers to see and aim at the pirates.

"Nilsa, be careful and don't hit any of ours!" Ingrid shouted.

"I can only see Norghanian heads and backs!" the redhead shouted back as she tried to aim without success.

"We're too close to shoot in an arc!" Ingrid cried. She had just tried and her arrow had gone into the sea.

"Not in an arc, but we can shoot upward!" Nilsa said, releasing to the sky above the stern. The arrow went up and up almost in a straight line, and when it reached the end of its momentum it turned down toward the deck. Nilsa watched it fall—it buried itself into a pirate's head and he fell dead.

"Good shot!" Ingrid cried.

"A very lucky one," Nilsa admitted.

They tried to mimic Nilsa's shot, and although some arrows hit the pirates' bodies, others did not, so ultimately it was not an effective strategy.

Aware of the difficulties, Egil was looking overboard at the enemy ship, trying to think up a plan to help them.

Viggo moved toward the pirates. "Come to me, little toothless sharks!" he taunted them, brandishing his two poisoned knives and looking grim. Two of the pirates slipped through the wall of soldiers and lunged at Viggo, who received them with sure thrusts, dodging their spears as they sought his chest and delivering poisoned cuts to legs and arms. He rolled to one side while the pirates looked at their wounds with surprise. Viggo's knife slashes had been so swift they had not even seen them coming. They tried to attack Viggo, yelling in rage, but as soon as they took two steps they fell down. The poison was beginning to have effect. "You'll soon be sleeping the eternal sleep, don't worry," he told the pirates, and then he hurried to face a group of three pirates who had cornered a Norghanian soldier against the port railing.

The pirates tried to reach the middle of the ship, but the Norghanian soldiers and the Panthers did not let them leave the stern, pushing them back with axes and arrows. The few pirates who managed to pass the soldiers' barrier were brought down by Ingrid, Nilsa, and Egil, who were forming a second defensive wall. Captain Ulmendren was behind them, sword in hand as he issued orders to the crew. He was bleeding from his right leg and had a nasty cut on his left side.

"Push back their spears with your shields!" he was shouting.

Lasgol could see that the pirates, short but stocky, were skilled fighters, and although they should not have posed a threat to the Norghanians who were bigger and stronger, they were causing many casualties with their spears. They launched powerful attacks with their long, two-handed spears, and they were managing to tear the Norghanian shields and armor. The defenders were not used to fighting enemies smaller than them who launched stinging attacks rather than the cutting slashes they were used to.

"Those spears are a danger," Lasgol said to Ingrid.

"I know, the scoundrels use them skillfully. Our soldiers are in a tight spot," she replied.

"Let's disarm as many as we can," said Nilsa.

Lasgol was moving from right to left to find a gap to release through and aim better. The thing was he had to shoot in between the soldiers without hitting them, and this was risky since they were constantly shifting back and forth defending and attacking. Nilsa's and Ingrid's technique of shooting at the sky was not working too well, so they decided to stop using it and Ingrid started to move from side to side, releasing the moment she saw a gap between the soldiers, being careful and only shooting if she thought she had a clear shot.

"Careful with our soldiers!" the Captain warned them when he saw they were releasing in between them.

Egil signaled Astrid to come over to where he was. The Assassin had just killed two pirates who had run toward them after breaking the defensive line, and she slid smoothly across the deck to stand beside her comrade.

"We'll end this much quicker if we can sneak over and take that position at the back," Egil told her, pointing at the stern of the enemy ship.

Astrid saw the gleam of intelligence in her friend's eyes and looked to where he was pointing and understood.

"I see. I'll do it, it's my specialty," Astrid said with a wink.

"Good luck," Egil said as he nocked his bow.

Astrid grabbed a rope from the sail, propelled herself from the railing, and dropped on the pirate's fore deck, right on the figurehead stuck into their own ship. Careful not to be seen, she walked across the deck to the starboard of the Zangrian ship. The assault was taking place from the port side, but she took a quick look anyway. The pirates were all facing the Norghanian ship and had their backs to her, but if they saw her she would have a hard time getting out alive because of their sheer numbers. She would have to use all her stealth and training as a Specialist to not be detected. She dropped down to the deck floor as if she were part of it.

While the pirates were boarding the Norghanian ship like madmen, she started crawling along the enemy deck without being seen, making her way toward the stern, using the shadows the sails made on the deck. Her goal was at the very end of the ship beside the rudder, and she had to reach it without being seen or things would get complicated for her, so she trusted her training and kept going.

Almost all the pirates were taking part in the attack, so she went fast, leaving behind the hull hatch and the main sail mast and crawling to the second mast, hiding behind the cargo bundles and barrels and whatever she could find to hide her presence from the enemy. She stopped for a moment to watch the fighting on the other ship and saw her comrades releasing and Viggo lunging with a combined attack of cuts and thrusts at two pirates before she lost sight of him. She was sure Viggo was enjoying himself—he loved messy, close fights, the messier the better. Those were his specialty, and he was an expert in these situations. She preferred stealth and surprise, finishing the target without them being aware or with as little noise as possible. They had different methods, different tastes.

She kept going and was close, but just when she thought she was going to make it and fall upon her target and surprise them, a pirate came out of the hull behind her and saw her. He ran to intercept her and she cursed under her breath. She could not foresee everything all the time. Not even the stealthiest Assassin could escape from bad luck—such was fate sometimes. She prepared to deal with the threat as fast as she could so she would not be found out.

An arrow from Egil, who was covering her from the afterdeck of the Norghanian ship, caught the pirate in the stomach, and he fell to the deck screaming in pain. The shot had not been so good, and the pirate's screams alerted his three comrades who were protecting their captain. That was Astrid's target—she looked at Egil and her friend apologized with a shrug. She waved it away, thankful for his help. At that distance, from one ship to the other, with all the sails, ropes, and other obstacles in between, the shot was not an easy one; besides, Egil was not the best of archers, but she would manage.

She stood up and glared at the pirate captain and his men.

"Drop your weapons overboard and surrender if you want to live," Astrid said in warning. She had no idea whether they understood her, but they would get the message from her body language.

The pirate captain pointed his sword at her and gave two of his bodyguards the order to attack. Astrid noticed they were big for Zangrians, larger than usual. They looked evil and seemed to know how to fight. They were not armed with spears but carried a short sword in one hand and a long knife in the other. Astrid waited for them to advance toward her, and the two men came under the second sail while the sounds of fighting came from the other ship.

"I warned you," she said, pointing her knives at them so they would have no doubts about what was in for them if they attacked her.

Both pirates lunged without a word. Astrid saw in their eyes that they meant to kill her and would do so if she gave them the slightest chance. But she would not—distractions were not a part of her training. The Zangrians delivered powerful crossed slashes, seeking her neck and torso. Astrid waited until the last instant to slip to the left with a swift fluid step, delivering at the same time a horizontal slash to the closest pirate's thigh. He did not seem to feel it and delivered a flat blow with his sword meant to behead her. Astrid crouched with tremendous speed and nimbleness and the sword swished above her head, brushing it. She delivered another cut with her right knife that caught the pirate in his other thigh, then rolled over her shoulder and to one side, since the second pirate was moving toward her, seeking to bury his sword in her back.

Two thrusts of the sword and knife tried to find her back, but she had already put some distance in between them to make sure the slashes did not reach her. She turned and countered with a fast movement toward the pirate who had just tried to skewer her from behind. She got him in the groin with her knife, and before her enemy could react she summersaulted backward. The two other pirates tried to catch her but could not—the first one fell under the effects of the poison which coursed up his legs, rendering them useless. He fell onto the deck, unable to move. The poison would soon reach his heart, also paralyzing it, leaving him with only a few breaths of life. The second pirate realized that the stab he had received was deadly and that he was going to bleed to death. He was not suffering, he barely felt the wound, so he sat on the deck and, with great resignation, waited for the moment to depart to the kingdom of the gods.

Astrid turned to the pirate captain and his last bodyguard. She pointed at them with her knives and then indicated the two defeated bodyguards.

"Last chance to surrender. Drop your weapons or you'll die," she told them in a cold, deadly tone.

The pirate captain shouted something in Zangrian which Astrid did not understand, but she had no doubt he did not mean to surrender. The two pirates advanced, glaring at her, intent on killing her. She did not move and waited for them to come as she had done before. Although this time she changed her tactics, since it was not a good idea to use the same attack or defense twice in a row. So, when they were three paces from her and preparing to attack, Astrid lunged forward, rolling over her head fast and nimbly.

The pirate captain and his bodyguard were taken by surprise since they had not been expecting that. They tried to react, but that instant was all that Astrid needed—she finished her move by delivering two ascending slashes with her poisoned knives while she stayed down. At the same time the bodyguard delivered a horizontal slash that only met air and the captain had to leap backward to avoid the blade.

Astrid attacked again and caught the bodyguard in the stomach, but the captain managed to block her knife with his sword and hopped back again to get out of range. Out of the corner of her eye Astrid saw the bodyguard collapse from the effects of the poison. He would not be getting up again.

"Don't make me kill you. Give orders to your men to withdraw," Astrid said, pointing at the stern of the Norghanian ship where the fighting was furious between Zangrians and Norghanians.

"I will not surrender," the pirate replied in a strong Zangrian accent.

"I see you do understand me. Order your men to withdraw and you'll live. Otherwise, you're a dead man."

The pirate captain looked at his dead bodyguards and seemed to hesitate. He looked down at the ship's deck, looked back up, and then lunged forward with a sword stroke directed at Astrid's heart. But the Assassin saw the attack, calculated the intersection, and, crossing both her knives, she caught the blade in between them and diverted it to the right. Then, following the block, she twisted her wrists and disarmed the captain. His sword flew in the air and fell on the deck.

"Fine, I surrender!" the pirate captain cried when he saw he had no chance.

"Order your crew to withdraw at once," Astrid told him, putting the tip of her knives on his chest.

"All right…" he said, his shoulders sinking.

A moment later the pirate captain gave the order to retreat with two sharp yells. The fighting was so loud he had to shout repeatedly before his pirates realized what had happened. They seemed confused by the order, but the captain went on shouting even louder. They finally started retreating in quite a chaotic manner, jumping back to their ship, running along the gangways they had set and some leaping directly into the water.

Astrid stayed on the enemy ship, ensuring the retreat was complete, and once she was satisfied she ran to the bow, grabbed a rope from the rigging, and leapt back to her ship. Egil saw her take the leap and went to help her, although Astrid did not need any assistance.

"They're withdrawing!" Captain Ulmendren shouted.

The Norghanian soldiers were now pushing the pirates overboard to their ship or the sea.

"Should we take them down as they run?" Nilsa asked.

"No, let them leave," the Captain said. "It would be worse if they turned on us in despair."

Ingrid nodded.

"Were do you think you're going?" Viggo asked the pirates when he saw them fleeing back to their ship. "Poor pirates fleeing in fear of Viggo, the amazing assassin?"

"Yeah, they're all fleeing from you in terror," Ingrid said.

"From the way you stink," Nilsa added with a guffaw.

"You can laugh all you want, but my fame grows by the moment. The   troubadours have another epic battle to sing about: Viggo the terror of the northern seas. The most ruthless pirates fled from Viggo the moment they set eyes on him," he said with exaggerated gestures as if he were narrating an epic battle.

"There's no doubt about it," Lasgol told him. "Can you please check that the pirates are indeed retreating and not playing us?"

"They're fleeing in terror," Viggo replied, watching them from the stern.

The pirates started pushing away from the Norghanian ship with their oars and shifted their sails in order to disengage their own ship and escape. There was a tremendous shattering sound of wood breaking on wood because of the pirate ship's maneuver.

"All hands to the oars, push away that ship!" Ulmendren ordered.

The sailors left their weapons and put their weight on the oars to separate the pirate ship from their own, but a part of it was stuck.

"Push back! Disengage it!" Ulmendren was shouting.

Lasgol and his comrades watched with their bows ready so the pirates would not attempt any last-moment treachery. The pirate captain was waving his arms around and giving orders to his crew, directing the maneuver.

"They're retreating," Egil confirmed as he watched and listened to their Captain.

"They'd better," said Viggo. "Otherwise they'll all end up as fish food."

"I'm going to help our wounded," said Egil as he ran to several soldiers lying on the deck with ugly wounds. There were about half a dozen who were not moving and looked like they had already departed to the kingdom of the Ice Gods. Egil checked them anyway and stated they were dead before moving on to help the others.

The two ships finally disengaged with another loud movement and the pirate ship headed fast to the east.

"The pirates are running!" Ulmendren cried, raising his arm in victory.

"Victory!" cried one soldier, and others followed, shouting, "Norghanian victory!"

Soon all the solders and crew members were celebrating the victory with shouts of joy and triumph.

Lasgol received a mental message from Camu. *Everything well? Need help?*

Everything's fine. We repelled the attack. Don't worry.

Everyone well?

Yes, everyone's fine, Lasgol confirmed as he watched his friends to make sure no one was hurt. The only one with blood on him was Viggo, and Lasgol knew it was not his own.

"Blast it! We're taking on water!" cried Ulmendren.

"We're sinking?" the Ambassador asked, who had come up when he heard the shouts of victory.

"We're sinking and we have no rudder!" the Captain cried.

Chapter 5

Lasgol ran aft to see from the starboard side the damage the pirate ship had caused to their own vessel. Egil went with him to assess how serious the situation was.

"Seal the hold! Quick!" the Captain ordered. "Don't let the hold flood, or we'll sink!"

A bunch of sailors went down to check the damage.

Lasgol and Egil were looking at the state of the hull on the stern and exchanging troubled looks. There was a huge hole, besides additional damage around the same spot, where they had been rammed by the enemy.

"That hole looks bad," Lasgol said.

"It does. Besides, part of the damage is at the waterline... we're taking in a lot of water.... A lot," Egil replied, half his body hanging over the railing to examine the damage. "It's going to be hard to sail and not sink."

"We'll have to fix that hole."

"It's not easy while at sea," Egil said. "Repairs are complicated in the middle of the sea, particularly if we're taking on water."

Lasgol looked toward the island. "I don't see any beaches, only cliffs. If we sink we'll have a tough time reaching the island."

"There has to be a more accessible part on the north side... if I'm not mistaken... I'm not sure, but I think there is. I need my maps."

"Let's hope we don't sink...." Lasgol was trying to think of a possible way out in case that happened. But nothing came to mind except swimming to the island and attempting to climb up the cliffs.

"There's still time to save the situation," Egil told him cheerfully. "Let's look on the bright side. The Captain is an expert seaman, he'll get us out of this."

Lasgol suddenly frowned, realizing Camu and Ona were in the hold and that the water could reach them.

Camu, how are you? he transmitted, trying not to feel too worried.

I fine.

And Ona?

Ona nervous.

Because of the water?

Yes, water come in below.

Has it reached where you are?

No, water come in behind. We're front. Sailors come and close half the hold.

They've done that so the water won't flood the hold completely. Are you sure you're okay?

We okay, no water.

Good. Let me know if water starts getting to you so I can get you out of there. I warn.

"They've sealed half the lower hold so it doesn't flood," Lasgol told Egil.

"Well done. They're good seamen, they know what they're doing," Egil said. "Are Camu and Ona all right? They're at the bow, right?"

"Yes, for now, but if the water keeps coming in…"

Egil nodded and looked at the Captain.

"I'm sure Ulmendren will know what to do. He and his crew were chosen for the mission, so they must be good. Thoran would only choose an experienced captain for one of his personal missions."

Lasgol relaxed somewhat and nodded.

"We'll see what he does and whether we can help."

"One third of the hands, bail out water! The rest to the oars!" the Captain ordered.

"We'll help with the bailing, come!" Ingrid said.

Nilsa nodded.

"That's not a job worthy of an Assassin of my category," Viggo muttered, looking unwilling to bail water out of the ship.

"A drowned Assassin loses all his glory," Astrid said with a wink as she put herself to the task.

Viggo thought for a moment. "True. We can't let the best Assassin in history drown. What a boring ending," he commented as he followed Astrid.

"Bail and row!" the captain was shouting at his crew.

Egil and Lasgol ran to help their friends, aware of the seriousness of the situation.

Ambassador Larsen walked up to the Captain as he was improvising a new rudder with three other men out of two oars and a few ropes.

"Captain, we can't sink. The diplomatic mission depends on us reaching our destination," the Ambassador said urgently.

"There's no need to remind me I need to save my ship!" the Captain barked back.

Larsen did not flinch. He stared at Ulmendren with poise and an air of being above the situation.

"Yet, I must remind you, my dear Captain, that the mission is highly critical for the kingdom. It can't fail."

"I know that! And I'm doing everything I can so we don't sink!" the Captain shouted back irritably. They managed to place the improvised rudder and secure it tightly with more ropes.

"King Thoran has entrusted us with an extremely important task. We can't fail him, especially not for a small maritime accident."

The Captain ignored the Ambassador like he would an annoying fly.

"We have a rudder!" he called to the crew.

"Great news!" Larsen told him.

"Not so great," Ulmendren snapped. "We're still taking on a lot of water and we're sinking."

"Oh...." The Ambassador looked dismayed.

"Western course! Keep close to the coast of the island!" he told the two sailors who were now at the helm.

Ulmendren rushed to check on the progress of those bailing water out of the ship. Two lines of people with buckets and barrels were bailing water from the hold under the deck. The Panthers had taken positions at the railing and were the end of the bailing chain. They were working as fast as they could to get all the water out of the ship and back to the sea where it belonged.

"Bail! Come on, bail!" Ulmendren shouted.

Larsen was watching the course of the ship and how they were moving parallel to the north of Fish Island.

"Must I remind you that we need to go to the Kingdom of Irinel and that is to the east, in the opposite direction?" the Ambassador said to the Captain as he trailed him everywhere he went.

"If you don't get out of my way and let me do my job, I swear I'll throw you overboard!" Ulmendren threatened Larsen, and since the Ambassador did not want any more trouble, he apologized and raised his hands.

"Of course, my dear Captain, of course, go ahead," and he stepped back.

Ulmendren went below deck to inspect the leak while the crew continued bailing water as fast as they could.

"We have to fix that leak," he commented, and his tone was troubled. "It's too large and there's too much water coming in for the ship to stay afloat." He chose four sailors and proceeded to search for boards to stop the leak. They worked on that for a long time while everyone else continued bailing water that by now was up to their waists. The ship's stern was sinking.

"Look, the figurehead is rising!" Viggo cried. "Now the ship looks more majestic, scarier."

"It's not rising or anything like that," Astrid said as she poured water overboard beside him.

"Then what is it?"

Ingrid and Nilsa were emptying a barrel of water overboard. They turned, intrigued.

"What it means is that since the stern is sinking and we're still going forward, the bow is rising," Astrid explained.

"Wow, what a disappointment, but it does make sense," Viggo admitted.

"That's not a good sign," Nilsa said, shaking her head.

"No. Bail faster!" Ingrid said.

They went on working, but the more water they bailed out, the more seemed to get in. It was not long before they realized this was a battle that, no matter how hard they fought, they could not win, and this was something the Panthers were not used to. They were always able to overcome any adversity, but perhaps this time they would fail. It looked like they would have to swim away from the sinking ship and reach Fish Island without drowning.

Lasgol put his head under the deck to see how the repairs were going. He could see the Captain and his men struggling with the leak. He had the impression of the leak as a sea creature, alive and made up of salt water that wanted to drown them all. As soon as they set down a plank, and before they could secure it, the northern sea hit the sailors with a wave and the plank flew out of their hands while more water came in. And not only the plank but also several sailors, since the strength of the waves was considerable.

"They're having trouble stopping the leak," Lasgol told his comrades.

"Why don't we stick Camu in the hole?" Viggo suggested. "They're about the same size—that way we'd stop taking in water."

"Why don't you shut your mouth, and that way no nonsense will come out of it?" Nilsa snapped.

Viggo stared at her as if what he had just said was not nonsense but a brilliant idea.

"I think it would work," he said...

"Don't be a dumbass. Keep bailing water," Ingrid said as she worked without pause.

"This is ridiculous: no matter how much water we bail out, more keeps coming in," Viggo protested. "I just don't see the point."

"So work faster," Ingrid chided.

Astrid was using a wooden box, and she looked at Lasgol and realized Viggo was right.

"We just have to keep working with all our might and we'll make it," Ingrid said.

Lasgol looked at Egil and he shook his head—if they did not close that hole, they would sink.

"Let's go and help with that leak," Lasgol said.

Ingrid looked at him, puzzled.

"The Captain's working at it with several crew members. He hasn't called for us."

"I know. But maybe we should take over. We're prepared and more focused than soldiers and sailors. In order to seal that leak we need teamwork. We're the best option for that. We're good at it."

Nilsa agreed, and even Egil had to admit it was a good idea.

"Let them bail and we'll close the leak," said Lasgol.

Ingrid nodded, and they ran to where the Captain and his men were fighting to fix the leak, past the men bailing the water out with boxes, buckets, barrels, and anything else they had found that might do the job. When they arrived they saw several sailors had been knocked down by the waves, utterly exhausted. The Panthers picked up the boards, nails, hammers, and other tools. "We'll take over," Lasgol told the captain.

"Go ahead... try... we're not getting anywhere..." Ulmendren replied—the water was already up to his waist and he was completely soaked. He looked extremely tired.

"Good. Everyone, get ready," Lasgol said to his comrades.

They waited a moment and a wave hit the side of the ship. A gush of water came in through the hole.

"Now!" Egil ordered.

Together the six friends, three on each side, placed two large planks and hammered them in place as fast as they could. It only covered one third of the hole, but it was a start.

"Another one's coming!" Egil warned.

"We have to make sure the planks don't burst," said Lasgol.

"Hold fast!" Ingrid cried.

"Push with your bodies, don't let the water burst the planks!" Lasgol shouted.

The wave hit the hull and the water poured in strong. One by one the Panthers used all their strength against the surging water. The wave passed and the planks held.

"Great work!" Ingrid cried.

"We need to cover more before the next one!" Lasgol cautioned.

The sailors handed them several boards while they urged them to hurry. The Panthers nailed them in place, covering another third of the hole in the hull.

"Wave!" Egil called as he counted in his head the time in between the waves.

"Everyone hold fast!"

"Piece of cake!" Viggo said, looking like an angry wet wolf, soaked from head to toe.

The wave hit and once again water poured in, but they held fast using their collective strength.

"We're almost done!" Ingrid shouted.

"Now for the last section!" Lasgol said, already motioning the sailors to bring them more boards.

"Egil, let us know. Now, all at once!" Ingrid said.

"Wait, there's no time. Let this wave break," Egil warned.

They all prepared to hold fast.

They bore the surge of the wave, which nearly knocked Egil down. Lasgol grabbed him hard with one hand while he set his strength against the planks. His friend and the wood held.

Ingrid gave the order. "Move on, now!"

They covered the last section just before the next wave broke against them. This time only a little water came in through minor cracks.

"You did it! Well done!" the captain congratulated them.

"It was nothing. We're the Royal Eagles. As far as we know, we can handle anything," Viggo replied as if it had been the easiest thing in the world and they had not had to make any effort.

Ingrid rolled her eyes and made a face of disbelief.

"Will it hold?" Lasgol asked the captain, not sure they had been able to fix the problem entirely.

Ulmendren evaluated the repairs for a moment.

"It has to be strengthened… it might hold well enough until we can make it stronger, but you've done a great job. I was beginning to think we were going down."

"Wonderful!" Nilsa said gladly, clapping her hands at the good news.

"It was nothing. Besides, it's been very pleasant," Viggo said with great sarcasm as he shook his soaking head.

"This has been an enriching experience," Lasgol told his friend, patting his shoulder. "Good team work always triumphs."

"And you're a weirdo with too many good intentions," Viggo replied.

"He's also a real charmer," Astrid added, winking at Lasgol.

"You might take note," Ingrid chided Viggo with a nod at Lasgol. "It would do you good."

Viggo raised his arms. "I'm already terribly charming," he said, smiling broadly.

"Oh yeah, terribly," Nilsa said with a look that said the opposite.

They were all soaking wet and, although Viggo did not want to admit it, exhausted from their efforts.

"Fighting against the sea is never a good idea, although sometimes you have no choice," Egil said.

"Very true," the Captain nodded. "Those who fight against the sea almost always lose, but those who don't fight always lose."

Egil nodded, understanding the meaning behind the Captain's words and smiling. "Indeed," he stated.

Viggo, on the other hand, was silent with his nose wrinkled.

"Words, words… just what we need…" he muttered under his breath.

The Captain turned to his crew.

"Six hands here, to relieve the Royal Eagles and secure those boards," the Captain ordered.

Six sailors rushed to strengthen the temporary leak cover, adding more planks and nailing them over the ones already installed.

Ulmendren motioned the Panthers to go back up on deck to let the sailors finish bailing out the water and strengthening the repair.

The cool breeze of the sea hit them the moment they came up on deck. They were soaked and the wind felt like knives with icy blades.

"We'd better wrap ourselves in blankets or we'll catch colds," Egil told them.

"Yeah, and they're dangerous if you catch them like this," Ingrid added.

They found the blankets they each carried in their packs.

"The weirdo doesn't need a blanket. He's a Forest Survivor, he can bear the cold and wet without a problem, am I right?" Viggo said with a grin.

"Don't pay attention to this fool and use the blanket, Lasgol," Ingrid told him. "You'll have plenty of chances to use Survivor skills when it's really necessary."

Lasgol smiled. "It's ridiculous to suffer just for the sake of it, and it's twice as ridiculous to suffer only for bragging rights," he told Viggo.

His friend made a face. "Really, what little sense of humor you all have. You're duller than Nilsa's soups."

"Hey, leave me alone," said Nilsa, who was already well bundled in her blanket.

They watched Ulmendren, who had also taken a blanket and, once wrapped in it, had gone to port side to look at the island with interest.

The Ambassador went up to him. "Is everything fixed? We're not sinking anymore?" he asked as if he expected just that.

"Not for now, but we have to find a place to land so we can repair the damage to the ship before we go on."

"That will delay us and cause trouble when we arrive. Delays aren't well accepted and least of all well understood," Larsen said.

"Well then, you can swim there if you want. I'm not going to risk my ship and my crew's lives to avoid being late."

"But it's an important appointment, of great significance. King Thoran ..."

"Yes, yes, I know!" Ulmendren interrupted. "You've told me that repeatedly, but even so, we have to repair the ship."

"Cove in sight!" one of the sailors called out from the crow's nest.

"Excellent! Set course to it!" Ulmendren ordered the helmsmen.

Amid the Ambassador's protests, the ship headed to firm land, the land of the Zantos.

Chapter 6

Captain Ulmendren directed the ship to the cove that opened before them. It was a secluded place, protected by tall cliffs on the sides which kept it hidden. Those rocky formations were covered in greenery and gray rock all along the northern side of the island. Beside the cliffs, the small cove with its secluded beach seemed designed to hide from the great northern ocean's wild waters.

"Captain, do you think it's safe to approach the island?" the Ambassador asked. "This is Zangrian territory, and while we're not at war yet, the situation between our kingdoms is more than tense. A Norghanian war ship like ours, heading to its coasts... might be misunderstood."

Ulmendren frowned.

"Fish Island has only a couple accessible spots. This cove halfway along the northern side is one of them. The other one is a port on the western side, but that's a fort of the Zangrian Army, so we'd better avoid it. That's why we're heading to that beach," he replied, pointing his finger at it.

A few paces behind the Ambassador and Captain, the Panthers were watching things unfold. They were interested in the new situation they faced. Things had gone awry and they were now heading to a Zangrian island—and knowing the Zangrians, things could get much worse, everyone was aware of that. The Panthers had already had some skirmishes with them and knew they meant big trouble.

The Captain went back to the improvised helm and maintained course toward the beach while the sailors finished bailing out the water from the hold. As they neared the beach they were able to see the inner landscape of the island. The vegetation was a lush green and quite sparse. They saw only a few trees in the area, but there were large, green-covered plains. It looked like the north wind had eroded the cliffs and the inside of the island during thousands of years and only a little vegetation had survived.

"He's not going to crash into that beach, is he?" Viggo asked, seeing they were heading straight to it.

"The Captain has to take the ship up to dry land in order to repair it," Egil explained. "Repairs at sea aren't usually good enough to continue navigating great distances. From what I understand you have to ground a ship in order to repair it properly in most cases."

"Yeah… but there's no port here to carry out the repairs," said Viggo as he scanned the coast.

"He's right, you know," Nilsa joined in as she watched the ship heading directly to the beach in a straight course. "What's the Captain going to do?" she asked in the tone of someone who would not like the answer.

"I'm afraid the Captain will have to do the repairs like they did in olden times," Egil said with a light shrug.

"By grounding the ship?" Nilsa asked, opening her eyes wide as they headed straight to the beach.

"Like a madman?" Viggo said.

Egil laughed out loud.

"No, he's not going to run the ship aground like a madman. What he's going to do is beach it without the ship suffering any damage, or at least that's what he's going to attempt."

"Wow, interesting maneuver," Ingrid said, scratching her chin, trying to imagine what it would be like.

"Bring down that sail!" the Captain ordered.

"Not interesting at all," Viggo replied. "D'you still have any of that anti-sickness potion, Egil? I think I'm going to be sick again with this maneuver."

"Yes, I do have some left," Egil said as he searched in his belt for the container, which he hastily handed over to Viggo. He drank it at once.

"Crew, oars up!" the Captain ordered.

Soldiers and sailors stopped rowing and lifted the oars.

"It seems the moment of truth has arrived," Ingrid said, raising her eyebrows.

"Crew, hold fast! Prepare to beach!" the Captain shouted.

"Well, this will be one more epic adventure that will be told about me—the time we took Fish Island with a sinking, drifting ship," Viggo said, puffing out his chest.

"The ship isn't sinking and it isn't drifting either, and of course we're not going to take Fish Island," Ingrid corrected him.

"Oh, but you have to color up events a little so they're more interesting, that's what the public wants," Viggo smiled at her.

"Don't color anything, and hold fast," she replied, raising an eyebrow.

Viggo gave her a wink and a smile and held fast to the mast, as if he were about to be shipwrecked and the great wooden pole would save him.

The Captain performed the beaching maneuver with great skill and the ship ended up with half the hull on the beach and the other half still in the water. The impact was minimal and the ship suffered no additional damage as it grounded. The skill of the Captain and his crew were evident.

"Soldiers, land!" the Captain ordered. "Protect the ship!"

"We should fetch our weapons," Ingrid suggested, looking inland.

Ambassador Larsen approached the Panthers.

"You're not to go ashore. You have to stay on board the ship and defend her. We're in Zangrian territory—anything could happen here."

"Defend the ship, or defend you?" Ingrid asked him with a cold glance.

"Both. It's crucial for the mission that the ship continues its journey and, of course, that I reach the Kingdom of Irinel safe and sound," Larsen stated.

"Fine. The Royal Eagles will stay and defend the ship," Ingrid said, glancing at her comrades out of the corner of her eye.

The soldiers, armed with axes and round shields, made a defensive half circle around the ship on the beach.

Camu, Ona, how are you?

We fine. Already land?

Yes, we're on a beach on Fish Island.

We come out? Tired of hold.

Lasgol looked around. All the crew members and soldiers were ashore—there was no one else on board but them and the Ambassador.

Yes, come up, but stay camouflaged, Camu. And only come above deck, don't go down to the beach. Okay?

Okay.

Ona appeared right away and came over to Lasgol, who dropped to his knees and petted her, giving her lots of attention.

"Ona, good girl," he said lovingly.

"Is that snow panther yours?" Larsen asked Lasgol.

"Yes, she's my familiar."

"Oh yes, I've heard that some Rangers have familiars. She's not dangerous, is she?" the Ambassador asked, raising an eyebrow.

"She isn't if you leave her alone," Lasgol replied in warning.

Larsen raised his hands.

"I wouldn't dream of bothering a big cat," he said and walked away to the stern.

Ambassador strange, Camu messaged to Lasgol.

He sure is different, Lasgol transmitted back.

Good? his friend wanted to know.

Well, I don't know how to answer that. He's a politician, a diplomat, so I guess he's not very trustworthy… in his world, lies and half-truths are common.

Then bad?

No… that doesn't make him bad… at least not for our interests or those of Norghana, but let's not trust him entirely for the time being.

Okay.

Lasgol hoped Camu would understand what he was trying to explain about Larsen. The creature did know right from wrong, he understood the difference. But when something was neither one or the other, but in between, he had more trouble understanding that. Unfortunately, there were many things and many people who fell into that "in between" category, which complicated things for Camu.

The crew brought out several ropes from the hold and proceeded to tie them to the figurehead so they could drag the ship up on the beach.

"Shouldn't we go down to help drag the ship?" said Nilsa when she realized what the sailors were going to do.

"Don't worry, they can handle the weight," Larsen said. "Your job is to defend the ship and my person—that's what's important."

"Look how nice this Ambassador of ours is," Viggo whispered into Lasgol's ear.

"Yeah… he's not very kind or considerate, that's for sure…" Lasgol whispered back.

"Politicians and diplomats rarely are, in my experience," Egil told them. "Luckily I haven't had to deal with them much, but I'm afraid we're going to learn a lot more about them on this mission. It might not be a very enriching experience, but I'm sure it will be useful in the future."

"But shouldn't they be kind, charming, and pleasant so negotiations go smoothly… and so they can obtain treaties with other kingdoms even if they're enemies?" Lasgol asked, puzzled.

"Yes, but we aren't kings or other diplomats. He doesn't need to be nice to us," Egil explained. "When the time comes, he'll use all his diplomatic arts, and I'm sure he'll ooze charm and kindness out of every pore."

"I think I'll like this fop even less then," Viggo said, making a face.

Following the Captain's orders, the crew organized into four teams and started dragging the ship up the beach. When the stern was completely out of the water the Captain gave the order to stop.

"We seem to be well grounded," Viggo said, looking over the gangway.

"I'm worried the ship will fall on her side," Nilsa said, also looking overboard at the sand below. "It won't, right?" she asked with fear.

Ingrid looked at Egil.

"Will it turn over?" she asked him.

Egil smiled, pleased they were asking him and that he was able to share his knowledge on the subject.

"Norghanian ships, particularly those designed for war, are built considering these circumstances. Assault ships don't capsize because they have a shallow draft. This one is slightly deeper since it has a cargo hold, so it could tilt to one side, but even so, I think it's unlikely to fall entirely on her side. In any case, I'm sure if Captain Ulmendren has decided to execute this maneuver, he knows how to finish it."

As if the Captain had heard Egil's words, he ordered his crew, "Prop her up!"

"Wow… sometimes I think you're some kind of seer," Nilsa said, smiling.

"Not at all, I simply love to read and learn different things that come in handy later on. Not everything is useful, but sometimes…."

"What he is, and we all know it, is a wise-guy know-it-all, but we love him anyway," Viggo said, beaming.

"It wouldn't hurt you to do as Egil does—learn more and speak a lot less," Ingrid said. Viggo put his hands to his heart as if Ingrid had wounded him with her comment.

"An arrow straight to the heart," he said with a charming smile.

"I wish they went straight to that melon head of yours."

"Then I wouldn't be the irresistible Don Juan, that I am. I'd become a boring know-it-all, and who wants that?" he cried, outraged.

"I don't understand what you see in him, I'm telling you," Nilsa told Ingrid, putting her hand on her friend's shoulder to comfort her.

Ingrid heaved a deep sigh. "Me neither. I swear, most days I don't understand it myself."

"To work, teams! Cut down those trees on the east side and prop both sides of the hull!" they heard the Captain's orders.

The sailors hastened to do as they were told. The soldiers protected those cutting the wood while they worked. There were few trees in the area, so they had to go quite a way off. The Panthers watched the vegetation carefully, since the situation was not ideal. They were beached and starting repairs, and if the locals appeared and attacked them they would be unable to flee. Besides, defending their position was not an easy task either—a half-propped ship was not the best fort.

No one was saying anything, but they were all aware. Lasgol used his *Hawk's Eye* skill all the time now. The moment it ran out he called upon it again, and he was doing the same with his *Owl Hearing* skill. He wanted to be able to detect any possible danger before it happened. He could see his inner energy consume itself with every summoning and the level of his inner pool drop. But he had a lot more energy now than before and it did not worry him so much that it was going down. He would not be able to replenish it until he slept, but for now he was okay and did not need to. The other reason he was draining his skills summoning was to see whether this had a positive effect on the consumption of energy required to do so.

He scanned the interior of the island and inhaled deeply, letting the air out in a long breath. He was not entirely sure whether he was right, but he had the feeling the more he used a skill, the stronger it became and the less difficult it was to call upon. Not only was it easier and faster to activate the skill, but it also required less energy. He had told Egil this and his friend had the same feeling. Hence,

Lasgol was experimenting to see whether they reached a final conclusion. Not that it was going to be easy, since everything that dealt with magic was complicated and slow—extremely slow in fact—but Lasgol knew he had to experiment to discover new things, and that was what he was doing. Every day he experimented a little more to continue learning.

The air coming from the sea ruffled his hair. So far they had not reached any conclusion regarding his suspicions about the decrease in energy used so, he kept trying to see how far he could go. One thing he was sure of was that the more he used a skill, the easier it was to call upon it, and of this he had plenty of evidence. He also knew that if he worked to strengthen a skill, in time he succeeded. The skills he used more often—like *Animal Communication, Owl Hearing, Hawk's Eye, Cat-like Reflexes,* and *Improved Agility*—were now more powerful than when he had started using them. They were also more powerful in that they lasted longer and their range was wider. With some skills like *Cat-like Reflexes* and *Improved Agility*, he even felt that his reflexes and agility were much better than before.

Egil came over and greeted him. His friend was sure that working on and using a skill improved the said skill in multiple dimensions. Lasgol always noticed the consumption of magic energy and how long it lasted, which were the facts that most concerned him when he called upon a skill. But he had not noticed other aspects, such as power. He smiled. He was amazed by the amount of things he still had to learn and experiment on with his magic. He had promised to tell Egil everything he found out, and his friend wrote down all their finds in one of his travel logs. He intended to write a big tome with everything they found out about Lasgol and his magic. It was going to be "fantastic," according to Egil.

"The ship is propped! Start the repairs!" the Captain ordered.

The cries brought Lasgol out of his reverie and back to reality. He had not detected any strange presence, so he relaxed a little.

"Everything all right?" Astrid asked, coming to stand beside him.

He nodded and smiled at her. "Everything is fine."

She nodded and gave him a wink and a smile.

The repairs began at once. They could hear hammering and sawing as the sailors on the beach cut the planks and shaped them.

"They're going to light a fire..." Ingrid said, looking displeased.

"They need fire for the repairs," Egil told her. "There's a substance they put on the repaired part of the hull, some kind of strong glue which seals the wood. It's necessary so the water won't get in."

"Well, but if the locals haven't found out we're here yet, which I doubt given the noise we're making and how unprotected the beach is, they'll soon know for sure," she replied.

"I was thinking the same thing," Astrid said. "The whole island is going to know we're grounded here and it won't be pretty."

"We need to be prepared," said Nilsa.

Ingrid nodded in agreement.

"I don't know why you worry so much," said Viggo. "If these scrubs attack us, these Zantos people, we'll finish them and that's that."

"It won't be that easy," Ingrid told him.

"I don't know why it shouldn't be, they're midgets," Viggo commented with a dismissive wave.

"Don't be too confident, you never know how formidable an enemy can be," Astrid said, putting a hand on his shoulder.

Viggo nodded. "When you're right, you're right. I'll wait and see."

As they had feared, the fire attracted the locals. Lasgol was the first to see them thanks to his skill and gave the alarm.

"Captain, armed men are approaching!"

On the beach, Ulmendren turned to Lasgol.

"I don't see them, from where? How many?"

"From the south. About fifty, maybe more," Lasgol told him.

"Keep going with the repairs!" Ulmendren ordered the crew currently at work. "The rest of you, arm yourselves!"

"It looks like there's going to be a party," Viggo commented.

"Let's hope not," said Nilsa.

"Everyone, get ready. Use the composite bows, we have the advantage of position since we're above and we have a longer range," Ingrid told them.

Lasgol nodded, then he turned to Ona. *You'd better hide in case everyone comes back on board,* he transmitted to Ona and Camu.

We stay, help if we can.

Lasgol did not want to argue, since he could now see more than fifty natives advancing determinedly toward them.

It did not seem that the presence of the Norghanian ship and the soldiers defending it intimidated the approaching Zantos: they were all armed with small bows, similar to Ingrid's bow, Punisher. *Okay, but if the Captain orders his men to come back on board, you go below deck before they arrive.*

Okay, Camu messaged.

Ona chirped once.

The Zantos continued to approach the beach. The situation was going to get tense at a moment's notice.

Chapter 7

The Zantos arrived at the beach. They were a large group. They did not look like soldiers but rather gave the impression of natives coming to investigate. They were all armed with their short bows though, which was troubling. They seemed to be the warriors of their tribe and were wearing tribal clothes made from the skin of some wild boar or another similar animal native to the island. Now that they were near, the Panthers could see that they were indeed shorter than the Zangrians although they belonged to the same race.

Lasgol watched them, intrigued. They looked similar to Zangrians: ruffled, thick dark hair on their heads and fair skin. Their faces were not pretty. They had thick eyebrows and big, flat noses. They held their arms in the air, holding their bows, and he noticed they were quite hairy. The warriors' physique was strange—on the one hand they were wide of shoulder and strong-legged, and on the other hand they were short as if they were missing part of their leg and back.

"That's weird. It looks as if they had taken a Zangrian and shrunk him," Nilsa commented as she looked at them, intrigued with her head tilted to one side.

"Flattened rather than shrunk," said Ingrid, staring at their bows with concentration.

"Well, I get the impression they've been squished somehow, they're almost as wide as they are tall," Viggo said. "Like they were hammered on the head until they ended up this stubby."

"Yeah, but they're tough. They look strong and muscular," Astrid warned them as, with a critical eye, she examined a possible rival or enemy.

"Yeah, the lack of height is significant in the Zangrians, but in the Zantos it's decisive," Egil said, watching them eagerly. "How I'd love to spend some time on this curious island and live with these people. Their culture must be fascinating."

"You find everything fascinating," said Viggo. "They might even eat you! Wouldn't that be fascinating?"

"They can't be cannibals!" Nilsa cried, horrified.

"They aren't, don't worry," Egil said. "I'm sure of that. This is one of the oldest races of Tremia, and it's well known they live off the fish and shellfish abundant in these waters, as well as the small spotted boar native to the island. Furthermore, I can assure you there are no cannibals in all of north Tremia."

"Thank goodness," Nilsa breathed out in relief.

"And to the south?" Viggo asked just to put Egil in a tight spot. "Are there any cannibals to the south?"

Egil looked at his friend and smiled. "Yes, there are," he admitted. "There's evidence of cannibal tribes in the south. But, so you may rest at ease, they live in isolated places I highly doubt we'll ever get to visit."

"Hah! With our luck I bet we end up in some cannibal tribe's cauldron as the main course in a banquet," Viggo said with great irony. "Well, they'd probably grill me to enhance my exquisite flavor."

"What they'd do to you is cut off your tongue so you'd stop talking nonsense," Ingrid snapped.

"Oh, my tongue in a sauce would also be exquisite," Viggo replied, proudly poking out his tongue and holding it with two fingers.

"Focus on the warriors!" Ingrid shouted at him, pointing her finger at the Zantos.

The natives had stopped at the beginning of the beach in a large, disorganized group. An older man with pure-white hair was leading them. Now he took a couple of steps forward.

"Listen, it looks like there's going to be a negotiation," Egil said.

"Are you Norghanian?" the old man asked in Zangrian.

Captain Ulmendren stepped forward to speak.

"We are Norghanian," he replied in the same language.

"I am Chief Dorgaton, of the Zantos people," the leader introduced himself with a small bow.

"Ulmendren, Captain of this ship and part of the Norghanian Army," was the reply, also with a small bow.

"We do not usually have many Norghanian visitors. Are you castaways?" the Chief asked, switching to Norghanian.

"The group leader speaks our language!" Nilsa said in awe.

"The fact that they look primitive doesn't mean they're uneducated. Particularly tribal leaders," Egil explained. "He probably speaks some other language too."

"We're not castaways. We have grounded our ship in order to make an emergency repair," the captain told the leader of the Zantos. "We don't want any trouble with the Zantos people."

The chief smiled ironically.

"The Norghanians are always looking for a fight. Everyone in Tremia knows that."

"That is our reputation, but that is not always the case," the Captain replied in a conciliatory tone.

"I hope not, for your own sake," the Chief said in a threatening tone.

The Captain started to tell Chief Dorgaton they had no hostile intentions and only wanted to repair their ship and continue on their journey, and while he did this the Panthers commented on their situation.

"Look at the old shrunken man, daring to threaten us!" Viggo said, looking outraged.

"He has his reasons," Lasgol replied.

"We can deal with those little ones without any trouble," Viggo said confidently, sure of himself and his comrades.

"They're not alone," Lasgol informed as he nodded to the west.

"I see movement but I can't distinguish what it is well. Who's coming, Lasgol?" Ingrid asked.

"Another larger group of Zantos warriors is approaching."

"That explains the confidence that white-haired stub speaks with," Viggo complained, frowning.

"Wow… things are getting complicated," Astrid commented.

"Shouldn't you intervene, Ambassador?" Ingrid asked, turning toward Larsen.

"Me? Why?"

"Because you're an ambassador and your specialty is negotiation."

"Not with archaic tribes," Larsen replied, waving the matter off. "That's way below my level."

Lasgol looked at the Ambassador in complete disbelief.

Level? Camu messaged to Lasgol.

He thinks it's beneath him to speak to the leader of the Zantos.

Beneath him?

He considers himself too important to deign speaking with someone he sees as less than him.

Why less than him?

That's a good question. No one is less than anyone else, or more for that matter. We should all respect one another. Always remember that, and never consider yourself above anyone else.

I more than dragon.

Here we go… what did I just say?

I understand.

Once again Lasgol was left wondering whether Camu had really understood what he had told him. He certainly hoped so. They would find out later on, since he was sure that subject would come up again in their conversations.

Captain Ulmendren finished explaining himself.

"I can assure Chief Dorgaton that we'll repair our ship and leave at once."

"Very well. You will not set foot inside the island. If anyone leaves the beach we will consider it an act of war," the leader of the Zantos said.

"Act of war? Isn't that a tad excessive?"

"That is what the Kingdom of Zangria has stipulated regarding the presence of Norghanian troops on Fish Island."

"Oh… I see…"

"I can call on a detachment of Zangrian troops stationed at the western port. They will not be as kind as I am…"

"Understood. We won't leave the sand."

"Finish your repairs and leave," Dorgaton said, pointing to the sea in an authoritarian tone.

"We need to cut down a few more trees," the Captain said, indicating a nearby grove.

"You have permission but hurry up," the Zantos Chief accepted. "We will be watching you."

The repair work continued at once. The large number of Zantos warriors who had come to the beach troubled the Panthers. If things went wrong they were going to be in deep trouble. And they were not the only worried ones—the Norghanian soldiers protecting the ship in a half circle around it on the beach were quite tense. The arrival of the second group of warriors had made them more nervous. The

Captain tried to keep them calm while he gave instructions to the sailors working on the ship.

The Captain sent half his men to cut down the trees they needed. There was a moment of tension when the group started off—they were all waiting for the Zantos to jump on them. The Panthers each stood at the ship's bow with their bows, ready to cover the men's retreat if they were attacked. But the Zantos respected the terms and did nothing. The group came back with a dozen thick and sturdy trunks which they used to prop up the ship's stern. This way it was raised and afterward would be easier to push the ship back into the water. The tide had come up, and it was the time to prop up the stern since when the tide went out they would not be able to pass the trunks under the hull. The Captain skillfully directed his men so that in a short while they lifted the stern enough to put the dozen trunks under it. Here the Norghanians demonstrated their renowned brute force. There were no accidents, and that was in itself a success.

Egil did not miss a detail of the repairs. He was impressed by the great job the crew was doing, as well as Captain Ulmendren's knowledge. He now focused on understanding what the Captain was going to do next. Egil would have loved to be below on the beach, witnessing everything at the Captain's side. But he also had his orders and had to stay on deck. He noticed they had put a large cauldron on the fire where two sailors were preparing the sticky viscous substance used to seal the outside of the hull. They stirred the mixture with two large sticks and Captain Ulmendren directed them. So far they had been carrying everything they needed for the repair in the hold—the captain was a farsighted man, he had spent many years at sea and it was obvious.

Once the substance was ready, they carried it in buckets to the ship and started applying it on the hull, climbing down some ropes that hung from the stern. It looked like they were painting the hull.

Viggo could not help making a humorous comment about it. "It's going to look gorgeous with this new coat of paint."

"I'll be happy if it keeps the water out," Nilsa said, watching the sailors with interest.

"That's the idea, don't worry," Egil reassured her.

"You'll see, I'm going to have nightmares. I'll dream that water comes in while we sleep and the ship sinks before we realize it," the redhead said.

"You would notice, the water would wake you up," Viggo said.

"You're not helping," Nilsa replied.

"That wasn't my intention," he said, beaming.

Nilsa made a face as if he were a toothache.

"Their bows are very small, they can't have a long range," Astrid said with a nod. She was watching the crowd of Zantos warriors with her eyes half closed and an intense gaze.

"They don't look timid either," Ingrid commented, tilting her head.

"They look pretty grown up for their size," Viggo said.

"If they show such confidence they must have a reason, and it's most likely more than their superior numbers. They must be good warriors," Ingrid said, watching them. "Stay alert in case they try something."

"You think they might?" Lasgol asked her.

"Let's hope not," Ingrid replied, "but better safe than sorry."

"Agreed," Egil said, nodding.

The work continued well into the night. The Zantos lit a couple dozen bonfires along the beach and remained vigilant. Torches and oil lamps were lit on the ship so they could continue working in the dark. The Captain knew they had to finish the repairs as soon as possible, and he went from one end to the other, shouting instructions to his men. The Norghanian soldiers protecting the ship on the beach remained firm and did not let the greater number of Zantos intimidate them. They were all weathered soldiers who would not flinch even if the warriors attacked.

They were finishing the last touches when all of a sudden, Lasgol heard a strange sound coming from the sea. He was the only one to hear it because his *Owl Hearing* and *Hawk's Eye* skills were still activated. The sound surprised him,—it was like a steady "clacking." Lasgol had not heard anything like it before and could not say what it might be, so he thought it important and went to investigate.

"I'll be back in a minute, I'm going to the stern," he told the Panthers, who were focused on the Zantos warriors.

"Fine," Ingrid said, "let us know if you see anything odd."

"I will. Let's hope they don't try anything," he replied with a nod at the Zantos.

"So far they're not doing anything, let's hope it stays that way," Nilsa said.

"Speak for yourself, I'd welcome a bit of action," Viggo said, flexing his limbs.

"Shut up and don't provoke fate," Ingrid snapped.

Lasgol went to the stern while Ingrid and Nilsa argued with Viggo about his comments. Astrid came with him. He stood scanning the sea, which was calm and dark since the clouds covered the moon and barely any light came from it.

"D'you see anything?" Astrid asked. "I can't see a thing, it's too dark."

"Yeah, I see and hear something…"

"What is it?" Astrid asked, sweeping the sea with her gaze, unable to identify what Lasgol was picking up.

"Look out! There's a monster coming out of the water!" Lasgol cried.

Suddenly Astrid was able to see what Lasgol had felt. A huge creature came out of the sea at great speed, making a steady clacking sound. The monster was gigantic, three times larger than the Norghanian war ship, and it looked like a great crustacean, although the body was covered with seaweed that fell down to the ground and made it look as if it were covered in hair. Two huge, menacing pincers were revealed on a body that moved on about twenty long appendages. The whole monster was covered by a shell, and it seemed to get its bearings through two extensions on its head that ended in what must be eyes.

Astrid threw back her head with the shock.

"What kind of a monster is *that*?" she asked in disbelief.

The creature was coming up the beach toward dry land, by the port gangway. It was moving slowly, but it was so big that it covered a lot of ground in spite of its lack of speed.

"It's some kind of giant crab," Lasgol said as he followed it from behind the gangway.

"It looks like something out of a drunken fisherman's nightmares!" Astrid cried behind Lasgol.

"Beware! Monster coming!" Lasgol cried in warning again.

The Panthers, alerted by Lasgol's shouts, saw the giant crustacean on the beach and raised the alarm.

"Monster on the beach!" Ingrid warned the Captain, who was finishing several outer repair details with several crew members, right in the path of the giant sea creature.

"By all the Gods of the Frozen Seas!" the Captain cried when he turned and saw the monster.

The sailors screamed and ran for protection on the other side of the ship. The soldiers who had already seen it were staring at its advance with weapons in their hands and horror in their eyes and hearts. None moved—they seemed to be attempting to process what they were seeing and were unable to.

The Zantos, on the other hand, did react.

"Great monster! Karramarro!" the Chief called out in alarm.

All the warriors stood at once and prepared their bows to release at the monster.

"Royal Eagles, protect the ship!" Ambassador Larsen cried, waving his arms frantically.

Ingrid glared at him.

"Oh please, tell me how…"

"I don't know, but the ship must be protected! And me too!"

"Oh really, I'd already guessed that," she replied ironically.

The Ambassador stared at the abomination coming up the beach one last time and ran to hide in the ship's hold.

"What a hero," Nilsa said, shaking her head.

"He's not really brave or much of a fighter," Ingrid agreed with her friend.

"Let's see, who called that monster out of the seas?" Viggo asked, waving his arms and looking accusingly at Lasgol first and then at Egil.

"Don't look at me, I didn't do anything," Lasgol said, reaching them.

Egil raised his hands. "Me neither, I've been here with you the whole time."

"Then it had to be the bug!" said Viggo accusingly.

Not be me, Camu messaged to everyone.

"I bet you called it with your magic. Have you been using your magic?" Viggo said accusingly as he looked behind where he believed Camu might be since he could not see him.

I do nothing with magic, Camu messaged defensively.

"Leave Camu alone," Lasgol snapped, "this has nothing to do with his magic!"

"It doesn't? So how do you explain such a monstrosity?" Viggo asked, pointing at the enormous crustacean.

"You know very well that there are surprising creatures in Tremia, in appearance, size, and physiology..." Egil began to say.

"Yeah, yeah," Viggo interrupted. "We don't need a lesson in Tremia monsters, but we could use some advice for what to do with this one in particular."

"We have to think of something, and fast," Nilsa said.

To the Panthers' surprise, the monster ignored the ship and headed straight to the bonfires where the Zantos were resting.

"It appears to be more interested in them than in us," Viggo said, raising an eyebrow.

"It might be drawn to all those bonfires," Egil guessed. "We're certainly bigger but we're less in the light. It must be that."

"Or it simply doesn't like the Zantos," Viggo said with a shrug.

"It could be that too," Egil admitted. "They've been on this island forever and I believe that monster might be the one mentioned in their traditions."

"The one you told us about that would attack them if they left the island?" Nilsa asked.

Egil nodded, "Makes sense."

"But they haven't left..." Nilsa reasoned. "They're still here, like they said they would."

"Well, angering mythological gods and monsters is common in the legends of any culture," Egil commented. "It might be furious for some other reason."

"Well, it's heading straight for them," Astrid said.

The Captain ran to give his men orders in a low voice to avoid drawing the sea creature's attention. He kept cool in spite of the nightmarish situation they were in. His sailors were also withstanding, although they would not stay calm for long in the presence of that monster. Ulmendren came over to the bow and, looking up, he called to the Panthers.

"We have to get out of here, now!" he said.

Ingrid nodded.

"Cover us," the Captain said and ran off.

The Captain wants us to cover them," she passed on the order to the others.

"Cover them? How?" Viggo said blankly.

Chapter 8

The great monster was already approaching the bonfires when the Zantos warriors began to shoot at it with their small bows. Hundreds of arrows flew to hit the body of the gigantic crustacean but bounced off. They could not penetrate the huge shell that covered the creature. With a round movement of its pincers, it hit two groups of warriors and threw them off in the air. The rest started surrounding the sea creature while they kept shooting. They shouted the name of the creature at the top of their lungs as if they were calling it to them, which was madness. It dismembered several warriors and, to everyone's horror, ate them.

"There does seem to be a cannibal on this island after all," Viggo said as he watched the scene with his head to one side.

"It's come to eat Zantos warriors?" Nilsa said blankly.

"We'd better not stay and watch," Astrid commented.

The Captain already had all his soldiers and crew on the beach, and they were beginning to push the bow of the ship to drive it back into the water.

"Come on, push!" he ordered.

The Norghanians, as one, pushed with all their might, but the ship only shifted three fingers.

"All at once! On my count!" the Captain said, "One, two…"

While Ulmendren counted down to the next push on the ship toward the sea, the unequal fight between the strange giant crab and the Zantos warriors continued. They were releasing at the monster, trying to put their arrows in through some crack in its shell and wound it, but as they kept trying they continued to suffer casualties. The huge pincers caught or destroyed the warriors and then ate them.

"Well, the little ones have guts after all," Viggo said, pleasantly surprised to see them attacking the monster so bravely.

"What are they calling it?" Nilsa asked, listening as the warriors chanted a strange word over and over.

"I believe they're saying Kar-mar-o," Ingrid said.

"Karramarro," Egil enunciated correctly.

"It probably means 'monstrous crab from the depths of the sea,'" Astrid said, shaking her head.

"Should we shoot at the monster?" asked Nilsa. "I'd like to help those poor wretches."

"Yeah, we should help them before it eats them all," Viggo agreed.

"We can't draw its attention to the ship, or it will be our soldiers and sailors who are eaten," said Ingrid.

"If we use plain arrows I don't think it'll be able to distinguish where they're coming from in the middle of this darkness," said Egil, "although I doubt we'll be able to wound it."

"Let's try at least," said Astrid. "Those brave men don't deserve to die like that," she said, pointing at two warriors who were trapped in the nightmarish crab's pincer before it put them in its terrifying mouth.

Ingrid looked at Lasgol and he nodded.

"Let's do what we can."

The Panthers nocked plain arrows to their composite bows and started releasing. The target was so huge it was impossible to miss. They released several times without hurting the creature, which continued eating Zantos warriors.

"Keep shooting until you find a weak point where we can penetrate that armor," Ingrid told them.

"I have the feeling it's entirely protected," said Nilsa as she released again, only to see her arrow bounce off the nightmare's body.

Lasgol released repeatedly. He called upon his *Fast Shot* skill in order to release three times in a row at top speed at the lower limbs the creature used to move, intending to maim it. He managed to hit his target but did not hurt the monster.

While the Panthers were releasing, the captain and his men were pushing the ship with all their might to get it back afloat.

"All hands on my count! One, two, three, push!" he ordered.

The ship began to move and the Panthers felt the deck slipping under their feet. They had to keep their balance to keep releasing. Nilsa grabbed the railing and smiled when she did not fall.

Great crab very tough, Camu's message reached Lasgol.

Can you feel any kind of magic?

No. Not magic.

Then it's not a creature with power.

No. Be plain monster.

Well, I wouldn't call it plain exactly, but I see what you mean. Is there anything I can do to stop it? Can you think of anything?

No… not know. If have magic I cancel it but not have.

Okay. Don't worry. We'll think of something.

"We're not going to be able to wound it," Egil said. "The only part not covered by its shell is the mouth and those two antennae which might house its eyes. We should try hitting those."

"It might have eyes? You're not sure?" Ingrid asked.

"No, I'm not. I don't know crustaceans that well, and a weird one like this even less," Egil apologized.

"Look here, Wildlife guy, do they have eyes at the end of their antennae?" Nilsa asked Lasgol.

Lasgol thought for a moment, trying to remember what he had learned. His mind kept wandering to river crabs instead of sea crabs.

"Yes, there are some with eyes at the end of their antennae," he said at last.

"Good, so we'll shoot at the antennae and see if we hit an eye," said Viggo.

"Yeah, and see if we get lucky," said Astrid.

Ingrid nodded, already aiming.

They all released at the higher part of the two antennae. The arrows sunk and the crab gave some kind of scream.

"Good, we did something!" Nilsa cried.

The Panthers released at the antennae and what seemed to be the monster's eyes. They hit their target and the creature screamed again.

"Good, that's much better!" Ingrid cried.

"Keep releasing!" said Ingrid.

The Zantos warriors kept running around the huge crab, releasing from their bows in a fruitless effort as their numbers decreased. The monster was set on devouring them all in spite of the wounds to its eyes.

"That creature's really tough," Viggo said in frustration.

"Why do the warriors keep attacking it? Shouldn't they run away?" Nilsa asked.

"I'm getting the impression that this fight is something else, like they're trying to reject some kind of evil god," said Egil.

"They might be trying to protect the rest of the tribe. If that monster heads to their villages, it'll destroy them and eat anyone in its path," Lasgol said.

"Yes, that could be it too," Egil agreed. "The Zantos might be fighting to protect their own."

Suddenly the huge crab turned, trying to catch a couple of warriors with its pincers and stopped to stare at the ship.

"It's watching us…" Ingrid cautioned.

"It shouldn't be able to see us with all the arrows we've buried in its eyes…" said Nilsa.

"Only that there are no eyes on those appendages, they're just antennae," Lasgol said, using his *Hawk's Eye* skill.

"Well then you were mistaken," Viggo said.

"It looks that way," Lasgol had to admit. "There are many different species of crab…"

"Well, it looks like something's catching its attention," said Astrid.

"That's not good," Viggo said, wrinkling his nose.

The ship moved again, propelled by the Captain and his men. This seemed to draw the crab's attention even more. It started to move toward the ship.

"It's coming toward us!" cried Nilsa.

"Get ready to keep it at bay!" Ingrid said.

"Use Elemental Arrows, everything you have left," suggested Egil.

The huge monster was coming toward the ship, brandishing its two great pincers. If it reached them it would destroy the ship and anyone on it.

The Panthers started releasing their remaining Elemental Arrows, Water and Air.

"Aim at the legs!" cried Egil. "Try to maim it so it can't catch us before we escape."

Ingrid and Nilsa released Water Arrows, which hit two of the enormous creature's front legs. On impact the charges of ice and frost should freeze the legs long enough to delay its advance. But that was not the case—the shell which also covered its lower limbs protected it from freezing. Not entirely, but enough. Lasgol and Egil also released Water Arrows and hit two other legs, and the bursts of ice spattered several more.

Astrid and Viggo were releasing Air Arrows, seeking the monster's mouth. They managed to get three to hit the inside of the monster's maw and the creature gave out a loud shriek but did not stop. It continued advancing toward the ship. Still, they had managed to slow it down.

"Captain, we have to get to the water, now!" Ingrid called out.

The Captain looked back and saw the creature behind them.

"Push with everything you've got! We have to reach the water!"

The ship moved with the effort of her crew.

The huge crab was almost upon them.

"I see two eyes right above the mouth!" Lasgol cried.

"Yeah, I can see them too!" Astrid said.

"At last, real eyes," Ingrid muttered.

"Release at the eyes!" Egil shouted.

They all shot at both eyes. The crab tried to cover them with its pincers and blocked several arrows, but it could not avoid them all. Ingrid's, Nilsa's, and Lasgol's hit the eyes. Cheered by their success they kept releasing without pause while the monster shrieked in pain and rage. Even so, it still kept coming.

"How can it see anything? It has half a dozen arrows buried in each eye," Astrid said.

"I don't know, but it can see something, I swear," Viggo replied.

"Keep shooting until we blind it!" Egil cried.

They all released again, trying to hit the eyes. Some arrows did, but the crab quickly defended itself using its great pincers to block the arrows so they would not reach its eyes.

"There's no way to stop it!" cried Nilsa.

Viggo left his bow on the ground and drew his knives.

"Don't you dare jump onto that giant crab!" Ingrid snapped at Viggo.

"We have to distract it somehow, or it's going to catch us!" said Viggo.

"I know, but you're not going to jump onto it!"

"I'm the best one to do it!"

"It's crazy, don't you dare!" Ingrid told him.

Viggo already had one foot on the gunwale to jump.

"Viggo, wait! I have an idea!" Lasgol told him.

"Whatever it is, do it quick!" Astrid cried.

Lasgol concentrated with a deep breath and called upon his *True Shot* skill. The monster was close enough for the skill to work. The only problem was that the *True Shot* skill took the longest time to activate. He felt a part of his inner pool's energy get consumed, which indicated that the skill was activating—now he just had to wait.

"Are you going to shoot? You won't gain anything with it," Nilsa said, seeing Lasgol with his bow armed and aiming.

"Lasgol, you have to do it now!" Ingrid urged him.

"Let him concentrate," Astrid told her comrades. "Pressing him isn't going to help."

The creature's two huge pincers were coming down on the captain and his men as they kept pushing the ship with all their strength, avoiding looking back so they would not see the abomination coming to eat them.

"Do it now! It's on top of us!" Ingrid urged him.

Lasgol was trying as hard as he could to finish activating the skill, but as he expected, it took its time. He saw the pincers and the helpless soldiers pushing under his feet, and he felt terrible because he was going to fail them, when the green flash suddenly ran through his arm and bow. The *True Shot* skill came faster than usual and headed straight toward the chosen target: a second left eye on the monster's side. Lasgol had noted that the crab had two pairs of eyes, not just one. There were two more eyes on its sides, and it used those now that the main ones had been blinded. He hit his target.

The creature gave out another loud shriek and stopped.

"Where did you hit it?" Ingrid asked.

"I think he hit another eye," Astrid, who was watching attentively, said.

"He hit another eye!" Nilsa cried excitedly.

Lasgol called *True Shot* again, this time wishing with all his heart that it would come even faster than the first time. He had to manage to blind the monster, even if it were only temporary.

The ship reached the water and all on deck felt a tremendous shock.

"All on board! Quick!" the Captain ordered his men.

"Let's go help them!" Ingrid shouted.

The crew climbed aboard by ropes they had let down and were helping one another. They hurried for their lives, climbing fast, the last one to climb up was the Captain. The ship was afloat already.

"All hands to the oars! Let's get away from that thing!" Ulmendren shouted.

They started to row as the monster came at them again.

"Quickly, it's coming for us!" Ulmendren shouted to his men.

Lasgol finished calling upon his skill a second time and the arrow flew straight to the center of the eye on the right side of the creature. It reached its target, slipping through the open space left in the pincer it was trying to protect itself with. With a horrendous shriek, the huge crab stopped on the beach, half its body in the water and half on the sand. It did not continue moving forward but let the ship get away.

"You were wonderful!" Astrid praised Lasgol while the ship left Fish Island.

Lasgol snorted.

"I just remembered that some crabs have two pairs of eyes, conveniently."

"Well, thank goodness," said Nilsa.

"For a moment there I thought we wouldn't make it," said Egil.

"You're not the only one," Lasgol admitted.

"Bah, there's no need to exaggerate. If it had come a bit closer I would've dealt with it myself," said Viggo.

Ingrid raised her gaze to the sky and shook her head.

Chapter 9

"Well, this has been a blast," said Viggo, watching the huge crab on the beach as the ship headed out to sea.

"And this time you didn't have to jump onto the monster," Nilsa said, smiling.

"Yes, thank goodness Lasgol was able to deal with it," Ingrid sighed in relief.

"I would've done the same thing, only a bit closer and more personal," Viggo replied, tapping one of his knives with his fingers.

"The same thing?" Astrid asked him with a look that required further explanation.

"I would've jumped onto the giant crab and gouged out its eyes with my knives," Viggo bragged.

"For that you would've had to think of blinding it, and I doubt the idea even crossed your mind," said Nilsa.

"I'm not only good with knives, I'm also good with this," he replied, tapping his head with his finger.

Nilsa laughed out loud and Egil and Lasgol grinned.

"Don't be preposterous," Ingrid said, rolling her eyes.

"It's possible that after trying to stick his knives into several parts of the shell unsuccessfully our friend might have gone for the eyes," Egil defended him with a smile.

"See? The wise-guy knows, and he's rarely wrong. The idea would've come to mind and I would've done it," Viggo said, puffing up his chest.

"The thing is it was truly a daunting monster, where can it have come from?" Nilsa asked as the island slowly disappeared in the distance and the darkness of night.

"From the depths of some abyss in the bottom of the sea most likely," Astrid replied.

"Well, let's hope it goes back there," Nilsa said wistfully.

"It's blind, it'll go back to the sea to lick its wounds," Ingrid reasoned.

"Not sure it's entirely blinded. Maybe the wounds will only impair its sight for a while and that will bother it enough to stop attacking," said Egil.

"I don't think we blinded it permanently with our arrows either," Lasgol said. "Not such a huge monster."

"Well, it was enough and that's what counts," Ingrid stated.

"Tacking east!" the Captain ordered.

"It seems we're taking up our course," Egil commented.

Camu, Ona, are you down below? Lasgol transmitted. He had been so focused on the monster and on summoning his *True Shot* skill that he had not had time to worry about those two.

We below.

Are you all right?

Yes, okay. We come down when sailors board ship.

Wonderful, you did well.

Sad not to help with great crab.

I know, we can't always act and help everyone with everything.

I know.

Rest now. Recover your power and let Ona stand guard so the crew doesn't see you.

Okay. No one come when Ona growl.

I can imagine, Lasgol smiled. The crew had enormous respect for Ona. They knew a snow panther could knock them down with a powerful leap and claw their necks open if she became angered.

The Captain was giving orders to his crew and also congratulating them for the good work they had done. He was also proud of them remaining calm in spite of finding themselves before a sea monster. When he finished speaking and congratulating the whole crew, he came over to the Panthers. He looked like he had been defending from a thousand-day siege.

"Great job, Royal Eagles!" he said.

"No, sir, you did a great job, you and your crew," said Ingrid.

"It's my duty and that of my men to see to the ship. I've been told you managed to somehow prevent the monster from reaching us," Ulmendren said.

"Lasgol blinded it," Astrid said proudly.

"Well done! If it had reached us it would have destroyed the ship with those giant pincers."

"I'm glad we were able to escape alive thanks to our combined efforts," Lasgol replied humbly.

"Captain, have you ever heard of the existence of such a monster?" Egil asked him with interest.

"I had no evidence of such a creature, but I had heard the legends. The Zangrians and Zantos have several stories about this monster and other similar creatures that dwell in the depth of these seas. It's quite common—all the coastal kingdoms have legends about sea monsters. Most of the time they're just that, legends. In all my time as a seaman I had never seen one come true, but I guess there's a first for everything."

"Do you think the Zantos will survive the monster?" Lasgol asked.

"From what I saw on the beach I'd have to say the Zantos knew the monster and, not only that, but they had already encountered it before. Their fighting looked more like a ritual than a desperate defense, or at least that's the impression I had."

"Yes, I feel the same way," said Egil. "It's most fascinating."

"And now what, Captain?" Ingrid asked him.

"Now we go on to the Kingdom of Irinel and hope we don't encounter any more trouble. This journey is becoming too entertaining," Ulmendren replied, making a face.

"Oh, you have to travel with us more, Captain, it's a unique experience," Viggo said, chuckling.

"I'm beginning to see that. I'm going to rest, and I advise you to do likewise," the Captain said. "I'm only leaving the minimum crew necessary awake. We have to get our strength back."

They all nodded in agreement, "Yeah, we're going to rest too," Ingrid said.

At that moment Ambassador Larsen appeared on deck.

"Captain, a word," he called.

"By all the sea monsters, what does he want now!" Ulmendren left them, muttering under his breath while the Ambassador trailed him all over the deck.

"I don't envy the Captain," Nilsa said, shaking her head.

They followed Ulmendren's advice and went to rest. They established watch shifts as they always did, even if the Captain had already established his crew's. Lasgol used his shift to go and visit Camu and Ona, who greeted him with much licking and affection, happy to see him. Sea journeys were something they both disliked and Lasgol was well aware, so he tried to be with them whenever he could. When his shift ended, instead of sleeping with the rest of the Panthers by the main mast, he stayed with Camu and Ona. When morning came and he woke up he found that Astrid had also come down below and was sleeping beside him.

The following days were peaceful. There were no more strange incidents. They sailed off the Zangrian coast since the captain did not want to risk another encounter with pirates. Ambassador Larsen was not at all happy with this strategy, since it delayed them even more. He continued to follow the Captain all over the ship, torturing him with his constant complaints and comments.

The Panthers were enjoying the journey, waiting for the next complication which would inevitably arise. At least that was what Viggo was expecting and the reason why he continually sharpened his weapons and prepared poisons. Astrid joined him, and together they perfected the toxic compounds. Egil went from one end of the ship to the other, seizing every opportunity to learn new things about the vessel and the crew's functions. He tried not to get in the way and ask few questions, but there were days when, carried away by his urge to learn, he could not help pestering the sailors. They endured him for a while but then went away or ignored him so he would stop questioning them.

Lasgol spent his free time repairing the frozen bridge and experimenting with his skills. The former was arduous and frustrating, although he realized that not only did he have to do it, but that it was also good for him. It was teaching him something important which many people lacked, Norghanians in particular, and that was patience. Patience was a great virtue people had to work on to develop and maintain, as Egil had explained to him many times. Lasgol was quite patient, or at least he thought so. In any case, he knew it was good for him to work on it, and if repairing the mental bridge was helping him somehow, it was by improving his patience. Working with his skills was not as arduous or frustrating, even if he did not make great advances. He suspected and hoped he was right—that with every day he experimented and struggled he was getting a little further, even if he barely noticed any improvement. But he was sure he was making progress so he did not mind the work.

Ingrid and Nilsa prepared Elemental Arrows with the components they had left. They had already used many in combat so they needed to replace them or they would not have enough when the time came. Making them was no easy process, and they had to be careful since it would not be the first or last time a Ranger lost a couple of fingers from an exploding Elemental Arrow while making them. They worked with reinforced gloves, but even so they had to take extreme precautions. The wind was their worst enemy, so they were working in the hold.

The final days of the journey went by without any more encounters, and they reached the coasts of the Kingdom of Irinel at last. The captain took the ship to the port city of Kensale, one of the most western cities in the realm. They crossed with several Irinel war ships, and Captain Ulmendren hoisted a diplomatic flag so there would be no confrontations. Most likely the ships of Irinel knew of their arrival, but just in case. A couple of leagues from port, two war ships with the green and white flag of Irinel began to escort them. That would prevent any trouble.

They entered the port, which was quite busy with merchant ships. The Irinel fleet was small and mainly made up of fishing and merchant ships. It was not a trade-inclined nation like the City-States on the coast further east. The Captain brought the ship into the harbor and docked. Once the operation was over the Panthers were ready to leave, all their gear loaded on their backs. Ambassador Larsen was waiting for the gangway to be placed so they could go down to the pier where four dozen Irinel soldiers were waiting for them with one officer in command.

"A welcome committee? Or are they waiting to take us into custody?" Viggo asked with great sarcasm.

"They're here to welcome us," Ambassador Larsen said.

"Are you sure?" Viggo asked doubtfully.

"We Norghanians are not well received in foreign kingdoms," Ingrid said, raising an eyebrow.

"We have safe-conduct to reach the capital. Those soldiers have come to guard us as we travel there."

"I think I'd prefer to watch my own back," Viggo told him. "Having so many soldiers around isn't exactly my cup of tea," he said, making a face.

"We are in a foreign kingdom as emissaries of King Thoran. We must behave as such and maintain appearances," Larsen told them in a tone reserved for explaining something to a child.

"The only expected appearance from me is this," Viggo replied, passing his thumb from one side of his throat to the other.

Larsen's eyes almost popped.

"As Royal Eagles, you had better stay alert and let me do the talking, especially the negotiations. Do not say a word or act unless I tell you. You must proceed with great caution and discretion as if you were my shadows, otherwise we might start an international incident, which is the last thing King Thoran wants."

"Don't worry, we won't," Ingrid hastened to reassure him.

Captain Ulmendren came over to see them off.

"I will await your return here. The crew and the ship will be ready to leave when you return."

"Very well, let's hope we don't encounter any setbacks," Larsen said.

Ulmendren responded with a nod. "Let's hope not."

"See you soon," Ingrid said.

"Be careful on land," the Captain said to the Panthers.

"Don't worry, we will be," said Viggo.

Ulmendren smiled like he had not during the whole journey. "I have no doubt of that."

"Thanks for the journey," said Egil. "It's been a most fascinating one."

"I'm glad you enjoyed it, that's not usually the case you know," Ulmendren said.

"Understandable. After all, this is a war ship," Egil smiled.

"Exactly," the Captain agreed.

They placed the gangway and disembarked. Lasgol stayed behind, waiting for Ona to go down and also to make sure Camu left the ship without trouble.

Ona leapt down to the pier with her usual grace, then the gangway seemed to give out and nearly fall into the water. Lasgol stared at it in horror, knowing it was because Camu was walking down it even though no one could see him.

Everything okay? he transmitted, worried Camu might fall in the water.

Gangway narrow.

We all went down safely.

Narrow for me, Camu protested.

Okay, I understand. Have you landed?

Yes, almost fall in water.

Lasgol snorted in relief.

Thank goodness—that would have been hard to explain.

I happy on land.

Yes, it's nice to set foot on a firm surface, I'll give you that.

We far from home?

Well yeah… we're quite a distance to the east of Tremia, northeast to be exact. Ask Egil to show you one of his maps.

I like maps.

I know.

Soldiers friends or foes? Camu asked all of a sudden.

Friends, we hope. They're from the Kingdom of Irinel, which is where we are.

Okay.

Lasgol watched the soldiers and sighed. He hoped there would be no trouble with them. There should not be, but you never knew…

Chapter 10

Ambassador Larsen walked upright and with an air of pomp and circumstance toward the officer in command of the soldiers. From his armor and helmet it was obvious this was not a mere officer. He was someone who had earned his stripes, someone powerful. No doubt he was there to welcome them, which indicated that their mission was official and the Kingdom of Irinel was aware and part of it. This reassured Lasgol somewhat, since the last thing they wanted was another dodgy mission in a foreign land. The Kingdoms of Norghana and Irinel were not at war, but they also had not signed treaties of friendship or collaboration, as far as Lasgol knew.

"Ambassador Larsen, I am Commander Gared," the officer introduced himself. "Allow me to welcome you to Kensale, trading city of the Kingdom of Irinel."

Lasgol and Egil exchanged glances. A commander of the army of Irinel with his guard was waiting for them. This *was* important.

"It is a real pleasure to visit these beautiful green lands again," Larsen replied with an elaborate bow.

"Is that all your escort?" the commander asked, looking at the Panthers.

"Indeed. They are the Norghanian Royal Eagles of our beloved monarch, King Thoran. His majesty has sent his best Rangers to ensure the mission's success."

"I understand, Elite Specialist Rangers," the commander said, nodding.

Now it was Ingrid and Astrid who exchanged blank glances. How did the officer know about the Rangers' specializations? How did he know they were elite Rangers?

Larsen raised an eyebrow. "I see that in the precious kingdom of Irinel you have knowledge of our renowned Rangers," he commented, trying to elicit more information from the commander.

"We do," Gared nodded without any other explanation.

The Ambassador waited in silence for a moment to see whether Gared would add anything else, but the officer remained inscrutable.

"The Royal Eagles are the best among the Rangers, which is why His Majesty has sent them. They will do their duty," Larsen assured.

"No doubt. I don't think there will be any complications, but we appreciate having experienced fighters."

"And loyal to the Crown," Larsen added.

"An important aspect in this matter," Gared agreed.

"I trust the King of Irinel will also provide those loyal to the Crown," the diplomat said.

"By all means. His Majesty, King Kendryk of the Kingdom of Irinel, has provided a loyal and experienced group as well."

Lasgol had no idea what they were talking about, but he was beginning to realize that their mission was important and affected both royal houses: Norghana's and Irinel's. What was going on, and why were the Royal Eagles required to be there?

"Very well, Commander. Whenever you wish, we are ready to go on," Larsen announced.

Gared bowed lightly and then turned toward his men and gave them several orders in their own language which the Panthers were unable to understand. The group of soldiers occupied the whole pier, forming a human wall parted in two, leaving a corridor in the middle.

"Follow me, please," the Commander said, leading the way.

Larsen signaled the Panthers to follow them.

Ona, you're with me.

And me? Camu messaged.

You stay a little behind. I guess those soldiers are going to escort us, so follow us camouflaged behind them.

Okay.

The soldiers' formation stepped back when they passed by as they saw Ona and Lasgol watching them. Almost all of them had red hair in several shades, from lighter to fiery, and freckles. They were thin and not as strong or tall as Norghanian soldiers, and their eyes were livelier. They wore chain mail and a helmet without a visor and they carried steel spears and a tear-shaped shield also of steel. The uniform and shield were painted green and white, the colors of Irinel. There was a curious coat of arms with a strange six-headed white flower on it that caught Lasgol's attention.

Egil, who was walking beside him, did not miss a detail as he inspected the soldiers like Lasgol.

"Can you speak the language of Irinel?" Lasgol asked Egil in a whisper.

"I'm afraid I only know enough to ask for a room at an inn," his friend said apologetically. "I haven't had time to study the language of this beautiful kingdom. I hope to learn some more during this journey."

"Then we're not going to find out their plans…"

"We'll have to trust the Ambassador," Egil replied and looked ahead where Larsen was walking as stiff as the pole of a spear.

Lasgol frowned. "He doesn't seem like someone we can really trust."

"Let's not be too hasty in our judgment. He might not be the nicest or the most heroic of Norghanians, but that doesn't mean he's not trustworthy. Obviously I mean to King Thoran."

"Not necessarily worthy of *our* trust then…"

"Irrefutable, my dear friend," Egil smiled at him.

"I figured as much…"

"Take it easy. The Ambassador has a mission to carry out for Thoran, and he will. Diplomats live and die for the results they obtain for their monarchs," Egil explained.

"Tough life then."

"It makes them strive for the best with every royal errand," Egil went on. "They'll use all their cunning, knowledge, contacts, and skills to reach their goal."

"That includes betraying us if necessary, right?" Lasgol suggested.

"Indeed."

Lasgol snorted, "I guessed as much."

Commander Gared led them along the pier to the city, whose northern gate opened onto the docks. They went through the gate and entered the walled city. It was not a large city and the fortifications, although functional, were not high quality, at least compared to the Norghanian walls. The walls in Norghana were made of rock from the high snow-covered mountains and at least double the width and resistant as the Irinel fortifications. Contrary to Norghana, it was not as cold in this kingdom from what Egil had told them. It was not snow-covered most of the year as Norghana was, nor did they have strong winter storms. But they did have a lot of rain. This was a green land and it rained practically all year round. As if wanting to prove this and welcome them, it started to drizzle.

"Put your hoods on. It rains a lot here, and it's a rain that thoroughly soaks you," Larsen turned to warn them.

"Welcome to Irinel, the green and white land," Commander Gared said.

The Panthers pulled up their hoods and secured their weapons and arrows so they would not get too wet.

"What does he mean by green and white land?" Nilsa asked Larsen.

"That is what the Kingdom of Irinel is known as. The green is for the large plains and cliffs on the coast covered with beautiful greenery the whole year long. As you'll soon realize, it's because of the incessant rain. The white refers to some special flowers which only grow in this kingdom, the White Seiburu, which grow all year long and have healing properties."

"Wow, how interesting. I'd like to gather some," Egil said, "in order to study them."

"No, don't even consider it!" Larsen replied, visibly upset.

"Why not...?" Egil asked blankly.

"Because it's the flower of the realm, the same flower they wear on their shields, and only those born in Irinel are allowed to touch that flower. If a foreigner touches one of the six-headed flowers, he will have his hand cut off, no exceptions."

"No exceptions? Isn't that a little harsh?" Ingrid protested.

"That's the law here. This is how it's always been. Let me warn you that there have been most upsetting incidents because of this ban. More than one diplomat and even a ruler have lost a hand."

"Really? That can't be true," Lasgol, who was also listening, said.

"It can. Prince Cesareus III of the Kingdom of Erenal, for instance. There was a war between the two kingdoms for over ten years because of the incident."

"Wow... they take their flowers seriously..." said Viggo, "which is weird. Are these people in their right minds?"

"We'd better not even go near them," said Egil.

"Yes, don't let anyone touch those flowers. They are very easy to identify—they grow in the midst of the green plains forming a circle, and they have six white heads."

The Panthers talked among themselves about the peculiar flowers of Irinel and the punishment for touching one.

"I can't say I'm especially interested in the holy daisies they have here," Viggo said.

"They're not daisies, and they're not holy. Just remember not to pick one," Ingrid said.

"The only reason I would pick some would be to make a bouquet for you," Viggo replied in a charming tone.

"You'd better not, or we'll both end up without a hand."

"But we'd still be together, holding the other hand," he replied, blinking hard.

"I'm going to give you a black eye—stop talking nonsense! We're on a diplomatic mission!"

"Diplomacy doesn't agree with him," said Nilsa. "I think he should refrain from speaking for the duration of the journey, that way he won't get us into trouble with that big mouth of his."

"You're just jealous I freely express what I feel," Viggo retorted. "You should try to say what you think, it's quite liberating."

"Thank you, but I prefer to contain myself and get along with people, particularly when I'm away from my own land and I don't know the customs or the protocol to follow."

"Your loss," Viggo said with a shrug.

"We'll need to be alert and not make any mistakes in this kingdom," Astrid said. "Let the Ambassador deal with the matter and we'll keep in his shadow like he asked. We'll have fewer problems that way."

"I agree," said Ingrid.

They walked through the city along a couple of main streets roughly cobbled: construction was apparently not one of the locals' strong points. With the Commander leading and all his men behind them, the Panthers did not feel entirely comfortable. They had the feeling the Irinel soldiers were waiting for the order to skewer them from behind with their spears. The Commander led them to a fortress in the center of the city. It was not large like a castle, although it had four round towers which made it look like one. At the portcullis a dozen guards were waiting. Commander Gared saluted them and they were allowed into the fortress.

"Your horses are ready," the Commander said and pointed at the stables where seven magnificent horses waited for them.

"Are we leaving at once?" asked Larsen.

"Indeed. You are expected at the capital," was the reply.

"Very well. This is most efficient," the Ambassador said appreciatively.

"I'll be right back," the Commander said as he went inside the fortress.

Larsen turned to the Panthers. "You must understand, this is a diplomatic mission agreed upon by our beloved monarch King Thoran and King Kendryk of the green and white kingdom of Irinel. There's nothing to worry about."

"Every time someone says there's nothing to worry about, something bad always happens," Viggo replied.

"That won't be the case," Larsen assured him. "You simply have to follow my instructions. Everything has already been negotiated and agreed upon. There will be no problems."

"Yeah… yeah…" Viggo said. He did not believe a word the Ambassador said.

"Are we to understand that we're here to perform some kind of treaty between both kingdoms?" Astrid asked, raising an eyebrow.

Larsen was thoughtful for a moment.

"That is exactly what we're going to do," the Ambassador confirmed.

"Very well," Ingrid replied before Viggo could utter one of his caustic statements.

Larsen returned to the front with the Commander and began to chat about trivial things.

"Do you believe him?" Nilsa asked her comrades.

"Not a word," said Viggo.

"We have no reason to distrust him," Ingrid said.

"There's one small detail that has me worried," Egil commented.

They all looked at him at once and listened carefully.

"What is it, Egil?" Lasgol asked him.

"If a treaty's going to be signed… why did Thoran need to send the Royal Eagles?"

They were all thoughtful. They knew Egil was right, that did not add up.

Chapter 11

They were soon on their way to the capital, leaving behind the port city of Kensale and heading into the southeast quadrant of the country. Commander Gared rode at the head, together with Ambassador Larsen. The Royal Eagles rode behind, followed by fifty soldiers in green and white. The capital, Blindah, was about a week away from the coast according to what Ambassador Larsen had told them, so the journey would take them a few days since the retinue did not seem to be in too much of a hurry judging by their pace.

You're following behind the soldiers, right? Lasgol transmitted to Camu to make sure.

I come behind.

Are you all right?

I bored.

We're on a mission, so don't do anything stupid. This isn't the time to play with all these soldiers around.

Maybe bite one in the behind.

Camu! Don't you dare!

And leg?

Don't! Don't bite anyone anywhere!

I bored.

Behave yourself!

Astrid saw Lasgol looking back tensely and guessed something was amiss.

"Everything all right?"

"Yeah… it's Camu…. You know…"

Astrid nodded and smiled.

"He's being Camu, right?"

"You've got it."

Astrid laughed.

"He's adorable."

"Adorable, my foot! He's naughty, disobedient, and stubborn, that's what he is," Lasgol protested.

"And you wouldn't want it any other way," she replied with a smile.

"I think you put too much faith in my love for Camu."

"Indeed, all of it!" she replied, laughing.

Lasgol had no response to that.

"I don't know why you make things complicated. It's easy—leave the bug at home every once in a while instead of bringing him everywhere," said Viggo, who had been listening.

"I can't do that. His home is with us."

"You don't say," Viggo moaned.

"Keep going," Lasgol replied to avoid the uncomfortable conversation.

"You're also adorable," Astrid whispered to Lasgol.

Lasgol smiled back at her and felt better. He watched his horse as he cantered. He was riding a beautiful specimen of the land, a twelve hand, obedient sorrel, although the horse was not as good as Trotter. Thinking about his beloved Norghanian pony saddened him. He had not been able to bring him on this mission; the orders they had received had specified "no mounts" as they would be provided with rides whenever necessary, as was the case now. Lasgol always preferred to ride Trotter, even if he was not as fast as the horse he had been given, but his pony was at least as resilient and a lot more obedient, not to mention entirely trustworthy.

"Beautiful country isn't it?" Astrid commented to him.

Lasgol looked around at the landscape and had to agree.

"Very pretty. Such an intense green fills the soul. These endless flat fields make an amazing landscape, a visual feast," Lasgol replied.

"I find all those small stone walls they raise here very curious," Viggo said, pointing at the two low walls on either side of the road. "What's their purpose? I ask because they're all low and irregular, so they can't be defensive. Besides, what would they be defending? The layers of grass?"

"Those small walls separate properties," Egil explained. "The land you see between the walls, as a rule, belongs to one family. There are also families and nobles who own large stretches of land."

"Then if it's all theirs, why have these walls?" Viggo asked.

"It's a way of dividing the properties and a custom of these lands. These walls you see might be over a hundred years old."

"Wow, they must take good care of them, or else they'd crumble," said Nilsa.

"They maintain them so they remain standing," Egil replied, smiling.

"What shocks me is how flat this land is. There isn't a hill for leagues around. Everything is green fields and a few spread-out woods between rivers that aren't too mighty," Ingrid commented, rising in her saddle to see better.

"And sheep and goats," Nilsa added, pointing at a couple of flocks peacefully grazing on both sides of the road they were on. "They have a lot of goats and sheep around here."

"It does seem like the ideal surrounding for flocks with all the fresh grass everywhere," Astrid said.

"The Kingdom of Irinel has a lot of cattle and is well known for its great tasting meat and cheeses, among other things," Egil told them.

"Ha! I like that!" Viggo said cheerfully. "Let's see if we can get some good grilled steaks!"

"Tell Larsen, he might be able to get some for you," Nilsa said.

"You think?" Viggo's eyebrow rose.

"Why not? Ambassadors and their retinue are usually treated regally," Nilsa said, nodding.

"Oh well, I'll tell him then. After all, we're the Royal Eagles, let them pamper us a little," Viggo said, convinced. "What's the wine like here?"

"Viggo! You can't drink on a mission!" Ingrid chided him, glaring at him from her mount.

"I simply asked what the wine was like, I never said I was going to drink any. It's strictly general culture," he replied, looking saintly.

"Oh sure, I believe you entirely," Ingrid replied, annoyed.

"The wine here is quite bad… but they do have some special beer, very good and well known that you can only drink here," explained Egil, who had held back a chuckle at Viggo's prior comment.

"Special beer? Well known?" Viggo asked excitedly. "Oh, this sounds good. Tell me more, wise-guy."

"Yup, it's not like our beers, it's a lot darker and more tasty," Egil said.

"Oooh, that I have to try!"

"It's called 'Garagarbeltz,'" Egil went on.

"Don't you dare go near that beer!" Ingrid warned Viggo.

"But we have to familiarize ourselves with the culture of this country. We have to experience the culture, integrate into it. They'll be offended if we don't try their delicacies, both in food and drink," argued Viggo heartily.

"He has a point," Astrid said, smiling.

"Don't encourage him, he does that himself," Ingrid told Astrid. "No alcohol of any kind, no matter how exquisite and cultural it might be."

"Killjoy…" he moaned.

"Duty comes first, and don't you forget it you melon-head. The moment you have some distraction before you, you dive in headfirst," Ingrid scolded him.

"That's because I'm very forward," he grinned.

"And very much a knucklehead," she replied.

They went on chatting and laughing; it was always entertaining whenever Ingrid and Viggo argued. The landscape was beautiful, but by mid-afternoon it was raining again and they all understood why the kingdom was so green and pretty.

"I don't like this place so much anymore!" Viggo protested, adjusting his hood,

"Do you say that because of this fine drizzle?" Nilsa asked him.

"It seems like no big deal, but it gets you really soaked," he complained.

"Come on, you're a Norghanian for heaven's sake! Horrible winter weather is your friend," Astrid reminded him.

"Cold, snow, and ice are. This stupid drizzle isn't!" he replied, shaking his head.

They all laughed at his words.

At nightfall, the Irinel soldiers set up tents so they could take cover from the perennial rain. They were made of canvas covered with a treated material that repelled rain and humidity. The Norghanians had nothing like it and, of course, this fascinated Egil, who wrote it down in one of his travel notebooks. The Royal Eagles shared a tent. Ambassador Larsen, of course, had one for himself, much more elegant and comfortable.

Poor Camu had to look for shelter among some trees a little to the east that would protect him from the incessant rain.

How are you doing with the rain? Lasgol transmitted to him.

Okay. Rain not bother.

I'm glad. You won't get sick from being constantly wet, will you?
Not know. Not think.

Ona had come into the tent with them to seek shelter from the rain. The snow panther was not pleased with being wet the whole day. This made Lasgol worry about Camu.

You won't catch a cold, will you?
Cold? Not know.
I don't think so. If you can bear the cold without any problem you should be able to handle rain too.
I bear.

I hope so, Lasgol transmitted. He was not entirely convinced—the truth was, they did not know what kind of illnesses Camu might catch. In fact, he had never been ill, except at the Frozen Continent, and it had turned out he just needed to hibernate. There were so many things about Camu that were still a mystery that Lasgol always had some doubts.

If you need us, send me a message.
I send.

The soldiers only carried camp rations, similar to the Norghanian ones: salted meat, cheese, and black bread. They could not try any of the regional dishes and they were not served beer, although Viggo did ask for it on the side. It seemed the word for beer was understood in every language

They continued their journey with the first light of day. Luckily it had stopped raining during the night and they were able to start under a bit of clear sky. The temperature was pleasant compared to Norghana, and although there was quite a lot of humidity, it was comfortable. They went through several villages and towns, and except for the roofs being less steep than Norghanian design and the green and white ever present in the buildings, what they found was not so different from their own towns and villages.

By the fifth day of traveling they had already grown accustomed to the landscapes and peculiarities of the Kingdom of Irinel. Lasgol was calm and even happy—they could enjoy the beautiful green landscapes and being accompanied by the king's army without fear. This was a novelty. When he had seen the soldiers waiting for them he had feared they would have to fight them or trick them somehow. The King's and his brother's missions tended to be that way, but so far things were going well and Lasgol was happy. He was enjoying the company of Astrid and their friends and they had not had any mishap since they had landed. And really, being the Royal Eagles, this was something to rejoice about.

When they had been traveling for a week, they glimpsed a great city in the distance. It was unmistakable because it was built on a plateau, one of the few they had encountered in that flat country.

"Our wonderful capital city, Blindah," the Commander announced.

"And wonderful it is indeed," Larsen agreed with him in a tone that did not sound like a mere compliment.

"We will arrive at noon," the Commander told them. "I will send a rider to announce our arrival. His Majesty will want to give you an appropriate welcome."

"I appreciate it," Larsen said, appearing honored.

"It is the least courtesy requires; you are an envoy of the Norghanian Royal House."

Larsen bowed, clearly pleased with the acknowledgement.

The Panthers, who were following and paying attention to the conversation, exchanged intrigued glances.

"How exciting, we're going to be welcomed by King Kendryk!" Nilsa said in a whisper to her friends.

"Yes, it's a real honor to be received by a foreign monarch in his own realm," Ingrid nodded.

"It's going to be a fantastic experience," Egil said excitedly.

Astrid and Lasgol exchanged a smile.

"It'll be nice," said Lasgol, hoping nothing went wrong.

"I hope we'll be regaled as we deserve, particularly me," Viggo commented, rising on the saddle.

"Let's not get ahead of ourselves. Perhaps the King will only receive the Ambassador and we'll have to wait at the barracks," said Ingrid.

"That would be most discourteous to someone of my level," Viggo replied haughtily.

"You'd better bring it down a notch, or else you'll be greatly disappointed at any moment," Ingrid advised him.

"I'll try, but I can't promise anything," Viggo smiled.

They arrived at the northern gates of the city which, seen from outside, gave the impression of being rectangular and quite long. The wall protecting it was neither as tall or robust as that of Norghana, which surprised them a little. They were also surprised to see a moat full of water surrounding the wall. Its function was to make it harder for enemies to take the wall. To enter the city they had to cross a wide, quite sturdy wooden bridge.

"Fascinating defense," Egil commented as he looked at the bridge, the water-filled moat, and the walls with great interest.

"A whole regiment could drown in there," Ingrid pointed out, gesturing to the wide moat filled with greenish water.

"And they would if they tried to take the wall by the moat," Egil said. "From what I understand, it's about fifteen feet deep."

"That's quite deep," Nilsa commented, looking at the water.

"It's fantastic to learn they use the region's water as a defense. Because it rains so much all year round, they use it as a defensive measure. Very interesting," Egil said, rubbing his hands together.

"Everyone uses whatever their land offers to their advantage," said Astrid.

"True and fascinating," Egil agreed.

"With all the rain here, an army would drown simply trying to lay a siege. There's no need to defend the walls," said Viggo.

Lasgol smiled. "Also true."

"The best thing of all is that in case of a siege they simply have to destroy the bridges that access the gates," Egil explained.

"Not with fire I guess," said Viggo.

"It usually is, since they're made of wood. They pour oil on them and set them on fire so the enemy can't reach the gate and they fall into the moat," Egil said.

"Or you bring bridges down with this," Ingrid said, indicating her Ranger's axe.

"That too," Egil smiled.

Lasgol decided not to bring Ona into the city, especially not a foreign one. She would attract too many looks and create unease. He also did not know whether the Royal House of Irinel would accept a panther in the castle, but he did not think it was likely.

Ona, Camu, you'll have to wait outside the city.

Ona looked at Lasgol and moaned.

It's for the best. I'll call you as soon as I can.

We wait, Camu messaged.

I see a forest to the north—hide in there.

Okay.

Ona ran off and several soldiers jumped out of her way. Lasgol was sure his two friends were better outside the city. Humans were fearful and complicated creatures.

The retinue went over the bridge and into the city. The buildings they could see, including the Royal Castle whose towers they could already make out, seemed a lot smaller than their Norghanian counterparts.

"It doesn't look like a great capital, does it?" Ingrid asked, a bit miffed.

"This is a modest capital," Egil told her. "From what I understand, the Kingdom of Irinel is no friend of ostentation and her citizens are humble workers."

"Then they're not like the Norghanians," Nilsa said.

"You mean they're not bullies, noisy and brutal?" Astrid asked, raising an eyebrow.

Lasgol smiled—she was not wrong.

"Our reputation is a little exaggerated," said Ingrid.

"It should be even greater so other kingdoms would fear us more," said Viggo.

"That's a two-edged blade," Egil said. "In the same way, no one would want to make alliances with us."

"Well... yeah.... But what do we need allies for?" Viggo said.

"So superior military forces don't destroy us, numskull," Ingrid snapped.

"What superior forces?" Viggo asked blankly, not believing there were any.

"I'll leave that answer to Egil," Ingrid said, waving for him to explain.

"Regarding military power, we have the Nocean Empire, the Kingdom of Rogdon, the Zangrians, the Kingdom of Erenal... the eastern coast cities... want me to go on?"

"Are they all superior to us?" Nilsa asked, looking disgusted.

"Right now, as our kingdom stands after the civil war, I'm afraid they are," said Egil.

"Well, then our beloved King Thoran had better fix the kingdom soon," said Viggo ironically.

"I'm afraid it's not so simple," Egil said.

"He's the King. It's his problem, not mine. Let him fix it."

"What happens to Norghana is our problem," Ingrid corrected him.

"To Norghana and her people," Nilsa specified.

"Yeah, but there are certain things the person sitting on the throne is supposed to fix," Viggo insisted.

"That's also true," Astrid agreed.

They continued through the city at a good pace, led by the Commander and a dozen mounted guards with two officers at the head who had come out to greet them when they had arrived at the gates. Ambassador Larsen was chatting with the two officers, displaying his diplomatic skills. The Royal Eagles were riding behind and watching so nothing went wrong. The city turned out to be quite large with narrow cobbled streets. There were not wide avenues and the buildings had character.

They arrived at the Royal Castle, and it was indeed smaller and more simply built than the Royal Castle in Norghana. Just like the outer wall that protected the city, the King's castle was surrounded by a wide moat filled with water that looked deep.

"They seem to have taken a liking to moats," said Viggo.

"Yeah, I bet they don't waste water to fill up moats in southern Tremia," said Ingrid.

"I can see things moving in this one…" Astrid commented, pointing at the water.

"Better not fall in," Nilsa cautioned as she stared at the greenish water with horrified eyes.

In order to reach the walled gate of the castle, they had to cross a wide stone bridge over the moat. Seeing that the end of the bridge could be drawn up, they admitted the castle seemed more impressive than before. The fact that all along the bridge and before the portcullis, guards of honor were carrying spears with banners of the Kingdom of Irinel increased the feeling.

Ambassador Larsen walked with his back straight and his chin high between the honor guard, which had undoubtedly been formed for their arrival.

"We should've brought Norghanian flags," Nilsa said as they crossed the bridge.

"We Norghanians don't travel around with flags," said Ingrid.

"We're more of the kind who capture those of the enemy," Astrid said with a mischievous smile.

"Well said," Viggo cheered. "Lots of flags and little else," he commented, looking at the guards with their long spears with the banners at their tips.

Above the portcullis waved the green and white Irinel flag.

The drawbridge came down to let them through and then rose again, and the gate opened.

"Come along, the King of Irinel awaits us," Larsen told them.

Lasgol exchanged glances with his comrades as, filled with uncertainties about what awaited them, they entered the Royal Castle.

Chapter 12

The throne hall in the Royal Castle of Irinel was not like Lasgol had expected. The one in Norghana was dark, even grim, but this throne hall was well lit and gave off a feeling of light and harmony. The light came in through tall windows with colored glass and bathed the whole room. The murals on the stone walls did not depict battles but the green fields of the realm. There were paintings of large, green-covered cliffs the sea tried to climb unsuccessfully, and on another wall there were portraits of what must have been the royal family and their ancestors.

The great hall with its arched columns was guarded by the Royal Guard of Irinel. These soldiers were a little taller and stronger than the ones they had seen so far, although compared to the Norghanian Royal Guard, who were huge, these were much less intimidating. Like the rest of the soldiers they had seen already, they carried a narrow tear-shaped shield, but instead of a spear they each had a long narrow sword hanging from their waist. One thing that caught Lasgol's attention were also several javelins strapped on their backs. He guessed these guards fought with javelins at a distance and with swords at short range. He thought he would like to see them in action, in a competition or something similar, to see their fighting style. It was certainly very different from that of the Norghanian Royal Guards with their huge double axes.

Commander Gared and Ambassador Larsen walked to the center of the hall, followed by the Royal Eagles between two lines of soldiers from the Royal Guard in formation to honor the retinue. The atmosphere in the hall was not tense—the soldiers seemed to be honoring, rather than watching, the new arrivals. In any case, Lasgol and his comrades remained alert; if they had learned anything, it was that any peaceful situation could turn sour in the blink of an eye. No one had taken away their weapons, which was a good sign, but Lasgol noticed that the Royal Guard had their eyes on them and not on the Ambassador.

They reached the throne and stopped. Lasgol was not the only one interested and curious. Egil's neck was about to snap, he was straining it so. On the throne sat King Kendryk and Queen Gwyneth, the monarchs of the Kingdom of Irinel. King Kendryk looked more Norghanian than from Irinel—he was tall and strong, with long blond hair which showed some white from the passage of time. He looked Norghanian from afar, but once you looked at his face, you could tell it was pleasanter than a Norghanian's. The fine nose and brown eyes were not of the north, they were from the east. He seemed to be around fifty and had a powerful physique. Queen Gwyneth, on the other hand, was the true image of a woman from Irinel, with long beautiful hair the color of fire that fell in curls down her shoulders and back. Her face was beautiful, delicate, with very pale, almost translucent skin and lots of red freckles which decorated her nose and cheeks. Her delicate beauty drew the gaze of everyone present.

Behind their Majesties and on both sides, the Royal Guard stood to protect them. Two elderly men were beside the King. One was wearing a well-made dress armor with a green cape hanging from his shoulders. He was no doubt a general or admiral of the armies of the realm. The other elder was not in armor but wore elegant, quality clothes. Lasgol guessed he must be a counselor to the King.

The Commander and the Ambassador waited for a sign to step closer, having stopped at a prudent distance to show due respect. King Kendryk waved them to approach and Ambassador Larsen followed Commander Gared, who knelt before the King and bowed his head.

"Your Majesty, I bring you the diplomatic retinue from Norghana, as you requested."

"Very well, Gared, thank you," the King said and waved him to one side.

The Commander saluted and withdrew.

"Ambassador Larsen, I am pleased to see you again," the King said in a kind tone but not devoid of a certain harshness. "In honor to your visit we shall speak Norghanian."

"Your Majesty, it is an honor and a privilege to be able to be back in your wonderful kingdom and more so in your magnificent presence," the Ambassador said with a deep bow.

"I see your tongue is as sweet as ever. You must be careful it does not stick to your palate so you cannot speak," the King said in a sarcastic tone.

"Your Majesty, being in your presence, which radiates the power of this land, and in the uncontestable beauty of your wife," Larsen said as he bowed elaborately to the Queen, "renders my mind incapable of stopping the compliments from pouring out of my mouth."

"Oh Larsen," Queen Gwyneth laughed. She spoke Norghanian with slightly more of an accent than her husband.

"The incomparable beauty of this country pales in comparison to that of its Queen and Lady," Larsen said and bowed again to the Queen.

"You are nothing but a flatterer," the Queen replied, laughing, and it was obvious the Ambassador's flattery did not bother her at all, rather the opposite.

The King gestured Larsen to stop bowing. The Ambassador obliged and turned his attention back to the King.

"If I am not mistaken you already know Reagan, First General of the Armies of Irinel," King Kendryk said with a wave toward the elegantly armored officer.

"I do know the strategist Reagan, Your Majesty. His victories in the battlefield are legendary," Larsen said, with a nod to the First General.

"I wouldn't say legendary, but they served to keep the kingdom safe," the First General said with a nod back.

"And of course you know Kacey, my personal counselor, diplomat, and wise man, among many other things," the King continued.

"Of course, Your Majesty. Kacey and I have known each other for a long time and we have remained in constant communication working on the treaty I've brought you."

The King nodded repeatedly.

"Show us the treaty Thoran has written," the King demanded.

Larsen took out a round document case he carried on his back, similar to those used to protect maps, and approached the throne.

"Let Kacey read it first. I want his approval before I read it," King Kendryk said.

With a nod, Larsen handed the document to the King's counselor, who took it and proceeded to study it carefully.

Lasgol and Egil exchanged nervous glances a few steps behind Larsen. They were intrigued by what was going on and what kind of treaty this was.

"Boy would I like to know what it says," whispered Ingrid.

"Boring stuff about treaties," Viggo replied, also in a whisper. He did not seem at all interested in what the Ambassador and the King were talking about.

"How can it be boring stuff? It has to be important, matters of state," Nilsa whispered back.

"State matters..." Viggo yawned and covered his face with his hand.

"I have the feeling there's more than commercial deals in that document," said Astrid, who was watching the counselor with eyes half closed, trying to read some of the text unsuccessfully.

"Lasgol, couldn't you use your *Hawk's Eye* skill and read what it says?" Ingrid asked him. "I also want to know what kind of a deal this is."

"I'll try," Lasgol said and proceeded to call upon his skill. There was a green flash around his head and he tried to read the document without drawing too much attention.

"Is everything in order? Is that what we agreed on?" King Kendryk asked his counselor.

Kacey was still reading as he paced before the King.

"It looks that way, Your Majesty. Allow me to read it again to make sure."

The King waved for him to continue.

The counselor continued to pace while his eyes read every word with care. At the same time Lasgol squinted to catch what the document said. But the King's counselor was at such an angle that he could not read the text. Lasgol shifted slightly and strained his head, and just then Kacey changed the direction of his pacing.

"I could read something about a military agreement... protection against external invasions... open trade between the two kingdoms..." he told his comrades.

"And what else?" Ingrid asked eagerly.

"Something strange..."

"Strange? In what way?" Egil said.

"Something about joining the two royal houses... of Norghana and Irinel," Lasgol said with a shrug.

"That's strange, and highly unlikely," Egil commented.

"Yeah, it does sound strange. How are they going to join the royal houses?" Nilsa asked.

"Shut up and stand still, the queen is looking at us..." Astrid warned them.

They all stopped whispering and stood still, like statues.

At last Kacey nodded and handed the document to the King so he could read it himself.

"Everything is in order," he told the King.

Kendryk read the document quickly, as if he wanted only to get the gist of it and did not care much for the details.

"Very well, there will be an alliance," King Kendryk proclaimed.

"This is wonderful news," Larsen said, bowing happily. "We thank His Majesty King Kendryk for this alliance, which will strengthen our nations and which predicts glorious times for both kingdoms."

Queen Gwyneth nodded. "Let us hope they are glorious indeed."

"Both glorious kingdoms have similar enemies. Joining our forces is the best decision for our future," said Larsen.

"Yes, the Zangrians and the Kingdom of Erenal are a continuous nuisance and threat we must bury once and for all," Kendryk said.

"Once the alliance of our two kingdoms is made public, the Zangrians and the Kingdom of Erenal will not dare to antagonize us," Larsen said confidently.

"That is what I expect of this alliance. This, and that the City-States of the eastern coast don't try to sink their greedy claws in my kingdom."

"Just like his Majesty Thoran hopes to dissuade the expansion attempts of the Kingdom of Rogdon from the west."

"It will be a good alliance," Queen Gwyneth said, nodding. "The union of the Norghanian axes and the Irinel javelins will be a formidable force that should prove most dissuasive to our foes."

"Are these the famous Rangers?" King Kendryk asked, indicating the Panthers.

"Indeed, Your Majesty. King Thoran sends you his famous Royal Eagles, the best Rangers Norghana has, as you requested."

"Good, that is what he promised. Let us hope they honor their reputation," the King commented, not sounding very convinced.

"I promise you they will. I have had the opportunity to watch them in action during the journey, and I can assure you they are fearsome," Larsen said.

"Thoran had better be sure, or else our treaty will be nothing. I will tear this document into pieces and there will be no treaty between the kingdoms of Irinel and Norghana."

"That will not be necessary. The Royal Eagles will complete the mission just as his Majesty Thoran promised you, and the treaty will be signed," Larsen said.

"I hope so," the King said as he looked the Eagles up and down, assessing their worth. He signaled his First General to approach the throne and they spoke in whispers.

Larsen and Kacey watched the conversation.

"It's quite clear we haven't come here only to escort Larsen..." Ingrid commented in a whisper, unobtrusively.

"King Thoran has sent us to do something here... something special... for King Kendryk," Lasgol said.

"Irrefutable, my friends," said Egil.

"It makes sense, or else why send us? He could've sent the Royal Guard," said Ingrid.

"Those morons have no brains," Viggo said condescendingly.

"We do, and that's why we're here," Astrid said.

Nilsa rubbed her hands together. "We'll soon be told what it is they want from us," she said, trying to stay calm.

Lasgol guessed it would not be anything simple, since no King would ask another for help for something unimportant and, least of all, gamble on an alliance for it. "Yeah... it's going to be interesting."

"It should be—King Thoran wouldn't lend us to a rival kingdom if there wasn't something important in it for him... quite substantial, I'd dare say, for him to gain... And I have the feeling that in this case there's a lot at stake..." Ingrid said.

The King finished talking privately with the First General and gazed down on the audience.

"Reagan, my loyal general, tells me they've found her," said the King. "We finally know her true location. At last."

"We'll make sure to bring her back," Larsen promised.

"It must be done without her suffering a single scratch," the Queen intervened. "I will not accept her being hurt in any way."

"She won't be, Your Majesty," Larsen promised.

"As we feared, she is still sheltering with the Druids," the King said.

"That is unfortunate... it complicates things," said Larsen.

"It does, and that is why I asked Thoran to send me his Royal Eagles."

Larsen turned. He looked at the group as they listened carefully, trying to guess what was going on.

"The Royal Eagles will see to that, they won't fail you," he assured the King.

"I hope so. We have already made three rescue attempts and they have each failed dramatically," the King replied.

"The Druids are formidable adversaries," Reagan apologized.

"We also did not have all the information about the real location," Kacey added. "Now that we do, there's more of a chance that we'll succeed."

"What is more important is that my daughter suffers no harm," the Queen said.

"I promise Your Majesty that Princess Heulyn will suffer no harm."

Suddenly, the door at the far end of the throne hall opened and two people made their entrance. They approached the throne and the guards let them through, saluting respectfully.

"Father, Mother," the youngest of the two said. Without a doubt he was his parents' son. He had his father's physique and his mother's face, which made him a very handsome young man. He was in his twenties and moved nimbly. He was wearing the colors of the kingdom and heavy, elaborate armor bearing the Irinel coat of arms over the heart. His boots and part of his green and white cape were muddied.

"Kylian, have you just arrived?" his mother asked, surprised.

"Yes, Mother."

"How did it go?" his father asked.

"As we'd expected," he said and looked at the man with him. He was wearing a dark-green, hooded cloak and his face was hidden. He was tall and gaunt and in his right hand he bore a wooden staff as tall as him. It had symbols engraved along the wood which the Panthers were unable to identify.

"Then there was no luck," the King guessed, eyeing his son analytically.

"No, Father. They do not want to negotiate," Kylian said.

"I am the King! I should not have to negotiate anything! They should obey my commands!" the King cried angrily.

"My people are ancient and complicated…" the cloaked man said, leaning on his long staff.

"Your people, Aidan, are giving me a lot of headaches, and one day I will grow tired of bearing their insults."

Aidan, the man with the cloak and staff, pushed back the hood to reveal his face. The Panthers exchanged blank looks. He was a man in his fifties with copper-colored long hair. His whole face and neck were tattooed with runes and strange symbols in dark green.

"My most sincere apologies, my King. My people, and the Queen's," he said with a slight bow toward her, "have ancient traditions and laws which sometimes collide with those of the King."

"Your people do not respect my authority. I am the King of Irinel and that includes the Druids, since they live in the southern part of my kingdom."

"My people know they must obey the laws of the King of Irinel."

"So why don't they return my daughter when I ask them to?"

"The King's daughter has Druid blood. She can seek sanctuary and that is what she has done. My people cannot deny that sanctuary. It is a sacred duty of the Druids. They will not deliver her. Not as long as she does not want to leave."

"Is she all right?" the Queen asked Prince Kylian.

"She is, her inseparable bodyguard is with her."

"At least she is well and protected," the Queen said with a sigh of relief.

"Could you speak to her?" the King asked his son.

"I could not speak to my sister. She refused to talk to me," Kylian said. "She has asked for sanctuary and is staying with the Druids. I wouldn't have been able to persuade her anyway, you know what she's like… how she gets…"

"That girl is stubborn, selfish, and vain. She doesn't know what's best for her and for the kingdom," the Queen said, upset and disappointed.

"Heulyn is what she is, that we cannot change," the King said resignedly. "If she does not want to come of her own accord, she will by force," he finished.

"She has always been headstrong, my girl, too headstrong…" Queen Gwyneth said. "No matter how much I've tried to make her see…"

"It's not our fault," her husband said. "We tried to educate her and teach her what being a Royal means, the responsibilities and sacrifices implicit in the role. If she doesn't want to accept that and see reason, it's not our fault, it's hers. We're going to bring her back."

"That is not an advisable option, Your Majesty…" the Druid said.

"You will help the Norghanians rescue her," the King told Aidan as he pointed his finger at him.

"It will not be a rescue… it will be a kidnapping, Your Majesty," the Druid tried to make the King understand.

"It *will* be a rescue because my daughter has lost her mind and doesn't know what she's doing!" the King shouted.

The Druid was silent.

"As His Majesty wishes," Aidan conceded, and he glanced at the Panthers. An intense green gleam appeared in his eyes, one which Lasgol identified at once: magic.

Chapter 13

The scene at the throne hall had left the Panthers puzzled. They had not been expecting anything like what they had witnessed and did not know what it meant. Distraught, the King had ended the audience and had withdrawn together with his wife and son. From the way they had left the hall, they must have had a lot to talk about.

The King's counselor, Kacey, had asked the Ambassador and the Royal Eagles to accompany him so he might show them their accommodations. He had prepared comfortable lodgings both for the Ambassador, who was housed in a luxurious room for foreign dignitaries, and the Royal Eagles, who were led to a comfortable, large military bunkhouse inside the castle. Once the Eagles were settled, Kacey accompanied Larsen to his chamber, and as they walked away Lasgol could see they were already in deep conversation about political matters of interest for both nations.

"What a mess they've landed us in again," Nilsa said, shaking one hand once they were alone and Lasgol had shut the door of the bunkhouse.

"Yeah, once again we're faced with the difficult complexities of a mission," said Ingrid.

"What difficulties? To me it's very simple," Viggo said, while he chose the biggest and softest bunk and threw himself on it to rest.

"How strange you should find it so easy," Nilsa said sarcastically.

"But, really, what's so complicated about it? We just have to rescue a girl and return her to her parents. I don't even know why they've made us come all this way."

"I believe our friend Viggo is overlooking certain important aspects of the mission," Egil commented.

"I'd say *all* the critical aspects of the mission," added Lasgol.

"So, what are those critical aspects?" Viggo asked with indifference.

"In the first place, the person we're supposed to rescue is none other than the Princess of Irinel," Ingrid said.

"Who doesn't seem to want to be rescued," Astrid added.

"Why would that be, I wonder," said Lasgol.

"She probably doesn't get along with her family," Viggo guessed. "It's more common than you'd think. I'm a clear example."

"It might also have to do with the responsibilities of the crown," said Egil. "She might not want to assume them."

"So, we have a princess angry at her parents who doesn't want to come back to the castle, oh what a terrible complication!" Viggo said with great sarcasm, waving his arms as if he were going to faint from how serious the situation was.

"Don't underestimate her not wanting to be rescued. That's going to make our mission more difficult," Astrid said warningly.

"If she doesn't come willingly we'll bring her by force," said Viggo. "Problem solved. You always go over things so much."

"We can't use such methods with her, you heard her mother the Queen—she wants her daughter back without a scratch," Lasgol told him.

"No scratches, but what about a bump on the head?" Viggo suggested.

"No! You can't hit a Royal Princess of Irinel on the head!" Ingrid snapped at him.

"Because she's a princess? I don't make distinctions. I deliver bumps equally among common people and the monarchy."

Ingrid rolled her eyes and cursed the heavens.

"You can't touch a single hair of her head," Astrid told him. "Otherwise, her parents will hang us, and apart from that there wouldn't be a treaty so the mission would be a failure."

"Well, in that case, matters are a bit more complicated then," Viggo admitted, "But only slightly."

"The next great complication is that she has sought shelter south with the Druids," Egil commented. "That's a real problem."

"And why is that?" Nilsa asked, "Are they aggressive?"

"The Druids are a peculiar group of people..." Egil said. "They live in deep forests and underground in said forests. They live for and by nature and have strange, ancient rituals. They hold nature as sacred—she is their Mother Goddess."

"And they have the Gift..." Lasgol said.

"How do you know?" Astrid asked beside him.

"I saw it in Aidan's eyes, and I felt it," he replied, putting his hand to his neck. The hair on the back of his neck was still pricked.

"Are they magi?" Ingrid asked, surprised.

"Shamans rather than magi. They use Magic of Nature," Egil explained. "That's what I've read."

Wow..." Ingrid wrinkled her nose. "How many are there?"

"I'm afraid there are a lot," Egil replied.

"And all of them are shamans? They can all conjure?" Nilsa asked.

"I don't know whether they all can, but from what I've read, in order to be a Druid, they have to be of Druid blood, and it's said their blood carries the Gift, the Talent," Egil explained.

"I like that even less," said Viggo, making a face. "No one told us we'd have to face a bunch of conjuring shamans."

"Are they originally from Irinel?" Lasgol asked; he was interested in finding out more about the Druids.

"No one knows. But there are more of them here than in any other place, so people believe they at least settled here initially."

"Initially? Have they moved? Are there any other Druids in other regions of Tremia?" Nilsa asked.

"Yes, indeed. The Druids have traveled throughout Tremia along the centuries and have settled in several kingdoms and regions. But there are more here in the Kingdom of Irinel than anywhere else."

"I'm concerned that they're so powerful," said Astrid. "The King of Irinel himself doesn't seem able to bend them to his will, and that says a lot."

"If they have magic and there are many of them, it's more than likely they'll be powerful and difficult opponents," Ingrid concluded.

"Let's not jump to any hasty conclusions. We'll wait and see what Larsen tells us and what help, if any, we might get from Druid Aidan," said Lasgol.

"Yeah, let's rest. Tomorrow we'll find out more," Ingrid agreed.

The Panthers each took a bunk and rested peacefully, even if they were all thinking about what they had found out about the mission and did not sleep until late.

When they woke up, much to their surprise, they were not fetched immediately. An officer of the Royal Guard who spoke Norghanian informed them that Ambassador Larsen had several meetings scheduled for that morning. One was with Counselor

Kacey, another with First General Reagan, and yet another with members of the court, so he would not be available until lunchtime.

"That's quite a busy schedule the Ambassador has," Viggo commented.

"That's normal. He has to attend to several matters during this journey," said Nilsa. "Diplomats try to make the most of every visit. They don't know when they'll have the chance to visit the realm again. I've seen it in Norghania many times."

"Can we leave our rooms?" Ingrid asked the officer on duty.

"Of course. You can go down to the dining hall and enjoy a good breakfast. You can also take a tour of the castle. The areas you wouldn't be allowed in are watched by the Royal Guard, so they're easily identifiable."

"Much obliged," Ingrid replied with a nod.

"If there's anything you need, you can ask me. I'm Captain Jarith."

"I'd like to try the famous Irinel beer," Viggo said.

Ingrid glared at him.

"You can't drink while on duty…" Nilsa whispered to him.

"If it's so famous, I want to try it," Viggo insisted.

"For that you'd better go to the castle canteen at sundown. It's forbidden to have alcohol during the day," Jarith told him.

"I'll be there tonight!" Viggo said.

The Captain smiled. "I'll be at the Quartermaster's if you need me."

"Thank you, Captain," said Ingrid.

The Captain left and Ingrid glared at Viggo.

"We've talked about this!"

"I know, but I didn't like the conversation much," he smiled at her.

"Let's go and have breakfast before I bite off one of this dimwit's ears," said Ingrid.

They had some free time, so after breakfast at the barracks with the soldiers of the Royal Guard, who did not take their eyes off them, they looked around the castle. The guards let them go up one of the towers where they admired the beauty of Irinel's countryside. Since the capital was built on a plateau and the castle on another inside the city, they could see all around for leagues and leagues. It was all grass-covered plateaus of deep green decorated with small trees and bushes. There were no mountains wherever you looked, and the forests were small and scattered about.

"The watch has an easy job in this kingdom. You could see the enemy from days away," Viggo commented.

"It's beautiful… so flat… so green…" Nilsa said.

"It is. It radiates peace and quiet, which our mountains at home don't do," said Astrid.

"True. Mountains don't exactly radiate peace and quiet," Ingrid said, wrinkling her nose.

"Our snow-covered mountains show their strength and roughness and warn of their danger," Egil said.

"Even so, I prefer them to this," Lasgol commented.

They went down to the bailey and watched the soldiers training. They were practicing with spear and javelin, something that caught their interest since they were not familiar with Irinel fighting techniques.

"I think it'd be good for us to watch how they train," Ingrid suggested.

"Yeah, I'm interested in how they manage those javelins," Astrid said.

"Good idea. Let's learn something from these handsome Irinel soldiers," Nilsa said cheerfully.

"Handsome? They're ugly, with those pale faces and vividly red hair," Viggo said.

"Maybe they're ugly to you, but to me they're handsome," Nilsa replied, shaking her head to show off her red hair in all its glory.

Viggo feigned boredom.

Lasgol and Egil smiled and went over to see the soldiers' training.

They knew something about fighting with the shield and spear, but watching the Royal Guard doing attack and defense exercises gave them a better understanding of how they were used. It was quite different from fighting with axe and shield, which was practiced in Norghana. With a spear they delivered short, sharp, piercing blows straight ahead, whereas with the axe, attacks in general were downward diagonal blows, both from left and right.

What really impressed them was how the guards attacked with their javelins. They threw them hard and accurately. They used sacks filled with hay and sand hanging from posts as human targets. The soldiers threw their javelins, piercing through the sacks. They had also set up some targets similar to those the Rangers used to practice with their bows, and used these to practice throwing their javelins. The Panthers were highly impressed by their skill, since they launched their shots from over fifty paces and hit the target practically every time.

"Never in my life would I have thought it possible to throw a javelin so far," Ingrid said admiringly.

"Least of all that they would actually hit the target," said Nilsa.

"Yes, these Irinel soldiers deserve respect for their skill with the javelin," Astrid said, also impressed.

"Bah, it's nothing to write home about. One of those little spears wouldn't hit me even if I was drunk," Viggo said.

"Oh sure, because you're untouchable," Nilsa said mockingly.

"You said it yourself—I am."

Ingrid gave him a slap on the back of the neck.

Viggo eyed her, annoyed.

"If you can't see a slap coming, you don't have a chance against one of those javelins from a distance," Ingrid said, smiling.

Viggo had to admit she was right.

"I like your practical demonstrations," Nilsa told Ingrid with a laugh.

They stayed to watch the entire training session. When it finished they headed to the dining hall to enjoy the Irinel cooking, which turned out to be pretty good. They tasted a stew made with meat of the local stock and the famous dark beer which delighted everyone. The meat was good and the sauce was delicious, and the dessert was even better: apple tart with ginger, so good they all had second helpings.

After eating, they decided to go back to rest and wait for news of Ambassador Larsen. They all expected it would be interesting news.

Chapter 14

They were lying on their bunks when Ambassador Larsen came at last. He was accompanied by the strange Druid with green eyes, his face tattooed with curious runes and symbols.

"Royal Eagles," he greeted them as he walked in and shut the door behind him and Aidan.

"Ambassador Larsen," they all replied politely.

"I've been unearthing more information about the mission and dealing with several pending issues."

"Has the moment arrived when you explain what it is we have to do?" Ingrid asked.

"That is correct," the Ambassador confirmed. "It is a rescue mission, as you've probably guessed from the conversation in the throne hall."

"A royal rescue," Nilsa added.

"Exactly. Your mission is to rescue the Royal Princess Heulyn. Needless to say, she must be rescued without the least scratch. This is of capital importance. If the rescue should fail or if the Princess suffers any harm, the treaty will not be signed. And I cannot emphasize enough how unhappy King Thoran would be if that should happen. The alliance treaty between the two kingdoms is extremely important for the future of Norghana."

"We understand the importance of the treaty," Ingrid said seriously. "But it is a bit strange that it depends on whether or not we rescue the Princess."

Larsen smiled. "Treaties are agreed upon because both parties want something and have something to gain. In Norghana's case they want a military ally to stop the Zangrians and the Kingdom of Rogdon. In the case of the Kingdom of Irinel, they want to form a military alliance as well but also the Princess' rescue. She is the key to the agreement. Without the Princess there will be no military alliance."

"Well, it sounded like she doesn't want to come back," said Nilsa.

"Princess Heulyn has a pretty headstrong personality…" Larsen admitted.

"That won't make it easy for us to rescue her," said Ingrid.

"Indeed, it will not. You must understand that the Princess will resist being rescued," the Ambassador explained.

"Then we're going to kidnap her, which is very different from rescuing her," Astrid clarified.

"You could interpret it as such," the Ambassador acknowledged.

"It's strange that we have to kidnap a Princess in her own kingdom," Egil mused, "highly unusual."

"It is. But this Princess is not just any princess, and this is a different kingdom. The Druids live here," Larsen said with a wave at Aidan.

"Is the Druid going to help us with the mission?" Lasgol asked Larsen.

"Yes, he is."

"I will only help you get into Foraoise Naofa, the Sacred Forest, and then I will point you on your way, but I cannot be of more help. I cannot go against my people," Aidan told them with a heavy accent.

"Don't you serve the King of Irinel?" Ingrid asked.

"I serve him, but I also serve my people. I am the Druids' envoy at the King's Court. My function is to look after the good of my people and keep a cordial alliance with the King of Irinel."

"But he *is* your King," Nilsa said.

"He is not of Druid blood. The Queen is," Aidan said.

"So your people only serve those of their own blood," Lasgol guessed.

"Serve and respect," Aidan said.

"Your people aren't going to let us take the Princess?" Astrid asked the Druid, who shook his head.

"They will not allow it. She has Druid blood and has asked for sanctuary. They will not deliver her and will defend her to the death."

"Will they defend her with magic?" Ingrid asked.

"Yes, they will. Magic of Nature," Aidan confirmed.

"Do you all have magic?" Lasgol asked him. This had been on his mind ever since the conversation with Egil, and he wanted to make sure.

"All those of the blood have magic, with varying levels of power," Aidan confirmed. He hit the floor with his staff and uttered some arcane words. The symbols carved on it shone bright green and several snakes took shape. They coiled around the wood and their heads looked ready to attack. The Panthers all took one step back, moving away from Aidan.

"I hate snakes!" Nilsa cried.

Viggo and Astrid already had their knives out, ready to attack.

Aidan raised his left hand.

"Take it easy, this is only a demonstration of my people's magic. Do not come near and they will not attack you. They will remain coiled around my staff."

"Can you command them?" Lasgol asked, mystified.

"Of course." Aidan whispered some words and the snakes left the staff and coiled around his right arm.

"Impressive," said Lasgol.

"They are creatures of Nature, so our magic can control them," Aidan explained.

"That's neat. If the Druids start bringing out snakes, spiders, and other venomous creatures, this is going to be lots of fun. I love it when our missions get this complicated, they're a lot more entertaining," Viggo said with a smile.

"We're going to be at a clear disadvantage if we don't have anyone who can counter their magic," Ingrid said as she stared at Aidan, but he avoided her gaze and did not acknowledge her comment.

"The best option is a stealthy night mission," Larsen said. "Get in, rescue the Princess, and escape without being seen."

"That's a good idea, only those missions almost never go as planned," said Viggo.

"They have her in a forest. That's your ground, you're Elite Specialists. If anyone can do it, it's you," Larsen said. "That's why you're here."

"Oh, we can do it," Ingrid assured.

"But we have to prepare really well," Astrid added.

"Egil, we need a good subtle plan," Ingrid said.

"I'll start planning," Egil said, smiling weakly.

"Aidan is going to explore the terrain and see when we can do the job," Larsen explained. "Princess Heulyn moved to a new location when she found out about her brother's arrival."

"She's smart," Viggo commented.

"And cautious," added Astrid.

"So then, we'll wait for news?" Ingrid asked Aidan.

The Druid nodded. "I will find out where she is hidden and a little guarded route through the Sacred Forest to the place. Once I find out I will send you a message with a pigeon."

Ingrid nodded.

Aidan intoned a few words. His green eyes shone bright and the snakes vanished, joining with the symbols of his long staff. He gave a curt nod and left.

Lasgol was left uneasy, and he was not the only one.

"There's one more person who will help us with the mission," Larsen announced.

"That's good, the more help we have the better," Lasgol commented.

"Is it another Druid or someone local?" Ingrid asked with interest.

"Neither, it's a Norghanian. I have to find him. I have orders from King Thoran for him."

"I'm sure he's going to love the fact that the King has chosen him for this mission," Viggo said with a mocking smile.

"As soon as I find him and give him his orders, he will join us on the mission."

"Can you tell us who it is?" Astrid asked, raising an eyebrow.

"Better wait until I find him. If I do not, it makes no sense telling you who it is." And with these words as farewell, the Ambassador turned around and left.

"This Larsen of ours is an open book," Viggo said acidly.

"I'm afraid diplomats are like that," Egil said, scratching his chin, no doubt trying to guess who it might be.

"So many secrets and so much incomplete information make me nervous," Nilsa admitted, shaking her arms.

"You're always…" Viggo started.

"More nervous than usual, I mean," Nilsa cut in before Viggo could finish the sentence.

"Well, you're not the only one," Ingrid admitted in turn.

Chapter 15

The following morning the Royal Eagles received permission to explore the capital. This cheered the group, since being shut inside the royal castle waiting for news from the Druid Aidan was not something they relished much. Egil had managed to find a tome on the Irinel language at the castle library, and he was leafing through it as they wandered the streets of the city. The tome contained common expressions of the country, with translations into five other Tremian languages. Egil was thrilled with the tome and was smiling from ear to ear.

Ingrid had managed to get enough components from the castle quartermaster to replace the supplies used to make Elemental Arrows. Unfortunately, there were some things she could not find. The soldiers did not use them and she had not found them in the castle. So they had decided to visit several shops in the city which, based on what Captain Jarith had told them, might have what they needed. The captain had offered to come with them, but the Panthers preferred wandering the city on their own and had politely declined his offer.

The first shop they visited, that of "Dasi the Herbalist," had not been of much help, although it had many components for preparing tonics and potions against fever and other common illnesses in the kingdom. From what they had gathered from the old herbalist, the Green Fever, which attacked the lungs, was the most feared illness in Irinel. It was caught from being exposed to the realm's constant rain, caused by the dampness, and it was difficult to rid the body of it once it set in. Egil wrote everything down in one of his notebooks and asked for the composition of the tonic against the disease. Cautious Rangers had long and happy lives, in his experience.

They continued their search for the components. One thing they noticed was that the people of Irinel were pleasant and nice. Very different from the Norghanians who were rougher and bad tempered. The people they met in the streets greeted them, and when they realized the Panthers were foreigners they chatted with them and offered to help with anything they needed. This was complicated, since Egil only knew a few words in the language of Irinel. What they did understand was that many people invited them to go to the taverns to have a beer with them. Given that they were citizens of a rival foreign kingdom, the Panthers found it shocking the Irinel people should be so kind to them.

Another thing they discovered was that the people of this realm enjoyed going to the taverns, which were usually full. They seemed to be meeting places for the locals, both men and women, buildings where they would greet one another and chat endlessly. The conversations were animated since they all drank beer or the strong liquors of the country, especially one that was like schnapps but with a better taste and a yellowish color. Viggo had insisted they try it. The locals were proud of their dark beer and this strong liquor. The custom of going to the tavern to eat and drink and chat naturally appealed to Viggo. The moment they were invited to a beer he accepted immediately without heeding Ingrid's protests. He had already managed to try the famous local beverages, and he had found them both excellent and puzzling.

They arrived at a square with a fountain in the middle, looking for the shop "Aimil's Components and Other Precious Materials" when something caught their attention. A man in rags was standing on a barrel, crying out to the four winds with menacing arm waving. The citizens walked past him without paying him attention, except for two men who were clearly inebriated and were egging him on.

The Panthers went over to listen, Egil paying close attention to what the pauper was shouting. He listened and then searched in his tome to try and translate what he was hearing.

"What's he saying? Do you understand anything?" Lasgol asked him. The man's appearance and his manner of gesturing and speaking to the people gave them the creeps.

"Let me check," Egil replied, putting his nose in the book, searching its worn-out pages.

"Well, while you listen, I'm going to make some friends in that tavern over there," said Viggo.

"Stay away from the taverns!" Ingrid scolded.

"We're in foreign territory, I'd even say hostile—we should try and make friends," Viggo replied with a mischievous grin.

"Enough with the nonsense!" she replied, waving her arms.

"Just in case, you never know. They might turn against us," he winked at her and went over to the tavern.

"He's going to return to the castle in great shape," Nilsa said, shaking her head.

Ingrid snorted in frustration.

"I'm telling you, I'll put his head in a barrel of water."

"I'll go along and make sure he doesn't drink half the tavern," Astrid said and winked at Ingrid to appease her.

"Thanks. And stop him from getting into fights or pulling any of his tricks."

"Don't worry, I'll keep an eye on him," Astrid replied and followed Viggo.

"Look, there's the shop, on the other side of the square," said Nilsa.

Ingrid nodded, "Yes, that's it."

"We'll be right back," Nilsa said to Egil and Lasgol, and the two girls headed to the shop.

Egil and Lasgol were still trying to decipher what the man was saying. Lasgol had a bad feeling, and he needed to confirm it.

"He's saying something about the end of man..." said Egil, listening to the message attentively as he glanced down at his tome.

"I was afraid of that... what else is he saying? Do you understand anything else?"

"Give me a moment," Egil said. "It's not easy to understand the words..."

They both listened intently.

"Based on all his waving and the reaction of those two drunkards, he seems to be proclaiming something bad..."

"The new lords... arrive..." Egil said, translating the man's ravings with the help of his book.

"That's the same message we've already heard..." Lasgol said ruefully. "Why is it here too?"

"... new era..." Egil translated. "That's all I understand. I can't make head or tails of the rest, sorry."

"That's okay, we get the gist. I don't understand a word. I have a terrible ear for languages."

"It's a matter of paying attention to the intonation of the words. That's the trick," Egil said, smiling.

"I think it's a lot more than that," Lasgol smiled back.

They listened a bit more to make sure.

"End of man, new lords, new era.... It's the same message we heard in Norghana," Egil said. "I'm surprised the same apocalyptic message is being shared here."

"I'm beginning to worry about all this talk of the end of man," Lasgol admitted. "This is more than a coincidence, and I have the feeling that something's going to happen. Something terrible…"

"Yeah, I also think it's something we should pay attention to. The fact that these doomsayers are throughout Tremia can't be a coincidence. There has to be a reason behind it."

"And a sinister one," Lasgol said with a shiver.

"That's what I fear. We have to find out what it is before it's too late."

Lasgol nodded.

"As you usually say in similar situations, this isn't a coincidence."

Egil nodded repeatedly. "No, unfortunately it's not."

Ingrid and Nilsa returned after a while, and from Nilsa's smile it looked like they had found the components they were looking for.

"What an experience," Nilsa said.

"What happened?" Lasgol asked.

"Well, the owner spoke a little of our language, although quite badly, and we speak none of his," she laughed.

"Did you manage, or do you need me to go and act as an interpreter?" Egil offered.

"We managed in the end," Ingrid said, showing them several leather pouches with the materials they had bought.

"Wonderful," Egil smiled.

"What about the pauper?" Nilsa asked, wrinkling her nose at his ragged features and wild gesturing.

"He's shouting the same message we heard in Norghana…" Lasgol said.

"The end of the era of men?" Ingrid asked.

Egil and Lasgol nodded.

"That's bad business…" Nilsa muttered.

"That's what it's beginning to look like," said Lasgol. "Whatever's spreading, it's not good thing."

Ingrid nodded heavily. "Let's fetch Viggo from the tavern before he creates a situation of his own."

"If Astrid's watching him, everything will be all right," Lasgol said, grinning.

It took them a while to get Viggo out of the tavern though. He had begun a beer drinking competition, and he had five rivals who swore they were going to drink him under the table. Of course, Viggo was swearing he was going to drink his beers plus those of his rivals. They managed to drag him out before he got completely drunk.

They continued wandering through the capital, enjoying the jolly people. It also did not rain much, so they were quite pleased. They arrived at another square with a couple shops Egil had been recommended with antiques and tomes on local folklore. Egil wanted to check them out and see whether there was anything in them about orbs. They were in a distant kingdom and they might have some information that could shed some light on the matter. The fact that they were on a mission did not mean they had forgotten the matter of the orb, not at all. The mission simply came first. Unfortunately, he did not find anything of interest in either shop.

"What now?" Ingrid asked him.

"There's still one more I want to check," Egil replied.

"Then off we go," Lasgol said cheerfully.

The antiques shop was called "Alun's Enchanted Objects." It took them several wrong turns and asking five or six locals, but they finally found it. According to Egil's trusted sources, this was a respectable shop and the objects sold in it were authentic. After all, you had to be wary of anything that had to do with enchanted objects and magic since there were swindlers in all of Tremia's kingdoms. And not only that, but many crooks traveled the cities and villages, selling fake objects and tomes which supposedly had magical properties.

What puzzled them was that a group of armed men was standing in front of the shop. Six soldiers wearing white and gray were waiting for someone who must have been inside the shop. They wore heavy armor and had large rectangular shields that covered half their bodies. Traditional, long, single-handed swords hung from their waists with a pommel shaped like a cross. They all wore square helmets that covered their heads and had a cross-shaped opening to let them see. They also wore steel gauntlets on their arms and boots, which completed their heavy armor.

"What a strange group..." Ingrid commented.

"They're wearing full heavy armor and carrying long swords and large shields. They look well protected," Astrid said.

"Are they from around here? They don't look like Irinel soldiers," said Nilsa.

"No, they're not from here," said Egil. "They must be with some important lord or some group…"

"Group?" Lasgol said.

"Yeah, they're all dressed alike, and if you notice they have some kind of badge… I don't recognize it…" said Egil.

"They do draw attention," said Nilsa.

"Our attention, but if you look at the people here you'll notice they pass the group by and don't seem surprised. They've seen them before—I'd say quite often from their lack of interest," Egil reasoned.

"Then we can assume they're from here," said Ingrid.

"It looks that way."

"I'll go over and talk to them," Viggo offered.

"Oh, no way. That group isn't the kind that wants to make friends," Ingrid told him.

"You'll see. I'll invite them to some beers, and done."

"Don't you dare move," Ingrid snapped.

"They've noticed we're staring at them," Astrid said.

"Just act normally," Egil suggested.

They all nodded in agreement.

They headed to the shop, leaving space between them and the armed group. Ingrid nodded to the rest not to go any closer. Lasgol knew it was a good habit to keep their distance, especially with military groups. You never knew what a simple glance might trigger. That was something which, with consideration, should be unconceivable but happened more often than expected. People with bad manners and people who were aggressive for no real reason were a lot more common than you would expect in civilized culture. Although, as Egil had told them, it was true that most of the cultures and kingdoms in Tremia were only slightly civilized, with Norghana toward the bottom of the list. Irinel seemed quite civilized in Lasgol's opinion so far, more than Norghana. On the other hand, it was still too soon to form an opinion. They still had a lot to see and experience in Irinel.

Suddenly, a figure came out of the shop. It must be the lord the soldiers were waiting for. Lasgol watched him. He was wearing a white hooded cloak which hid his features. What caught their attention first was the fact that he was not armed with sword and shield, nor was he wearing heavy armor. He was carrying a white staff with silver symbols and a jewel at its tip.

"It's a Mage…" Nilsa whispered as she recognized the look.

"He is indeed," Egil nodded.

From pure instinct, Astrid and Viggo stiffened and their hands reached for their knives.

"Attention…" Ingrid warned under her breath.

The stranger looked up. His gaze swept the square in front of the shop and he noticed the Panthers.

"I should have guessed it would be you," the Mage said, nodding heavily.

As soon as he heard the voice, Lasgol thought it sounded familiar. He could not see the hooded figure properly, but he had the feeling he knew the man.

"Do you know us?" Ingrid asked, one eyebrow raised.

The Mage pushed back his hood, revealing his face.

"Of course I know you, and you know me," he said firmly.

"Eicewald!" Lasgol cried, surprised to recognize the Ice Mage.

Chapter 16

"What a surprise!" Nilsa cried.

"Yeah, we weren't expecting to see you here," said Ingrid.

"I was hoping to find you here," Egil said, smiling. He didn't seem as surprised as the other Panthers.

Eicewald motioned his escort to wait aside and came over to greet the Panthers. He hugged them all.

Lasgol looked the Ice Mage up and down and found him the same. Everything on him was snow-white. He had the snow-white hair of the Ice Magi but, unlike the other Norghanian Magi, he was as impressive as a Royal Guard instead of being gaunt and fragile looking. The dark gaze of his eyes, which were black as night, did not fit the pale Norghanian features, but Lasgol was already used to their glare and he knew there were no dark intentions behind that gaze.

"I see that Astrid's rescue from the Turquoise Queen was successful in the end," he said as he greeted the brunette.

"Yes it was," she replied. "And you missed an intense adventure."

"Aren't all the adventures you find yourselves involved in exciting?" the Ice Mage said.

"Absolutely right," Lasgol nodded.

"That's right, we parted ways with you just before we went to rescue Astrid," Viggo recalled.

"Our good Ice Mage came up with an excuse so Orten and Thoran wouldn't suspect us when we stole the Star of Sea and Life," Egil reminded them.

Eicewald nodded. "That's true. I told the King I needed time to do an important arcane study and left. That was true. I had wanted to continue with one of my studies for a long time but the Norghanian wars had stopped me. I came here to the Kingdom of Irinel, and I have also visited the Confederation of Free Cities on the east coast where the continent ends."

"That's right, I remember now," Viggo said, throwing his head back.

"Don't pay attention to him, he's had quite a few beers with the locals," Ingrid told him. "Tell us, were you followed after you left?"

"Yes, indeed. Orten sent a couple of his spies after me. But it turned out I was doing exactly what I'd said I was going to do, so they left me in peace after a while. I didn't have any other trouble," the Mage explained. "I guess the plan worked."

"It did, and I'm glad you didn't have any trouble with the King or his brother," Lasgol told him.

"So far that's been the case…" Eicewald said in a troubled tone.

"So far?" Nilsa asked, arching an eyebrow.

"King Thoran has just sent for me," the Mage said. "He made contact through one of his loyal men."

"Ambassador Larsen?" Egil asked, although it was more a statement than a question.

Eicewald nodded. "That's correct. I was given a message from him this morning at first light, with orders from the King. I'm to report at the Royal Castle for a meeting with the Ambassador, who will deliver them."

"So, you must be the Norghanian who's going to help us with our new mission," Ingrid said.

"That's right!" cried Nilsa, who had just realized.

"I guess so. I still haven't got my orders, but finding you here everything fits—King Thoran wants me for an important matter, which no doubt has to do with your mission."

"No doubt about it," Egil stated.

Eicewald nodded and smiled.

"Well then, welcome to the group, you're going to love the mission, it'll be quite entertaining," Viggo said ironically.

"We'll appreciate your help," said Lasgol. "There's an important factor you'll be able to help us with."

"I understand you mean magic," said Eicewald.

"Exactly."

"I'll do whatever is in my power," the Mage promised.

"I'll rest easier if Eicewald comes with us," said Nilsa. "The best thing to counter magic is a Mage—and me, of course. I'm a Mage Hunter."

"One might think you were beginning to like magic and magi," said Viggo.

"As long as the mage is good and uses his magic to do good, I don't have a problem," she replied.

"I really am happy to see you," Eicewald said suddenly, looking each one up and down.

"We're glad to see you too," Ingrid said, nodding.

"The mission that brings you here must be political, and important," the Mage said thoughtfully.

"A mission for King Thoran colored by politics, yes," Lasgol confirmed.

Eicewald nodded. "I'd guessed as much. There are rumors in the capital that Norghana and Irinel are finally going to sign a peace treaty."

"Rumors which aren't far from the truth," Egil said.

"I see," Eicewald nodded.

"And what's an Ice Mage doing with an armed escort?" Lasgol asked with a wave to the heavily armed soldiers.

Eicewald looked at them for a moment and nodded.

"It might seem strange, but they're helping me with my studies."

"They don't look too scholarly, to be honest… they kind of look like the sort who enjoy stabbing the enemy in the back," Viggo said in a biting tone.

"They might appear that way, but they're actually members of the Brotherhood of Custodians."

"Brotherhood? A religious order?" Egil asked with interest.

"No, we're not a religious order like the Order of the Temple of the Light in Rogdon, or others of men of faith," Eicewald explained.

"The fact that they're already armed rules them out as dangerous, right?" Nilsa asked.

"It's an armed order whose aim and function are the search and protection of valuable Objects of Power."

"Objects of Power… that explains why a mage would be interested," Egil commented.

"Exactly. Objects of Power are of great interest to me. Some in particular," Eicewald told them. "The Brotherhood of Custodians seeks, studies, and protects Objects of Power so they don't fall into the hands of evil. They seek to maintain the delicate balance between good and evil in the world, a balance which might be affected by certain great Objects of Power depending on whose hands they fall in. Their mission is to prevent this from happening."

"So if a powerful object falls into their hands, is it safer with them than it would be with others?" Viggo commented as he eyed them with distrust. "I'm not convinced."

"I trust the Brotherhood. They follow a strict code of conduct imposed by the Grand Meister of the Brotherhood, whom I know personally," Eicewald explained.

"In that case they must be trustworthy," said Nilsa. "I think it's a good thing these warrior priests look for magic artifacts to keep them from harming the weak and innocent. I even find it noble and honorable."

"That's how they see it too," Eicewald said, nodding at the redhead.

"Well, then I already like them," said Nilsa.

"Don't be so quick to trust them, remember they're an armed group," Astrid warned.

"I think it's logical that they're armed," Viggo said. "No one's going to give them an Object of Power just because they ask nicely."

"They don't take them by force either," Eicewald assured them. "What does happen, unfortunately, is that there are forces of evil, armed and dangerous, which will stop at nothing to get what they want. That's why it's necessary for the order to be armed and have a military bearing."

"That's fascinating, you have to tell me more about them," said Egil, staring at the members of the Brotherhood of Custodians. He seemed eager to find out more about them.

"I'm going to need some time," Eicewald replied with a smile.

Egil nodded and smiled back.

"Were you here looking for one of those Objects of Power?" Astrid asked the Mage.

"That's right. I was looking for information about a specific Object, to be precise. This shop and two or three others have tomes with information that's not found in libraries or scholars' studies."

"Interesting. What a coincidence that we've run into each other," Ingrid said.

"Were you also looking for information?" the Mage asked, looking at the shop.

Egil confirmed it with a nod.

"Anything to do with the mission?" Eicewald wanted to know.

Egil shook his head. "Something that has to do with everything, personally."

"Understood. If I can help I'm at your disposal," the Mage offered.

128

"Thanks. You very possibly can," Egil said.

"By the way, where are Gerd, Ona, and Camu?"

Lasgol and Egil exchanged a glance.

"I think we'd better get together and talk about our respective circumstances and everything that's happened since we last saw each other," Lasgol suggested to Eicewald.

The Ice Mage nodded. "That's a good idea. I'll dismiss the members of the Brotherhood and go to the Royal Palace to see Ambassador Larsen, but afterwards we can have dinner at a place I know and talk quietly."

Egil agreed. "It'll be good to catch up."

"The more information we have, the better," Ingrid said.

"Then this evening we'll have dinner at the Tavern of the Jolly Dancer. It's well known. It's in the center of town, not far from here. Ask the locals, they'll help you find it."

"Make sure they have that great local dark beer," Viggo requested.

"They do," Eicewald promised. "As well as good food and dancers."

"Dancers? Wonderful!" Nilsa said, clapping her hands in excitement.

The Ice Mage said goodbye and left with the soldiers of the Brotherhood of Custodians. The Panthers watched them leave.

"That's curious," Ingrid said as her eyes followed them.

"Not something you see every day," said Astrid, who was also watching them leave with an intrigued look on her face.

"And what a surprise to meet Eicewald again!" Nilsa cried.

"I think it'll prove fortuitous indeed," Lasgol said. "We're going to need his experience and magic."

"And knowledge," Egil added. "I also think his help will be invaluable to this mission."

"I wonder what Eicewald was looking for in that shop," Lasgol said, scratching his head.

Egil looked back at the store. "It probably has nothing to do with what we're looking for…"

"Aren't you the one who says situations like this aren't coincidences and that there's always a reason behind them which links and explains them?" Ingrid asked.

"True. In this case I still can't guarantee it's anything more than a mere coincidence. I need more information and some connection to rule out coincidence. Like the Mage already said, there are two or three more places with interesting information about Objects of Power. But we're looking for specific information about one in particular, a dragon orb. I don't think Eicewald will be looking for the same thing."

"We'll find out soon enough," Lasgol said.

"We will for sure. And now, if you'll all excuse me, I'll go and see whether I can get some information about magical orbs in this place."

"I'm coming with you," Lasgol joined him.

The two friends spent quite a while seeking for tomes and objects which might shed some light over the mystery of the dragon orb. Egil did his best to make himself understood, and the truth was he did quite well considering he only knew a few words and the rest he referenced from his tome on the language. Unfortunately, after many questions and studying several interesting tomes and objects, they had to give up. There was nothing there that might be of use to them.

"No need to feel frustrated. Achieving a difficult goal requires a lot of effort. There'll be many times when the cause might seem lost and you want to give up. But if we persevere and keep working despite the obstacles, we'll reach the desired goal," Egil told Lasgol, seeing the resignation on his friend's face.

"You're a true philosopher," Lasgol said with a smile.

"Not yet, but I hope life's experiences teach me a lot so that I can share my knowledge with future generations."

"I'm sure that'll be the case," Lasgol said, putting his arm around his friend's shoulder. "You're an example to follow, you just don't realize it yet.

Chapter 17

The Tavern of the Jolly Dancer was a much bigger and nicer place than they had anticipated. That evening it was crowded and they found it difficult to get a table. The place was famous and the locals often frequented it, as did foreign visitors and travelers passing by. Apparently the tavern was well known in and out of the capital, and it was considered an obligatory stop for anyone passing through the capital.

Finally after waiting for quite some time, they managed to get a sought-after table. Eicewald had not arrived yet, so they passed the time drinking some of the famous local dark beer at Viggo's insistence.

"I'm only trying it to shut you up," Ingrid told him.

"And I am too, so you stay quiet the whole evening," added Nilsa.

They both tasted the beer, and to Viggo's great surprise they liked it.

"It's quite good," Ingrid commented approvingly.

"It has body," Nilsa added. "I like the taste and the texture."

"I can't believe it!" Viggo cried. "They actually like it!"

Lasgol and Egil tried it and did not like it that much.

"I prefer Norghanian beer," said Lasgol.

"Me too, it's more refreshing and has a lighter taste," Egil joined him.

Astrid tried the Irinel drink and reached the wise conclusion that the light Norghanian beer was better in the summer and the dark Irinel one for winter.

Eicewald appeared right before the tavern owner asked them what they wanted for dinner.

"I'll order for everyone," the Ice Mage said. "There are some exquisite specialties of the area you must try."

Ingrid nodded.

"I hope they won't be too eccentric dishes…" Nilsa said.

"Trust me, you're going to love them. The food in this kingdom is excellent," the Mage assured them. He then proceeded to order food for the group in the Irinel language.

"You speak the language of the realm very well," Egil congratulated him. "I'm quite envious. I wish I could communicate with the locals as well as you."

"That's the advantage of years and experience," the Mage said, almost apologetically. "I've lived a lot and traveled to this kingdom plenty of times and that has taught me several things, among them the beautiful language spoken here."

"How come an Ice Mage has visited this rainy green land so much?" Astrid asked, looking surprised.

Eicewald smiled and nodded repeatedly.

"The first time I came I was like you, on an official mission," he explained. "Many years ago when I was only an apprentice, I had to come with my lord Ceaice, the King's First Ice Mage, on an official visit. At that time my power was still small, and my master, tutor, and lord used me as a valet rather than a mage." He was thoughtful at the memory. "I advise you to enjoy this first visit, because the next ones won't be as impressive. When you discover a new land, a new culture, the first time is the most exciting, the most enjoyable, and the one that remains in your memories. Especially if you're no longer a young apprentice as I was. Here, sitting around this table, I see Ranger Specialists with proven character and experience. You can fully enjoy this visit."

"Honestly, visiting Irinel so far has been quite enjoyable," Nilsa said in a lively tone.

"I'm thrilled no one has tried to kill us while we've been in the kingdom—that's something to celebrate already," Ingrid said, widening her eyes.

"These people and this country are most fascinating," said Egil, smiling as he watched the locals in the tavern.

"And in later years, different duties and studies brought me to this land I enjoy so much," Eicewald continued.

"It seems to me that certain studies can take people to some very strange places, like the turquoise realms lost in the middle of the sea and kingdoms where it never stops raining," Viggo commented, taking another swig of his beer.

"And you would be right," Eicewald replied. "My studies have taken me to unique places. Also my duties to the crown, like in your case," the Mage said.

"And it seems like we still have a lot left to visit and experience," Lasgol commented with a look that made it clear they had seen nothing yet in comparison to all they would discover in the future.

"You can swear to that," Astrid nodded.

"It will be fantastic," Egil confirmed with the same feeling.

"I love traveling, meeting new people and seeing new lands," said Nilsa. "It's so exciting."

"Yes, because excitement suits you best," Viggo said, making a foolish face.

"Look who's talking—you have the most ridiculous moustache of black beer foam that suits you like a glove decorating your moronic face," Nilsa shot back, pointing at his face with her finger and chuckling.

"He does look quite handsome," Ingrid agreed.

"I do? Really?" Viggo tried to see himself in some mirror or reflecting surface. He got up and went to the counter where there was a mirror hanging beside it.

"He is fearless, and handsome and dashing, but when it comes to brains…" Ingrid said with a loud snort of despair, "he has none!"

"He certainly is… special," Astrid said to Ingrid with a broad smile.

"That's right," Nilsa said, laughing.

"How did your meeting with Ambassador Larsen go?" Lasgol asked Eicewald to change the subject.

The Mage put his hand inside the leather pouch he carried at his waist and pulled out a sealed parchment. The seal was broken, so the Mage had already opened it. Eicewald read out loud.

"*By Royal Decree, his Majesty King Thoran of Norghana orders his Ice Mage Eicewald to renew his obligations with the throne and kingdom. He is to report to Ambassador Larsen and receive orders for the mission he must perform in the Kingdom of Irinel. Once this mission is over, he must return at once to Norghania to serve in his post as Ice Mage of the King.*

Signed His Majesty Thoran, King of Norghana."

"Wow… the King claims you…" Nilsa said as if this was not good news.

"It would seem my season of studies has ended abruptly," Eicewald said. "I'm not surprised—I'm not usually allowed much time for my personal studies. The needs of the Kingdom come first for an Ice Mage."

"Just like for a Ranger," Ingrid noted.

"Has Ambassador Larsen explained to you what the mission entails?" Lasgol asked.

"He has. It's a complicated mission… and delicate…" Eicewald commented with a look that said he was not at all happy with having to carry it out.

"Delicate?" asked Astrid, intrigued.

"Yes… a crucial treaty is at stake for our king and for the future of the Kingdom of Norghana. If it gets signed, King and country will have some time to recover. The Zangrians and other kingdoms will think twice before attacking Norghana, knowing that Irinel is her ally. If we don't get the treaty signed, Thoran will be in a disadvantageous position difficult to escape. Still, rescuing the Princess is going to be complicated…"

"From what we witnessed in the throne hall, the Princess doesn't want to be 'rescued,'" Nilsa commented.

Eicewald nodded. "Princess Heulyn is quite headstrong…"

"That means she'll cause trouble," Viggo guessed as he returned from examining himself in the mirror. "And by the way, I look terrific," he said nonchalantly. He had not wiped the beer foam from his upper lip.

"I think we're more than capable of dealing with a princess, no matter how stubborn she might be," Ingrid said, crossing her arms over her chest.

"So… it sounds like relations between the Princess and her parents are not ideal," Astrid commented, phrasing her comment almost as question.

"No, they are not," Eicewald confirmed. "The Princess has always been a rebel and very obstinate. She has her own opinions, and from what those in the palace say, she has a bad temper and is a sore loser. She doesn't usually obey her parents or anyone else, as is the case now."

"That's all we need, a bratty Princess," Viggo said, raising his arms to the sky.

"It can't be that bad," Ingrid said, looking at Eicewald. But the Mage said nothing, just lowered his gaze.

"We'll be able to handle her. I'm pretty good at relations between or with people, and I've served at court," said Nilsa.

"So you deal with her," Viggo told her.

The tavern owner brought their food, which smelled so delicious their stomachs began to rumble. The conversation stopped while they enjoyed the tasty dishes. They started with a cream of mushroom soup fresh from the farm, with leeks, celery, onions, milk, and butter. They all enjoyed it and liked the thickness and consistency of the dish. Soups in Norghana were not creamy like this one. Then followed a meat pie, which surprised them all because it looked like a round cake; inside the pie, instead of something sweet, there was a meat stew with carrots, peas, and spring onions seasoned with thyme and bay leaf. Viggo was delighted with the idea of putting stew inside a pie that had then been baked. Nilsa thought it was a hit and a pleasant surprise. Lasgol tried it and decided it was one of the best things he had ever eaten, and Egil found it fantastic.

"Now, would you mind telling me what happened with the Turquoise Queen and afterwards?" Eicewald asked when as they finished their delicious meal.

"Egil, you'd better tell him, you're good with words and details," Ingrid suggested.

"It would be my pleasure," Egil replied. And while they were all licking their fingers, Egil told the Mage all their adventures and experiences, as well as everything that had happened in Norghana while the Ice Mage had been away. Eicewald barely touched what was left on his plate, he was so absorbed in Egil's story, and Egil did not tell him everything. He did not mention the Dragon Orb and the Pearl portals. Lasgol noticed this; it was not that they did not trust the Mage—they did—but it was too much to trust him with and for now they would rather only the Panthers knew. They figured it was a good idea to be prudent before trusting someone with something so important. The fact that Eicewald was a powerful Ice Mage was something Lasgol kept in mind. After all, the Dragon Orb was an Object of Power, one with a lot of power, and this was sure to interest someone like Eicewald, or any other mage. Egil was also aware of this, and they both thought it was better to withhold this information for the time being. If they changed their minds later and felt they should tell him, there was plenty of time. The last thing they needed was the Ice Mage turning against them because he wanted the orb for himself. Besides, the strange company he was keeping did not help.

When Egil finally finished recounting all their adventures, except those that had to do with the orb, Eicewald asked him tons of questions which Egil answered to the best of his ability.

"I see you've been busy," Eicewald said. "Congratulations on the Specializations you've obtained. That's a truly impressive achievement. I wonder whether this higher training system might be applied to the Ice Magi…"

"I don't recommend it!" Nilsa cried, looking distressed.

"It is dangerous. Engla and Gerd are still recovering from adverse effects caused by the training," Lasgol told him.

"Yes, when you manipulate the mind you run serious risks. Although the benefits might be worth it. But I understand it's better not to take risks until the matter is more under control," the Mage reasoned.

"It's better to leave the head in peace," Viggo stated.

Eicewald nodded heavily.

"And what adventures has the great Ice Mage had all this time?" Astrid asked him.

"Well, I've been searching. What I told King Thoran and his brother, Duke Orten, was not untrue. I really wanted to come to this kingdom to continue an important study. Important for me, of course, not for them."

"What study is this, if we may ask?" Egil said, intrigued.

"Well, the Brotherhood of Custodians has been chasing a special object, one of great power which they believe, if it fell into evil hands, might create a catastrophe."

"Uh oh… here we go again…" Viggo said, waving his arms.

Eicewald smiled and went on. "Our search made our paths cross a long time ago. It led to them contacting me in Norghania, and we've been collaborating ever since, as I was also interested in the same Object of Power."

"What object is this?" Lasgol asked.

"It has several names in different cultures," Eicewald explained. "I call it the Hand of the Master."

"That's a fascinating name," Egil said, thoughtful.

"The object is too. It is believed to be the hand of what once was a very powerful being, or god, which contains a part of his power. Hence why several forces are so intent on possessing it."

"Did you find it?"

"We were close, but the object is no longer in Irinel. It's been moved."

"By whom?" Egil asked.

"That's a good question. We don't know who, but the Brotherhood of Custodians are following some clues. They'll inform me as soon as they find out who's taken the object and where it is now."

Suddenly there was music in the tavern, and they all turned to see what was going on. At the back of the establishment they saw three people, two boys and a girl, dressed in local garb. Beside them several musicians were playing. The three young dancers started to dance without moving from their place.

"Wonderful, there's dancing today," Eicewald said cheerfully and applauded.

"What kind of dance is this? They dance alone?" Nilsa asked blankly.

"Alone and in one spot," added Astrid.

"They only move their legs fast, and in all directions," Viggo said, frowning.

"I find this method of dancing most fascinating," Egil said, smiling and nodding to the beat.

"It's a dance style typical of Irinel and only practiced here. The young dancers train endlessly," Eicewald explained.

"I like the music, but this dancing... I don't know, it seems like their feet are on fire..." Ingrid said.

"I like that they dance like that, I find it a lot livelier than our boring ballroom dance," said Lasgol, who did not miss a detail.

And as they enjoyed the music, dancing, and wonderful atmosphere of the tavern, they forgot about their mission for a while, with all its complications, mysteries, and plots, and simply enjoyed a well-deserved good time.

Chapter 18

It was raining when dawn came, typical of the Kingdom of Irinel, and the Royal Eagles were preparing to set out on their rescue mission. They had received Aidan's pigeon with directions. They were to meet the Druid at a specified point, east of the sacred Druid forest.

In the bailey of the Royal Castle Lasgol was feeling restless, which surprised him since he usually was in command of his nerves. But he noticed he was not the only one—he studied his comrades and noticed Nilsa was way more nervous than him, although this did not surprise him since the redhead was a natural nervous wreck, even though she always made great efforts to control herself. She had actually improved a lot since the early days at the Camp. The one who was as calm as could be, as if this had nothing to do with him, was Viggo. He was playing with his throwing knife. Ingrid was going over their weapons and gear with Astrid. They were both nodding, which was a good sign.

Egil was talking to Eicewald while they waited for Ambassador Larsen to arrive with the latest instructions. They both seemed to agree on the plan they had thought out the night before.

"Is everything okay?" Ingrid asked the Ambassador when he arrived with Kacey, the King's First Counselor.

Larsen and Kacey exchanged glances, then Larsen nodded. "Everything's fine."

Lasgol was left feeling uneasy after that exchange; it looked foreboding. He thought they both looked worried, and it had to be about the outcome of the rescue mission.

"Everything is in order. The place where the Royal Princess is hiding has been located," Kacey informed them.

"Good, then we should go and rescue her," Ingrid said determinedly.

"I must emphasize one last time that it is essential that absolutely nothing happens to the Princess," Larsen told them.

"Her Majesty the Queen will not tolerate any harm done to the Princess," the King's counselor insisted.

"We know. We'll be careful," Ingrid promised.

"But unexpected events can always happen in these types of missions," Viggo said sarcastically.

"That had better not happen," Kacey threatened him with his finger.

Viggo smiled and made a face, as if he was not fazed by the counselor's threat.

"We're leaving," Ingrid ordered so Viggo would not say anything else inappropriate.

"Good luck. For Norghana!" Larsen said.

"Luck is for the unprepared—we don't need it," Viggo replied.

Nilsa threw him a glance that said, "we do need it," but Viggo ignored the redhead and mounted his horse.

The group set off and Lasgol led them north, to the small beech wood where Camu and Ona were waiting. He asked the others to hold back a moment when they reached the trees and went in to look for his friends. As soon as he did, Ona came out to greet him with a growl of recognition.

Ona, beautiful, I'm here now, Lasgol transmitted to her and dismounted to pet her.

The panther approached Lasgol and rubbed her head on his outstretched hands while she chirped lovingly.

You take long, he received Camu's complaint.

I came as soon as I could, like I always do. You know that, Lasgol replied.

You take very long, Camu protested again as he revealed himself further in, between two trees. There were leaves on his head and mud on his face.

What on earth have you been doing?

Chase squirrels.

Lasgol rolled his eyes.

I've told you a thousand times you're never going to catch a squirrel and to leave them alone.

I catch one day.

Ona growled twice.

Your sister also knows you won't.

You see, Camu said stubbornly.

And anyway, what have the poor squirrels ever done to you?

Nothing, Camu said nonchalantly.

The more reason to leave them alone, just like the trout!

I great hunter, you see.

But you don't even eat meat! Lasgol transmitted to him in frustration, as he remembered all the times he had had the same conversation with Camu without success.

Not matter. I great hunter, like Ona.

Ahhh… now I see, you want to be like your sister.

Better than Ona.

But Ona hunts for food.

I too, feed Ona.

Lasgol snorted. It was pointless to insist. Camu would do whatever he wanted until the idea stopped being appealing, and that might take months or years.

Leave now?

Yes, we have a mission south of the kingdom.

I help.

Yeah, we might need your help this time.

I powerful.

Well… we're going to face the Druids and they have magic.

Ona moaned twice. She did not like the idea of facing someone with magic.

Not know.

Well, neither do we, but the Druids have Magic of Nature. How can I explain… they're like a tribe where everyone seems to be a shaman with some magic. They live in forests and under them.

Under forests?

In caverns or tunnels under the woods. Most likely built by them with the help of magic. At least that's what we've been told.

I understand.

Stay alert when we reach their domain and let me know when you detect magic.

I tell.

Let's go, our friends are waiting.

Lasgol went back to the group with Camu and Ona.

"Here are our reinforcements," Nilsa said cheerfully.

"Those two? Reinforcements?" Viggo protested. "They don't do anything but get us into trouble, particularly the bug."

I no bug.

"Yes you are. Or do you see any other creature as weird and ugly as you around? And please wipe your face off."

I handsome. You weird and ugly.

Nilsa burst out laughing, and Ingrid and Astrid joined her.

"I see things haven't changed much in the group after all this time," Eicewald commented, amused.

"And may they never change," Egil said. "Everything's more bearable and fun this way."

"I don't doubt it for moment," the Mage said. "Hello Ona, Camu, I'm glad to see you again," Eicewald greeted them. "Do you remember me?"

Ona chirped once.

We remember Ice Mage.

"Lasgol and Egil have already told me you've developed a new skill to communicate with everyone through open messages. That's a great achievement."

I much achievement.

"So I've been told. It seems you're also learning to fly; that must be an impressive skill. That's something I'd like to witness. It's a skill many dream of having and which no mage, sorcerer, shaman, or person blessed with the Gift has ever managed, at least as far as I know."

I more than dragon, Camu messaged proudly and lifted his head, straining his short neck and showing his muddied face.

"That's saying a lot. The dragons in our mythology and in many of the cultures in Tremia were powerful beings and they could indeed fly, but with physical wings."

I not need wings.

"As soon as we have the time, I'd love to see how you do it."

I show. Not land well, Camu admitted, hanging his head mournfully.

"Well, I might be able to help with that. After all, I am a Mage."

"If not him, I'm sure you could help me," Lasgol told Eicewald.

"Do you need help? Are you having trouble?" the Mage asked him, surprised.

"Yeah, I'm having a small problem with my power... several problems to be precise, and I'd benefit from the help of a mage with your experience and knowledge."

"Of course, you can count on me. It will be a pleasure to help you if I can," Eicewald offered.

"Thank you, as soon as we have a moment I'll explain what my problem is and ask some questions I have about magic and how to improve my skills..." Lasgol said, a little embarrassed about asking the Mage for his help.

"I'm glad you're asking me. There's no reason to be ashamed of asking for help when you need it, in magic or in any other aspect of life. Timely help might mean the difference between a happy, prosperous life and a short, sad one."

"Wise words," Egil nodded.

"Age brings with it some wisdom—not too much, but enough if one has met several obstacles on the way and been able to overcome them."

"And those you don't overcome are also good teachers," Egil added.

"That's right, often better than those we do overcome," Eicewald nodded.

They went on to the south, following the Royal Road that crossed the kingdom from north to south and east to west, according to the map which Counselor Kacey had given them. They headed straight south. As they typically did when on missions, they avoided all cities, towns, and villages to avoid raising unnecessary suspicion. Because they were a group of Norghanians, they were going to draw attention wherever they went in this foreign kingdom.

They went as fast as they could. They had several days of traveling ahead of them before they reached the Sacred Forest of the Druids, so they tried to waste as little time as possible. They only stopped at night to rest and used the light of day to advance as far as possible. As they traveled, their unease decreased and the group began to feel a little more relaxed. Already being on a mission, instead of waiting for events to develop and going over every possible scenario in their heads, made them feel better. When they were together and had a goal to accomplish, everything seemed to fit and harmony returned to the group. It was not that they were unaware of the danger awaiting them in the forest, but being together on the road with a definite aim made everything better.

They barely spoke at night because they knew they had to rest as much as they could before continuing at dawn. Besides, although Eicewald was a well-traveled and experienced mage, it was hard for him to keep up with the pace Ingrid set. So they tried to let the Mage rest as much as he could. He thanked them, alluding to his age. Of course, everyone pretended otherwise because they did not want the Mage to feel bad.

The journey was shorter than they had expected initially. They reached the southern part of the kingdom and found that a quarter of the country was indeed the territory where the Druids lived. It was a lot of land, more than they had imagined, occupied by the mysterious people. Most of the southern land of the kingdom was a huge forest, seemingly without end. It contrasted with the rest of the realm's landscape, which was flat and green with few woods. The only similarity between the south and the rest of the regions of the Kingdom of Irinel was that there were no mountains here either. In fact, there were no hills or plateaus worthy of mentioning. The enormous forest extending before them was absolutely flat, and the tops of the trees seemed to have been trimmed at the same height, giving it an unnatural look. Forests were not usually like that.

They arrived at the first trees and stopped. The road ended there and did not go into the forest. They all guessed the reason. Druid territory began here—this was their domain. They dismounted and Lasgol walked into the trees to take a look around. It was a large oak wood, at least in this first part of the forest. He went in deeper with Ona on his right. Suddenly the hair on the back of his neck stood up. He put his hand on his neck and felt it strongly.

"Magic…" he said under his breath.

Camu came in after them and stood on Lasgol's left side.

I feel magic too.

Do you know where it's coming from?

Camu remained silent for a moment and strained his neck, sniffing hard. Then he walked a little further into the trees as if trying to detect the magic's origin.

Not one place only.

The magic isn't coming from one place?

No. Many places.

That's weird, what do you mean by many places?

Magic coming from whole forest.

Oh… I see…

And ground of forest, Camu messaged, sniffing at the roots of a tree.

Eicewald came in after them. He looked around and half-closed his eyes, trying to perceive something.

"I feel much power emanating from this place," Lasgol

143

commented. "Camu says it's coming from the forest itself, all of it."

"And he's not mistaken. This is a place of power, all of it," the Ice Mage confirmed.

"Wow... that's not good news."

Eicewald nodded. "This is a special place. The Druids hold it sacred, and there's a reason for that. This is not a regular forest, it's a forest with a great amount of magic. Let me show you." Eicewald closed his eyes and murmured some enchantment as he circled his staff in the air. Lasgol watched him, enthralled. All of a sudden, there was a white flash and a wave surged from the Mage's staff, which spread throughout the forest around them. The wave seemed to spread a cold mist, like frost. As the wave went through the trees and the ground below, apparently freezing them, green emanations became visible. It was as if a green vapor were coming out of the trees and the ground and becoming visible against the freezing frost the Ice Mage had created. Lasgol realized what they were witnessing was the magic power the trees and forest floor emitted.

"I see it, it's amazing. You can almost reach out and touch the power this place emanates," Lasgol said as he reached out his hand to close it over a column of the greenish power coming up out of one of the roots. His hand closed on emptiness, unable to grasp it, and he felt a great shiver run up his arm to the back of his neck.

"That's what I felt the first time I was here."

"Do you know these woods?" Lasgol asked as he withdrew his hand, since touching the mist Eicewald had created froze his skin.

The Mage shook his head. "I've been here on three different occasions, always with the Druids' permission, but I wouldn't say I know them, rather that I've visited them."

"Did they grant you permission to enter their Sacred Forest? I thought they never permitted visitors."

"You're right. They don't, as a rule. They don't like strangers or anyone entering their forest. I visited them because of my studies and asked for permission to carry out my research in their woods. Surprisingly, they granted me access."

That's weird, isn't it?" Lasgol asked.

Eicewald nodded. "It is, and yet there's a reason that explains why. They didn't do it out of the goodness of their hearts. Afterwards I found out the real reason why they had granted permission—they were interested in the same study I was working on. In fact, their scholars were studying the same thing I was. In this life it's rare for someone to grant something without asking for something else in return."

Lasgol nodded.

"I was able to carry out my studies with the help of several of their scholars. They are shamans of power, some very powerful, as much or even more than me…. They use the magic this place offers them in combination with their own, which makes them formidable adversaries, especially within their forest."

"That's not good news either," Lasgol moaned.

"I also visited this place because it greatly intrigued me and I wanted to study it, find out where the power you see comes from. I wanted to know whether it's intrinsic to the forest or if there's something else under the trees that generates and emanates all this magical power. It's an interesting question and it could be of great significance if it's ever discovered."

"And what happened?" Lasgol asked, intrigued.

"They didn't allow me to research this—in fact, they forbid it. They found me trying to investigate the forest's power and threw me out rudely. That was the last time I came here, until today."

"We're now entering without their permission…"

"And that's something that troubles me a lot. They will not permit it, and if we're discovered we'll pay with our life for our intrusion. This is their sacred forest, and they will not allow us to taint it with our presence."

"We should assume it'll be well watched."

"Yes, it is. There are lookouts throughout the forest."

"They might not detect us," Lasgol said, but as he was speaking he realized this was wishful thinking.

"Oh, they definitely will. Not only do they have lookouts posted throughout the forest, but the magic itself will let them know."

Lasgol's eyes opened wide. "How's that possible?"

"The Druids can speak to the forest, and they do that through this power," he replied, indicating the magic emanating around them. They can ask the magic whether there are any intruders and the forest will let them know we're here."

Lasgol took a step backward.

"Then let's get out of here!"

"Relax, it's not imminent. We still have some time before that happens."

Ona uneasy, Camu messaged them.

Lasgol looked at the panther, whose hair was standing on end along her back and was growling.

Easy, girl, is the magic making you nervous?

"It takes a while to get used to this place," Eicewald commented.

"Magic makes them nervous," Lasgol said, indicating Camu and Ona.

"Fine. Let's get out of the forest and go back with the rest," the Ice Mage said.

Lasgol nodded. *Come, let's go back,* he transmitted.

They went back to the group, who were waiting expectantly.

"So, what do you think?" Ingrid asked.

"It's complicated. There's a lot of magic in this forest," Lasgol told them.

"That makes the mission more difficult," she replied.

"I still don't understand why the king of Irinel needs us to rescue his daughter," said Viggo. "If it were me, I'd send an army and raze this forest, problem solved. I bet the Druids would never dare to dispute me on anything ever again."

"You and your measured and intelligent methods..." Nilsa said.

"It's not right to destroy people for having discrepancies," Ingrid snapped.

"Several kings have already tried in the past," Eicewald explained.

"And what happened?" Astrid asked as she watched the forest with great interest.

"No one ever heard anything of the armies that entered the forest," said Eicewald.

"Nothing?" Viggo asked.

Eicewald shook his head.

"They never found a single body."

"See, Viggo? You and your great ideas," Nilsa said reproachfully.

"Are they so formidable then?" Ingrid asked, concerned.

"They are in their forest. The magic of this place helps them and turns them into fearsome opponents."

"So, then we draw them out. Problem solved," said Viggo.

"And how would you propose we do that?" Ingrid asked him.

"We start a fire and wait for them to come out," he replied calmly.

"You'd better leave the plans to Egil, yours are too brutal," Nilsa snapped.

"Brutal? Why's my plan brutal?"

"Because you'd have to burn a forest the size of south Norghana, that's why!" said Ingrid.

"It can't be that big," Viggo said.

"Her approximation is quite correct," Eicewald said.

"Setting fire to such a massive swath of land would be difficult with this weather," Egil said, pointing at the sky. It was beginning to rain again.

"Well, that, yeah… this blasted rain which won't stop falling would ruin my plan, but otherwise it was a magnificent plan."

"From a strategist's mind," Ingrid said ironically.

"So what are we going to do then?" Astrid asked.

"We'll head to the east, following the edge of the forest. The meeting point with Aidan is there," Egil pointed on the map.

"Very well, let's keep moving. We'll ride twenty paces from the forest." Ingrid then added the warning, "Don't get any closer."

Chapter 19

They waited at the meeting point, which turned out to be a depression in the terrain east of the forest, with a winding stream running through it. This place was the only hollow for leagues around, and Aidan had chosen it on purpose. Once inside the creek, the group vanished as if it had been swallowed by the earth.

Night fell, covering the green fields and the arcane forest. The horses were drinking from the stream and the group was waiting, sitting on the moist soil. The rain kept falling and there was no way to shelter from it. If they set up a tent, even in the bottom of the hollow, they might be seen by some Druid watchman, so they decided not to, since they did not want to risk being detected from the forest's edge. Viggo was thrilled with the whole situation.

"Isn't it ever going to stop raining for a single moment in this blasted region?" he protested, shaking the rain off his Ranger's cloak.

"You complain too much, it's only rain," Ingrid told him.

"Rain that gets into your under... your bones," he replied.

"This time I'm with Viggo, this ceaseless rain is a nuisance. You don't notice it at first, but it slowly leaves you soaked through," said Nilsa.

"Let's look on the bright side, at least it's not ice and snow. For a Norghanian the temperature is very pleasant," Astrid argued.

Lasgol was sitting against the side of the hollow with Camu and Ona lying beside him. He smiled at their banter. He also thought the rain was annoying, but considering how beautiful this country was, with its intense green and the fact that it was not cold, at least not like in Norghana, he felt the rain was a lesser evil.

Astrid sat down beside him.

"What do you think?" she asked with a nod toward the great forest.

"Well, to be honest... I think it's complicated,"

"Even with his help?" Astrid asked with a nod at Eicewald, who was sitting beside Egil and commenting on a possible escape plan while consulting the map Egil was carrying.

"Even with his help," Lasgol admitted.

"In that case, I'll have to start worrying," she replied tenderly.

"No, what I meant was… I don't want you to worry…"

"Take it easy," she smiled, "I'm not worried. I was joking, I have faith in us."

"Ah… it's just that the rescue in this forest is going to be quite complicated."

"Have I told you I love you today?" she asked him, tilting her head and smiling.

"Errrr… I don't think so…" he replied, feeling the heat rush to his face.

"Well then, I love you," she said and kissed him.

Lasgol became lost in the kiss for a moment. When their lips parted, he saw Astrid's gaze and could not help but return the feeling in it.

"I love you too," he said and kissed her in turn.

The two became lost in a moment of profound love.

"This is no time for turtle doves, we're on a mission here," Viggo chided, watching them kiss.

"Leave them alone, you're just jealous," Nilsa said.

"Me, jealous? No…" Viggo did not finish the sentence and was thoughtful. "Wait a moment, you're right, I am jealous. Ingrid?" he called, staring at the blonde archer.

"If you dare kiss me I'll give you a black eye. We're in danger. Focus and behave yourself."

"But they're kissing," he protested. "This is discrimination," he cried.

"Discrimination? Discrimination against what?" Ingrid cried, raising both arms.

"Discrimination for being handsome and breathtaking," he said, beaming.

Nilsa burst out laughing and Ingrid could not help but chuckle.

"Shut up and focus on the mission, you're impossible, you fool," Ingrid said, unable to erase the smile from her face.

"I see things are the same as always," Eicewald told Egil with a big smile.

"And may they stay that way," Egil replied, beaming.

The Ice Mage nodded repeatedly.

"This is where you think the place is?" Egil asked him, pointing with his finger on the map.

Eicewald nodded. "I'm not a hundred percent sure it's there…"

"I understand, but in this life there are few things apart from death we can be sure of," Egil replied, raising his eyebrows.

"Very true."

"Or irrefutable, as I like to put it."

They both laughed and continued planning the escape.

Astrid stroked poor Ona, who was drenched from the persistent rain. Even her fur, which seemed to handle snow and cold with ease, did not seem to do well in the incessant rain she had to put up with.

Camu, are you okay? Does the rain bother you at all? Lasgol transmitted.

I very well. Rain is nothing, I scales of dragon.

Yeah, yeah…. Lasgol waved his hand so he would drop the subject.

"This mission is a little strange…" Astrid commented to Lasgol.

"Why do you say that?"

"Because we're doing a dangerous job for a foreign king in his own kingdom. Not exactly what you'd expect of a Ranger."

"Isn't it? We're doing our King's will…"

"We're doing it because it's our duty to protect the kingdom from internal and external dangers."

"We're doing this to protect the kingdom…" Lasgol replied. "This is something the King needs done to make Norghana stronger and defend her from greedy rival kingdoms," He reasoned.

"It is… taking quite a few turns…" Astrid said, frowning.

"It's also true that the king will use the Royal Eagles to obtain fame and wealth. We know that, it's no secret."

"I know, and I don't really like it."

"But we can't refuse either, we serve the King."

"That's even worse," Astrid was shaking her head.

"In the end our duty is to protect Norghana, and that's what we're doing," Lasgol told her. "Maybe not how we would choose to do it, but in the end, it is protecting Norghana and her people."

Astrid stared at Lasgol thoughtfully.

"Is that what you really want to do?"

Lasgol tilted his head, surprised by the question.

"What do you mean?"

"When you joined the Rangers your desire in life was to clear your father's name, and you did it."

"Not without the help of all of you," he replied with a wave at the rest of their comrades. "I succeeded because of you, and I'll always be grateful for it."

"Yes, but... your goal in life now, what is it?"

Lasgol thought for a moment.

"When I cleared my father's name and that of my family, after what happened with my mother... after her sacrifice for the good of Norghana..."

"Her way of bringing peace to Norghana and freeing the kingdom from the impostor wasn't very subtle, to be honest..."

"I know, but in the end it's the thought that counts, and she wanted the best for Norghana, just like my father."

"Just like you..."

Lasgol nodded. "Yes, and I realized that the best way to do that was by following my father's footsteps: to become a Ranger and fight for the good of Norghana and the Norghanians."

"That's why you're a Ranger, that's why you don't question the King."

"I do question him, don't think I don't, but I have to trust that he's trying to save the kingdom from being conquered. As a Ranger and a Norghanian, I owe him my loyalty. We all do, even if we don't like what he is or his way of ruling."

"Yes, but you owe yourself not to be deceived and used because your mission in life is to help Norghana."

"I see what you're trying to tell me and I appreciate it. I won't follow the King's orders blindly. I have my own criteria and I know which lines to never cross."

Astrid nodded. "Don't betray your principles for a greater good, because that good might not be what it seems, and there'll be no turning back once you're left without honor," she advised him tenderly.

"Don't worry, I'll be careful not to betray my honor and my principles."

"Okay, I like that," she said, smiling.

"I have you to help me reach my goals."

"Your goal, your destiny, is a lot greater than being a Ranger and protecting Norghana. I've told you as much before, and I stand by it. You're special. The things that happen to you are part of a greater destiny that's still to come."

"Is that what you think of me?" Lasgol looked at her with wide eyes.

Astrid nodded repeatedly.

"I'm positive. Your destiny is greater than you think. A lot greater."

"Don't say that, I get the shivers just thinking about it."

"One day your destiny will be revealed to you and then you'll realize, I know. I'll be at your side and help you achieve it, because it'll be a destiny of unthinkable proportions."

"What's the matter with you today? Why are you like this?" Lasgol asked her, puzzled.

"It might be because I've been thinking about my own goals, my destiny… after what happened with my uncle."

"Oh, I see. What have you been thinking about? Tell me, I want to know."

"I've been thinking that we all have a destiny to fulfill in this life, some goal to reach, dreams to accomplish. You, myself, Ingrid, Nilsa, Viggo, Egil, Gerd, and our friends lying there too," she said, stroking Camu and Ona.

"You really think so? All of us?"

"Yes, I do. And the Panthers' destiny is important, beginning with each member of the group. Important and special, even if we don't know what it might be. That's the feeling I have."

"Are you saying this because we're not farmers or miners with a much quieter life?"

"Because of that and because each one of us is special. If you think about it we're all unique, each in our own way, but I believe there's something more to us, something that will make our destinies so important that we can't even begin to imagine it."

"Wow, you've been thinking about this a lot, but maybe you're going over the matter too much," Lasgol smiled, trying to wave it off.

Astrid noticed.

"Yes, maybe my feelings are exaggerated," she smiled back.

"What is your goal, your destiny?" he asked her, interested in whatever answer she might give.

Astrid sighed. "To protect Norghana and you."

"Me?" Lasgol asked blankly.

"Yes, because I love you, and because without you there won't be a great destiny you must fulfill."

Lasgol mused for a moment.

"Maybe the great destiny is yours and not mine, have you even considered that?"

"Don't try to turn the tables on me, you know perfectly well that the destiny I'm talking about is yours and not mine."

"I don't see why, it could just as easily be yours. You're capable of fulfilling any epic destiny awaiting us. Besides, you're a lot more capable than I am," Lasgol said firmly.

Astrid smiled at him, gazing on him lovingly.

"Thank you for those words, they mean a lot."

"It's the truth, it's what I think."

"It might be, but that's not what'll happen. It's you who will fulfill the great destiny, not me, no matter how capable I am," Astrid said determinedly.

"And why's that? Why do you think it'll turn out that way?"

"Of the two of us, who has the Gift? Who has a magical Creature of the Ice? Who has a snow panther to protect him? Who comes from a lineage of proven worth and powerful blood? That's not me, that's you."

"Even so, that doesn't mean my destiny is what you're saving."

"No, but it's pointing that way."

"Often what something appears to be, or initially looks like is different from what it actually is," Lasgol said.

"Besides, it's what my gut tells me," she concluded.

"You wouldn't happen to be a witch, would you?" he asked her with a mischievous smile.

"I've always been one," she replied with an even more mischievous grin.

Lasgol chuckled. "That's good to know."

"Look out!" Ingrid warned.

"Something's coming," Nilsa added, staring into the forest.

Lasgol was surprised by the choice of words. They all reached for their weapons and prepared for action. Lasgol poked his head out of the hollow to see who or what was coming, and what he saw puzzled him. An enormous boar was approaching them.

"Take it easy, it's a boar," Ingrid waved it away.

"A large one," Nilsa specified.

"I'll scare it off if it comes closer," Lasgol said, figuring the animal would not come out.

"Don't draw attention," Ingrid warned. "There might be

watchmen in the first line of trees ahead."

Lasgol signaled her not to worry.

The boar stopped a few paces away, and Lasgol thought it was going to leave. If it detected their scent it would. It was alone and probably coming down into the hollow searching for water. The beast lifted its snout and seemed to sniff the air. Surely it had caught the group's scent and would turn around. Boars, contrary to what many people believed, did not attack unless there was a reason, like protecting their brood or lair. Lasgol knew this and was at ease. But, to his great surprise, he realized he was wrong. The beast approached the edge of the hollow.

Ona growled—she had detected it too.

Easy, Ona, don't come out, don't let it see you. Camu, hide.

Me hide.

Lasgol was sure that now the boar would go away. It had heard Ona's threatening growl and would leave.

Once again he was wrong. The boar came even closer. To avoid making any sound Lasgol decided to use his *Animal Communication* skill to try and scare it off. It had worked in the past, so he was pretty confident it would work again. He lifted his head just enough to see the beast and tried to capture its mind's aura. He used his *Aura Presence* skill to try and detect its aura. Suddenly a green color appeared, forming an arch over the animal's head which indicated he had located it. It was different from Camu's and Ona's, which puzzled him since, in his experience, auras were pretty similar. He attributed it to the influence of the nearby forest's magic; it had to be that. There was too much magic here, and it had most likely spread beyond and was affecting the way he was catching the boar's aura. It had to be that.

He concentrated and called upon his *Animal Communication* skill. To his great surprise, the skill failed him.

"What the..." he muttered under his breath.

It had to be the forest's magic. He tried again, but he also failed.

"Wow..." he murmured again.

Astrid, who was still beside him, glanced at him, concerned.

The beast was a few paces away from Lasgol; he could see its mind aura which, although different, he could focus on. So why was his skill failing him? He tried a third time. He concentrated as hard as he could on the animal's aura and called upon his skill but failed once more. Taken aback, Lasgol hid as he pondered about what was happening and why his magic was not working.

All of a sudden, the boar came down the side of the depression to the stream and stared at them. Nilsa and Ingrid had their bows ready to release if the animal suddenly attacked. Lasgol also nocked an arrow and Astrid reached for her knives.

Then Lasgol felt the hair at the back of his neck stand up.

Magic, Camu warned beside him.

"Don't release... there's something strange going on here," Lasgol warned.

Eicewald was watching with narrowed eyes.

"That beast's not natural," he warned them.

Suddenly, the boar started to blur as if their vision were failing them, but it was impossible for it to fail them all at the same time. Lasgol immediately thought of a magical illusion. Maybe they were seeing an illusion and not the real animal. They were being tricked.

"It's an illusion! There's magic here!" he told his comrades.

The boar began to slowly shift before their eyes. The fur vanished and the shape of the snout, head, and body changed among distortions that seemed to affect everyone's vision. It was an almost grotesque spectacle, the way it shifted, the abrupt change and the bones and muscle that seemed to break to re-form into another shape after a moment.

"What on earth is happening to that beast?" Viggo cried.

"Everyone, be alert!" Ingrid urged.

The boar finished its transformation and lay on the ground, still on all fours. They saw not an animal but a man. He was stark naked and his body was tattooed all over with strange green runes. Until he stood up they could not tell who he was.

"Aidan!" Lasgol cried when he saw the face of the Druid and the green flash of his eyes, still filled with sparks of the magic he had used.

The Druid put a finger to his lips and moved away a little, turning his back to them. From under a rock by the stream he retrieved a leather bag. Inside were his clothes. He began to get dressed nonchalantly while they all watched him in awe. Once he had finished putting his clothes on, he went over to another larger rock, and from behind it he retrieved his wooden staff with carved runes similar to the ones on his face.

"Aidan, that was risky," Lasgol told him.

"More than risky, it's dangerous," Astrid added.

"Norghanian Rangers tend to not attack animals just for fun," the Druid told them.

"That's true… but in this situation…" Lasgol rebutted.

"It didn't seem to me that any of you had intentions to attack me," Aidan said, sure of himself.

"Even so, it was very risky," Eicewald said.

"But necessary. There are watchmen of my people nearby. I couldn't approach in human form."

"I don't know whether you all realize this, but the Druid here just transformed from a boar into a human. Don't you find that a little twisted?" Viggo said with wide eyes.

"I think it's awesome," said Nilsa. "He looked like a real boar, and a big one at that."

"That's because of my human size. I can't make myself smaller when I turn into an animal," the Druid explained.

"That's fascinating," Egil said eagerly, "magic that allows a human to change shape and turn into an animal. It's simply fantastic!"

"It's one of the skills of Druid Magic," Aidan explained.

"Druids can really do that?" Ingrid was mystified.

"Yes, almost all of us can, at least those with enough magic to call on this skill. It's one of the skills my people prefer to use. It allows us to be more in touch with nature, to fully enjoy absolute freedom, like a wild animal does in the forest."

"I didn't know anyone could do that. It's one thing to create an illusion and make someone believe they're seeing an animal when it's actually a person they're seeing, and a very different thing to take on its true shape," Lasgol said, "Because that was its true shape, right?"

"It is, except for the mind. You keep your human mind."

"That explains why the aura I saw was so strange—it wasn't an animal one. Now I understand why my attempts to use my *Animal Communication* skill failed. I can't use it on human minds, only on animals."

"I had already heard of the Druids' shape-shifting skill but had never witnessed it before. I had trouble recognizing the magic used," said Eicewald. "I can tell you it won't surprise me so much again," he smiled. "I'll remember."

"Good, remember it, because in this forest you might encounter it again."

"Were you able to locate the Princess?" Lasgol asked him.

"I could. I'll lead you to the place, but I won't intervene. If you're discovered, I'll vanish. I can't be involved."

"We understand," Egil said. "Guide us to the Princess and we'll do the rest."

"Good, very well. Get ready. We're going in, and that's going to be risky."

Lasgol felt a shiver run down his back.

Chapter 20

The group approached the edge of the forest in single file, with Aidan leading them, and went in. As soon as they did they all stiffened—entering the arcane forest in the middle of the night was not at all soothing.

Aidan stopped after a dozen paces and crouched. He placed his left hand on the ground and began to move his staff with his right hand as he murmured arcane words.

Magic, Camu, hidden, messaged to Lasgol in warning.

Aidan is with us, don't interrupt his magic.

Sure?

Yes, let's just hope he doesn't betray us.

I watch.

Yeah, me too. We're entering a dangerous place guided by a Druid of the forest, not the best of situations.

Ona growled once.

Be alert, both of you, but don't act without asking me first. Okay?

Okay.

Ona chirped once.

Lasgol watched Aidan as he continued conjuring. In some weird way he could feel the magic around him, more than he usually could. He did not know whether it was because the place emitted so much power that it was impossible for someone with the Gift not to feel it, or if it was for some other reason. He could even feel and make out Aidan's magic easily. He saw how a way cleared before the Druid, a path about two paces wide, marked by a deeper green than what he had glimpsed when Eicewald had shown him the magic coming out of the forest. He was surprised he could pick up the Druid's magic so easily.

"Follow me carefully," Aidan whispered, "In a single file. You can't see it, but I've cleared a path we'll be able to walk along without the forest detecting our presence. If anyone leaves the path for whatever reason, the forest will know we've entered. If the watchmen ask it to alert them to intruders, it will inform them and this mission will be over."

"The forest's a snitch!" Viggo growled, and he struck the underbrush on his right with his knives.

"Stop saying and doing stupid things and pay attention," Ingrid scolded him.

"This forest is fascinating," Egil said, "although I must admit it's not good for us right now. It would be fantastic to understand how this magic works and the relationship between the forest and the Druids."

"That would take us an eternity. To understand the magic and its connection with the Druids is a study of many years," Eicewald replied. "Although I must admit I share that interest."

"Now's not the time…" Ingrid told them.

Egil and Eicewald nodded.

"We'll follow your footsteps, Aidan," Astrid promised and signaled him to start.

The Druid nodded and began to march through the trees, the rest following behind single file. They stepped carefully in the footprints of the person in front. It was the only way they could keep to the path cleared by the Druid without deviating from it, since they could not see it. Ona and Camu brought up the rear with Lasgol, who had explained to them the situation and told them to step only where he did. Having four legs complicated this for them, but they made their way, making sure their front legs stepped exactly where Lasgol had stepped.

As they went further into the forest, Lasgol could feel its magic around him more strongly. With every step further in, he felt the magic of that arcane place more and more. His concern increased with each step they took.

All of a sudden, Aidan stopped and crouched, and as if moving in unison they all imitated him. The entire file remained silent and crouched. There were oaks on both sides and little other vegetation, so they could not hide well. Suddenly, through the trees to the west they saw a large wolf, and then five more. They were all a bit bigger than a regular wolf, even the wolves of northern Norghana. Aidan made a sign and they all threw themselves on the ground.

Wolves magic, Camu's warning reached them.

You pick up their magic? Lasgol asked him.

Magic of wolves like Aidan.

"They're Druid watchmen," he received the whisper Aidan had

159

passed on.

Do you detect any more magic?

Much magic in forest. Difficult.

Okay. Be alert in case you detect more Druid magic and let us know.

I warn.

They had to wait for the patrol of Druid wolf-guards to go by before they could continue.

They all had their weapons ready but Egil had instructed them not to use them unless it was absolutely necessary, since if they lost the element of surprise they would not have a chance to rescue the Princess. The Druids would raise the alarm and move her to a different hiding place at once. If this happened they would fail their mission, and if it was already complicated to begin with that would complicate it even more.

At a signal from Aidan they kept going. Everyone checked every shadow, noise, or possible presence. They were all too aware that the forest could swallow them and no one would ever hear from them again. Lasgol had several of his skills activated and he had seen Eicewald and Aidan cast spells on themselves, so he assumed they did too. Their progress was slow since they had to be careful and remain on Aidan's invisible path, and this increased their tension. It was going to take them forever to reach the place where the Princess was hiding.

Aidan made them stop a couple more times to avoid other Druid patrols. These were not in animal shape but human, and they had with them large predators like hunting dogs. They saw tigers and black panthers. Lasgol guessed they must be familiars, like Ona. Or perhaps they used their Magic of Nature in some way to bond with such beasts. He found it amazing and at the same time akin to his own magic. The magic the Druids used was similar to his own, at least in part, and this made him think. Perhaps he could learn something from them, if the Panthers survived the experience of course, which was becoming less certain with each step.

Suddenly, Aidan raised his hand and they all stopped. He crouched and pointed at a huge tree to the south. It was an oak several centuries old. Part of its trunk, which had dried up, was the size of a cart, and it looked like it had been emptied, leaving part of the trunk hollow. The branches remained firm, and in the distance it looked like just another oak. You had to get close to it and look carefully to notice the anomaly in the trunk. Lasgol saw it at once since he had his *Hawk's Eye* skill activated. The others probably had not seen it since they were not close enough, and the fact that it was the middle of the night did not help either.

There were two large bushes on either side of the tree. The place was quiet and the nearest trees were several paces away with little vegetation around them. The place seemed clear and not dangerous. Aidan signaled to the group that this was the spot. Lasgol called on his *Owl Hearing* skill just in case. He did not want any surprises or scares. He decided to keep it active along with his *Hawk's Eye* skill—this forest filled with magic and powerful Druids had him on edge. He looked around but did not see or hear anything that drew his attention, so he relaxed a little. Even so he called on his *Animal Presence* skill; he did not trust the Druids—if there were any in animal shape his skill would detect it. He sent forth a green wave which spread all around him, and at once he picked up the whole group and all nearby animals. They were all small rodents, he did not detect any large animal or human that was not part of their group. He snorted. There were no Druids here, in human or animal shape.

Can you detect anything odd? He asked Camu in case his friend could pick up something else.

Magic everywhere, difficult to make out.

Yeah, same here. I have terrible goose bumps on the back of my neck and all along my back. There's too much magic here.

You well?

Yeah, I'm fine, don't worry. It's just that I'm not used to feeling so much magic around me, and I don't understand why I feel it so strongly. I shouldn't, really. I'm not particularly sensitive to magic like you are.

Maybe type of magic.

What do you mean?

I feel all magic, you little magic.

Yeah, I'd guessed as much…. Lasgol figured Camu was bragging once again.

Magic here like your magic.

Really?

Yes, I feel, similar.

Wow, that's odd.

Not odd. You magic of nature. All magic here of nature.

Lasgol was left with questions. Camu might be right. Most of his skills had to do with nature. Only those related to archery were not, and he had developed these out of sheer necessity. He thought about it and decided Camu was right. The strong feelings were because he was sensitive to Magic of Nature and this forest emanated it from every tree, bush, root—even the moist soil itself.

Ingrid stepped up to speak to the Druid. She whispered something in his ear and Aidan nodded. He indicated the tree and then under it at its roots, which were large, long, and twisted above and under the ground all around the huge tree. Ingrid looked at him, puzzled. Aidan nodded again and pointed at the same place. Then he made a sign they all understood: wait. They looked at him blankly; there was no danger in sight but they were not to advance. Aidan repeated his gesture, and Ingrid looked into his eyes before finally withdrawing to where Nilsa was standing.

Lasgol was intrigued. What was going on?

Then Eicewald began to cast a spell, moving his Ice Mage staff in circles.

Ice Magic, Camu messaged Lasgol.

I see that, but what's he doing?

Not know, but ice magic powerful.

Lasgol watched Eicewald cast his spell for a long moment, and then something unexpected happened. From the tip of the Mage's staff two rays of ice issued forth. They split as they left the jeweled tip of the staff and headed to both sides of the oak. They were steady rays, like white beams of light that went straight to the two tall bushes that seemed to decorate the sides of the oak. Upon contact the bushes began to freeze, ice covering the plants from root to the last leaf. Freezing those two bushes did not seem to make much sense—why was Eicewald doing this? The only reason Lasgol could think of was that there might be a Druid hiding in the bushes. But he had already used all his skills to detect any guards and had not detected anyone, so that could not be the reason.

What happened next left him dumbfounded. The bushes froze completely and for some weird reason collapsed forward, as if the ice had severed their roots, which made no sense. Eicewald had only frozen them. Lasgol had already witnessed this Ice Mage spell, which froze whatever the freezing beam touched. But it did not sever. So the fact that the bushes collapsed frozen puzzled him.

Eicewald stopped casting the spell and the two rays of ice

vanished. But if what he had already seen seemed strange, what happened next was even stranger. The frozen bushes on the ground began to transform. Lasgol could not believe his eyes—the bushes shifted into human form and before them appeared two entirely frozen Druids.

"It can't be…" Lasgol muttered under his breath.

Bushes be druids. Surprise, Camu messaged to him, along with a feeling of great amazement.

Ona chirped twice, unable to believe it.

I can't believe it either. My skills didn't detect them.

Be bushes.

True, that's why I didn't notice them. My skills detect humans or animals, not bushes.

You improve.

Thank you, I know I need to improve. Remind me that I have to develop a skill that detects humans in bush form.

I remind.

I was being sarcastic.

Oh, I no good sarcastic.

Yeah, no need to swear to that.

The power of the Druids was truly remarkable. If adopting the shape of an animal was an impressive achievement, assuming the form of plants seemed unbelievable. To make sure Lasgol used his *Animal Presence* skill once again. He detected both Druids on the ground without any trouble. They were frozen but alive. He had learned another lesson. His skills were good but not infallible. He would remember. He was left wondering how he might have detected the two guards in bush form and found no answer.

Aidan indicated that the way was clear by pointing to the tree. Ingrid went over to inspect it. She walked between the two frozen guards and checked inside the trunk before signaling the others to approach. It looked clear. The Panthers followed and Lasgol saw steps inside the tree that went underground. The tree seemed to be the entrance to some tunnel or underground chamber, as he had already guessed.

The time had come to enter the secret entrance in the midst of the huge tree to the Princess' hiding spot. The group knew this and exchanged glances, waiting for the sign to go in.

Eicewald was the last to approach. He checked the entrance and cast a spell, which Lasgol guessed was to detect any kind of magic trap or alarm. The whole interior of the tree was immediately lined with frost. Eicewald studied it and finally nodded his approval. They were free to go inside.

Ingrid made a sign for Aidan to come forward.

The Druid shook his head and did not move from where he was standing, about thirty paces back. He had not approached the tree.

Ingrid glared at him to come in.

The Druid shook his head and indicated he was staying right there and would not be going in.

Ingrid did not insist further. She looked at her comrades and motioned them to go in. She went first, leading the group.

Lasgol snorted. They were entering the strange lair. What awaited them down below?

Chapter 21

They went down the steps carved in the soil. Ingrid motioned Nilsa to her side and they led the descent together, with Astrid and Viggo behind. Eicewald and Egil followed two steps back. Then came Lasgol with Ona and Camu bringing up the rear. The stairs were wide and went down deep. They did not lead to a natural cave or animal lair, but to a place fashioned by people. The darkness was close and they had to follow the walls to avoid tripping and falling.

They went down what Lasgol calculated would be two whole stories, the stairs ending in a round chamber. A wooden door on the other side stopped their advance. The walls of the chamber were covered in green moss, and they could see the great oak's roots through the four walls. The door was also covered in the same bright, intense green moss that seemed to give off some kind of phosphorescent light which allowed them to see in that hall.

Lasgol noticed that even underground and with the closed darkness enveloping them they could glimpse the gleaming brightness coming from the walls covered in the strange mossy layer and he wondered how it was possible.

Moss magic, Camu messaged.

Are you sure the magic you're picking up isn't the chamber itself? Lasgol asked him.

Chamber magic too. Moss closer magic.

That explained why they could see it.

"Beware, the walls emanate magic," Eicewald warned them, having noticed too.

"It might be some kind of detection system," Egil commented in a whisper.

"The door is covered in moss. If we open it, the moss will tear," Astrid murmured as she studied the door carefully.

"What do you want to bet it triggers some kind of alarm?" Viggo said in a low voice.

"Yeah, most likely," Ingrid agreed, studying the moss.

"We could burn it," Viggo suggested.

"No!" Eicewald stopped him, "the fire would destroy the moss,

165

and it would be the same as opening the door and tearing it apart. Either would trigger an alarm."

"So then, what are we going to do?" asked Nilsa, who was beginning to get nervous.

"The task is not to tear the moss. We'd have to take it off all in one piece," Egil said. "It's thick and solid, but our two assassins who are so talented with their knives might be able to do the job."

"They're great to dispatch enemies, but not to take moss off a door," Viggo replied.

"Great for everything," Ingrid told him, "get to it."

"I'll start," said Astrid and began to take the moss off the upper right corner carefully using her curved knife.

"How will we know whether we trigger the alarm?" Nilsa asked, hopping from one foot to the other.

I know, I pick up alarm magic.

"Okay then, you warn us, or better yet, let's hope you don't need to warn us," Nilsa said.

I warn or not warn, Camu confirmed.

Viggo started to loosen the mossy canvas of the lower right corner of the door. Both assassins worked, using their weapons carefully and with great skill. They managed to meet midway, and with great delicacy they pulled away the layer of moss and freed the front of the door. They did not hurry, since they knew if they pulled too much or cut where they should not they would be in a tight fit. As if they were two furniture-upholstering experts, they managed to remove the whole layer of moss until the door was entirely free.

"Great work," Egil congratulated them.

"Such a long time and so much training to end up doing this," Viggo protested.

"This is how legends of the Assassins are forged," Astrid told him. "You could sell it by saying your skill with knives was so impressive that you were capable of dismantling the most advanced traps, even the magic ones of the Druids."

Viggo bowed his head and rubbed his chin.

"Seen like that... I like it, yeah,"

"Let's see if the door has any other traps," Eicewald said as he cast a spell on the handle. A cold frost covered it.

"Is there a trap?" Nilsa asked.

"No, but we need a key," the Mage replied.

"Bah, I'll take care of that," Viggo said, crouching before the lock. "I have the missing piece of key here!" He took out his lock picks and tried them, but they were too small. He switched to his knives then, using them like his pick locks.

"Don't force it, that'll be worse," Ingrid cautioned.

"I know how to force a door, I've done it thousands of times," he replied.

"I'd rather not know why," she said.

"For stealing of course, what else?"

"Didn't I just tell you I didn't want to know? Shut up and work," she snapped.

"The fact that you don't want to know doesn't change the fact that in my past life I was a bit of a thief," he smiled at her as there was a metal click and the door opened.

"I find your past as a thief great," Nilsa told him, patting him on the back.

"Yeah, because it comes in handy now."

"Precisely," Nilsa replied, "or as Egil likes to say, irrefutable, my dear friend."

"Sure…" Viggo made a comical face.

"Come on, door's open, let's keep going," Ingrid said.

"Put on your hoods and scarves so they don't recognize us," said Egil.

"I don't see why. Who'd be so crazy to come all the way here? Only a handful of Rangers," said Viggo. "Us, to be precise."

"Shut up and do as Egil says," Ingrid ordered him.

They went into the next chamber and it was more like a corridor, long and narrow and ending in another door. The dirt floor was covered with sticks and branches, and they walked in pairs cautiously. The walls were still covered in the strange moss that emitted a greenish light.

"I could create a star of light to brighten our way, but its light is too harsh for this place, it would draw too much attention," Eicewald told them.

"I think we can see well enough," Ingrid said, looking everywhere with narrowed eyes.

Eicewald nodded.

They reached the second door, and this one was covered by some kind of creeper plant which seemed to have a life of its own because it moved up and down along the door, covering its entire width.

"This is odd indeed," Nilsa said, grasping her bow tight.

"It's Magic of Nature. These plants aren't natural," Eicewald said, examining them with interest.

Egil picked up a long stick from the floor and touched the creepers. At once, one of them coiled around the stick like a snake and began to squeeze until it broke the stick in two.

"Charming plants," Viggo said with great sarcasm.

"If we touch that door we'll be literally torn apart," said Ingrid.

"I'm afraid so," said Egil.

"Fire?" Viggo suggested.

"Ice would be better," said Eicewald, and he began casting a spell on the door's guardian creepers. A cone of ice shot out of the Mage's staff, hitting the plants. The Mage kept the ice steady and the plants froze in the blink of an eye. They dropped from the door like a layer of ice and remained on the floor, frozen solid.

"I like these ice spells of yours," Viggo said to Eicewald.

"And I like your skill in knife combat," the Mage returned the compliment.

"That's because I'm the best Assassin in all Tremia."

"One of the best," Astrid corrected him with a wink.

Ingrid opened the door carefully and they saw another deserted corridor. It seemed to end in another chamber, and this time there were no doors or plants preventing their passage.

"Let's go, the way is clear," she said.

They began to walk along the tunnel, careful of where they stepped. They did not trust this place, which was the only one not covered in moss. Suddenly Ona growled loudly in warning.

"Watch out!" Lasgol said.

They stopped and Ingrid asked, "What's the matter?"

Before anyone could react, Ona leapt to the front of the group. Ingrid, Nilsa, Astrid, and Viggo had to crouch as she flew over their heads.

"What the…" Viggo cried.

They had not noticed two holes on the side walls, and all of a sudden two huge tigers jumped out of them. They roared threateningly, showing their teeth. They seemed to have come out to protect their lairs.

"Tigers!" Ingrid called.

"Or Druids!" Astrid warned.

Lasgol called upon his *Animal Presence* skill and confirmed that the tigers were indeed animals.

"They're real tigers!" he warned his comrades.

Ona faced them, showing her teeth and clawing the air threateningly.

The two tigers, both larger and more powerful than Ona, did not cower. They roared loudly, showing their deadly fangs.

"Help Ona!" Lasgol cried.

The tigers, enraged by their intrusion, jumped on Ona.

Lasgol released instinctively at the tiger on the right and Egil did the same. Nilsa and Ingrid released against the one on the left with tremendous speed. Eicewald started to cast a spell and Viggo and Astrid lunged at the tigers, one at each. Before the Ice Mage could finish his spell, both tigers were dead.

Lasgol ran to Ona.

Ona well? Camu messaged him anxiously.

Ona is unharmed, Lasgol transmitted back as he examined the panther.

"You at the back, next time release more carefully, one of your arrows grazed my ear," Viggo complained.

"I'm sorry, it was me," Egil apologized, "they attacked so suddenly…"

"If you're not ready don't release, you nerd, or I'm going to end up with one of your arrows in the back of my neck."

"The tigers are dead," Astrid confirmed.

"Let's keep going, if these are their guardian dogs I don't want to imagine what's waiting ahead," said Ingrid.

"Everyone, be alert," said Astrid as she pointed at the end of the tunnel with her knife.

They arrived at the entrance that accessed the next cavern. It was oval in shape, quite large, and deserted. In the middle was a tree trunk that seemed to go up through the ceiling to the floor above. They went in and studied the chamber. It was clear that the earthen walls had been dug out by magical means, because they did not have a single flaw. They were smooth and curved where they joined the ceiling, which was also smooth, as if it were the house of a noble, only they were underground, under the huge oaks.

They walked over to the tree trunk in the middle. The fact that it was growing there was strange. It had a hole in the middle of the trunk the size of a melon that looked like a bird's nest. Ingrid looked in carefully but it seemed empty. She turned around and signaled for them to keep going. They could see a narrow opening on the other end of the chamber, although it appeared blocked with something like resin.

They neared the trunk. Nilsa was leading the group, followed by Astrid and the rest. All of a sudden, a hum came from the hole. The group stopped with their weapons ready. It might be some kind of alarm. The humming quickly grew louder.

Ingrid, who was closest to the tree, turned to look.

"That doesn't sound good at all…" Nilsa muttered under her breath as she aimed at the hole.

"Watch out!" Ingrid warned as she also aimed at the hole where the sound appeared to be coming from.

The humming grew louder, and suddenly what appeared to be wasps poured out of the hole. But they were not regular wasps, they were three times the size of a regular one. Ingrid realized something weird was going on and spun round. The wasps attacked her aggressively. She was stung in her left arm as she covered her face.

"Watch out! Huge wasps!" she warned her friends as she tried to rid herself of the group that had lunged at her by shaking her arms and hitting them with her bow.

"They're attacking us!" cried Nilsa as another swarm of wasps stung her right arm.

Astrid, who was behind Ingrid and Nilsa, was also defending herself from the wasps, which looked for victims to attack as soon as they left the tree.

"They're aggressive and their stingers go through our clothing!" she warned as she realized their Ranger clothing did not protect them from the insects.

More and more wasps streamed out of the hole, like guardians of the underground cavern rejecting the intruders they had detected.

"Relax, they're just wasps," said Viggo, making light of it. Then two stung him in the leg and he leapt almost to the ceiling.

"They're not regular wasps," Egil said when he was stung in the back. "Their stingers shouldn't go through our cloaks, and the prick hurts."

"They're not regular-sized either," Eicewald added. "I'm afraid they've been created by the Druids as a defense system."

Lasgol called upon his *Cat-like Reflexes* and *Improved Agility* skills and tried to avoid the wasps' attacks. Beside him, Ona leapt and clawed the air right and left, killing the wasps she caught. Camu was camouflaged and was not being attacked, so it seemed the wasps could not detect him.

Eicewald conjured quickly and created a protective ice sphere around him. When the wasps attacked him their stingers got stuck in the ice.

More and more wasps flooded out of the hole in the trunk, filling the chamber, their humming echoing deafeningly throughout the room.

"Block the hole!" Egil shouted, pointing at it.

"Yeah, block it so no more wasps escape!" Lasgol joined him as Egil tried in vain to get close and do it himself.

The deafening humming stopped them from thinking clearly. Ingrid, who was closest, realized it was up to her. Her arms were a mess of stings and the pain she felt was terrible. She left her bow on the floor, took off her backpack, and stuffed it into the hole of the tree. She stayed there, pushing with both hands in case there was some force inside the tree that might push her pack back, but that did not happen. Although as she held it there the wasps riddled her back with their stingers.

Viggo was running around the room, chased by a hundred wasps. He got to the opening at the far end of the chamber and found it blocked by the strange resin.

"There's no way out!" he cried and ran in the opposite direction, the wasps chasing after him.

"What do we do about these wasps? They're killing me!" Nilsa shouted, desperately hitting anything that flew by her with her bow.

Astrid was defending herself from the wasps trying to sting her from every direction. She hit them with her cloak, striking left and right and up and down.

"I'll deal with them," said Eicewald, and he started to cast a spell at once. He moved his staff above his head and the temperature in the chamber began to go down.

Lasgol was slapping the air like a maniac, trying to kill wasps all around him. He followed Ona's example, who had a large number of dead wasps around her from all her clawing.

The temperature dropped drastically and the wasps began to fly slower, their wings heavy. With each turn of the Mage's staff they moved slower. Eicewald continued conjuring and the temperature dropped even more. Lasgol felt his cloak covering with frost. The wasps began to drop to the floor. The humming died out, and as it did the wasps fell to the floor, frozen.

The Mage continued casting his spell until the last wasps had dropped dead.

"They're all dead," Lasgol informed the Mage.

"Stop the spell, you're freezing us to the bone," cried Viggo.

Eicewald immediately stopped the movement of his staff and the spell.

"How are you?" Lasgol asked his comrades.

"My whole body hurts like crazy!" Viggo said from the entrance door. "I've even been stung in my butt! My whole butt!"

Ingrid had one knee on the floor and Nilsa was sitting beside her. They seemed to want to speak but were unable to.

"They're not well," said Astrid as she bent to take a look at them.

"They received the brunt of the attack, they were closer to the hole the wasps came out of," said Lasgol.

"Let me check on them," Egil said, stepping over. He knelt beside the two girls and began to examine them. He lowered their Ranger scarves so they could breathe better.

Eicewald was examining the dead wasps.

"I've never seen wasps like these before... I wonder how they bred them."

"There's nothing magical about them, is there?" Lasgol asked, intrigued.

No magic. Wasps not magical, Camu messaged him.

Thanks, Camu. Are you all right?

Wasps not see. Not sting. I well. Ona yes sting, poor Ona.

Lasgol knelt beside Ona, who was licking her legs.

"Don't worry, it'll pass soon," he told her, although he had no idea whether that was true. It was wishful thinking.

"I doubt it'll pass quickly. These wasps must have been bred by the Druids. They're skilled at anything to do with nature," Eicewald commented. "I'm afraid their venom might cause us problems."

"I can corroborate that," said Egil. "Ingrid and Nilsa both have a lot of venom in their systems and their organs are slowing down. I'm afraid if they slow down too much they might begin to fail. It's a dangerous venom. My legs are also starting to go numb, it's where I got stung the most."

"What do you mean dangerous? Isn't it wasp venom?" Viggo asked, going to Ingrid's side, worried.

"I have to analyze it, but I'm sure this isn't your regular wasp venom. The swelling has turned blue with a yellow pinpoint where the stinger went in. That's not a normal sting," Egil concluded.

"How's my precious blondie?" Viggo asked Ingrid, taking her hand. She was now lying on the floor and could barely open her eyes.

"I can't feel my arms… or my back… a lot of pain…"

"Don't worry, everything's going to be okay," Viggo promised with a troubled glance at Egil.

"Everything will be fine," Egil assured them as he checked Nilsa.

"I thought… they were going to kill me with their stingers…" she muttered. "Everything hurts terribly…"

"Yes, it does hurt a lot," Astrid said to Nilsa, stroking her forehead, "But that's nothing for a bunch of Ranger Specialists like us."

"It's significant they didn't sting us on the head, only our limbs and backs…" Viggo commented.

"They might have been aiming at areas with more flesh where it's easier to insert their stinger and inject their venom," Eicewald reasoned.

"That's a possibility, yeah," Egil said as he extracted venom from several of the dead wasps to analyze later. "That would mean they've been bred with a specific purpose, which is impressive."

"And a problem for us," said Astrid.

"How's my tough northern beauty?" Viggo asked Ingrid, who was looking at him, unable to speak.

"I can't… feel…" is all Viggo could hear.

"The venom is paralyzing their organs, and it's possible it'll make them faint," Egil explained.

Astrid and Lasgol exchanged worried glances.

"I'm going to give them a generic antidote I have with me. Let's hope it can counter the venom's effects," said Egil.

"Can't you do anything?" Viggo said with a troubled look.

"Not without analyzing the venom, and even so it's possible I'd have to create a new antidote, which is out of the question here," Egil explained as he administered the tonic to Nilsa. Then he dragged himself to Ingrid's side and gave it to her. Finally he drank some himself.

"How's everyone else?" Lasgol asked, noting Egil was having trouble with his legs.

"I can't feel my butt and part of my back, but otherwise I think I'm okay," said Viggo after doing several squats to see whether his legs would respond.

"One of my arms and a leg are half-numb, but I can still move them for now," said Astrid, also moving them to see if she still had control of them.

"I'm the same," Lasgol said to Astrid.

"They didn't manage to sting me," said Eicewald.

"My legs and back are bad," said Egil as he continued to work. "But my arms are working, so that's good enough for now."

"What do we do now?" asked Viggo.

"We have three injured," Astrid said, indicating Nilsa, Ingrid, and Egil.

"The rest of us could go on," Eicewald suggested.

"Continuing without these three is risky," Astrid replied.

"Needless to say, I don't want to leave them," Viggo said, looking at Ingrid.

"None of us want to leave them," Lasgol assured him.

"It's a difficult decision… I believe we're close to the Princess," said Eicewald.

"We don't know that," said Viggo.

"We don't, but I don't think they've gone much further down. It's one thing to hide a refugee and another thing entirely to hide a Royal Princess," the Mage commented.

"If we go back now, they'll know we tried to rescue her and the mission will fail. They'll move her and we won't be able to find her again," Lasgol reasoned.

"True. This is our only opportunity," said Astrid.

Viggo glanced at Ingrid as she lay there. He did not look eager to go on.

"The mission… comes first…" she told him.

"You and your blasted sense of duty and honor," Viggo protested.

"The mission… complete…" she whispered with difficulty.

"All right! Let's finish this quickly!" he growled.

Astrid nodded.

Ona, you stay here and look after them.

Ona moaned twice.

I need you to take care of them in case a Druid appears. They're not in any shape to fight.

Ona chirped once.

Good girl, Lasgol transmitted. He also wanted her to stay because she did not seem to be feeling well either.

They went over to the resin-blocked opening. Before they could discuss a way to get through the opening, Viggo was already hacking at the resin with his knives.

"The fastest course is direct action," he told the others.

Astrid looked at Lasgol and shrugged. She took out her own knives and started to help Viggo clear the way.

Chapter 22

They worked eagerly to clear the passage between the two rocky walls, making enough space for a person to squeeze through.

"This resin blocking the way is some kind of door the Druids use," Eicewald said, examining one of the pieces that had fallen to the floor.

"Door or no door, we're going to tear it down and get to the other side," Viggo said as he went on hacking at the remaining resin.

"I'm not saying otherwise, it's just that breaking down a door to get into a house doesn't seem to me like the subtlest approach," Eicewald commented.

"The time for subtleties is over, we're taking direct action. We rescue the little Princess and get out of here like lightning," Viggo replied.

"When he gets this way it's difficult to reason with him," Astrid told the Mage.

"Sure... what worries me is that they could detect us breaking in," Eicewald said.

"You think they will?" Lasgol asked him.

"We'll soon find out... one way or another," the Mage replied with a shrug.

"Passage cleared," said Viggo, who had just finished clearing the opening. Without waiting for anyone, he went into the next chamber.

"Let's follow him," Astrid said and followed Viggo.

Go? Camu messaged, surprised by Viggo's action.

Yes, let's go, we can't let them go alone.

Okay.

Can you get through the opening?

I get through.

Lasgol signaled to Eicewald, and they went in after their comrades. The scare Lasgol got was tremendous—they skidded and went down a polished rock incline, falling into a new and much deeper chamber. Lasgol jumped to his feet and nocked an arrow. Eicewald also got to his feet quickly and stood alert, brandishing his Ice Mage's staff. Camu came down shortly after. He had some trouble getting through.

"Nice place," said Viggo, gazing at the chamber they had fallen into.

Lasgol stared at the place with his mouth open. They were in an underground chamber, massive in length, width, and height. It consisted of different gardens with all kinds of colored flowers and streams crisscrossing them. There were even half a dozen trees scattered about which almost reached the lofty ceiling.

"Worthy of a Princess," said Eicewald.

"There are three doors—one north, another east, and a third to the west," said Astrid.

"The Princess has to be behind one of them," Eicewald reasoned.

"Get ready," Astrid warned.

"Stunning poison?" Viggo asked her.

"It's the kind that works best on Magi," Astrid confirmed.

Viggo nodded and both Assassins began smearing their knives with poison.

Lasgol searched in his quiver for three Earth Elemental Arrows. They were good against Magi, because like the stunning poison, they left them confused and unable to cast spells, which gave the Panthers an advantage when confronting them. Nilsa had been developing other more effective arrows against Magi, but she kept them with her because they were not fully tested and might fail in real combat.

"Should we split up and open all three at once?" Viggo suggested.

"I know you're in a hurry, but that's not the best option," Astrid told him.

"In fact, it's the worst option," Lasgol said. "It makes more sense for us to open one door together and face whatever might be behind it."

Viggo was about to object when the three doors opened at the same time.

"Watch out!" cried Astrid.

Lasgol readied his weapon.

Camu, hide and move away a little, just in case.

I hide.

"We've got company," Eicewald said, who at once conjured an anti-magic protective sphere.

A Druid appeared out of each of the doors. They were unmistakable with their attire, similar to Aidan's, and in particular their green tattoos with rune symbols. The Panthers could only see the tattoos on their faces, neck, hands, and feet since they wore sandals, but they knew the tattoos probably covered their whole bodies. Two of the Druids were in their fifties, while the third was older, about sixty-five. They approached the group calmly, leaning on their long wooden staves with carved runes on them until they were in the middle of the chamber.

"You are trespassing, foreigners," the oldest of the three told them.

"We're here to take the Princess back to her family," Eicewald said in a calm tone.

The elder observed him. "You are the Ice Mage who visited us before," he said to him.

"That's right, I am Eicewald," the Mage said and saluted the Druid.

"I am Colin, leader of this part of the forest. We have not been introduced, but I have heard of you."

"And I've also heard of the wise leader of the forest."

"You cannot be here without my permission, and you know it."

"I do, and I apologize. I am sent by King Kendryk who wants his daughter, Princess Heulyn, back home."

"Did the King of Irinel send you, or was it the King of Norghana?" the Druid asked with curiosity.

"On this occasion it was both," Eicewald admitted.

"I assumed as much. An Ice Mage owes his loyalty to his King before that of any other kingdom."

"Yes indeed, as it should be," Eicewald confirmed, nodding.

"You are not of the blood, and neither are those with you. I do not grant permission for you to be here. Go back the way you came and take the Rangers with you."

Lasgol was surprised to hear that. How did the Druid know they were Rangers? Had someone betrayed them? Perhaps Aidan? Someone at the Court?

"With all due respect to the Druid people, I must insist that we are allowed to take Princess Heulyn back to her family."

"The Princess is of the blood and has requested sanctuary. We, her people," he said, pointing at his fellow Druids, "have granted it to her and are protecting her as her people. We will not let anyone take her from us."

"That makes things more difficult…" said Eicewald.

"Not at all. Mother Nature teaches us that the wise thing to do in impossible situations is to turn away. The wolf doesn't go into a bear's den."

"These wolves must get to the Princess and take her with them," said Eicewald.

"Then these wolves will die at the hands of the bear," Colin said, ending the conversation.

The three Druids started to conjure at once, moving their wooden staves. Lasgol could see the green flashes of the runes on the Druids' bodies and the symbols of their staves. He did not know what spells they were casting, but it was Magic of Nature and no doubt it would be deadly for him and his friends. He did not think twice and nocked an Elemental Earth Arrow, aiming at the Druid on Colin's right since he figured Eicewald would deal with the leader, and released. The Druid he attacked finished conjuring and a thin tree with long, almost-ethereal green branches appeared before him. Lasgol's arrow flew straight at the Druid's chest, the tree's branches shielded the Druid. To Lasgol's surprise, the branches moved swiftly and hit the arrow, stopping it from reaching the Druid.

"I wasn't expecting that…" he muttered as he nocked another arrow.

Astrid and Viggo lunged forward to attack, and as Lasgol had guessed they left the leader to Eicewald and went straight for the other two Druids.

The one on the left aimed his long staff at Viggo and cast a spell as he sprinted toward the Druid like lightning. All of a sudden the ground around Viggo sprouted roots, which reached up, searching for the Assassin's body. But he noticed and jumped out of the way of the roots, which seemed to have a life of their own as they sought to trap him. As he was in mid-air he focused on finishing the Druid before the man could cast another spell. He fell on the Druid with his knives before him. In the middle of his jump the roots trapped his legs and pulled down hard. Viggo's flight was interrupted abruptly and he fell a foot away from catching the Druid. He remained trapped on the ground by the creepers that held both his legs.

"Blasted plants!" he cried as he tried to free himself of the roots by slashing at them.

Instead of jumping like Viggo had, Astrid opted for an attack with cartwheels in order to confuse the Druid she was up against, making it more difficult for him to defend himself. She started her cartwheel as the Druid began conjuring. She had to reach him before he finished his spell or things would end badly. She also had to avoid the tree he had put a spell on since she did not trust its long branches—she had the bad feeling they could trap her. She ended her approach, veering to the right side of the Druid and avoiding the tree. She was about to deliver two slashes to the Druid's legs when from his staff, whose symbols shone deep green, erupted a wooden stake of considerable size. Astrid saw it at the last moment, and instead of completing the attack she threw herself to one side to avoid it. The stake brushed her side. She rolled over and continued rolling defensively on the floor while the Druid conjured again.

Eicewald attacked the leader, aiming at his torso and conjuring up an ice beam. The beam issued from his staff and the Mage kept it steady to freeze the leader. But Colin had cast a spell on himself and covered his entire body with a thick, hard tree bark. The beam tried to freeze the tree bark but found it very difficult. Eicewald sent more energy and power when he realized the bark was beating back the icy cold of his spell. He maintained the beam on the Druid's torso, who was staring at him.

"The tree bears the winter, no matter how freezing," Colin said with a smile as he sent more energy to strengthen his bark cloak. Every time he used his magic some of the runes on his body lit up a deep green.

Eicewald realized he was not going to be able to freeze Colin and changed his spell. He sent a frozen javelin to see whether he could pierce through the bark's defenses. The ice javelin stuck in the tree bark but did not pierce through.

"You will not be able to bring down an oak with a javelin, even one of ice," Colin said.

The Mage nodded and changed his strategy again. He created two large ice axes with long edges and began to swing them in the air before striking both sides of the Druid.

"The woodcutter with a powerful axe will bring a tree down no matter how robust it is," Eicewald told Colin as he wielded the axes with his staff. They struck right to left and left to right, as if the Druid were a great oak they were going to fell.

I help, Camu messaged Lasgol.

But be careful and don't interfere with Eicewald's magic, or you might make the Druid kill him.

Oh, I understand…

Lasgol ran to one side and released, avoiding the defensive tree guarding the Druid. The arrow flew straight at the Druid—the tree reached out with its branches to divert it but could not. The arrow hit the Druid as he was casting a spell on Astrid. It hit him full in the chest and there was a small explosion of dirt and smoke which stunned and half-blinded him. Lasgol rapidly released again, this time using an Elemental Air Arrow. The Druid tried to recover, but the arrow hit him before he was able to. It hit his chest again and this time the burst was followed by a discharge which made the Druid shake uncontrollably.

Seeing that Lasgol had hit the Druid, Astrid took advantage of the distraction and came at him at great speed. She delivered two strikes to the Druid's legs, and after blocking the attack of the defensive tree branches, ran like lightning to the Druid who was attacking Viggo. The defensive tree vanished when the Druid fell to the ground, unconscious.

Viggo had already managed to free one leg from the entrapping roots and was hacking at them with his knife to free the other. The Druid finished his spell and Viggo noticed that dozens of flowers similar to poppies had sprouted around him.

"Flowers? What nonsense is this?" he cried as he continued freeing his other leg.

Then the flowers began to exude a strong, sweet smell. It entered Viggo's lungs and went to his head, making him dizzy. He delivered one more strike to free his leg and tried to stand. He only managed to sit up, swooning from the flowers' perfume.

"That smell… it's some kind of poison or drug…" he muttered.

Astrid changed direction when she saw Viggo swaying. She went for him as the Druid began conjuring again. Viggo managed to get to his feet but he was left bent over; he could not stand up straight, his head weighed too much.

"Darned… poppies…"

With a tremendous leap Astrid pushed Viggo forward, getting him out of magical plants' area.

Lasgol released his Earth Arrow and hit the Druid as he conjured magic against Viggo again. The arrow hit his shoulder and the small explosion filled his face with dirt and smoke, blinding and stunning him. Lasgol nocked an Air Arrow and got ready to release and knock him out.

Astrid had got back on her feet and with a leap and a pirouette headed to the Druid. Viggo was gazing at the ceiling with an unfocused gaze.

"Pretty... ceiling... how beautiful..."

Lasgol's arrow hit the Druid on the right side of his chest and the discharge left him shaking. Astrid reached the Druid and cut his thighs. She turned to Lasgol and signaled to him that the Druid was no longer a threat. An instant later the Druid dropped to the ground.

Eicewald was still locked in combat with the Druid leader. Colin had cast a spell on the Mage and around him three incorporeal, translucent, green and brown trees had sprouted. They were clearly magical. They had thick leafless branches which closed around Eicewald's anti-magic sphere like a sea monster's tentacles. With a wave of the leader's staff the branches began to squeeze the sphere, trying to burst it. Eicewald noticed and concentrated, sending more energy to strengthen his sphere since if the branches broke through he would be exposed to the Druid's magic.

Lasgol signaled Astrid to attack the leader. She nodded.

Colin realized they were going to attack him and that he was at a disadvantage. He raised his staff and cast a spell, moving it in circles above his head. All of a sudden the six trees pulled their roots out of the ground with a loud crunch and started to move as if they were alive.

"The trees are moving, how funny," said Viggo, whose mind was still hazy.

Lasgol reacted and released against the nearest tree. He had an Earth Arrow nocked, and it burst when it hit the tree but did nothing to it. Astrid lunged at the one closest to her, but her knife strokes, although poisoned, did nothing to the tree either, which defended itself by hitting her with one of its branches as if it were an arm. The other two trees were moving slowly with heavy swaying movements toward Viggo and Eicewald.

Lasgol watched them and knew they could not stop them with regular knives and arrows since they were trees. He thought of using his Ranger's axe, which was more for chopping and cutting small trunks than for felling giant trees. He wondered what could cause the most damage to a tree and the answer came at once: fire. He switched to Fire Arrows and, concentrating, called on his *Fast Shot* skill. He focused on the three trees attacking Astrid, Viggo, and himself. There was a green flash, and in the blink of an eye three arrows flew one after the other from his bow. The three arrows found their targets in succession. The trees were struck by the explosions followed by flames, and several of their branches caught fire.

The burning trees stopped their advance—they had not liked that at all.

"Viggo, knives of fire," Astrid told him as she poured the compound on hers.

"Fire… how pretty…" Viggo said, staring at the trees like a loon.

"Viggo! Come back to us! Knives of fire!" Astrid yelled at him.

I help Viggo, Camu messaged them.

Lasgol had no idea how Camu was going to help him, but he encouraged his friend regardless.

Do what you can.

I do.

The farthest trees kept coming, getting closer. Lasgol knew he would have to use the same tactic again. He concentrated and called on his *Fast Shot* skill once more. This was a skill he had difficulty summoning, and it took him a while to do it. He knew this was not the time to dwell on it but he certainly had to be faster at summoning his skills, especially powerful ones like this *Fast Shot.* Luckily, the trees were moving slowly. The three Fire Arrows hit the trees and burst into flames which caught in the branches.

Astrid was fighting them off, delivering strokes of fire to the branches the tree was trying to hit her with. Its movements were slow but powerful, the branches thick and strong.

I with Viggo. Help, Camu messaged them.

"What a pretty tree," Viggo was staring at the flaming tree coming toward him.

I cancel magic. A silver flash enveloped Viggo and he suddenly blinked hard.

"What on earth…?" he said blankly.

You free of magic of flowers, Camu informed him.

A branch came straight down to strike Viggo on the head. With a swift movement, he stepped aside and avoided the branch.

"Can someone tell me why the trees are attacking us?" Viggo asked, already pouring fire on his knives.

Not trees, be Druids, Camu messaged.

How do you know that? Lasgol asked him.

Trees not have magic, these yes. Not trees, be Druids.

"So they've turned into trees," Astrid cried as she fought.

"They won't be able to handle the fire!" Lasgol told them as he looked for more Fire Arrows on his quiver and realized he had run out.

Viggo leapt onto the top of the tree on the side that was not burning and started hacking at the branches with his knives of fire.

"Little trees to me! Ha!" he mocked as he fought with all his might.

The fire from Lasgol's arrows, combined with Astrid's and Viggo's attacks with their knives of fire, made the three trees burn entirely. Suddenly a Druid came out of a tree, shaking off the fire that had caught on his clothes. The tree he came out of was soon consumed by the flames. Lasgol had no time to react and released a Water Arrow, which put out the fire and left the Druid half frozen from the burst of ice and frost.

The Druids inside the other two burning trees came out when the fire had almost entirely devoured them. Viggo and Astrid did not give them time to react and knocked them out with blows to the nape and temple with the butts of their knives.

"Let's attack the other three," Astrid told Viggo.

"These Druid-trees are going to get what for," Viggo said.

While Lasgol, Astrid, and Viggo fought against the three remaining trees, Eicewald was trying to bend Colin, who was turning out to be a tough rival to defeat. The Druid's magic was powerful and Eicewald was in a tight spot. His ice axes were bothering the leader but he still stood firm. For his part, Eicewald had to defend himself from the suffocating pressure of the trees trying to break his defensive sphere. But then something surprising happened. A silver flash appeared behind the leader, Colin. The spell crushing Eicewald's barrier vanished, and the three incorporeal trees trying to reach the Mage's body to break it in two, burst into nothing before his eyes. It was as if the leader had stopped his attack. But Colin's look of surprise and anger indicated that he had not done it of his own will.

I help Eicewald, Camu told the Ice Mage.

Eicewald understood that Camu had canceled Colin's magic and nodded, smiling.

Colin conjured another spell against Eicewald, and this time he created a waterfall which fell directly on the Mage's sphere, weakening it with its pressure. Eicewald sent more energy to strengthen it.

There was another silver flash and the waterfall evaporated over Eicewald's head.

"How are you cancelling my spells?" Colin asked in surprise, his eyes wide.

"It's not me who's doing it," the Mage admitted. "You'd better surrender before my ice axes finish piercing through your defenses and kill you," he said as his axes kept striking the leader's body like pendulums of icy death.

The leader looked around. His last three tree-Druids were falling down, defeated. Astrid, Lasgol, and Viggo, who had beaten them, turned now to the leader.

"I see I've been defeated," he said and dropped his staff.

Eicewald stopped striking with his icy axes. He cast one last spell on the leader and ice bars surged out of the ground, forming an icy cell that imprisoned Colin.

"Don't touch the bars or you'll freeze," Eicewald warned him.

The leader nodded.

Astrid, Lasgol, and Viggo came over to Eicewald.

"I hope you haven't killed any of my people, or you will not leave the sacred forest alive."

"We've scorched them a little, poisoned them a little, but they'll live," Astrid said.

"I hope so, for your own good," Colin threatened.

"We don't kill if there's no need. You know that," Eicewald told the leader.

Colin did not look convinced as he eyed Viggo.

"I do, but today you've been lucky because I haven't," Viggo smiled.

"Which of the three doors is the right one?" Lasgol asked the leader.

"I cannot help you with that. You have defeated me, but I will not cooperate."

"Then we'd better kill him, right?" Viggo asked.

"We're not going to kill him," Lasgol said in a serious tone.

"But he doesn't want to help us and he's going to kill us as soon as he's free! Leaving enemies alive isn't good for our health," Viggo replied.

"He's not our enemy," Eicewald corrected him. "It's just that we have to recover something he doesn't want to give us."

"You'll see, we'll regret leaving him alive," Viggo said, raising his arms to the heavens.

"Let's try the door on the left," Lasgol said, pointing at it with his bow.

Come on," Astrid agreed.

Chapter 23

Lasgol stood in front of the door and called on his *Animal Presence* skill to see if he could determine who or what awaited them beyond. He could not detect anything, but he thought it might be the magic of the place interfering with his own.

Do you pick up anything strange? he transmitted to Camu.

No, only magic of forest.

Yeah, me too.

"Let's proceed carefully, I can't determine what's on the other side of the door," he warned his comrades.

"No problem," Viggo said, and he kicked the door open, lunged inside, and did a somersault.

"Could he be more of a brute..." Astrid muttered, following him in with a silent somersault.

Lasgol followed them, aiming his bow. Eicewald came in next, and Camu came last.

Before Lasgol could release, Viggo and Astrid had a Druid flat on the floor with their knives at the man's neck.

"Don't hurt him," Eicewald cried.

Lasgol looked at the Druid and realized he was an old man. The room they were in was a library study with a large desk and shelves full of books.

"The Princess?" Astrid demanded.

"This is her study... she must be in her chamber," he said, glancing at a door which must lead to the room in the middle.

Viggo went to hit the old man but Astrid stopped him. She tied his hands behind his back, tied his feet, and put a gag in his mouth before strapping him to the table.

"It would've been easier and more efficient to strike him on the head," Viggo told her.

"He's an old valet. He's not a danger, he couldn't even fight back. You have to respect the elderly," she said.

Viggo rolled his eyes.

They went into the next chamber, the one in the middle, following the same procedure. The inner door was not locked so they made no noise, something Astrid was thankful for. The central chamber was a large hall with several spaces. One section was a tea parlor, another a dining room, and a third a resting space with soft sofas. It was deserted. They checked it, just in case, but found no Druids or animals which presented any threat, only furniture. An inner door led to the third chamber. Lasgol guessed, after seeing the first two chambers, that the third one would be the bedroom.

They went to the door. It was locked.

"I'd rather you used your lock picks than your foot," Astrid said to Viggo.

"As you wish. Of course," he smiled and proceeded to pick the lock. It did not take him long. There was a metallic click and the lock yielded. They opened the door carefully without going in, since the Princess and whoever was guarding her must be in that room and they were all aware of it.

Viggo poked his head in a little and looked inside.

"It's a luxurious bedroom, but it's empty," he told his comrades.

"Let's go in quietly," said Astrid.

Both Assassins went in first, stealthily. They each went to one end of the large room. An enormous, royal, four poster bed occupied the middle of the room. In front of the bed were three mirrors, also large, and on each side two wardrobes that seemed to have no end. On the right and left walls without wardrobes were creepers laced with hundreds of different colored flowers. They appeared to line the walls with a beautiful tapestry, as if they were a garden with flowers from different kingdoms. Once again, the walls gave off that greenish luminescence, but here in the bedroom it was more rose-toned.

Lasgol and Eicewald went over to the bed, on alert for any surprises. But the room was deserted. Camu came in last and remained behind Lasgol, who was scanning the enormous bedroom, which was indeed worthy of a princess, even if it was underground. The Druids had lodged the Princess in style.

Astrid threw herself on the floor to look under the bed.

"Clear," she confirmed.

Viggo opened the wardrobe on the right, but it was so large it took him more than a moment to search.

"Nothing," he confirmed at last, looking frustrated.

Astrid searched the other wardrobe.

"She's not here either."

"That's weird…" Lasgol said. He was not happy, the Princess should be there.

All of a sudden an arrow flew out of the left wall creepers, straight at Eicewald's chest.

"Watch out!" Lasgol warned him.

Eicewald made a swift move with his ice staff and raised an ice sphere around him. Lasgol knew this kind of sphere protected him from physical harm.

The arrow hit the sphere and, just as Lasgol was expecting, it could not go through the Mage's protection. Eicewald had raised it with amazing speed, and judging by the thickness of it, the sphere would protect him from any physical attack, whether sword, arrow, or staff. Lasgol was impressed. Only a powerful Mage with great experience could do such a thing in the blink of an eye. But then something strange happened—when the arrow hit the sphere, instead of trying to pierce it there was a small explosion and a dark substance began to taint the sphere black.

"What's that?" Astrid asked, frowning.

"I don't know, but that wasn't a regular arrow," Lasgol replied.

He turned to the spot where the arrow had flown from, but he could only see the creepers that covered the wall entirely from one end to the other.

"I'll deal with it," Astrid said and went to the creepers determinedly.

A new arrow flew from the creepers straight at Astrid's body as she approached at a run. The brunette threw her body to the side in a swift, nimble move and the arrow brushed her head.

"Come out and fight, you coward," Viggo dared their attacker as he followed Astrid to help her.

Astrid went through the creepers and vanished, as if they had swallowed her.

"Astrid…" Lasgol panicked and aimed his bow, although he could only see flower-filled creepers and nothing to shoot at.

"It's a false wall!" Astrid warned them.

A second arrow flew from the same wall, but on the opposite side to where Astrid had entered. The arrow flew toward Viggo.

"Watch out, Viggo!" Lasgol cried.

The arrow was swift and it had a short way to go—Viggo would not be able to dodge it, even with his amazing agility and reflexes. He realized this and instead of trying to dodge he blocked it by crossing his knives over his chest. The arrow hit the edge of one of his knives, but instead of diverting it there was a small explosion and a purple-blue substance enveloped Viggo.

"Oh no..." he muttered when he realized he had fallen into a trap. The arrow was not a regular one but carried some kind of poisonous gas.

Lasgol saw the substance and also realized the trap.

He headed to help Viggo when a Druid came out of the right wall from behind the creepers and attacked him with his staff. Lasgol leapt to one side. The Druid cast a quick spell and a green flash ran throughout his body and staff, and suddenly Lasgol saw that his body and staff were entirely covered with great thorns, like those of a rose but huge. Even the Druid's face was covered in thorns. Only his eyes were visible—he looked like a porcupine-man.

Acting on instinct, Lasgol jumped backward and released at the Druid. The arrow hit the man's thorn-covered torso and did not go through. The Druid attacked with his thorny staff and Lasgol dodged him. Out of the corner of his eye he saw Viggo falling to the floor, subdued by the substance that had enveloped him.

"Eicewald, help Viggo!" he called.

"I can't, I can't see a thing," the Mage replied. His sphere was completely blackened.

Astrid came out of the creepers, dealing strokes at another Druid who must have been hiding in the wall.

"This is a trap room!" the Assassin cried as she made the Druid back up.

"Don't breathe the purple substance!" Lasgol warned her.

Viggo was crawling along the floor, trying to escape the gas that had affected him, and got under the bed.

Astrid had the Druid against the wardrobe and was trying to penetrate the protection of tree bark he was wearing. Every time he tried to cast a spell on her, Astrid hit him hard in the mouth. She could not knock him down, but she hurt him enough to interrupt his spell.

Lasgol left his bow on the floor and took out his axe and knife, since he was too close to the Druid to release. His *Improved Agility* and *Cat-like Reflexes* skills were active, so he could easily deal with the Druid and his thorny staff.

Eicewald deactivated his protective sphere in order to see. Immediately from a new position among the creepers another arrow flew, seeking his heart. The experienced Mage had to raise a wall of ice in front of him to protect himself. The arrow hit the wall and burst, splashing it black. Once again the dark substance started spreading all over the protection. Eicewald poked his head around one side of the wall and helped Astrid. He cast a spell on the Druid fighting her, throwing an ice trident at the Druid's head. He seemed to bear it well but he stumbled, looking dizzy. Seeing this, Astrid began to hit him on the head with all her strength.

Lasgol was defending himself from the Druid's staff strokes with his knife and axe. He diverted a new attack with his knife and hit the Druid on the right thigh with his axe. He did not manage to penetrate the thorns and reach the flesh, but he continued the movement with a stroke to the Druid's head which made him step back. He seemed affected. There was no blood, so it must have been the axe blow itself that had bothered him. The Druid launched another defensive blow with his staff and the thorns grazed Lasgol's shoulder.

I help, Camu's message reached him.

Lasgol did not know what his friend was going to do, so he remained alert.

Then suddenly there was a sharp blow and the Druid collapsed forward onto the floor. He tried to get up but for some reason could not.

What did you do?

I on top of Druid.

Did you throw yourself on him?

Yes, my scales stronger than his thorns. I scales of dragon.

Good idea—a bit weighty, but very efficient.

You tie I hold.

I see he can't get up. You weigh a ton.

I mighty.

And heavy.

Lasgol brought out some leather ligatures and tied and gagged the Druid while Camu held him down, all of his weight on the Druid's back.

Don't move. Keep him down, Lasgol told Camu.

My prisoner. Not worry.

The Druid tried to cast a spell but with the gag he was finding it hard. What the Druid did not know was that he would not be able to because Camu was cancelling his magic. The spell that covered his body with thorns vanished. Seeing himself defeated and not knowing how or why, he stopped resisting.

Eicewald made a stalactite fall on the other Druid's head and knocked him out. Unfortunately, just then the archer released behind Astrid and the arrow broke at her feet. The purple-blue gas rose and affected Astrid, leaving her a little stunned.

Lasgol looked at the two knocked-out Druids.

"There's still the archer!" Eicewald cried in warning, and as if he had heard the Ice Mage, the archer released again against Eicewald from another part of the wall. The Mage raised another ice wall, and just like before the arrow burst and the black substance began to climb the defenses.

"I'm not going to be able to see for much longer," the Mage warned Lasgol.

"I'll handle it," Lasgol said, and he ran into the creepers on the right side with his weapons in hand. Upon entering he realized that behind them was another wall with a space two paces from the creepers, which meant a secret corridor ran around the whole room. That's where the archer had been moving and releasing at will, but that ended now. He ran as fast as he could and, turning in the corridor, came face to face with the archer. He was surprised because the archer was clad in clothes similar to a Ranger's. The archer raised his bow, but Lasgol had been expecting it and threw himself down at his opponent's feet, using his improved reflexes and agility. The arrow went over his head. Lasgol hit the archer's ankles with his forearms, making him fall to the floor. Lasgol rolled over and sat on top of the archer, holding the man's arms with his knees so he would not knife his sides. With a quick movement, Lasgol put his Ranger's knife at the archer's throat.

"If you want to live, don't fight back," Lasgol warned.

"Well, well, who do we have here? If I haven't been beaten by the handsomest guy in Norghana," the archer said.

Lasgol was puzzled. It was a woman's voice, and it sounded very familiar. He pulled the hood off to see who it was and his eyes widened when he saw the blonde curls, pretty face, and sea-blue eyes of someone he knew quite well.

"Val!"

"In the flesh, my handsome Ranger," she winked at him.

"What...? You're here...?"

"I see I still make you stutter. What a compliment," she laughed.

"What are you doing here?"

"Waiting for you. Haven't you come to fetch me?" she replied mockingly.

"You know perfectly well I haven't come for you."

"Ohhh.... What a pity," she smiled. "Then you've come for my lady."

"Yes, he's come for me," a sharp, haughty voice said.

Lasgol saw another young woman appear behind Valeria. He lifted his knife toward her threateningly. Based on her physique and clothing, a younger copy of her mother the queen, there was no doubt this was Princess Heulyn.

"How dare you threaten a Royal Princess? Lower that weapon immediately!" she ordered him rudely.

Lasgol was confused.

"I don't want to hurt you," Lasgol said.

"Who are you?" Princess Heulyn asked.

"That's not important. What matters is that we're here to rescue you, Princess Heulyn," Lasgol said.

"Rescue me? I don't need rescuing. I'm here with the Druids of my own free will."

"Perhaps, but we've been sent to rescue you."

"You may return the way you came. I'm not going anywhere," she said sharply and folded her arms.

"Would you mind letting me get up? Not that I find this posture unpleasant, not at all," Valeria smiled charmingly and seductively at Lasgol, "but it's not the best one to negotiate anything."

"Do I have your word you won't try anything?"

"Yes," Valeria replied.

Lasgol stood up and let Valeria get back on her feet.

"Let's go back to the room. We'll talk there, with everyone," she said.

They came out of the creepers and Eicewald, who was helping Astrid, pointed his staff at them.

"Everything's all right," Lasgol hastened to say so he would not start a spell.

"What's that traitor doing here?" Astrid, who was already

recovering, cried with eyes like saucers.

"I'm the Princess's bodyguard," Valeria said.

"And my confidant," Heulyn added.

"Princess Heulyn, it's a pleasure to see you again," Eicewald said with a deep bow.

"You're the Norghanian Mage, I remember you. Ice Mage, if I'm not mistaken."

"That is correct, Royal Princess."

"Yes, I'm never wrong," Heulyn said, lifting her chin.

Viggo came out from under the bed.

"I'm good as new. Who do we have to kill?"

"About time," Astrid said, unable to believe how long he had taken.

"I had to withdraw for a moment," said Viggo. "So I could recover."

"Did you like my special arrow?" Valeria asked him.

"Well, well, look who we have here—the pretty blonde traitor," Viggo said, smiling.

"I see you haven't forgotten me," she smiled back coquettishly.

"Don't waste your charms on me, I'm spoken for," he replied, shaking the dust off his shoulder.

"It wouldn't be by a blonde Archer?"

"Precisely," Viggo said proudly.

"Congratulations. I'm happy for both of you."

"Thanks, have you already tried the weirdo?" he said, indicating Lasgol with his thumb.

"If she tries I'll cut her throat," Astrid snapped with a furious glare.

Val raised her hands.

"He seems to be spoken for too. I'll let him be," she said in a pacifying tone.

"You'd better. If you get close to him you'll die," Astrid promised.

"What character," Princess Heulyn said. "I like it, but I forbid you to lay a finger on my confidant. If you do, I'll demand your head."

"You can say whatever you want, but I'll kill her regardless."

"You should know your place. You're addressing the Royal Princess of Irinel, show me the respect you owe me," Heulyn said, lifting her chin even higher.

"I only owe respect to the throne of Norghana," Astrid replied.

"So, this beautiful damsel is the Princess of Irinel," said Viggo, looking at her sensually. "Allow me to introduce myself…"

The Princess raised her hand and put it in front of Viggo's face.

"I don't deal with men, and least of all men without good breeding. Don't you dare address me, ever."

Viggo turned his head and looked at her, dodging her hand.

"We're going to get along just fine, you and me, Princess, you'll see," Viggo said in an acid tone.

"We must leave before the Druids realize what's going on. We haven't been exactly silent," Eicewald said.

"Leave and you'll keep your lives. If you touch me I'll have you beheaded, all of you," the princess threatened scornfully.

"She's so sweet, isn't she?" Viggo said, blinking hard and glaring at her.

"If I were you, I'd do as the princess says," Valeria warned them. "She's serious."

"Your father sent us, you won't do anything to us. We're only carrying out his orders," Lasgol explained.

"I'll make sure you're all killed if you don't leave at once, with or without my father's approval."

"Absolutely charming. What a pity I already have a girlfriend," Viggo said, blowing a kiss at the princess.

"I'll have them cut off your tongue before you're beheaded," Heulyn said.

"Astrid, gag and tie her up. You, Viggo, the same with Valeria," Lasgol said.

"Were not taking this one, are we?" Astrid asked, pointing at Valeria with a look of enraged disgust.

"Yes, she can help with the princess," Lasgol replied.

"That's not a good idea!" Astrid protested.

"She's her bodyguard and confidant, better bring her too," said Eicewald.

Astrid muttered under her breath but did as she was told.

"If you so much as brush against me I'll have your arms torn off, Norghanian," the princess threatened coldly.

"I'm not in the mood for little princesses," Astrid said and tied and gagged her unceremoniously.

Viggo went to tie and gag Valeria.

"Are you already the most fearsome Assassin in all Norghana?" she asked him with a smile.

"Of all Tremia," he assured her while he tied her.

"I see you progress fast in life. It doesn't surprise me either—you've always had great talent," Valeria said with another smile.

"And a poor head, according to some," Viggo replied, tying her with double knots just in case.

"I absolutely agree," Valeria nodded repeatedly.

Viggo started to gag her. "Don't try any nonsense. You know us, you won't get anywhere and the brunette will slit your throat if you give her an excuse."

Valeria nodded. "Don't I know it," she said, looking at Astrid out of the corner of her eye.

"By the way, good arrows," Viggo admitted to her.

"Aren't they? I call them Purple Dream and Squid Ink. They're my personal creations. I like to experiment with arrows, elements and compounds."

"You can give us the recipes, they're useful," Viggo said and put the gag in her mouth.

"Come on," Lasgol said, and they left the bedroom.

Chapter 24

Princess Heulyn struggled against them. Astrid pushed her forward unceremoniously, but even so she was delaying them with her rebellious attitude. Valeria did not struggle and kept close to the Princess. They arrived back at the wasps' chamber. Egil was still tending to Nilsa, Ingrid, and Ona, who were lying on the floor with painful looks on their faces. He was on his knees beside them.

"How did everything go?" he asked when he saw them arrive.

"We have the Princess," Astrid said, and she gave her a good shove to prove it. Heulyn mumbled threats that could not be heard through the gag.

"Fantastic!" Egil cried, pleased.

"And someone else," Viggo added and showed them Valeria.

"Isn't that...? Val!" Nilsa cried, recognizing her.

"What are you doing here?" Ingrid asked, frowning as she recognized her too.

"It appears the Dark Ranger is the Princess's bodyguard," Astrid said in a tone of great frustration.

"Tremia is small indeed," Egil said, nodding. "I'd be fascinated to hear how that came about. Truly singular, and more so that our paths should cross again here," he commented, staring at Valeria.

Valeria shrugged and said something unintelligible because of the gag.

"How are you doing?" Lasgol asked, concerned as he knelt to check on Ona.

The snow panther moaned twice.

"I've managed to revive their systems by combining several tonics, and with a bit of improvisation," said Egil, who had his components' belt and the book of remedies open before him. The book was now his inseparable companion, although they all believed he had memorized it already.

"Can you walk?" Lasgol asked. "We have to get out of here before all the Druids fall down on us."

"Yes, we can," Ingrid said determinedly as she stood with difficulty.

Lasgol waited to see whether Nilsa could get to her feet; it took her a little longer, but she did.

"Yes, we can," she confirmed.

Ona also stood and growled once.

"How are your legs, Egil?" Lasgol asked his friend as he put away his utensils.

"So... so, but I think I'll be able to walk."

"Good, then let's get out of here. We've already had enough fighting for one day," Lasgol declared.

"I don't think we'll get out of these woods without more fighting," Astrid warned him.

"We might get lucky," he replied, although he did not really believe it.

The group set off. Lasgol and Eicewald helped Ingrid and Nilsa to keep going. Although they could walk, it was hard for them and they could barely keep their balance, not to mention that their arms were useless. They were not going to be able to shoot. Lasgol begged the Ice Gods they would not have to fight, because their comrades were not in a state to do so. Even Ona, although she was walking, was moving slowly and clumsily.

They retraced their way to the entrance. Lasgol took a look outside and did not detect any threat, so he signaled the others to follow him out to the sacred oak wood of the Druids.

They exited and looked for Aidan but did not see him. He was not waiting for them where they had left him on their way in.

"Aidan isn't here," said Nilsa, who was looking in every direction for him.

"Maybe he ran into trouble and hid, or fled," Egil reasoned.

"There are no signs of struggle," said Ingrid as she looked at the ground and the nearby bushes.

"So, how are we going to get back if we can't see the path the Druid opened?" Viggo asked.

"I can track our trail," said Lasgol.

"Now you're talking, Tireless Tracker," Astrid said, and shoved the princess, who was trying to go back inside the tree they had come out of.

"We have a problem. Even if you manage to follow the trail, without a new spell by Aidan the Druids will find out we're in the forest," said Eicewald.

"True…" Lasgol was thoughtful.

"Isn't the path cleared still?" Egil asked. "Or has it been too long for the spell to still be active?"

Camu, can you pick up Aidan's magic? Lasgol transmitted to him.

No, magic of Aidan disappear.

"That poses a serious problem," Lasgol said as he bent over to check the ground. "I can see our trail all right. I can guide you, but they'll discover us without the spell."

"Eicewald, can you cast a spell like Aidan's?" Ingrid asked him.

The Mage shook his head. "I'm afraid not. My spells are Water-Magic based. I can open a frozen corridor, yes, but I fear the Druids would pick up on it since it's magic they don't use. Aidan's magic is Magic of Nature, the same running throughout this forest. That's why they don't detect it."

"Well, that's great…" Viggo commented. "Besides, we can't get out running with four cripples and two prisoners—we'd be caught at a moment's notice."

"But we can't stay put either, I'm afraid. Druids will come," said Eicewald.

Lasgol had an idea.

Camu, can't you cancel the magic and open a corridor like Aidan did?

Not know.

Try and see.

I try.

Ingrid and Nilsa encouraged him, "Come on, try it. See if we're lucky."

Camu stepped forward. They all waited. Suddenly there was a silver flash, and after a moment there was a second one.

Not work, Camu messaged.

It doesn't? Why, what's the matter?

I cancel magic, but only a moment. Then magic come back.

Why's that?

Much magic, everywhere.

Oh yeah… I see… you can't cancel it all, of course.

Can't, too much, come out again from ground, and trees.

I see…

"At least you tried," Astrid told Camu.

"If the origin isn't stopped, the core won't stop emanating Magic of Nature," said Eicewald.

199

"So what are we going to do?" Nilsa asked.

Lasgol turned to Egil. "Any plans?"

Egil smiled. "Yup, I made an escape plan in case things went wrong, in case of trouble after the rescue. We'll go south, crossing the forest as fast as we can."

"There's an area to the south where the Druids don't set foot—the forest's magic doesn't penetrate there," said Eicewald. "That's what I wanted to visit to do my study, but they refused. No matter how much I insisted, they wouldn't let me go."

"Well, it looks like today your wish will come true," Viggo told him.

The Princess began to struggle. She kicked and wriggled with all her might. She was trying to shout, but the gag did not let her.

"We have to do something with her or she's going to cause us trouble," said Nilsa.

"I suggest a sharp blow to the back of the neck. Fast and efficient," Viggo said, making the gesture with his hand.

"We can't hit her," Ingrid said, shaking her head.

"I could freeze her so she stops causing trouble," Eicewald suggested, "but I'm afraid her parents the King and Queen would interpret it as me hurting her. Freezing someone isn't deadly, but it does leave certain burning marks from the ice on the body."

"No, that's not good either," said Ingrid as she helped Nilsa contain the enraged prisoner.

"I have the solution," said Egil, searching in his Ranger's belt.

"Hold her tight, she's slippery," Viggo told Astrid.

Valeria stiffened when she saw Astrid holding Heulyn tight.

"Watch out! A Forest Ogre!" Egil said, pointing behind the Princess with a look of horror.

They all looked in that direction, including the Princess. But there was nothing there.

"What on earth..." Ingrid started to protest.

With quick movements, Egil applied a scarf to the Princess's nose which he had soaked in Summer Slumber liquid.

Before she could realize what was happening, the Princess lost consciousness. Astrid held her so she would not fall.

"Good idea," Ingrid told Egil.

"Thank you, I had it planned already. It will keep her unconscious for half a day."

"Well, you'd better prepare more of that for when she wakes up," Viggo said. "She's insufferable."

Egil smiled. "I'd also counted on that," he said and showed him two more phials of the blue liquid.

"I'll carry her," Astrid said, slinging her over her shoulder as if the princess were a sack of hay.

"When you need me to take over let me know," Lasgol told her.

"Don't worry, she's not that heavy. She's really skinny," she said with a wink.

They set off at once. Lasgol helped Ingrid lead the group. After them came Eicewald, helping Nilsa. Viggo followed, helping Egil with one hand and with the other guiding Valeria. Astrid followed, carrying the Princess. Camu and Ona brought up the rear. The panther still struggled to walk and Camu, now in his visible state to preserve his reserves of energy, was licking her lovingly with his blue tongue.

Lasgol could not distinguish the green power of the forest but he knew it was all around them, emanating from trees and soil alike. The Druids would soon discover that the Princess was missing or the forest would alert the Druids to their intrusion. Either way, he was expecting problems very soon. He tried to lead the group as quickly as possible but Ingrid, Nilsa, and Egil could barely walk straight and moved with a lot of difficulty. Lasgol could see the frustration on Ingrid's face, who was clenching her jaw and leaning on her bow to advance. Nilsa was doing the same, and between the bow in one hand as a staff and her comrade's help they went on.

All of a sudden, through the trees a group of Druids appeared at a run.

"We've been discovered," Astrid warned the moment she saw them.

Lasgol looked back using his *Hawk's Eye* skill and saw they were Druids indeed, female Druids. They had not seen any so far, and he was surprised. They were wearing simple short tunics halfway down their thighs in forest colors. What surprised him more was their hair, which was long and braided and adorned with leaves and branches from the forest. The color of their hair was also odd, somewhere between green and brown.

"That's a group of Druid Mothers, they're powerful forest witches," Eicewald warned them.

"Hurry up! Keep going!" Lasgol cried, trying to make them go faster before the Druids reached them.

They all went as fast as they could, but the Druid Mothers were gaining on them. The women were not very fast, but in the group's condition they could not manage to lose them.

"Eicewald, you and I will stay back to delay them. The rest of you, keep going south," said Lasgol, letting go of Ingrid.

"All right," the Mage agreed, also letting go of Nilsa's hand.

"D'you want me to stay as well?" Viggo asked.

"No, you'd better make sure the group gets to the place Egil mentioned."

"Okay, if a Druid comes close I'll kill him," Viggo said as he went on with the group.

"Be careful," Astrid said as she went after Viggo, hauling the unconscious Princess.

I stay. Help.

Okay, but Ona, you go with the rest, you're in no shape to fight.

Ona moaned twice.

Ona you not well. You go, Camu messaged to the panther.

Ona moaned once and left.

"Let's do this," Lasgol told the Mage, who nodded.

I ready, Camu messaged.

202

Chapter 25

Eicewald summoned a protective anti-magic sphere. Lasgol began to call on his skills in order to fight better and nocked an arrow. Fighting was inevitable, and it was going to be complicated since the rivals possessed the Gift and would use it against them.

The Druid Mothers got within three hundred paces of them and stopped. There were a dozen women, and they started to cast a spell in unison.

Magic of nature, Camu messaged them.

"Can you hit them with an arrow that'll interrupt their spells?" Eicewald asked. "They're too far for me to reach them with one of my spells. That's why they stopped there."

"I can try. We're also too far away for them to reach us with their magic, right?" Lasgol asked, noting the distance that separated them.

"True, but they're not conjuring against us."

All of a sudden, halfway between the Druid Mothers and them a sort of whirlwind began to take shape. As it formed it started to emit a strange sound, like a sustained lament only feminine voices could manage.

"There it is."

"They're attacking us with a whirlwind?" Lasgol asked blankly, not grasping the strategy being used against them.

"No, what you're witnessing is a summoning spell," the Ice Mage said.

Lasgol aimed his composite bow and used an Earth Arrow, one of the few he had left. He released at the Druid Mother in the middle. The shot seemed well aimed—it was going to hit the witch in the torso, or perhaps the stomach if it lost height, but at least it was not deviating. When the arrow was about to hit the Druid, two of them made a move with their staves and caused a gust of wind with leaves that pushed the arrow up high.

"That's not good…" said Lasgol, unable to believe they had diverted his arrow with their magic.

"Druid Mothers rule over the forest and everything in it," Eicewald explained. "Their Magic of Nature is powerful and this forest is their ally. They'll use everything in it against us."

The whirlwind they had summoned continued spinning without moving from the spot where it had risen; it was still emitting that penetrating, high-pitched lament.

"I'm guessing we don't want to move forward and attack..." Lasgol said to the Mage, phrasing it more like a question than a statement.

Eicewald shook his head. "There are too many—they'd tears us into shreds. In fact, it's a blessing they don't want to fight us directly. I find it quite strange, since they know they're more powerful than we are."

Be for me, Camu messaged, straining his neck proudly.

You think so? Lasgol replied, not convinced.

"It might be... they've never seen a creature like Camu. Maybe they respect him and they're being wary for some reason..." Eicewald guessed.

I more than dragon.

Yeah, but even so—and I'm not saying you're not—how would they know?

They know.

"Perhaps Camu's not all that wrong..." Eicewald said thoughtfully.

"He's not?"

"They see something strange and dangerous in the creature, otherwise we'd already be in direct combat. They're being wary, and it can only be because of him. They don't have that much respect for me and your magic isn't developed enough for them to fear you. They don't fear an Archer either, as you've seen. It has to be because of Camu."

I know, Camu said and wagged his long tail in a dignified manner.

"If they advance, we must retreat. As long as we make them waste as much time as possible so our friends can escape, we'll be achieving our goal. The fact that Camu's presence is confusing them is good for us."

"Understood," Lasgol said as he released again, this time using a regular arrow, sensing they would divert it. He was right—the Druids seemed to control the breeze that ran through the trees of the forest and they blocked his next shot with ease. He shot a third time to try and distract them while they continued conjuring the whirlwind that was making some high-pitched summons. Lasgol had the feeling that the whole forest was going to answer the spell's call. With every spin of the whirlwind, which did not move from its spot, the sound spread all around.

Suddenly, Lasgol felt the ground shaking.

"What's happening?" he said, looking all around.

"I don't know, but they're tremors at intervals," said the Mage.

"Weird…" Lasgol commented, uneasy.

Eicewald bent down to touch the ground, trying to feel what the tremor was. Lasgol noticed how a tree seemed to move closer to the Druid Mothers. It had to be an optical illusion. He focused and saw the tree move again. Against the background of the other trees it seemed like he was not seeing clearly, as if his eyes were tricking him.

"Something strange is going on… I see a tree moving toward us," he warned Eicewald.

The Mage narrowed his eyes to try and make out what Lasgol was seeing. He did.

"Yes… an oak *is* moving. It's coming toward us," he confirmed.

"A Druid in the shape of a tree, like the bush guards?" Lasgol said.

"It could be, yes… and now I see three more following."

"There's six more," Lasgol corrected him, using his *Hawk's Eye* skill.

"Astonishing. They're large, strong oaks… I don't know how a Druid could adopt a shape like that, the size is too big… I've never seen anything like this before," Eicewald admitted.

The trees were moving toward them with steps that made the ground shake. They used their roots as feet and took strides. They did not drag themselves, which made it disturbing and somewhat terrifying.

"Camu, can you tell whether these oaks are Druids using their magic?" Lasgol asked him.

Camu closed his eyes and flashed silver.

Not be druids.

"What do you mean they're not Druids? They have to be," Lasgol said.

No magic in tree.

"You don't pick up any magic in the trees?" Eicewald asked him, also puzzled.

No, not be magic.

"So, if they're not Druids using their magic, what are those walking trees?" Lasgol asked blankly.

"They must be some kind of beings who live in this forest that the Druids have called to help them fight us," said Eicewald.

"They can't be living beings…." Lasgol watched the six oaks walking toward them with slow, powerful strides, and the more he looked at them the harder he found it to believe that they were some kind of creature from the forest.

"Tremia is full of special creatures and beings," Eicewald said with a nod to Camu. "Maybe we're in the presence of some of those other beings."

"Well, that's a major problem then, because I can't think of how to stop them. They're huge, tough, powerful oaks."

"Do you still have Fire Arrows? the Mage asked him.

"I'm afraid not." He replied checking his quiver, just in case, "Hang on I think I do have a couple left."

"Camu, does your magic allow you to create fire?" Eicewald asked him.

No, I cancel magic.

"In that case, we're in trouble," the Mage said. He began to cast a spell on the first of the trees that were already upon them. He aimed his staff at the roots and began to freeze them with a steady ice beam.

Lasgol released a Fire Arrow against a tree to see what would happen, in case it was a trick or an illusion. The arrow stuck in the trunk, and there was a small explosion and a flame rose to the first branches, which caught fire. To Lasgol's surprise the tree grunted, a deep sound. Using its branches, it hit the arrow and shook it off, then tried to put the fire out with its branches.

"I'm beginning to think they actually are living creatures of the forest in the form of great oaks," Lasgol said, nodding. He released at the second tree as it approached him with the same result. The fire caught on several branches and the tree-being tried to put it out by shaking its branches. Lasgol had the feeling they would manage to put the fire out, and that things were going to get even more complicated since they would need a lot more fire to burn one of those enormous walking trees.

Eicewald managed to freeze the tree's roots, creating a large block of ice that held it in place. The tree grunted with rage, although they could not tell where the sound came from since it had no mouth.

They did not know how it could see them either, because it did not have eyes.

"I managed to stop one. I'll get the second one," the Mage said and proceeded to cast another spell.

The tree trapped in the block of ice began to punch the block using its branches as if they were arms and fists.

"Those tree-beings are incredible," said Lasgol as he checked to see whether he had any Water Arrows left to help Eicewald. He found one and released it against the first tree and its frozen roots to prevent it from freeing itself. There was a small burst and ice and frost covered one of the roots the tree was liberating.

Eicewald managed to freeze the second tree by creating a block of ice at its feet and started at once on the third. Lasgol watched the two trees grunting angrily and punching the ice holding their roots and could not believe his eyes. Egil would find this fascinating and fantastic—these forest creatures were just that. Lasgol found the fact troubling. He released several regular arrows against them, but he had the impression he was like a mosquito biting a pair of oxen.

Suddenly, there was a *crack* and the first tree-being freed part of its roots. It took a step and began to pull forward with all its strength. Lasgol noticed that the tree-beings were tremendously strong and that they had to be intelligent and sentient, which indeed made them fascinating. With one last strong pull, the tree-being freed the rest of its roots. Eicewald had just finished freezing the third tree and noticed that the first one was already free again.

"I'm not going to have enough time to freeze them all before they free themselves," the Mage said with a worried look on his face.

"I know, we have to retreat," Lasgol urged the Mage as he released his last Fire Arrow against the tree-beings, hoping the fire would delay them.

"Yes, let's go to the meeting point."

"Could you raise a high wall of ice here?" Lasgol said once he had released.

"I doubt it would do any good…" Eicewald replied.

"It's a distraction. I have an idea."

Eicewald trusted Lasgol and said no more. He began to cast the spell, moving his staff in circles as if he were drawing the wall before him. Lasgol put his satchel on the ground and started removing his traps.

Eicewald finished raising a spectacular wall of ice that separated them from the trees.

"Perfect," said Lasgol as he placed the first of his traps hidden by the wall. Once he had it set he concentrated, searched for his inner energy, and called on his *Trap Hiding* skill. The trap vanished before their eyes.

"Oh, I see…" the Mage said.

"Let's escape. While they're busy with the wall I'll set more traps."

Eicewald nodded and they ran off. The first tree-being reached the wall and stopped. The wall was as tall as the tree, and it seemed to be wondering whether to go around the obstacle or do something different. While it decided, Lasgol had already set another trap and continued his flight.

A second tree arrived beside the first one and they heard strange sounds, like snapping sticks. These were followed by similar sounds like branches breaking.

Tree-being speak.

"Are they talking?" Lasgol said as he placed another trap and manipulated it with some components from his belt.

I think yes.

"That's awesome. It shows they're intelligent and capable of communication, apart from the fact that we're facing sentient beings," Eicewald said, impressed.

"Trap set, let's keep going," Lasgol said, and they continued running away.

The two tree-beings beside the wall seemed to reach some kind of conclusion and started to punch the ice wall with their branches and trunks. They could hear dull blows that made the frozen wall shake.

"Quick! They're going to tear it down!" Eicewald urged.

Lasgol set the last trap he had left and, using his magic, he hid it just as the barrier began crumbling. Three trees stepped over the icy remains and continued pursuing them with powerful strides that caused tremors in the forest ground.

Lasgol, Camu, and Eicewald ran south, glancing back over their shoulders to see what the tree-beings were doing. All of a sudden they heard a small burst and Lasgol stopped to look back. One of the trees had stepped on one of the fire traps Lasgol had placed. The flame from the trap had reached several of its lower branches and they seemed to have caught fire.

"Did it work?" Eicewald asked, stopping further ahead.

Tree-being on fire, Camu messaged him.

Suddenly they heard a scream, a mixture of a tree splitting and a cry of rage. The tree-being was shaking its branches from side to side and beating branches against others, trying to put the fire out without succeeding.

"It looks like it," Lasgol replied.

Another of the trees tried to help, beating it with its own branches, but to its chagrin, instead of helping extinguish the flames the second tree caught fire too.

Another scream of rage reached them.

The third tree continued its pursuit, with strong steps and faster strides. It seemed to run, although it did not lift its roots off the ground.

"That one's coming pretty fast," said Lasgol.

"Run!" Eicewald cried.

A little further ahead Lasgol heard another one of his traps bursting and the third tree-being's cries of rage as it stepped on it. Lasgol had his *Owl Hearing* skill activated and could clearly hear what was happening behind them. He heard running steps among the strong strides of the three remaining tree-beings, which surprised him, so he looked back after calling on his *Hawk's Eye* skill.

"The Druid Mothers are running to help the three trees in trouble," Lasgol told Eicewald.

"They'll put out their fires," the Mage replied as he kept running.

Lasgol kept looking back as he continued running. The Druid Mothers reached the tree-beings whose branches were in flames and started conjuring at once.

Magic of nature, Camu warned.

"I see them. They're using their magic to help the tree-beings."

Lasgol was able to make out several of the Druid Mothers emit green flashes that ran throughout their bodies. Suddenly the forest ground opened amidst the burning trees and a river of clear water appeared, springing from the depths of the forest. The Druid Mothers continued conjuring, and then amid green flashes, the river water transformed into large waves that rose high. At an order of the female Druids, the waves broke against the three trees. An enormous amount of liquid doused the flames that assailed the three trees, and part of the fire died upon contact with the water.

"Well, aren't they powerful…" murmured Lasgol.

"They're forest witches… powerful and wise…" Eicewald said, panting from the strain of the run.

A second set of waves rose from the river and broke again against the tree-beings. The remaining flames died out and the trees were soaked with water. They did not continue their pursuit, but the other three did and two more traps exploded. One of fire and the last one of earth, since Lasgol had run out of fire traps or components to make them.

After the two explosions, one of the tree-beings stayed back so the Druid Mothers could help it. The other two kept coming after them.

Eicewald stopped and took a deep breath.

"How are you doing?" Lasgol asked, stopping beside him.

"Not as well as a Forest Survivor," the Mage winked at him.

Lasgol grinned. "You'll make it."

Eicewald was panting heavily.

Already near place, Camu messaged them.

"How do you know?" Lasgol asked.

Feel power place.

Oh, you feel magic?"

Yes, much magic, much power.

"I don't know if that's a good thing…" Lasgol said.

Suddenly, several male Druids appeared at a run and joined the tree-beings in the chase.

More Druids coming, Camu warned, having seen them too.

Eicewald watched them for a moment and started casting a spell, moving his staff in circles and aiming it at the skies.

"Ice doesn't affect them, but I can try and delay them," he said and shut his eyes. "We're close—if I can manage to delay them, we'll all get there."

Lasgol looked south with his *Hawk's Eye* skill and was able to see Ona looking over her shoulder. Yes, they were near.

"What are you going to conjure?" Lasgol asked him as he saw the white flashes of the Mage's power around his body and staff.

"I'm calling up a great winter storm."

Suddenly there was a great white flash and a winter storm formed above the pursuers. The temperature dropped drastically, thunder and lightning crackled, and billowing winds began to fall upon the tree-beings and the Druids as frost and ice began to form around the pursuing group.

"That should delay them for a while," said Lasgol.

"Let's hope so," Eicewald said wishfully.

The Druids raised defenses over their bodies, covering themselves with the tough tree bark. Then they covered themselves with shrubs and creepers that surged from the forest floor to protect themselves from the strong icy gusts of the winter storm. The wind lashed at them and the freezing cold punished them—the storm was powerful and it would have killed a whole regiment of men, but the Druids and the tree-beings seemed capable of bearing both the strong winds and the icy temperatures. They did move more slowly because of the wind's force and they had trouble staying upright but kept coming.

"It will delay them, but it won't stop them," Eicewald said.

"It's enough, we're close."

Very close, big power.

The three ran south.

Chapter 26

Lasgol, Eicewald, and Camu crossed the last trees, and what they found left them with their mouths hanging open. A great expanse entirely free of trees and shrubbery was before their eyes. Not a single plant, only clear ground as far as the eye could see. They stopped to look in awe.

"This is weird," Lasgol said, scanning the place. It seemed like nothing grew in this area. He was aware they were still inside the sacred Druid forest which was full of trees, bushes, and life, but this place was some anomaly of nature.

"It is," Eicewald agreed as he bent over to touch the earth with his hand. He closed his eyes and, concentrating, cast a spell. Freezing energy issued from his hand and spread, covering a small area around his palm. He raised his hand and looked at it. The layer of frost he had created was already fading, as if another, stronger force was destroying it.

Lasgol felt the hair at the back of his neck stand on end and a shiver run down his spine.

Powerful magic, Camu messaged.

"It is, it devoured my spell in no time," Eicewald replied as he scanned the clearing. "This place is special… as I had expected…"

Lasgol saw two figures appear in the horizon, Egil and Ona.

"Let's keep going, they're further ahead."

The three walked briskly toward their friends. Lasgol kept glancing back in case they were being chased. Eicewald had told them the Druids never entered this place and he was hoping they would not, but just in case he looked behind them. It did not take long for him to see the Druids, and they were remaining at the edge of the trees. The tree-beings also appeared but did not come forward. Lasgol snorted in relief—they were safe for the time being. Then he thought again and became uneasy. If the Druids were unwilling to enter this place, it must be for a reason, and it would not be a good one considering how powerful they were and that this was their forest.

They reached the rest of the group. Nilsa, Ingrid, and Egil were sitting on the ground, Ona lying beside them. Astrid had left the unconscious princess on the ground too. Viggo and Valeria were on their feet, looking at them as they arrived.

"High time!" Viggo said in welcome but smiled to show he meant it as a joke.

"Trouble?" Astrid asked them, coming over to Lasgol and stroking his hair tenderly.

Meet tree-beings, very fascinating, Camu messaged, explaining in his own particular way.

Egil's eyes widened at once.

"Tree-beings? Very fascinating?" he asked eagerly.

Lasgol explained succinctly everything they had been through and the tricks they had used to escape.

"It certainly sounds most fascinating," Egil confirmed. "It would've been fantastic to see."

"They're already at the edge of the trees, but you'd better not go near, just in case. I'm not a hundred percent sure they won't come into the clearing," Lasgol said as he looked to the north. With his *Hawk's Eye* skill he could see them amid the trees.

Egil got to his feet and started looking around in the hopes of seeing some tree-being.

"How are you doing?" Lasgol asked the group.

"A little better," Ingrid replied.

"But not much better," Nilsa clarified.

Lasgol understood and nodded. He went over to Princess Heulyn to see how she was; she seemed to be sleeping peacefully.

"This strange clearing is in truth a circle," Egil explained. "I've taken some measurements, approximate mind you, but I can't do more, my legs aren't responding properly. I'm sure it's a massive circle in the southern part of the Druids' Forest,"

"It's a place of great power, that's why the Druids don't come near," Eicewald explained. "What I can't determine is where the point of greatest power is... I'm trying to pick it up but I don't seem to be able to. This whole place emanates a strange power, alien to me..."

I know, Camu messaged to them.

"Do you, Camu? How do you know?" Eicewald asked blankly and turned to the creature.

I know magic.

"The magic in this place?" the Mage asked him.

Yes, be magic family.

"Oh no! Don't let the bug say another word. I know what's coming next!" Viggo protested.

"Shut up, you numskull, and let them talk," Ingrid snapped. "We have to find out whether we're safe or not."

"Of course we're not safe!" Viggo said firmly.

Ingrid put her finger to her lips.

"Drakonian magic you mean?" Lasgol asked him.

Yes, magic Drakonian.

"Well, then we're screwed!" Viggo cried.

"That's most curious and interesting," Egil commented thoughtfully. "If you think about it, this means that Drakonian magic is more powerful than the Druids', even than the magic of the sacred wood itself.... That's why this circle is in the middle of their forest but hasn't been overtaken by it."

"I'm afraid I'm not familiar with the term 'Drakonian Magic,'" Eicewald said. "You mean the mythical Dragon Magic?"

Yes, magic of dragon, magic Drakonian, Camu explained.

"We believe, from what we've found out so far, that it's possible dragons were not one single family of creatures," Egil explained. "We're working with the possibility that there are several families and subfamilies of creatures within what are known as dragons. It's only a hypothesis, of course—we can't prove it yet."

"That's quite interesting," Eicewald said. "Dragons are not a subject I've studied or that have particularly interested me, except in relation to an Object of Power believed to have something to do with them. My interest and most of my studies are about objects of great power. But, the mythology of several kingdoms of Tremia does establish different varieties of dragons. It used to be believed that they all referred to a single kind of creature, but they might have been different kinds. That is if dragons and similar kinds ever existed, something I seriously doubt."

Yes exist. I Drakonian, Camu messaged him.

"You might be, I'm not saying otherwise. As I said, my area of interest has always been Objects of Power, and I've devoted my studies to them."

"Like the Star of Water and Life," Lasgol said.

"Exactly. That's why I collaborate with the Brotherhood of

Custodians and other organizations and magi or collectors who search for Objects of Power."

"In that case... if you asked the Druids' permission to come here... it's because you thought there was a powerful Object of Power in this place," Lasgol guessed.

Eicewald nodded. "Indeed, that's right. Otherwise I wouldn't have come. Like I said, I'm interested in Objects of Power, or true power, not the ones that have a little magic like enchanted swords and bewitched jewels. There are objects so powerful that they can change the destiny of a kingdom. I want to find them for Norghana."

"For Norghana, or for Thoran?" Lasgol asked him.

"For Norghana. Kings come and go. In the end they all disappear, even the oldest lineages. But the strongest kingdoms remain, even in spite of their monarchs."

"That's a good dream for our country, but as long as Thoran and Orten lead the Kingdom it's not likely Norghana will become a great and powerful kingdom," said Lasgol.

"True, but one day they'll be gone, just as those who reigned before them are gone," said Eicewald, "And most likely it will be because of their own greed and lack of intelligence."

"One can only hope," Egil said to Eicewald with a smile.

"Be careful what you say, those words might be interpreted as treason," Ingrid warned with a nod toward Valeria.

"True. Some wishes might be interpreted as a betrayal to the crown," Eicewald said. "I'll put it another way. Whatever happens to the king, whether he lives and reigns for a century, the Kingdom of Norghana will remain if it's strong and powerful, and magic can ensure that is so."

"Then you're hoping Norghana becomes a strong kingdom through magic?" Nilsa asked.

Eicewald nodded. "The most powerful kingdoms with the greatest probability of surviving are those which either have a lot of gold or a lot of magic power, in my experience. The former buys armies, the latter destroys them."

"Interesting view..." Ingrid said. She seemed to like what she was hearing.

"Not a bad goal," said Astrid.

"It seems strange to me that this place might hold such an Object of Power," Lasgol said.

"More than strange," Egil intervened. "Now that we're here, we have another piece of important information our dear friend the Ice Mage didn't have before."

"What information?" Viggo asked, frowning.

"If what Camu picks up about the power of this place is correct, and we can assume it is because he isn't usually mistaken about this type of things…" Egil began to explain.

"Then the Object of Power I'm looking for," Eicewald continued, "has to do with dragons, since the magic Camu picks up is Drakonian Magic."

Viggo raised both arms in the air.

"The bug, the weirdo, and now the Mage… all of you are looking for trouble at every corner. Let the dragons be! And everything that has to do with them!"

"It's not trouble, it's an opportunity," Eicewald told him. "An object of great power that can save Norghana from her enemies."

"Yeah, or create a ton of headaches, which is what usually happens," Viggo said and went on waving his arms.

"I think if the Object of Power can help Norghana, even if it's magical, we need to have it," Nilsa said frankly.

"You too?" Viggo said, surprised.

"Remember that magic isn't bad in and of itself, it's whoever uses it that makes it good or evil. Better that we use it for good," Nilsa told him seriously.

"If you go down that path of thinking, I see you joining the Brotherhood of Custodians," Viggo said.

"There's already a lot to protect around here," Nilsa said with a look that said "or not?"

"Well, you're right there," Viggo had to admit.

I feel point of magic strong, Camu messaged. He had his eyes shut and his neck strained.

"Is there a stronger point?" Lasgol asked him.

"Isn't it like the forest where the magic is everywhere?" Eicewald asked, also intrigued.

Magic stronger in one point, Camu replied without opening his eyes, feeling it.

"Lead us to that point," Eicewald told him.

"Won't it be dangerous to get close to the magic? Look what this clearing is like," Viggo warned.

"We're already in it. If it's going to affect us, it's already doing so," Eicewald told him. "I don't think getting closer to the point where it's stronger will make any difference. But if you feel uneasy, I'll go alone."

"Good idea, I'm staying here," Viggo said, his arms folded. "I'm not afraid, but I don't trust it."

"It would be better for us to rest and watch," Ingrid said, scanning the edge of the nearest trees. "I think I see movement among the Druids," she said, pointing at the trees.

Lasgol looked in the direction Ingrid was indicating and saw that indeed there was a group of Druids watching them.

"The Druids aren't coming into the clearing for now, and we're out of reach of their magic," Egil said, calculating the distance.

"They don't use bows either," said Nilsa, "so we should be okay if they don't come into the clearing."

"Let's hope they don't," Astrid said. "I'll keep watch," she said and threw a glare at Valeria and then at the Princess on the ground.

"It'll be better if I go by myself," Eicewald decided. "Camu, would you mind showing me where it is?"

I lead, the creature messaged him and started to walk with his eyes closed, following the magic he was picking up. They all looked at him, intrigued. Eicewald walked behind him. Lasgol made to join them, but Eicewald gestured him to stay behind. Lasgol knew the Mage thought it was for his own good, but he had magic, just like Camu and Eicewald, so he had to go. He followed the Ice Mage, who nodded when he saw him approach.

Camu led them a little more to the east inside the clearing. He was walking with his eyes shut, which intrigued Lasgol. Not that he was going to trip, because the ground was absolutely flat and there were no obstacles to trip on. At last, Camu stopped.

Be here.

"Exactly where you're standing?" Eicewald asked him.

Yes, be here.

"Funny… I can't tell where the energy is coming from, although I can feel it," said Eicewald.

Lasgol, whose hair was standing on end all over his body, felt the same.

Be here, I feel. Magic family, powerful.

"Before we do anything, let me check whether Egil's theory is

217

correct," said the Mage, and he started to cast a spell. Lasgol watched him, intrigued without understanding exactly what he meant. He moved his staff in circles as he intoned words of power. All of a sudden four balls that seemed made of ice came out of the tip of the staff and shot off in the four directions.

"Now what? What do we do if we can't see how far they go?" Lasgol asked blankly.

"We wait until they reach the edge of the forest. Once they do that, they'll come back. If they do so at the same time, Egil's theory will be correct and this place is a large circle. On the other hand, if they don't come back at the same time, then it's not a circle."

"Oh, I see…"

Eicewald smart, Camu messaged.

"Thank you, but I'd say learned rather than smart," the Ice Mage smiled. "In this life the more you learn the better prepared you are to face whatever the future brings."

"Very true," Lasgol smiled. He knew the Mage was absolutely right.

The four balls arrived back at Eicewald's staff at the same time.

"We are in the center of a large circle, Egil was right."

"A large circle of power," Lasgol added, looking all around.

"That's right," Eicewald agreed.

Drakonian power, added Camu.

"Seeing the power is latent and there's nothing on the surface to cause it," Eicewald said, looking in every direction, even up to the sky, "it has to be under us, beneath the surface," the Mage said.

"I was thinking that too."

Yes, under, Camu confirmed.

"I know we're here by accident," said Eicewald, "but I can't let this opportunity fate is offering pass me by."

"Are you going to try and get the object?" Lasgol asked, guessing that was exactly what the Mage was going to do.

"Yes. It's going to take some time though. I think the best thing to do is for you to lead the group through the southern area of the forest before the Druids decide to enter the clearing. And I believe that as soon as they have a good number that's exactly what they'll do."

"Don't they fear this place?"

"They do, but I doubt their fear will stop them from coming once there are a hundred of them. They'll feel strong enough as a group. That's what I think at least."

"Then we have to leave," Lasgol agreed.

Eicewald nodded and started casting a spell with his eyes shut, moving his staff right above the point where the object of Drakonian power was buried.

Come, Camu, let's go back to the others.

Okay.

They ran back to where the rest were waiting and Lasgol explained the situation.

They all listened carefully while Eicewald continued conjuring, oblivious to Lasgol's explanations.

"I bet that's a blasted White Pearl buried here," Viggo said as soon as Lasgol finished.

"This is really amazing," Astrid said.

"It makes sense that the Druids don't set foot here," said Nilsa, "because of the artifact's magic. And I also agree that the moment they've gathered a big enough number they'll come for us."

"We're jinxed… why do we keep finding such things? The Ice Gods really want me to prove my exquisite skills at every twist and turn!"

"If there really is a Pearl like the Shelter's buried down there, it would certainly be most fascinating," said Egil.

"You weren't really expecting to find something like that, were you?" Ingrid said.

"This is all the bug's fault!" Viggo said, glaring at Camu.

Not my fault, and I not bug.

"Of course it's your fault. If we find a Pearl it's your fault for sure."

"The thing is, if it turns out to be a Pearl we weren't even looking for it. Don't you find that a tremendous coincidence?" Astrid asked.

"That's no coincidence," Viggo said, shaking his head. "We're under some curse of the Ice Gods for something either the weirdo or the bug has done."

"Whatever it is, we'd better run before the Druids decide to enter. I'm beginning to see a lot of movement on the northern and eastern edges of the forest," Lasgol warned them.

Egil checked the southern edge of the clearing.

"From the edge of the clearing to the end of the forest there can't be more than five hundred paces of forest. We'll have to run through it. Once we're out of it I doubt the Druids will continue hunting us. They don't usually leave the forest."

"Sounds like a plan," Ingrid said as she stood up, propping herself up with her bow.

Nilsa imitated her and said, "Let's get out of here."

Astrid went to pick up the Princess.

"I'll take her," Lasgol said. "You make sure no one jumps on us."

Astrid nodded.

Lasgol slung the Princess over his shoulder and noticed that she really did not weigh much.

"Run!" Ingrid said, and their escape began.

They all followed her. Ingrid, Nilsa, Egil, and Ona were in the lead since they were the slowest, so they would set the group's pace. Lasgol followed with the Princess over his shoulder. Valeria, with Viggo and Astrid behind her, brought up the rear.

They passed by Eicewald, who was concentrated, casting his spell. They did not stop to see what he was conjuring up, but based on the time it was taking the Mage and his look of effort, it was going to be a powerful spell. The group ran as fast as they could and Lasgol saw that, at the east, the Druids were also running to intercept them and prevent their escape to the south. The Druids had a longer way to go since they had to go all around the circle. Unfortunately, although the Panthers were running straight they were much slower than the Druids because the injured could barely run and seemed to be about to fall with each step they took. Especially Nilsa, who was having a hard time not stumbling or losing her balance and falling.

They were about to reach the southern edge when they heard a powerful blast. Lasgol looked back and saw that Eicewald's spell had been completed. A huge waterfall had formed over the Mage, and he was directing the falling water at the ground, right on the spot where Camu had told them the object was buried. The water from the big cascade was hitting the ground with tremendous force, pounding the earth with terrible force and making pieces of the ground fly into the air. Then Eicewald focused and directed all the might of the fall of the water to the spot, pointing his staff. Another chunk of earth flew up in the air. Lasgol quickly realized what the Mage was doing.

"The Mage doesn't fool around," Viggo said.

"I've never seen anyone dig a hole using the power of a

waterfall," Astrid commented.

"Every day is full of surprises," Lasgol said with a shrug.

They headed into the forest, and Lasgol told Astrid to take the lead in case they came face to face with a Druid. The Assassin did so and they began to make way through the trees. They soon met several Druids who were waiting to stop their advance.

"Astrid, watch out!" Lasgol said. "Three Druids behind the trees."

"I don't see them!" she replied.

The Druids were using some kind of camouflage spell which made them hard to distinguish from the oaks.

"Camu, help Astrid!"

I help.

"They're ten paces to the right!" Lasgol called. For some reason he could see them pretty well. It must be his *Hawk's Eye* skill.

"Viggo, three others running from the east!"

"I'll deal with them," said Viggo. "Now, don't make me go looking for you and cut your throat, because I'll do it without hesitation," he whispered to Valeria.

She nodded.

Lasgol was left with Valeria beside him and the Princess on his shoulder.

"You're not going to give me any trouble, are you?" he told her.

The blonde beauty winked at him and shook her head.

Astrid and Camu had arrived where the Druids were hiding and from where they had sent a spell at them. Creepers climbed up Astrid's legs and coiled around them like snakes. The spell against Camu failed. The Druid stared at him with eyes wide open and his comrade also cast a spell at Camu, which failed too. The two Druids looked at one another, puzzled. Camu ran at them and brought them down by jumping on them. As he jumped there was a silver flash and the third Druid's spell came apart.

Astrid found herself free of the creeper-snakes. With a great leap she fell onto the Druid that had cast the spell on her and punched him senseless with her fists, holding her knives. The Druids got back to their feet and began to beat Camu with their staves. The creature whipped them with his tail, catching them in their torsos and knocking them down again. Before they could get back up, Astrid was on top of them and knocked them out in the blink of an eye with blows to their temples and noses.

"Hurry up! We have to get out of the forest!" Ingrid shouted as she pulled at the rest of the group. Her face showed the frustration of not being able to fight. Nilsa, who was stumbling behind her, was not capable either and had enough trouble keeping her balance and the pace.

Viggo and the Druids met at a run. The three stopped abruptly when they saw him coming and started to cast a spell. The first one took Viggo's throwing knife in the shoulder and cried out in pain, stopping his spell. The other two Druids saw Viggo lunge at them like a tiger upon its prey. They could not finish their spells. Viggo knocked them down so forcefully that they fell backward, hard. They tried to recover, but it was useless. Viggo rendered them unconscious with powerful blows.

"Trying to use Druid spells on me... hah, please..." he said, pulling his throwing knife out of the Druid's shoulder, who cried out in pain. Viggo shut him up with a fulminating right punch.

He looked up and saw another dozen Druids running toward him.

"Better get out of here," he muttered to himself and ran to his friends.

Ingrid arrived at the edge of the forest and gestured for them to get out of the trees.

"We made it!" Nilsa cried.

"Remind me never to come back to this forest!" Viggo said as he arrived.

"A fascinating and fantastic place," Egil told him as he ran out of the forest as fast as he could.

"Let's get as far as we can in case they keep chasing us out here," said Lasgol.

They all agreed to that.

The group ran until there were three hundred paces between them and the forest's edge. Astrid, Lasgol, Viggo, and Ingrid picked up they bows. At that distance they could release at the Druids and they would not be able to reach them with their spells.

The dozen Druids chasing after Viggo came out of the forest at a run. Astrid, Lasgol, and Viggo aimed their bows threateningly.

The Druids stopped. They looked at one another and calculated the distance, realizing they were out of range. Without a word, they turned around and went back into their forest, vanishing among the trees.

Nilsa gave a long whistle.

"It's been entertaining," Viggo said, lowering his bow.

"Very entertaining," Astrid agreed.

"What do we do now? Do we wait for Eicewald?" Nilsa asked.

"No, we can't stay here. They know where we are," said Ingrid.

"Let's go back to the meeting point. Eicewald will join us there if he manages to get out," said Egil.

They got ready. They had to go around the forest on the outside, reach the ravine, get their horses, and go back to the capital. After what they had experienced in the forest, Lasgol felt blessed to be returning.

Chapter 27

They found the horses in the hollow just as they had left them. Aidan was not there, but Lasgol found his trail and it was recent. Aidan had covered his tracks well, but Lasgol did not miss the Druid's footprints. He had been looking after the horses, which they appreciated. The group lay down to rest and re-hydrate. They were tired; even Lasgol, who at first had not felt the weight of the Princess, was now exhausted. The only ones who did not seem tired were Camu and Viggo.

"I see Aidan has left us," said Viggo as he told Valeria to sit down beside the still-unconscious Princess and stay put.

"He can't give himself up," Egil told him.

"Yeah, I guess so. Someday this double life is going to catch up with him."

"He's a good man, he tries to prevent bloodshed between the Druids and the King of Irinel," said Egil.

"Some things are inevitable no matter how much you try to avoid them," Viggo commented with his peculiar philosophy of life. "Now we're missing the Mage. It would be nice if he came quickly, because we're still in danger. That twisted forest is still too close for my taste."

"We're aware of that, but we're going to wait a little while," Lasgol told him. He did not want to leave Eicewald to his fate.

"I don't understand why he had to dig out a White Pearl in the middle of a chase. These Magi are crazy," said Viggo.

"It was a once-in-a-lifetime opportunity and he didn't want to miss it. He'll probably never set foot in that place ever again," Egil told him.

"If the Druids catch him, I tell you, they'll bury him alive," Viggo said.

"Don't be a bird of ill omen," Ingrid said.

Viggo shrugged. "There's a time to run and another to look for Objects of Power. The Mage has them mixed up."

"Magi in general don't let the opportunity of obtaining Objects of Power pass them by, least of all one that can create a clearing like the one we saw in the Druid forest," Egil explained.

Much power, Camu added.

"Yeah, I hope it serves him in the grave," Viggo said nonchalantly.

They waited a while longer for the Mage and finally started getting nervous. Viggo might very well be right, and if so they would never see Eicewald again.

Suddenly a figure came out of the forest at a run. It was Eicewald.

"Get ready to ride," Lasgol said when they saw him running toward them.

"At last," said Viggo.

The Mage had finally arrived, panting and ghostly white.

"We… have to… escape…" he muttered.

"Ride!" Lasgol ordered.

They all did. They tied the Princess to Astrid's horse since she was still unconscious, even though they had brought a horse for her. The Assassin would be in charge of carrying her. Valeria, who had no horse, would ride with Viggo, who made a gesture to her that meant "no nonsense." As soon as they were mounted the Druids appeared. Coming out of the forest in a large group, they tried to cast a spell on the group. Once again they had to run away from them, on this occasion at full gallop heading north. They missed the attack by a hair's breadth.

They rode for a good while until they left the great forest behind and felt they were safe at last. They looked for a river where the horses could drink and replenished their water-skins. They dismounted and Egil tended to the injured.

"Shouldn't you look after yourself first?" Ingrid asked him.

"He should, yes. If the Healer Guard isn't healed first, how is he going to heal the rest of us?" Nilsa said with a smile.

"Well, yeah, maybe you're right," Egil said, giving in. He treated himself first and then took care of the others.

"Did you get the Object of Power?" Lasgol asked Eicewald. He was curious about it.

You get? Camu asked, equally curious.

"How could he get the White Pearl if it's a huge chunk of rock?" said Viggo.

"Maybe it wasn't a White Pearl…" Astrid said.

"Yes and no," Eicewald said with the air of someone keeping a secret.

"Well, now the Mage gets all mysterious on us," said Viggo.

Eicewald smiled.

"I had a hard time digging it up. It was quite deep, but I got it," he said and put his hand in his traveling pack. He brought out an object wrapped in a bright white scarf. He put it in the palm of his hand. Very delicately, he unwrapped the object and let them see it. In the Mage's hand was a pearl the size of a large apple, all silver, which shone with silver flashes. It was spherical and beautiful. It did not look real, it was so perfect and precious.

"Wow!" Lasgol cried, dropping his jaw.

"It's beautiful," Astrid said.

"It must be worth a fortune," said Nilsa, staring at it wide-eyed.

"It's a pearl, like I told you," Viggo said.

"Sure, because you always have to be right, even if you're not," Ingrid chastened him.

"That's not a white pearl, it's silver. Not to mention the size, which is much smaller," Nilsa added.

Much power, Drakonian, Camu messaged in warning.

Egil stepped over to look at it.

"Fantastic and fascinating. It's latent, isn't it?" he asked Eicewald.

"Yes it is, it's power is latent, and as Camu said, quite powerful," the Mage replied.

"Do you know what kind of power it is? What it can be used for?" Egil asked Eicewald eagerly.

"I'm afraid it's too soon to assume anything. I'll have to study it long and carefully in order to understand what this Object of Power is and what it's for."

"Perhaps it's only an expensive jewel," said Viggo.

"Some jewels have enchantments and spells in them, but that isn't the case here. The power it emanates is its own. It hasn't been enchanted or charmed," the Mage told them.

"Well, it must have some purpose," Nilsa said. "We have to find out what it is."

"That's exactly the question," Egil said.

At that moment Princess Heulyn woke up and looked around. She seemed to realize what was going on.

"How dare you touch me, you Norghanian scum! I'll have your heads removed for this!"

"Astrid, would you mind gagging and tying her up?" Lasgol asked her.

"No problem."

"Don't you dare touch me! I'll have you skinned alive!" the Princess yelled at Astrid.

"A charming woman, really," Viggo said, covering his ears.

Eicewald put the silver pearl away. "I'll begin studying it as soon as possible," he told them.

"Be careful," Lasgol said to him. "Just in case."

The Mage nodded.

They rested as much as they needed now that they were out of danger. When Egil thought they were fit for travel, after examining everyone, they set out again. Lasgol told Camu to remain invisible, he preferred the princess not to know of his existence and, for the time being, she had not noticed him. Valeria, on the other hand, was already aware of Camu's presence as she had seen and felt him during the escape. She hadn't said anything about it, but Lasgol knew that the perceptive and intelligent blonde would be wondering about the creature.

The return journey to the capital, Blindah, was miserable. On the one hand, the presence of the Princess and Valeria, whom they kept gagged most of the time, did not make the journey easier. On the other hand, the object Eicewald had found and which he studied whenever he had a moment, gave off bright flashes which made the horses and some members of the group nervous. Princess Heulyn never missed a chance to insult them and threaten them the moment they took off her gag. Unfortunately, they had to feed her and give her water, so they had no choice but to bear her verbosity. Valeria was much more restrained and tried to defend the Princess as she advised the Panthers on how to treat the Princess so her parents would not take it out on them afterwards. Astrid put the gag back on Valeria as soon as she could.

Nights were especially uncomfortable because they had to watch the Princess, since she had already tried to run off more than once. No matter how rebellious and foul-mouthed she might be, she would never be able to escape the Panthers, but she was a nuisance. Viggo had suggested his "blow on the back of the neck" strategy several times, but it had been rejected. They also could not carry her unconscious the whole way. Egil's tonics could be noxious if used in excess. So they had no choice but to bear her tantrums and verbal attacks.

The journey seemed too long, but they finally arrived at the capital of Irinel at sundown. Lasgol asked Camu and Ona to wait in the northern forest as they had done before. It was the safest option for them. The group took their leave, promising to be back soon, and headed to the Royal Castle without taking any detours. If they did stop and someone recognized the Princess, they would have a lot of explaining to do and things might get tense. The citizens of the capital would not understand what they were doing with their Princess, they were sure of that. You did not gag and tie up Royal Princesses.

When they arrived at the castle they identified themselves and were let in without a problem. The guard had orders to let them through. Even so, the soldiers were puzzled and surprised to recognize their Princess.

"Everything's all right," Eicewald assured them.

The soldiers nodded, even if they were not fully comfortable, and called the officer on duty as soon as they had entered.

They headed to the entrance of the main building without dismounting. By the time they arrived, the officer on duty intercepted them with a dozen soldiers. They asked the officer to announce their arrival and that of the Princess. The officer sent two soldiers to give warning of their arrival and waited with them. He was concerned about the Princess but he did not dare intervene.

"There's nothing to worry about," Eicewald said to the surly officer, who was glaring at them.

First General Reagan and the King's counselor, Kacey, came out at once to welcome them, accompanied by a dozen Royal Guards.

"Mission accomplished," Ingrid informed them, indicating Princess Heulyn and Valeria on their horses.

"Is she all right?" Kacey asked, eyeing the Princess with concern.

"She hasn't suffered any harm," Eicewald confirmed.

"The Princess is just slightly upset," Viggo added.

"It's only natural, given the circumstances," Counselor Kacey excused her.

Suddenly Ambassador Larsen appeared at a run from the castle and stood beside the counselor, looking concerned. When he realized the group had the Princess with them, the Ambassador gave a loud snort and smiled in relief.

"Great job, Royal Eagles," he congratulated them.

"We always fulfill the mission we're given," Ingrid told him.

"King Thoran will be pleased," Ambassador Larsen told them. "I will send a pigeon this very evening."

"Perhaps you should wait and see how their Majesties react," the First Counselor advised him.

"True, very true. I will simply let the King know that his Royal Eagles have done what was promised and therefore, without a doubt, their Royal Majesties will also be pleased," the Ambassador said, implying that they had done their part and now the King and Queen must do theirs.

"I understand," Kacey said, nodding.

"Help her dismount and take the gag off carefully," the First General ordered two of the soldiers.

The moment the gag was off the Princess started giving orders, filled with overflowing fury and rage.

"I want them executed at once!" All of them!" she yelled at First General Reagan.

"It's a pleasure to see you safe and sound," the General said and made a small bow.

"Your Royal Highness, we are so glad to see you safe and sound," Counselor Kacey said.

"Kill them all, right way! All of them!" Heulyn shouted at the top of her lungs, pointing her finger back and forth at them as she yelled.

The Royal Guard looked at the General without knowing whether to follow the Princess's orders or not. The general, unobtrusively, gave them the order to ignore her requests.

"As you can see, we've fulfilled the mission entrusted to us by the King," Ingrid said.

"Yes you have, you may retire and enjoy a well-deserved rest," General Reagan told them.

"Thank you, sir, we'll do that," she replied.

"General Reagan! Lock them up or I'll make sure they take away all your stripes and that you end up scrubbing the palace's latrines!" Princess Heulyn threatened him.

"They're your father's wishes, Your Royal Highness, I can't disobey them," the general said in a kind tone.

"We'd better go inside, you must be exhausted from the journey,"

Counselor Kacey said to the Princess. "I'll order a perfumed bath and an exquisite dinner for when you finish getting changed and groomed."

"What I want is the heads of these filthy, depraved Norghanians!" she yelled, pointing at the group as they retired to the stables to leave their mounts.

"I'm afraid you'll have to talk to your father about that," Kacey replied in a kind, soothing tone.

As they were leaving, Viggo blew a kiss at the Princess and made a lovelorn face.

"You'll pay! I swear you'll pay!" Heulyn yelled, completely beside herself.

They rested all night and part of the morning, something they appreciated after the intense mission.

Ambassador Larsen came to see them around noon with tons of questions about the mission, which the Panthers declined to answer. They informed him that how they had carried out the rescue was irrelevant—it was done and everything had gone well. The Ambassador ceased his questioning and left them. They thought they would not see him again for a while, but they were wrong. After lunch he came back to inform them that King Kendryk wanted to see them in the Throne Hall.

When they arrived, they were glad to see that Princess Heulyn was not present. The King and Queen of Irinel were sitting on their thrones, and with them were Counselor Kacey and First General Reagan. Kylian, King Kendrys's son, was also present, and they were surprised to see Aidan there as well. He was standing beside the King's son.

"Your Majesty, the Royal Eagles and the Ice Mage Eicewald," Ambassador Larsen presented them.

"First I want to thank you for rescuing my daughter from the Druids," King Kendryk told them.

"And without her suffering any harm," added Queen Gwyneth. "That has gladdened my soul. I was afraid some misfortune might have happened."

"From what I hear it was not an easy task," the King said.

"You heard correctly, Your Majesty, it turned out to be a difficult mission," Ingrid confirmed.

"That's why I asked for the best, and I see Thoran was not exaggerating when he told me he had them. Entering that sacred forest full of magic, rescuing my daughter without harming her, and escaping from the Druids and their magic is a real achievement. I will not lie to you, I had my doubts whether you would make it."

"Doubts which are entirely understandable, given the difficulty of the mission," Ambassador Larsen defended.

"We've talked with my daughter and her protector, Valeria, who told us how complicated the rescue was and what excellent warriors you are. She also confirmed they did not suffer any harm at any time and that they were well treated."

"The Princess, though, does not see it that way… as you can well imagine, but given her character we understand her reaction. I myself have been able to confirm that she has suffered no harm, no matter how much she protests and rages about it," Queen Gwyneth explained.

Egil and Lasgol exchanged glances. Valeria had spoken well of them to the King and Queen, and that pleased Lasgol. If she had spoken ill of them, they would now be in serious trouble. Considering she did not have to do so, it was something to be thankful for.

"It's been a difficult experience for her and it's only natural she should have mixed feelings," said Larsen.

"More than mixed," said the king. "It's something we'd already expected. The Royal Princess must take over her responsibilities to the crown, just like my son, her brother is doing. He's already leading the kingdom's armies. He will lead them in the next confrontation, and he is training for that with all his will. The wounds I received in the field of battle have left me with some serious injuries, I cannot wield a sword," the King admitted. "Therefore, my son will assume his duty and do so in my place. Unfortunately my daughter does not seem to understand what her place is, but she will. You have my word that she will."

"It's an honor and privilege to lead our kingdom's armed forces and defeat our country's enemies," said Kylian.

"Well spoken, my son," his mother said proudly." As for Heulyn, she will understand one way or the other."

231

"Any way, those are private matters of the House of Irinel which do not concern the Royal Eagles and the Ice Mage, who have fulfilled the mission we asked them to," said the King.

"Is Your Majesty pleased with the services rendered by the Royal Eagles?" Larsen asked.

"I am, very pleased," the King nodded.

"That being the case, will his Majesty sign the treaty of friendship and collaboration between the kingdoms of Norghana and Irinel?" the Ambassador asked.

"I will sign the alliance and we will reach an agreement. Tell your King I will comply with the last part of the agreement. I will soon send him what we stipulated and a long-term alliance will be sealed between our kingdoms."

"I will do that, Your Majesty. Thank you, Your Majesty, it's an honor," Ambassador Larsen made bow after bow.

"And to you, let me express my gratitude. You will always be welcome in the Kingdom of Irinel," the King said and bowed his head slightly toward the group.

"You have been named honorary guests of the kingdom," Counselor Kacey said. "You may come and go whenever you please, and you will always be welcome in this castle."

"We appreciate it, Your Majesty," said Ingrid and bowed. They all imitated her.

Lasgol was pleased with the King and Queen's appreciation and knew his comrades were too. They were not used to receiving congratulations in Norghana for the missions they carried out. Besides, this allowed them to visit the beautiful kingdom whenever they wished which Lasgol thought of doing in the future, if they ever had enough free time. He was hoping King Thoran would grant them some. Visiting Irinel in the summer with Astrid, when the rains relented, could be a beautiful journey.

"Ambassador Larsen, return to Norghana with the Royal Eagles and the Ice Mage and inform Thoran that he has fulfilled his part of the deal and that I will fulfill mine."

"We will leave at once," Larsen assured him with repeated bows.

They left the Throne Hall and headed to their rooms. Once they were alone, they asked Larsen what would happen next.

"Are we going back to Norghana?" Ingrid wanted to know.

"We are. Our work here is done," the Ambassador replied with a big smile.

"Back to the ship, then?" Viggo asked.

"We leave at dawn. I'm going to finish a couple more commercial deals with Kacey which depended on this mission being successful and on having the King's good will, then we can go back home."

"I feel a bit sad to be leaving already," said Nilsa.

"Me too. I'll miss the country, but knowing who's here in the palace, I'd rather not be anywhere near," Astrid said, looking at Lasgol.

"Perhaps the blonde will come by to say 'hi,'" Viggo said in a tone that begged for argument. "Well, not to all of us perhaps, but to the weirdo?"

"She'd better not. I'll send her back with a pretty necklace around her neck, and it won't be pearls," Astrid snapped.

Lasgol looked at Astrid, hoping she was exaggerating, but unfortunately he could see in her eyes that she was more than capable of carrying out her threat.

"Valeria's appearance has been an unexpected surprise," Egil said in a quiet voice. "We have to admit she's helped us, apart from our feelings about her past betrayal."

"One for which we already tried and sentenced her," said Lasgol, who did not want anything else to happen, especially bloodshed.

"I agree with Lasgol on this. We tried her and sentenced her to exile. She's done her time and helped us. On my part, I don't see a problem," said Ingrid.

Lasgol snorted under his breath; the fact that Ingrid did not want bloodshed was an improvement.

"I kinda like the dark blonde, but I still think we should've killed her," Viggo said nonchalantly. "She'll bring us trouble in the future, I tell you."

"I share Viggo's opinion. Killing her now is what we should do, before we regret it, and I'm sure we will," Astrid said.

"I want to give her the benefit of the doubt. Yes, she betrayed us, and we sentenced her for it. I want to believe she's learned from her mistakes and that she'll redeem herself," Nilsa said.

"That's because you're a goody-two-shoes, like the weirdo," Viggo said.

"And naïve. People don't change. They improve a little or pretend, but if their heart's rotten, it will always be," Astrid said firmly.

"I know it's not my place, and perhaps you don't want my advice on this matter…" Eicewald began.

"Go ahead, speak, we respect your opinion," Egil said.

"The Princess's bodyguard is entirely faithful to her. We can't touch her as long as she's under Heulyn's protection. It would be like making an attempt against the life of an officer of the Irinel Army."

"More than that, you shouldn't even go near her," Larsen added. "The Royal Family holds her in great esteem. Not only the Princess trusts her, but the King and Queen as well. They will not tolerate any aggression against her."

"I wonder how she gained the Princess's trust. Heulyn isn't exactly easy to please," said Ingrid.

"With treachery and foul play, for sure," Astrid said.

"Regardless, she has the approval of the Royal Family of Irinel and cannot be harmed," Larsen said in warning.

"We understand," Ingrid said and glanced at Astrid and Viggo.

The two Assassins held her gaze; they were not convinced.

Larsen took his leave. Eicewald went to the far end of the room to continue his research. He was engrossed in his discovery and was eager not to waste a single moment. Egil went over and sat down close to him, watching the Mage work. If Eicewald was engrossed, Egil was pretty intrigued too.

Lasgol was worried Valeria might visit them—it would not be a good idea. They were getting ready to go to bed when the room's door opened slightly. They all turned.

A figure entered the room.

Chapter 28

"Aidan!" cried Nilsa when she saw the Druid come in.

Lasgol snorted in relief—he had been sure it would be Valeria.

"High time you showed up!" Viggo said reproachfully from his bunk, pointing an accusing finger at him.

The Druid came in and shut the door.

"I had to leave or I would have been found out," he told them.

"Couldn't you use the magic that allows you to camouflage?" Astrid asked him.

"Yes, I do have that, but it allows me to camouflage from foreigners, not from my own people. Fellow Druids recognize that magic. They would have discovered me if I had camouflaged or hidden."

"Well, you could've told us that beforehand," Viggo said reproachfully.

"I warned you that I could only lead you to the place where they had hidden the Princess, nothing more."

"He's right, he warned us of how much he could help us," Egil defended their new arrival as he came to talk to the Druid.

"He did what he could, we have no reason to attack him," Eicewald said, also defending the Druid as he came over with Egil.

"But you might have come back to help us escape," Ingrid said, standing up, "We nearly didn't make it."

"A patrol appeared; I could not stay. And I wouldn't have been able to help you anyway. If I had been seen with you the repercussions would have been very serious."

"What do you mean?" Ingrid asked blankly.

"My position at Court as a representative of my people before the King of Irinel would have been compromised. My people would've realized my collaboration in the rescue—or kidnapping, as they see it—and they would have taken it as treason. I would have lost my post, and if I had gone back to the sacred forest I would have been exiled, or even worse. Besides, if they had discovered that I was involved, there would be a serious political problem, possibly a war, since my conspiracy with King Kendryk would have been deemed treachery and an aggression to the Druid people."

"It's absolutely understandable that you didn't want to risk your position," Eicewald said.

"You did what was expected of you," Egil told him. "Without your help we wouldn't have been able to carry out the mission."

"Will there be war?" Lasgol asked, wanting to know what would happen now that the Druids knew that the King had sent foreigners to rescue his daughter.

Aidan sighed. "I'm working to prevent it. My people are furious. They consider what happened as premeditated and an almost practically open act of war. There are many voices demanding we rise in arms against King Kendryk because of the outrage committed. They accuse the King of having desecrated our sacred forest. I must prevent that from happening. That's my duty, and because of that I couldn't be compromised."

"King Kendryk risked a lot when he chose you for the mission," Eicewald told him.

"That's right, but he doesn't trust anyone else of my people. That's why I couldn't get even more involved. I must appear as neutral as possible or else I'll lose my people's support and war could break out," Aidan explained.

"Well, as for being neutral, in this case you leaned a little too much toward the King's side," Viggo told him acidly.

"The same way that, when necessary, I'll lean toward my people's side," Aidan assured.

"Understandable," Egil nodded.

"I'm now trying to prevent open conflict. I've been able to persuade the leaders of my people to sit down to dialogue."

"That's a great achievement," Lasgol said. "I hope you can persuade them so there's not a war."

"I'm going to try with all my strength and influence," Aidan said.

"So King Kendryk risked a lot to rescue his daughter," Ingrid said with her head to one side.

"The King was very aware of the risks," Eicewald said.

"He was," Aidan agreed.

"Then, if he was willing to risk a conflict with the Druids, even a possible war, it's because he has a lot to gain," Astrid said.

"Maybe he did it out of love for his daughter..." Nilsa commented. "He wanted her to come back to her family."

"Oh boy, are you gullible," said Viggo. "You and the weirdo are so upright and candid that a two-year-old would rob your money bag."

"It's a political maneuver," Ingrid said. "He's looking for Norghana's support. As far as wanting his daughter back, I understand that must have had something to do with it."

"Not only that, but also an internal maneuver. The King has sent a clear message to the Druids. He will not let them ignore him, and this mission is exactly that: a show of force. He's gone into the heart of the sacred forest and stolen away their protégée, showing them he has the means to do so," Eicewald explained.

"What a fascinating world, that of politics and power, always opposite strengths fighting, trying to find a balance only to break apart an instant later," said Egil.

"I don't find it fascinating at all," Ingrid said, shaking her head. "Clear speech and weapons, that's how people understand one another. All these treacherous political games played behind the back are hateful."

"I find it quite fascinating," Nilsa admitted, "how twisted the rulers of kingdoms and nations in Tremia can be…"

"My task now is to reestablish the peace broken by the King's actions," Aidan told them.

"I hope you achieve it and that this doesn't end in bloodshed," Lasgol said.

Aidan nodded heavily.

"That's my wish and goal."

"Kings risk a lot with some of their gambles…" Astrid commented.

"That's the only way kingdoms endure," said Eicewald. "Without great risks there are no great rewards. When the future of a kingdom is in the balance, kings and queens will do whatever they can to win, both in the political sphere and on the battlefield. They both depend heavily on one another."

"We appreciate the help you've given us," Egil told Aidan and bowed his head to him.

"What I do, I do for the good of my people," the Druid said and returned the bow.

"We wish you success in persuading your people not to rise in arms against the King," Ingrid said.

"Thank you. Before you leave I wanted to know whether I could be of further assistance. I heard you had some trouble and might need my healing knowledge of the forest."

"Oh, that would be great," Nilsa said. "We're still suffering from the aftereffects of the wasp poison in our bodies."

Aidan nodded. "I'll help you, I know the antidote."

"We appreciate it," Ingrid said.

The Druid left them and came back after a while with the antidote prepared in a potion. He gave it to all of them, because although some had no apparent aftereffects, the wasps had stung them all and the poison was still in their bodies, which might cause trouble in the long term. Once the potion was administered, he also shared with Egil how it was made, which the Healer Guard appreciated greatly, since he did not know the remedy.

"Thank you. I will have more made and I will give it to Ona."

Aidan then took his leave of them.

"Have a safe journey home!" he wished them.

"Good luck with the negotiations," Egil wished him.

"I hope our paths cross again someday," Aidan said.

"Yes, but not in that blasted forest," Viggo said.

Aidan nodded and left them. He had some complicated and important days ahead of him.

"Well, I'm trying to rest. Now that we've had that antidote, let's see if we can," Ingrid said. She had been having trouble sleeping.

"Yeah, I'm dying to sleep throughout the night until morning," Nilsa joined in. She had not been sleeping well either because of the poison.

Egil wrote down in his medicinal notebook how to make the antidote.

"Fantastic," they heard him mutter.

The group got into their bunks and all slept well that night, finally getting proper rest.

Morning came without Valeria appearing, which made Lasgol happy. That way they would avoid an altercation. They prepared for the journey and gathered all their equipment. An officer of the Royal Guard provided them with everything they asked for and food for the journey. With their packs and saddlebags full they headed to the stables, where Ambassador Larsen and the King's Counselor were waiting to see them off.

They mounted and took their leave of the Counselor, who wished them a good journey and good luck in future ventures. They left the Royal Castle and went through the city one last time, contemplating its people, streets, and peculiar buildings. Viggo wanted to stop for one last dark beer, but Ingrid would not let him despite the protests of the Assassin.

They left the capital and went to look for Camu and Ona; it was time to return to the ship and sail to Norghana. They found them peacefully lying down in the middle of the grass. Camu had covered Ona under his Extended Invisibility Camouflage as soon as they had detected any presence, so it was extremely unlikely for anyone to have found them. It could happen if Camu was distracted or playing, which was often the case, but so far it had not happened.

The journey to the harbor city of Kensale went without incident. It was a pleasant ride, since they had already completed their mission successfully and could relax and enjoy that beautiful green landscape. Besides, a good mood reigned among the group and there were many jokes that demonstrated the camaraderie they enjoyed. The Panthers and Eicewald were chatting about the region. Nilsa and Egil had already recovered from the wasp poison completely. Aidan's potion had finished healing them along the way, so their mood was even brighter.

The only one who broke the harmony and camaraderie was Ambassador Larsen, who revealed himself as pompous and vain as usual, and perhaps even more so since he was returning to Norghana with several signed deals and the success of the mission, which meant Thoran would not only not punish him, but reward him, or at least that was what he said. The Panthers did not believe the King would reward the Ambassador's efforts, and Viggo told him so on the first occasion.

Camu and Ona were, as usual, at the rear of the group and always seizing any chance to make an escapade, play, and enjoy the surroundings. Since there was no danger there and because for as far as the eye could see, there was only a plain filled with green grass and they did not fear any encounters, Lasgol let them play to their hearts' content. A little relaxation was good for them now and then.

They arrived at Kensale and the harbor without any delays. Just as

Captain Ulmendren had promised, he was waiting with his ship, ready to depart.

"Welcome, all of you!" he shouted from the gunwale.

"Captain Ulmendren," Larsen greeted him with a nod.

"Ambassador, Royal Eagles," the Captain returned the greeting nod.

"Everything ready to leave?" the Ambassador asked.

"Are we in a hurry?" the Captain asked.

"Absolutely," the Ambassador replied.

"I take it then that the mission was a success?"

"Of course it was," Larsen confirmed, puffing up, as if any doubts were offensive.

"Then we'll cast off at once. Everything's ready."

"Wonderful," Larsen said smugly.

The ship left the harbor with the evening's first winds. The Panthers said goodbye to the Kingdom of Irinel from the gunwale.

"Until next time," Lasgol whispered, hoping to return someday.

Chapter 29

Lasgol was sitting at the bow of the ship as he did every morning to work on his inner bridge. The breeze was pleasant and the sea was calm. They had already been sailing for several days and had not encountered any significant mishap other than the changes in weather. Seeing the journey was peaceful, Lasgol did not miss the chance to use the time to work on his magic. It was something that required effort and concentration but which had become a daily routine, and when he could not do it for whatever reason he sorely missed it. It surprised him, since he had never imagined he would enjoy spending long periods of time doing hard work.

He sighed. He felt good, comfortable. He realized it was not exactly the effort he liked, but rather the satisfaction of every little improvement he made. Every small section of the bridge between his mind and his pool of power that he repaired and transformed into his own magic was an achievement. And that was what gave him the pleasant feeling of satisfaction he missed when he did not work on it. Although he knew he could not always work on his magic because of the missions' requirements and his duties as a Ranger, it always made him feel bad. It was as if he set aside that part of himself, the Gift, to do other tasks more important at the time, and it left him with a bittersweet taste in his mouth.

Eicewald came over and sat beside him.

"How are you doing?" he asked, putting his hand on Lasgol's shoulder.

"Fine. It's funny. It's terribly hard and painful, but when I manage to repair the bridge a little I feel great satisfaction."

"And I bet that when you're not working you miss getting that small satisfaction," the Mage said.

Lasgol looked at him, surprised.

"Exactly. How do you know?"

"Because it happens to all of us," Eicewald smiled. "In fact, it's one of the first lessons you have to learn about magic. No one is born with great knowledge or power. No one is born with a hundred powerful skills to use against their enemies, no matter how much we'd like that or what we might have read in some fable or legend. We all have to work to develop our Gift, our Talent, the Magic we have within ourselves that we were born with."

"I didn't know that… Egil has found books that talk of powerful magi born with already-great powers."

"Don't believe everything you read," Eicewald chuckled. "It's true that some people are born with greater power than others, and even a few are born with impressive power. But that power must be developed to be used, and that takes time and sacrifice. No-one's free of this law of nature, no matter what certain tomes say which praise certain famous personalities or myths that have been created."

"Then I guess all of us who are born with magic must learn to develop and use it."

"That's right. It doesn't matter what race you belong to, the kingdom you're born in, the region you grow up in, or the type of magic you develop. We all start from the same place—we are born with magic, with the potential to develop it, and we must go through the process of developing and perfecting it. It's a similar process for everyone, though not the same."

"Not the same?"

"No, and therein lies the beauty of the human being and magic. There are no two identical people, and neither are two magics alike. The reason is simple: every person is born different, with their own peculiarities and different Gifts. That's why every person develops the Gift they were born with in a different way from others. Therefore there are no two identical magics. Similar? Yes. The same? No."

"I'm not sure I fully understand…"

"I'll explain with an example I think you'll easily understand. You and I are Norghanians and we were both born with the Gift. Seen from the outside, someone might think we possess the same magic, but that's not the case. You and I are very different, both as people and regarding our magic. This is because we were born different— both as human beings and regarding our Gift. Not only that, we then developed even more differently. Something we will continue doing until the day we die. We are unique individuals in every aspect, the magical one included. In fact, the Norghanian Ice Magi, although we study and practice the same form of magic based on the same principles and studying the same tomes of magic, are unique individuals, even magically, with different powers and skills."

Lasgol was thoughtful for a moment.

"I thought Ice Magi all had the same power and used the same magic, or if not the same, very similar."

Eicewald shook his head.

"We don't have the same power because we're all different people born with different power and we've developed it individually. We followed the same principles and teachings that led us to become Ice Magi, and in that sense our magic is similar, but still not the same. Every human being is different and individual, and magic is one more component which makes us even more special and unique."

"I think I understand. Thank you. Your explanations have helped me a lot. I'm full of doubts… I've never been able to count on anyone to clear them up before."

"No need to thank me, and it's natural that you have questions since you've never been instructed in the art of magic. With each step you go up the long ladder to obtaining control of your Gift. You'll receive a reward, the satisfaction of obtaining an achievement."

"Oh… I see. May I ask then? I have so many questions…"

"Go ahead, I'm here to help you as much as I can. The journey is long, and we have time. I'll answer your questions and try to solve your doubts. It's the least I can do."

"I'm deeply thankful. I know it's not something a Mage usually does lightly."

"True, but your case is special."

"Special?"

"Yes, because you have amazing potential. You're self-taught. And most of all a good person. That's why I'm compelled to help you, whether I like it or not," Eicewald chuckled.

Lasgol laughed out loud.

"Thank you, I mean it."

"Not at all. I'd be doing the kingdom a small service if I didn't help you with your magical potential."

"Limited magical potential," Lasgol specified.

"For now. That's something we'll change with time and effort," Eicewald promised.

Lasgol was not at all sure his potential could grow, he did not believe it.

"Trust me. It won't be easy, but we'll succeed."

"I trust you," Lasgol nodded, wishing it was so.

"The great problem we magi have—and by magi I mean whoever possesses magic, including sorcerers, shamans, warlocks, and others blessed with the Gift—is that we're too self-centered to pay attention to the world around us. Or to those who need our help, as is your case. You have to understand that we are selfish, Lasgol, self-centered, most of us."

"I doubt it... I don't see you like that..."

"Yes, we are," Eicewald nodded. "That's something you must accept. Magi don't help other magi as a rule. Very few do so, and those who train other magi do so to strengthen their own group. The Ice Magi are a clear example. We train other Ice Magi to strengthen our numbers."

"And fight for the realm against the kingdom's enemies."

"That's right. That's why they train other magi to defeat the enemy in battles, not out of a desire to help another. Those blessed by the Ice Gods with the Gift spend most of their life, if not all, focused on developing their own power or on obtaining more power to use together with their own. Magic makes you selfish, because the more you have, the more you want. The more skills you develop, the more you want, and then you begin seeking more powerful abilities. It happens to all of us. It's inevitable because those of us who have the Gift are powerful, and power calls to power."

"I've never seen it as a negative thing... hated by others, yes, but not negative in and of itself."

Eicewald smiled indulgently.

"It's refreshing to find someone like you, with your kind spirit," he told Lasgol. "Beware of those who seek power and riches, because their souls aren't noble," Eicewald recited.

Lasgol nodded—he knew the saying.

"I'm really not different from my comrades," he said, waving at them by the main mast. "We're all Rangers."

"Yes and no. On the one hand you're all Rangers, but you're different because you have the Gift. The thing with you and what makes it refreshing to teach you is that you have had no previous instruction. The people who are born with the Gift—with very few exceptions, as in your case—are instructed either by tutors or at schools of magic. You haven't been taught. What you've learned is through experimenting and with the help of some tome of magic you

244

got your hands on. That's not common. And you're not even a Mage, you're a Ranger, which is even more curious."

"When you say I'm not even a Mage but a Ranger, do you mean I can't be both?"

"That's right. A Mage is a Mage," Eicewald pointed at himself. "A Ranger is a Ranger," and he pointed at Lasgol and his comrades.

"Oh… so I have to choose between the two?"

Eicewald smiled. "You're smart, nothing gets past you. In my opinion you're a Ranger. You've prepared yourself for years to become one. More so, you've achieved higher specializations with more training and practice. You've spent a great part of your young life training to become a Ranger. I did the same, but to become a Mage. Once I did that, I spent much of my life studying and learning. I'm still doing that and will go on doing it until the day I die."

"You mean that because I'm a Ranger that's what I should choose because that's what I've studied and trained for?"

"Not necessarily. Nothing's written in stone in this life. You can be whatever you want to be, as long as it's possible. You're a Ranger by profession and training, but with the small difference that you have the Gift. That opens a whole new range of possibilities for you. You can study magic and train to become a Mage, since you have the Gift. Your friends can now train in a new profession, if they wanted to, but they can't become Magi because they don't have the Gift."

"You're saying that in order to develop my magic I'd have to leave the Rangers and follow the path of magic and train as a Mage?"

"The path of magic," Eicewald said with a wink. "Well yes, that's what you should do. Magic requires all your effort, all your being, if you wish to develop its full potential. It isn't that different from becoming a Ranger. How much have you fought and struggled in order to become one? And a Specialist with several specializations?"

"A lot…" Lasgol admitted.

"Well, the same or even more would be required of you to develop your magic and become a Mage."

Lasgol lowered his gaze and his face shadowed.

"I see…"

"That's not the answer you were expecting."

Lasgol snorted.

"I want to develop my Gift, for my magic to be powerful, to be able to discover amazing skills that will help me…"

"But you also want to continue being a Ranger," Eicewald guessed.

Lasgol nodded.

"I'd like to say you can do both because I know that's what you want, but if I'm honest, I don't think that's possible."

"Do I have to give up one?"

"No. You're a Ranger. Don't give that up. It's cost you great effort and I know that's what you want to be. Besides, you're a sensational Ranger. Your Gift will always be there. You won't be able to develop it completely, but you can make slight progress. The skills you manage to develop will help you become a better Ranger. They're already doing that."

"Could I be an Ice Mage?"

"If you left everything and came to the tower to learn day and night for years, you might, yes."

"Oh... that's not exactly what I want..."

"Anyone with the Gift can learn some magic specialty, but as I've told you, it takes years of hard work and apprenticeship."

"I see. It seems my Gift is more aligned to Magic of Nature, from what I've seen and experienced so far," Lasgol explained.

"Then you shouldn't try to become an Ice Mage. You could be a Druid or any other specialty of Mage more in agreement with the Magic of Nature."

"But I could be an Ice Mage?"

"Yes, because if you have the Gift you can learn any specialty of magic that exists. From Water Magic, which is what I use, to Fire Magic, or Blood Magic or even Death Magic. These last two I don't recommend though, since you can end up losing your own soul. But we are all born with a Gift that aligns more with one type of magic than others. That eventually makes your power greater in that area of magic. Someone like me, born with an inclination to Water Magic, will always be more powerful with that magic than with Fire or Death Magic. You see? Does that make sense?"

Lasgol nodded. "Yeah, it does."

"Most of us born with the Gift only specialize in one type of magic, because it's easier for us and because we can make more progress in it."

"But there are magi who practice more than one type of magic, aren't there? I've heard of such."

"There are. Few, but there are. There are even some who are Magi of the four elements."

"Water, Fire, Air, and Earth?"

"Exactly. It's rare to find one, but they do exist. There are also Sorcerers of Blood and Curses Magic. Very dangerous and sinister."

"Yeah, I can imagine…"

"But one is always more powerful in a specific area of magic. If you study two, you won't be as powerful as if you'd specialized in only one of them."

"Thank you for all the explanations, now I understand better," Lasgol said as he tried to assimilate everything Eicewald had told him.

They went on talking well into the night, and Astrid had to come and remind them they should eat something. They had to interrupt the session but Lasgol felt content, because it was a conversation he had enjoyed very much. Most of all for the feeling of being able to count on a tutoring figure, something he had always wished he had.

Chapter 30

The journey's mornings were now training sessions for Lasgol. He seized the opportunity to get as much information as he could from Eicewald, and the Mage had started helping him improve his skills. Not only him, but he had also started working with Camu, which although was a lot more difficult, Lasgol really appreciated. He knew it was the only opportunity the creature would have of learning something from a Mage.

Egil asked Eicewald for permission to join his sessions with Lasgol and Camu as a listener, strictly to learn. He was aware that magic was not taught to those who did not have the Gift, since the Magi considered it a waste of time. But Eicewald appreciated Egil a great deal and granted his request. The words "fantastic" and "fascinating" echoed throughout the deck of the ship.

Astrid let Lasgol have all the time in the world he needed to spend with Camu and Eicewald working on developing their magic. She knew how important it was for Lasgol and also for Camu and did not want to rob them of their time or be an obstacle, which Lasgol appreciated from the bottom of his heart.

Eicewald focused on helping Lasgol and Camu improve the skills they already had. It was the simplest way to teach them, considering they were on a ship in the middle of the sea and the Mage did not have any tomes on magic study with him. He showed them how to do it correctly in a practical way, since both Lasgol and Camu, in their own way, had tried to improve their skills without much success so far. They had achieved small advances, but not what they were aiming for.

They had been practicing Eicewald's teaching for days with him. They practiced Lasgol's *Animal Presence* skill and Camu's Extended Invisibility Camouflage skill since, they were both interested in improving them. These were two useful skills—the first one to detect enemy presence and the second one to hide from said enemy.

That morning it was Lasgol's turn to go first.

"You must call on the skill by focusing on a goal, a tangible goal," Eicewald was explaining to Lasgol.

"But it's a skill that spreads on its own…"

"Precisely. You must make yourself get it to reach a specific distance. If you only want it to go farther you won't make it or the improvement will be small. It's like when you release at the bull's eye with your bow. It's only a good shot if it hits the bull's eye, and this is the same. Mark a distance—it has to reach there."

"All right. I want it to reach from bow to stern," Lasgol said.

"Very well, now we need a volunteer," Eicewald asked.

Egil offered himself at once, since he was always "glued" to them. He ran to stand at the farthest point of the ship. Captain Ulmendren looked at him with a puzzled expression but said nothing. He was already used to his passengers doing strange things.

"Concentrate on reaching Egil. If you come short and don't reach him you're not fulfilling your goal. It's essential."

Lasgol nodded at Eicewald and then looked at Egil. He shut his eyes and focused on reaching him with his skill. He knew how far he had to go. He was well familiar with his skill, it was only a matter of making the extra effort. He called upon his skill and felt how a small portion of his inner energy pool was consumed. The skill was activated and a green wave issued from his body, spreading around him in a large circle. It fell two paces short of reaching Egil.

"It didn't make it…"

"Don't worry, you're close. You just have to make a bigger effort. Force your magic to make it. When you feel the skill starting to activate, I want you to force it to consume more energy."

Lasgol nodded.

He followed the Mage's instructions, and when the skill started to activate he tried to give it more energy. But he could not. He refused to become frustrated, however, and tried again. Once again he was unable to do it. He persisted over and over. He could not do it.

"It seems to always pick up the same amount of energy…"

"Yes, magic is smart and always seeks to use the minimum amount of energy for any spell or summons. That's why it's you who must force it."

"Oh, I see."

"Keep trying."

It took Lasgol two days to get his skill to use more of his inner energy. Even so, he did not reach Egil, who every day stood at the end of the ship and waited patiently for success while he wrote down his ideas in one of his notebooks.

"Now you must focus on two things, gathering more energy and reaching Egil. Both at the same time," Eicewald said. You already have one, the other will come."

Lasgol tried for another whole day without success. He could tell the skill was becoming more powerful since it used more of his inner energy, but he could not make it spread to where he wanted. The following morning he succeeded at last.

"I reached Egil! I detected him!" he cried joyfully.

Eicewald smiled. "Congratulations. I knew you could do it."

"Thank you so much for teaching me how."

"Now you know what you have to do with all your skills. Set an obtainable goal and force your magic to use more of your energy."

"I'll do that."

"It's a slow process of repetition, of trying and trying again, but that's how you move forward."

"There are no shortcuts for magic, right?" Egil said as he came back.

"Irrefutable, dear Egil," Eicewald replied, and the three burst out laughing.

They went to see Camu. They went down to the hold where Camu was resting and hiding and continued practicing with the creature. The goal was the same but with the Extended Invisibility Camouflage skill. Camu had been working on it with unequal results. In the creature's case it was not only that he did not manage to extend his camouflage, but it was also unstable and prone to failure.

I try. I sure success.

"We don't doubt it," Lasgol told him.

I powerful. I success.

"You must focus on camouflaging Lasgol and Egil completely and maintaining the spell."

I know.

"Good, make sure you gather a large amount of your inner energy, of your magic energy, to do so."

And gather a lot.

"That's it, the more the better."

"Courage, my friend, you'll make it," Egil told him.

I know I do.

"He doesn't lack confidence," Eicewald joked.

"He's the same with everything."

Camu concentrated and, following Eicewald's instructions, called on the skill. Egil vanished before Lasgol's eyes.

"Very good, now keep the skill active and feed it more energy," Eicewald told him.

Not success, Camu said regretfully.

"You have to keep trying," the Mage said kindly.

Camu tried three more times without luck. He started to get anxious. But since he was so stubborn he kept trying. After four days of continuous failure, Lasgol vanished along with Egil.

"Hold the spell," Eicewald told him. "Feed it more energy to hold it."

Suddenly Lasgol's head became visible and then Egil's feet.

Go well? Camu asked still with his eyes closed.

"You're doing very well. You need to stabilize the spell. Concentrate on sending more energy and making it stable," Eicewald instructed.

I do.

It took Camu the whole day, but he finally managed to maintain the spell and Lasgol and Egil vanished from Eicewald's sight completely for a good while.

"You did it, Camu, congratulations," Eicewald told him.

I know, I powerful.

"Nobody beats him at self-confidence," said Lasgol.

"It's the self-confidence of born winners," Egil said.

I winner.

"Don't encourage him, that's worse," Lasgol said to Egil.

The three laughed and Camu stared at them, not understanding what they were laughing about.

Ingrid, Nilsa, and Viggo were not interested in magic, so they spent their time under the main mast chatting and commenting about their interests. One subject Ingrid and Viggo found interesting, particularly after the recent incident with the Druids, were the new anti-magi arrows Nilsa was developing. The idea was simple and at the same time very efficient, and both Ingrid and Viggo saw their potential use.

"The concept is simple," Nilsa was explaining. "The idea is that a Mage can't hurt you if he can't conjure. And to keep him from conjuring, we have to interrupt his spell and leave him unable to try again."

"Or kill him," said Viggo.

"Yeah, but if you can't kill him, the next best thing is stopping him from casting a spell," Nilsa went on.

"And that's why you've created those anti-magi arrows..." said Ingrid. "They distract them so they can't conjure?"

"That's the basic idea, yes. I thought that if a Mage for example has his defenses raised..."

"Like those blasted elemental spheres," Viggo said.

"Or tree bark," Ingrid added.

"Yes, any defense against physical attacks that we can't break down with conventional weapons, like our arrows or knives or axes."

"I see what you're getting at... go on, do tell..." Viggo encouraged her.

"Yes, what have you come up with?" Ingrid asked eagerly.

"I've taken an Earth Arrow and an Air Arrow and combined them, doubling the sound and the stunning effect with other components."

"That sounds interesting," Astrid said, coming closer to listen.

"I'd better show you. I need a volunteer," Nilsa said, looking at Viggo.

"Me? Why me? Ask either of them."

"Aren't you the most fearsome and famous Assassin in Norghana? You wouldn't be afraid of a small test, would you?"

"Me afraid? Never!"

"Perfect. Stand over there beside the gunwale," Nilsa told him, indicating a few steps away.

"You're not really going to shoot at me, are you? With your nerves you might pierce my ear."

"Which would suit you well..." Nilsa muttered in a low voice.

"What did you say? I can't hear you with the sea breeze."

Ingrid and Astrid smiled.

"Nothing, don't worry. Now get ready. I want you to whistle some tune."

"Why? What for?"

"Shut up and whistle!" Nilsa shouted at him.

"What a temper…" he protested, but he started to whistle.

Nilsa picked one of the ceramic loading containers for the Elemental Arrows which contained her new mix. It had not yet been added to an arrow. With a swift movement she threw it at Viggo's feet. The container broke and there was a small explosion, followed by a thundering noise.

Viggo leapt so high he almost touched the sail. When he fell back on deck he was stunned, blinded, and half deaf.

Captain Ulmendren came running to see what had happened. The whole crew turned toward Viggo and reached for their weapons. Ambassador Larsen was already running to the hold to hide, just in case.

"Everything all right?" the Captain asked.

"Everything's in order," Ingrid replied.

"Huh?" Viggo said, unable to hear properly.

"That everything's in order," Ingrid shouted so Viggo could hear her.

"What do you mean everything's in order? I'm blind, deaf, and my head hurts like crazy," Viggo said, wobbling.

"As I said, everything's perfect," Nilsa smiled.

Astrid could not help laughing when she saw Viggo stumble.

"Whistle, Viggo," Nilsa asked him.

"What?"

"I said whistle!" Nilsa shouted.

"No way… my head's killing me."

"Try to whistle," Ingrid told him.

Viggo finally tried to but could not.

"Between the stun and the headache he won't even be able to think," Nilsa told them.

"You could've warned me!" Viggo complained.

"If it's not a surprise it doesn't work so well," Nilsa apologized.

"I see… if you can't whistle you can't cast a spell either…" Astrid reasoned.

"That's the idea. It doesn't kill magi, but it renders them useless for a while."

"I like it," Ingrid said.

"Yeah, I like it a lot," Astrid agreed. "I have a couple additional ideas."

"Let's hear them," Nilsa motioned for her to sit beside her.

While Nilsa and Astrid were planning uses for Nilsa's invention, Ingrid went over to Viggo's side.

"You were splendid."

"What?"

"Nothing, handsome," Ingrid said and gave him a kiss.

The days went by on the ship between the lessons in magic; Lasgol's, Camu's, and Egil's questions; and the development of new arrows and other anti-mage weaponry by Nilsa, Astrid, and Ingrid. Viggo kept apart from them and went to play dice with the crew to try and win away their salary.

The return journey turned out to be quite productive. Some gained knowledge, others specialized in weapons, and Viggo earned a good bit of money.

Chapter 31

Their welcome at the Royal Castle in Norghana was somewhat different from what they had experienced in Irinel. King Thoran did not even see his Royal Eagles because he was too busy with matters of state of the utmost urgency, or so they had been told by the officer in command. As they were crossing the bailey in the direction of the Rangers' Tower, they saw Duke Orten mounting, getting ready to leave with about fifty riders. They were his personal guard, as big as they were ugly and matching the manners of their lord. The King's brother looked them up and down for a moment.

"I heard you completed your mission successfully," he barked at them.

"We did, sir," Ingrid replied politely but sternly, ignoring the Duke's surly tone.

"A magnificent success," Ambassador Larsen added. "The Royal Eagles were magnificent, just like the King's Ice Mage," he said, pointing at each one of them.

"You like to dress up the truth. You talk too much but say few true things," Orten attacked him.

"I swear, my lord, it has been a great success. You must have received the royal pigeons from the Kingdom of Irinel announcing the good news," Larsen said defensively.

"They have come, but I'm someone who doesn't believe something until I see it. My brother is more gullible. I am not," the Duke said from his mount.

"The mission has been completed successfully and the treaty will be sealed," Eicewald said coldly.

"I hope so. I don't like surprises and reversals," Orten said as he stared at Eicewald. "You spend too much time away for a Royal Ice Mage, procrastinating and neglecting your responsibilities and duties to the kingdom. I don't like that, and I know my brother doesn't either," the Duke said, pointing an accusing finger at him.

"Well, now I'm back and I'll resume my duties at once. My studies sometimes take longer than I'd wish, and for that I apologize," the Mage said and bent over in a deep bow.

"There won't be any more studies in your future for a long time. We've already been too lenient with you. Your duty is to lead the King's Ice Magi and protect the throne. Never forget that."

"I never do, sir, I assure you."

"For your own good, and for everyone's, I hope the mission has indeed been a success," Orten said, looking at all of them accusingly. "Things are getting difficult with the north and mid-east."

"This new alliance will surely dissuade the Kingdom's enemies from making any compromising moves," Larsen assured.

"We'll see. Not everything is finished. Return to your duties. There's a lot to deal with."

Larsen did another elaborate bow. "Right away, my lord." The Royal Eagles and Ice Mage gave small bows.

The Duke left with his men at a gallop, and they lost sight of him as he went down the main avenue of the city.

"As charming as always, our good duke. He raises our spirits with his charismatic words," Viggo said with a lot of sarcasm.

"Don't forget good looking and breathtaking," Nilsa said and made as if to puke.

"The weight of the throne's responsibility is a difficult load to carry. The Duke and his brother, his Majesty the King, do a laudable job," Ambassador Larsen said, nodding and with a look of regret for the load the two brothers shouldered.

Viggo was about to say something but Ingrid covered his mouth. They were in the Royal Castle, and there were Rangers and soldiers nearby who might hear. In all likelihood he was going to voice one of his acid comments, and it was not the place or the time. Complaints against the King or the Royal Family were treated as treason, and even more so since the civil war, so there was no place for them.

"No doubt," Eicewald agreed, nodding, but out of the corner of his eye he looked at Lasgol and Egil so they would know he did not agree.

"Let's take the horses to the stables so they can be taken care of," Ingrid said.

A Ranger came over to them and saluted them with a nod.

"Gondabar wants to be informed at once," he told them.

"How timely…. I wanted to go and have a beer and rest a little…" said Viggo.

"Don't you want to tell your feats to our leader?" Nilsa asked him, looking exaggeratedly surprised.

Viggo was thoughtful for a moment.

"Now that you mention it… who better than myself to tell of my adventures and prowess? Yeah, let's go and see Gondabar. I'll tell him what we did."

"Sticking to the facts, of course," Ingrid told him, arching an eyebrow.

"Of course, without diverting an iota from what really happened," Viggo said in an unconvincing tone.

Ingrid shook her head and snorted.

They left the horses in the stables and headed to the Rangers' Tower while Eicewald headed to the Tower of the Magi.

"I'll see you soon. I'm off to resume my position among the Magi," he said as he took his leave.

"Be careful," Egil said in a warning tone.

"Of course, very careful," the Mage replied, and he walked away, leaning on his ice staff.

When they left the horses, Lasgol went looking for Trotter. He had him in a stall at the back of the stables. He had spoken to the stable master so he would look after his pony, and apparently he had done a good job.

Trotter! How are you? he sent a mental message.

The Norghanian pony recognized the message from Lasgol and greeted him with snorts, shaking his head up and down.

Happy to see me?

Trotter nickered and rubbed his muzzle on Lasgol's torso as he stroked the horse's mane and head.

I see you've been well looked after, Lasgol transmitted while he checked him over to make sure.

I bring you greetings from Ona and Camu. They stayed outside the city, in the eastern woods. They're doing well and will be happy to know you are too. I'll see you soon, I have to go and report.

Trotter nickered again and shook his head up and down as Lasgol left.

As they were approaching the Rangers' Tower, they saw a large number of comrades coming out of the building. There were newbie Rangers, veterans, and royals. It appeared that the arrival of the Royal Eagles had drawn the attention of their own people. Then, without anyone saying a word or giving an order, they started forming two lines like a corridor.

The Panthers walked toward them with puzzled looks. They arrived at the first two, who saluted them with a nod and gestured for them to walk through the corridor they had made. Ingrid looked at her friends, then the corridor they had made to the door, and nodded.

"Let's go," she said to the Panthers.

They started walking between the two lines of Rangers, who watched them briefly and then turned their heads to the front. "Are they making us an honor walk?" Nilsa asked, looking at both sides as they went along the corridor of Rangers.

"That's what I think," Ingrid confirmed.

"It's the least they can do when the hero returns with another great achievement," Viggo said, puffing up his chest.

"I'm sure you mean the Panthers' return with another success under their belts," Astrid corrected him.

"I don't mind sharing the glory, I'm not greedy," Viggo replied with a huge smile.

"What you are is so vain," Ingrid snapped at him as she walked among her comrades with a determined step.

The Rangers remained firm, forming the two lines and looking straight ahead. They were whistling an old Ranger song: The Return of the Brave. They were doing it in unison and without too much volume, as if it were a private ceremony for the Rangers.

"I think it's an honor they're making this corridor and welcoming us with that song," Lasgol said, feeling honored and a little emotional from the recognition they were receiving.

"It's one of my favorite Ranger songs," said Egil.

"I guess they know we finished the mission successfully," said Astrid.

"News flies in the Tower," Nilsa confirmed. "At least when I was here, and this, being good news, will be widely known."

They went into the Tower, leaving the warm welcome behind, and the Rangers on duty greeted them soberly. They wasted no time and went to see Gondabar. They ascended the stairs to his office and were admitted at once, since the leader was waiting for them.

They knocked on the door and Gondabar's voice reached them from the other side.

"Come in."

The Panthers went in and formed a line before their leader, who was sitting behind his work desk filled with scrolls and tomes.

Lasgol was taken aback by the look of Gondabar. The leader of the Rangers was not exactly the image of health. He was thinner and seemed to have aged. They had seen him shortly before leaving on the mission, so finding him like this surprised him greatly. Lasgol was not the only one who noticed—he saw Egil was watching Gondabar with a worried look on his face and that Nilsa and Ingrid had exchanged a quick glance of concern.

"Welcome, Royal Eagles, or Snow Panthers as I know you prefer to be called," the leader of the Rangers said in greeting.

"We come at the request of our leader, as the path teaches us," Ingrid said.

Gondabar nodded. "So teaches the path, and so it must be done," he recited.

"Are you feeling well?" Lasgol asked him, worried about Gondabar's deteriorated look.

"Actually not really…. Age isn't forgiving, and I already have too many springs behind me…"

"And a lot of daily work to do," Egil said.

"Complicated and important work," Nilsa added.

"True, it's my responsibility and I wouldn't want it any other way," Gondabar replied with a tired smile.

"Then you're not ill, sir?" Astrid asked him, also looking concerned by Gondabar's appearance.

"I'm not ill as such. My body is beginning to fail me and I don't look well, but with a little rest I'll soon be better," he explained.

"If our leader allows me, I could examine him," Egil offered, "my knowledge of healing isn't extensive, but it's growing."

"I have no doubts, what with that brilliant mind of yours and the ease with which you retain information," Gondabar smiled at him. "I assure you it's not necessary, I've already been examined by the King's surgeons and a veteran Healer Guard. There's no illness in my body—it's just age and exhaustion. They've changed my diet and given me revitalizing tonics to take every day. I'll soon be fine. Don't worry."

"We're only concerned about our leader's health and well-being."

"I appreciate your concern about my health and the good cheer you bring."

"Always, sir," Ingrid said.

Gondabar smiled gratefully.

"I see you are all well. I'm very glad to see it, because this mission was complicated and might have ended badly."

"We're perfect, and the mission was a piece of cake," Viggo said, puffing up like a peacock.

The leader looked at Viggo and tilted his head.

"A piece of cake? This isn't what I would have expected from such a mission. Will you please tell me what happened on the mission, with as much detail as possible? I'd appreciate it."

"Well, we went..." Viggo started.

Gondabar raised a hand to interrupt him.

"Could you tell me, Egil? I want to have the facts and everything that happened from the most accurate point of view possible."

"Of course, sir," Egil replied.

Viggo made a face but kept his mouth shut.

Egil proceeded to tell Gondabar everything that had happened with his usual attention to detail and focused on the facts, without any personal opinion. Facts, data, and results. The others watched Egil explain, noting his way of detailing everything without beating around the bush and always seeking the heart of the matter.

Gondabar waited for him to finish and then asked a dozen questions which sought to elicit more detail about several points that had raised his curiosity. When Egil had cleared them all, the leader of the Rangers looked at Viggo.

"So, that was a piece of cake?" he asked sternly.

"Well... there were *some* difficulties..." Viggo admitted.

"I've noticed that."

"What's important is that we did it and came out unscathed," Ingrid said.

"Poisoned, but unscathed in the end," Gondabar said.

Ingrid and the others nodded.

"I've always been fascinated by the world of the Druids," Gondabar admitted. "We don't know much about them and they are a people with magic and wisdom that would come in handy."

"I don't think they'd be willing to help us with anything, not after what happened on the mission," Lasgol said.

"No, they won't. They'll hate us for profaning their sacred forest. They won't forget it was Norghanians who did it."

"Do you think they knew we were Norghanians, sir?" Nilsa asked, rubbing her hands together nervously.

"If they didn't know at first, they'll have found out by now. You used Rangers' weapons, Rangers' traps, and you were accompanied by an Ice Mage…"

"So if it comes out of a cow and it's white and warm, it's milk," said Viggo with a shrug.

"Pity. The Druids are a powerful people, it's not good to have them against us," Gondabar said.

"The King of Irinel is who they should consider an enemy, not us," Astrid said. "He sent us."

"Even so, it was you who infiltrated their forest and kidnapped their protégée, you Norghanians. They'll remember. The tension between the Druids and the King of Irinel has always been high, and this raises it even more."

"Will they retaliate? Will they rise up against Norghana or the King of Irinel?" Lasgol asked, nervous at the prospect.

Gondabar looked out the window and thought for a moment. Then he turned back to them.

"I hope not. But we can only wait and see how they decide to act."

"Let's hope it won't be with bloodshed," said Astrid.

"Let's hope so," Gondabar agreed. "The Zangrians are doing military maneuvers at the border, with all that entails… and there are rumors that, in the Frozen Continent, there have been internal fights for power among the different peoples of the continent…"

"Wow, that's bad news," said Lasgol, wondering how Asrael was doing and whether he would be having problems. They would have to find a way to contact the Shaman of the People of the Glaciers to find out what was going on. The Zangrians were a constant threat, so there was little they could do about that.

"We're not expecting an invasion, are we, sir?" Ingrid asked.

"For now our spies haven't confirmed any dangerous movement of troops, so no. But the possibility is present. Our Kingdom is weak, and other kingdoms will seek to benefit. It's always like that. It's the law of life in the fight for power in Tremia. That's why we must be more vigilant than ever—it's our duty as Rangers."

"We will be. We always are," they all replied.

"It is in times of need, when the kingdom is weak, that we are more valuable to Norghana and the Norghanians," Gondabar said. "Right now is the time to put a stop to our enemies and help the throne and realm."

"We understand and will do so," Egil said.

Gondabar was silent for a moment.

"It's funny that a Dark Ranger is now serving in the Royal House of Irinel," he said, looking at the group.

"It is surprising indeed," Ingrid agreed.

"Life takes many turns, and some are very twisted," Egil said with a smile. "None of us really knows where we'll end up one day."

"As long as it's not dead…" Nilsa murmured almost like a prayer.

"I'm not going to die," Viggo said confidently.

"No one can swear such a thing," Gondabar told him.

Viggo made a face as if he could but said nothing.

"I want to congratulate you for completing the mission successfully," Gondabar told them. "I'm sure King Thoran is happy too. Unfortunately he doesn't have time for celebrations."

"We appreciate our leader's congratulations, they're more than enough," Ingrid said.

"We serve the realm with honor," said Nilsa.

"And you do it with courage and success, and I congratulate you for it," Gondabar said as he bowed his head to them.

The Panthers returned the gesture.

They all thanked Gondabar for his words.

"You may rest until the next mission. You have a few days off, but don't stray too far from the capital, we might need you soon."

"We're at our leader's disposal," Ingrid said,

"Go and rest, enjoy a few days of leisure. You've earned it."

The Panthers left Gondabar, happy to have a few days off which would be great for them all. Although, thinking again, it was rare they should have any rest. Something always came up to spoil it.

Chapter 32

They rested all night without waking once. Nilsa had got them the large room in the Tower so they could share it and not be disturbed. She had never had any trouble getting favors for them—Nilsa knew practically everyone in the Rangers' Tower, as well as many Royal Rangers. Now that they were the Royal Eagles, it was even easier to get things; whatever she asked for she was given. The respect others had for them grew greater every day, and even the Royal Rangers, who were the best of the best, treated them with deference.

At dawn, rested and hungry, they went down to enjoy a good breakfast in the Rangers' dining room. They had thought they would go into the city afterward to deal with several things. The mood of the whole group was excellent. They were back, they had well-deserved days of leisure ahead of them, and Gondabar had congratulated them for their good deed. Nilsa had gone to deal with several things in the Tower, or so she had told them as she shot out of the room like lightning.

"I bet the redhead is talking to every living being in the building," Viggo said as he sat down to eat a bowl of porridge.

"She has a jovial, friendly character. Unlike you, who are like an angry black cat," Ingrid told him.

"Black panther you mean," he corrected her.

"Nilsa is a charmer, that's why she gets along with everybody," Lasgol defended her.

"The best trait to make friends is a jovial, open personality like our dear Nilsa's," said Egil.

"And honesty," Astrid added.

"Very true, that too," Egil nodded.

"A letter from Gerd! A letter from Gerd!" Nilsa arrived at the dining table where they were sitting, running and shouting.

Viggo choked on his porridge from the shock.

"Can she be… clumsier…. Agh!"

"I hope it's good news."

"Read on, please!"

They all wanted to know how the giant was doing.

Nilsa read:

Dear friends, I hope you are all well. I guess you're still on the mission since I haven't received any news in quite a while, which is strange. You always send me a few lines to cheer me up, and when I didn't get any I asked the Mother Specialist Sigrid. She told me you are indeed on a mission as I had suspected. She didn't say anything else, of course—I know what missions and secrets are like. She told me to relax and wait patiently for you to write to me when you finished and that there's nothing in Tremia that can defeat you, so that made me feel more at ease.

I only wanted to let you know that I'm progressing quickly and my rehabilitation is going very well, better than expected. Healer Edwina is like a goddess of goodness and kindness and she's managing to heal me in a really impressive way. She's working with me and Elder Engla to exhaustion, and she does this every single day without complaint and with no regard to the great sacrifice it is. I'll never be able to repay her for her efforts and charity. Sigrid and Annika tell me not to get carried away, that although I'm progressing a lot, the way is still long and hard. I can't help but be optimistic, you know me. I know the road is long and hard, I suffer it every day, but I'm positive because things are going very well. I just wanted you to know this and to ask you to please write to me as soon as you can. I know you'll be all right, but it'll put my mind at ease. Send me crosspatch Milton, who knows the way and will deliver the message.

A great bear hug to all.

Take good care of yourselves,

Gerd.

"What great news!" Nilsa cried, clapping her hands, delighted and hopping all over the hall.

"Our Gerd's great," Ingrid said, smiling.

"And a good person," Astrid added.

"He's a mountain of muscle without a brain. I'm sure he believes he's improving a lot while he's actually progressing like a snail," Viggo commented and waved the letter aside.

"Only you could make such a comment about someone as good as Gerd," Ingrid scolded.

"Yeah, because he's an idiot," said Nilsa.

"You'll see how I'm right," Viggo said, unmoved.

"Don't be such a killjoy!" Astrid chided.

"I'm sure that Edwina's help and Annika's care are helping him improve," Lasgol said.

"Says the goodie weirdo," Viggo said acidly.

"Why on earth are you in such a bad mood this morning?" Ingrid asked him.

"Me? In a bad mood? Never," he said, shaking his hands in denial.

"Yeah, and cows fly over the full moon," Nilsa snapped.

"What's important is that our friend is improving. Whether it's a lot or very little, what matters is the healing," Egil told them. "Imagine if we'd received news from the Shelter saying he wasn't improving at all...."

"That would be devastating," said Lasgol.

"Don't make me cry," said Nilsa, whose eyes were moist only thinking about the possibility.

Viggo had no choice but to change his discourse. "Well, if he says he's improving it's likely that he is, even he could be right in that," he said, seeing he had gone too far.

"I'm glad you see it that way," Ingrid smiled at him.

"So, with this excellent piece of news we can start off and go into the city," said Egil. "I have several errands to run."

"I also have something to do," said Astrid in a serious tone.

"I'll take a walk around the Royal Castle first," said Viggo.

"And may I ask what for?" Ingrid said with a raised eyebrow.

"I'm going to make my presence known," he said, lifting his chin.

"How will you do that, and why?" Nilsa asked.

Viggo started pacing with his hands on his hips, flexing forward a little as if to show off his muscles. He took a couple of strides and looked angry.

"Are you really going to strut like that throughout the Royal Castle?" Ingrid asked him, following him with a blank gaze.

Viggo did not reply and went on walking pretentiously. They noticed that the Rangers who came out of the Tower and the soldiers stared at him in surprise.

"He's delirious again," Nilsa said, shaking her head.

"That's not new with him," Lasgol commented.

Viggo walked in a circle around the group.

"These people don't know who I am. They don't appreciate that I'm a figure to admire," Viggo said casually, as if speaking to himself. "They don't know they ought to treat me with the utmost respect. I don't expect anything less."

"You don't expect anything less?" Ingrid said in a shocked tone and with a look of utter disbelief at what she was hearing.

"Absolutely. I'm the best Assassin in Norghana and a hero of the nation who has just returned from another successful mission of great importance for the kingdom," he said calmly and continued strutting.

"I think many already know that," Lasgol said, trying to make him stop strutting so ridiculously.

"Not enough," Viggo replied. "I'm going to go and talk to the court's troubadour and tell him of my heroic adventures myself. I don't think they're making enough songs and poetry about my amazing self. That's unacceptable, and I'm going to make sure it changes right away."

"How can you be such a narcissist and so impossible?" Nilsa asked him, raising her arms to the sky.

"He's a fool and a numbskull," Ingrid said. "More and more every day," she said, also raising her arms in frustration.

"I'm unique and irreplaceable. I'll see you later. I'm going to speak to the troubadour," Viggo said and left, still strutting like a peacock.

They left Viggo and his delusions at the Castle and headed into the city. They decided none of them should go alone, just in case. They should not need to fear anything in their own capital, but still. Lasgol had been attacked from behind and by surprise the last time he had been walking through the usually safe streets of the capital. No matter how safe the capital of a large kingdom might be, there were always thieves, thugs, unscrupulous traders, rascals, quarrelers, and other scum of society, in Norghania like in any other of the great cities of Tremia.

"Nilsa and I are going to check a couple of shops with bows and components. We want to see what's new and interesting," Ingrid told the others.

"I want to perfect my anti-magi arrows. I need them to be even louder," Nilsa said.

"Good, we're going to do a couple of errands," Egil said, indicating himself, Astrid, and Lasgol.

"We'll meet this evening at the Tower," Ingrid said.

"Very well, be careful," Astrid cautioned.

"You too. I find it strange and disappointing that I have to say that in our own capital," Ingrid said ruefully.

"I do too, but I have the feeling that times are changing, and not for the better," Egil said, looking sad.

"I think so too," Ingrid agreed.

Astrid, Lasgol, and Egil headed to the south of the city while Ingrid and Nilsa went east. The streets were busy and the people went about their own daily tasks. Norghana's capital was a crowded city and the Rangers, used to smaller groups, always felt a little out of place among so many people, who never stopped going here and there like ants in their colony.

They arrived at a small square and Egil stopped suddenly. Astrid and Lasgol almost bumped into him. The place was quite busy since it opened onto three wide streets of the commercial area. Lasgol knew at once why Egil had stopped. At a corner, in front of an inn was a man who looked like a beggar, preaching to the passersby and waving his arms madly.

"Let's go over and listen," Egil said.

Astrid and Lasgol nodded. Half a dozen people were listening to the man, who did not look Norghanian but from the lands of the south, since his skin was quite a bit darker than that of the northern people. The three friends watched the man as he waved his arms, proclaiming his apocalyptic message.

"And the deserts of the south and the mountains of the north, everything will burn with true fire that will consume the impure! Only those who embrace the new order will be saved!"

Lasgol and Egil looked at one another.

"It's the same message again," Lasgol told Egil.

"Very similar, yes…. Let's hear what else he says," Egil suggested.

"It won't be pretty, I'm afraid," Astrid commented with a look on her face that said she expected the message to be predominantly negative.

"The end of the era of men is coming with giant strides!"

The people present were listening with attention and cried in alarm, some frightened and others dismissing the terrifying news the preacher delivered to them.

"Men will be defeated and a new order will rule over Tremia and the whole world!"

"I don't like all this talk about a new order one bit," Astrid whispered to Lasgol and Egil.

"It's significant," Egil confirmed and signaled her to keep listening.

"Only those of the ancient blood will share the new world with the all-powerful lords!"

"The more I hear, the more troubling I find it..." Lasgol whispered as he watched the preacher pointing his finger at his audience, the sky, and the earth.

"The all-powerful lords will return and reign! The day is coming!"

"That's important," Egil commented. He had brought out one of his notebooks and begun to write.

"No kingdom that resists the designs of the new lords will be saved! They will perish in flames! Everything must burn and be purified before the new order is established and the lords reign!"

Several men and women who were listening left, some horrified and others with gestures of disbelief.

"The message is horrifying," Astrid commented as she watched the messenger with a frown.

"Those who oppose the new order will end up consumed by the scorching fire of a new era that's fast approaching. The time of men will come to an end!"

All of a sudden a patrol of the city guard appeared in the square. They were doing their rounds and consisted of six soldiers and an officer. When he saw the preacher, the officer halted his men. He approached the man and, after listening to what he was preaching for a moment, he spoke.

"Stop that nonsensical blabber!" he told the preacher.

"I am a messenger, and my task is blessed by the lords of tomorrow!" the man cried.

"Shut up right now or I'll cut your tongue out!" the officer threatened.

The preacher hesitated, deciding whether to go on or not.

"Throw this lunatic out of the city," someone with a surly look said to the officer. He was one of the people who had been listening.

"He says nothing but horrible things," said a woman.

"The new order..." the preacher began to say.

"Not another word, or I swear I'll cut your tongue out right here!"

The preacher shut his mouth.

"And what if he's telling the truth?" a man asked, looking frightened.

"How are we going to survive fire and destruction?" another one asked.

"We should give ourselves up to the mercy of the new lords," a woman shouted.

"It's forbidden to preach death in Norghana!" the officer informed, shouting.

"My message isn't of death, it's of rebirth," the preacher replied.

The officer reached for his sword and pointed it in the direction the man ought to follow.

"Get out of the city. If I ever see you again, it'll be the last thing you ever do!"

The preacher left quickly, making his way through the throng.

"Let's follow him," Egil told his friends.

Both Lasgol and Astrid nodded.

Chapter 33

The preacher took the street to the left and went along it at a quick pace. The officer and the guard dispersed the crowd that had been listening to the apocalyptic message. Lasgol went down the street the preacher had gone and looked back. Several of those who had been listening were walking away in a group, commenting on what they had heard. That was not good—if the message influenced the people it might be dangerous.

They followed him along several streets and alleys, keeping a safe distance and without the man noticing he was being followed. He quickly moved away from the city's good neighborhoods. He went through several quarters where the working people lived, miners and woodcutters mostly. Finally, he went into the lowest slums of the city. They followed him through ill-looking parts of the city where they glimpsed seedy characters posted on every corner. The preacher headed quickly toward an area where there were only huts. It was a depressing area with lots of poor people trying to survive in bad conditions, such as filth, rot, and sickness.

They watched him enter a wooden hut that was barely standing, close to one of the city walls. The hut seemed to have enough space for four people. They got closer and Egil stopped by a half-broken door hanging from an old rusty hinge.

"Are we going in?" Astrid asked.

Egil nodded. "I want to speak to him."

"This place is quite depressing," Lasgol said, looking around. "D'you think this preacher, living here like this, will tell us anything of interest?"

"It's not only what he tells us, but how he knows what we're interested in," Egil told him.

Astrid and Lasgol looked at one another. They did not fully understand what their friend meant.

"Didn't you notice he wasn't carrying any tome? How does he know the message he's preaching? What's his reference?"

"That's true. Priests and the like usually carry a tome with the scriptures they preach from," said Astrid. "They consider them holy."

"It's true that none of the preachers we've seen so far were carrying anything with them..." said Lasgol.

"How do they know what to preach?" Egil asked

Lasgol shrugged.

"I see what you want to find out. Let me open the way," Astrid said, reaching for her knives. "You never know what you might find in a place like this."

Egil nodded and motioned for her to go first.

Astrid kicked the door open and entered like lightning.

Lasgol adjusted his bow and quiver on his back so they would not bother him in case of a fight, took out his knife and axe, and went in with Egil following.

Inside the hut there was nothing but a pair of improvised bunks with cloth and wool that had been picked off the remains of some old mattresses and piles of filth of all kinds in two of the corners. The roof was dilapidated and must have had a thousand holes through which light filtered, and therefore so did rain. Three men in rags were sitting on one side of the hut with the preacher on the other side. The stench was so strong that Astrid and Lasgol put on their Ranger scarves to protect their noses.

"You three, out!" Astrid told them, pointing at the door with her knife.

The three men did not protest and went out on all fours. The preacher eyed them warily from his bed where he had sat down.

"What do you want?" he asked distrustfully.

"We want to speak with you about the message you've been preaching in the square. We're interested," Egil said in a kind tone.

"You are not believers in the new all-powerful lords," he said in an accusing tone.

"Let's say that we want to better understand who they are and why they're coming," Egil went on. "We're interested in knowing what's going to happen."

"And the deserts of the south and the mountains of the north, everything will burn with the true fire that will consume the impure! Only those who embrace the new order will be saved!" the man cried out loud.

"Yes, yes, you said that before, we heard you..." Egil said.

"It's what will happen," the preacher said.

"Do you really believe that?" Lasgol asked him.

"With all my heart and soul," the man replied.

"You believe it's the end of men?" Astrid asked.

"The end of days is coming! The great awakening is already happening! The new order, a new era is fast approaching and the time of men comes to an end!"

"You said that before too…" Egil said. "You're repeating the message word for word."

Astrid and Lasgol had also noticed this and exchanged glances.

"It's what my soul tells me. The message I must preach to the four winds," the preacher said,

"Why?" Egil asked as he squatted until his eyes were level with those of the preacher who was sitting on his ruined bed.

"I have to preach the message, it's my sacred duty."

"How long have you been doing it?" Egil asked him.

"Since… since…." The preacher was thoughtful, as if trying to remember without being able to.

"You don't remember?" Egil was looking fixedly at his eyes.

"No… since…. I don't know…"

"What's your name?" Egil asked him with his head to one side.

"I… my name is…." The man could not remember his own name. "My name doesn't matter, what matters is the message."

Lasgol and Astrid exchanged a blank look.

"Who gave you the message?" Egil continued his interrogation.

"Give?"

"Who told you what you had to say?" Egil said patiently.

"I… don't… remember…" the preacher searched his mind with his gaze lost and could not find the answer.

"You don't remember who gave you the message or when?" Lasgol asked, intrigued. That was weird, since the man had been preaching his apocalyptic message with all his being. He had to remember who had given it to him and when.

"I don't… I don't remember…"

"Are you lying to us?" Astrid asked, pointing one knife at him.

The preacher did not flinch at the threat. He was lost in thought, seeking to remember and unable to do so.

"I'm not lying… I can't remember…"

"Interesting situation," Egil said, scratching his chin. "He doesn't remember his name or the origin of his speech. Being one of such tremendous importance, he should remember it."

"He could be lying to us," Astrid said.

"Indeed. But I doubt he's lying."

"I'm not lying," the preacher said, and his eyes came back to the present moment. "Those who oppose the new order will end up consumed by the scorching fire of the new all-powerful lords!" he cried with renewed energy and passion.

"Once again he's repeated it word for word," Egil said as he compared the man's words to the notes in his notebook.

"He's memorized the message and repeats it like those birds that always repeat what they hear a human say?" Astrid said, frowning.

"Like a parrot, a bird of the south of the continent. Yes, something similar," said Egil.

"So, if he's repeating a memorized message, that's not good for us. What are we going to do? How can we get the answers we want?" Lasgol said.

"Leave me alone with him," Egil said as he took a metallic box out of the satchel he carried on his back.

"Oh oh... is that what I think it is?" Lasgol asked uneasily.

"You're going to introduce him to your two little friends?" Astrid asked with a lethal gleam in her eyes.

"That's right. I'd already foreseen that we'd find ourselves in a situation like this   where it would be necessary to obtain information by unconventional means. I've brought Ginger and Fred with me. They'll help us solve the problem," Egil said, grinning.

"I'd rather not be present for this," Lasgol said, shaking his head. He did not like to see the tiny pink viper and the king scorpion in action. It gave him the willies and   he got a knot in his stomach every time Egil brought them out to intimidate someone.

"I do want to see this," Astrid said, and Lasgol looked at her in disbelief. "You learn a lot by seeing Egil in action," she told him.

"Better if you let me work alone," Egil asked. "This is going to require all my concentration. I have the feeling that it's not that this preacher doesn't want to tell us the truth but that he really doesn't know what that is."

"Oh all right, in that case I'll let you work in peace," Astrid accepted. "But I want you to tell me everything later."

"Deal," Egil promised.

Lasgol and Astrid went out of the hut, leaving Egil to do what he must, alone and in peace. As he himself used to say, the art of extracting information from people who refused to talk was complex and fascinating at the same time. Lasgol worried that his friend might make a mistake, or that an accident should happen, since Egil did not make mistakes and that they might have to regret the loss of a life. He hoped that would never happen, but there was the old saying that went, "those who play with ice a lot end up losing their fingers." Egil risked a lot with his interrogation game, and one day he could suffer a serious mishap.

They heard screams of fear and begging from the preacher. Lasgol wanted to go in, but Astrid grabbed him by the arm.

"Let him do his thing," she told him, nodding.

"What if he goes too far?"

"You know him well, he won't. Egil knows what he's doing and how far he can go," Astrid assured him.

There were cries of terror from the preacher, who seemed to be having a panic attack.

"Don't worry, Egil's in control of the situation," Astrid assured Lasgol again to calm him.

Lasgol was not so sure. Using such dark methods did not please him. On the other hand, he was with Astrid and Egil, who were the two people with the darkest tendencies in the group, so he would not find support for his well-intentioned concerns.

After a period of silence and screams of terror, Egil came out of the hut.

"He doesn't remember anything of how he got the message or who gave it to him," he told them. "He repeats it as if it'd been engraved with fire in his mind. It's most fascinating."

"He doesn't remember anything?" Astrid asked, frowning.

"How's that possible?" Lasgol asked, puzzled.

"There are several possibilities. I've been thinking about them. The most likely to have occurred in this case is that his mind's been manipulated."

"That's not something many people can do," said Lasgol.

"A Mage?" Astrid suggested.

"I'm guessing a sorcerer or a shaman," Egil replied. "You need specific and specialized knowledge of the human mind."

"A Dominator? An Illusionist?" said Lasgol.

"Someone like that, or with similar magic and power. It's as if his memory had been erased. Part of it, that is. He remembers the message he must spread but little more. He doesn't remember his past life—it's as if he never existed."

"I didn't know it was possible to do that to another person," Astrid said. "He doesn't remember anything from his previous life?"

"From what I gathered, only a few details before the moment he became a preacher."

"Did he tell you how it happened?"

"He barely remembers. I must say I find this dilemma most fascinating. If it weren't against our interests, I'd say it was fantastic."

"Yeah, but it's really bad for us. We need to know what's going on here," Astrid said in a tone of frustration.

Lasgol shrugged. "Things are getting complicated."

"Yes, the situation is quite complex. A witness who barely remembers who he is or what happened to him isn't much to go on with," Egil admitted.

"So we leave empty-handed, what a disappointment," Astrid said ruefully

"Yeah… this doesn't help us understand what's going on…" Lasgol added.

"Not completely. I did manage to get something out of him though. It was difficult, but there's an important detail he does remember."

Both Lasgol and Astrid turned to him eagerly.

"I found out that he remembers a significant detail, an object," Egil told them.

"An Object of Power?"

"Most likely. He remembers the head of a large reptile," said Egil.

"A great snake?" Astrid suggested.

"Possibly, yes," Egil said.

"Interesting…." Lasgol was thoughtful.

"Well, it's a clue. Now we know we have to find the head of a great reptile in the form of an Object of Power," said Astrid.

"Irrefutable," Egil smiled broadly.

"Very well, shall we continue the search?"

"As soon as you wish," Egil nodded.

"Is the preacher okay?" Lasgol wanted to know.

"As well as he might be given the circumstances," Egil replied as he bent over to organize his satchel where he carried the box with Ginger and Fred.

Lasgol went into the hut to see how the preacher was doing. It was not that he did not trust Egil, but just in case. He found him as they had left him, sitting on his beggar's bunk with his gaze lost and a look of horror on his face that Lasgol did not like at all. He snorted. At least he was alive. He was glad Egil's interrogation had finished without incidents. Lasgol knew that Egil could cope with a slip, a death. He would get over it. He was hardened, very hardened inside. Life had delivered many blows to him, tragic ones. He had lost his father and brothers in a violent way, and that left its mark.

The preacher sighed deeply and lay down in a fetal position. Lasgol pondered on what he was witnessing. That man was not well, he had suffered a great deal. He guessed the man had also lost his parents violently and it had marked him forever. But somehow Lasgol knew his friend was harder than he, himself, in that sense. Egil would recover from any mishap, blow, or reversal of fate, no matter how strong that life threw at him unexpectedly. Lasgol knew that although he would also bear them well, he had seen the lethal gleam in Egil's eyes and knew his friend would overcome them much better than he would.

He sighed. The suffering and unfathomable pain of losing dear ones marked the soul of a person in ways that were difficult to understand. He left the hut and, with a glance at Astrid, let her know everything was all right.

"Let's get out of here, this stench is beginning to affect me," Astrid said and made a face. Her head hurt.

"Come on, we need to continue searching," Egil said cheerfully with a big smile.

Egil had found something, some clue he thought was important. Lasgol recognized that smile of triumph.

Chapter 34

Egil told them he wanted to visit a couple of places of interest where he might find some useful information. Lasgol thought they would leave that depressed area and return to the commercial section of the city. He was wrong. They went further into the southeastern part of the city, the poorest and at the same time the most dangerous. Lasgol said nothing to Egil, although it surprised him that he was willing to go deeper into those little recommended parts of the city. Going into the worst areas of any capital in Tremia was never a good idea. But both Astrid and Lasgol trusted their friend and they knew that if they were heading that way it was for some important reason. Egil was not one to run unnecessary risks; on the contrary, he weighed them all and made well-thought-out decisions before taking any risks.

Astrid and Lasgol remained alert as they walked since they were beginning to notice several thugs with more than likely bad intentions.

"If anyone approaches I'll deal with them," Astrid told Lasgol with a deadly gleam in her deep-green eyes.

Lasgol nodded; he knew Astrid would end any threat in the blink of an eye.

They followed Egil's indications to the first place he wanted to visit. Astrid and Lasgol were surprised and exchanged blank looks. It was a tavern in a grim and dangerous part of town. Egil did not frequent taverns and least of all in such an unfavorable section of the city with so many criminals lurking.

"I'm going to go in for a moment," Egil told them.

"Aren't we all going?" Lasgol said.

"No, I must go in alone."

"Isn't it dangerous? I can watch your back," Astrid said as she saw an ill-looking character exiting the establishment.

"These places always entail a certain risk since they're frequented by ill-looking locals with dishonorable intentions, but don't worry, I can take care of myself."

"As you wish…" Astrid replied. But she was not at all convinced.

Egil went into "The Red Bat" and Astrid and Lasgol stayed outside, waiting for him. A moment went by and they saw two scoundrels that might have been slum thieves or robbers come out. Lasgol could not help but worry about their friend.

"I'm going to see what's going on," Astrid whispered to Lasgol. A moment later she was climbing the side wall of the tavern and went inside through a window to the upper level.

"I'll watch the door..." Lasgol whispered back. There was not much else he could do.

It was a long time before Egil came out from the establishment. Almost at the same time Astrid appeared, pretending she had been watching the surroundings.

"Wasn't there a better tavern for a meeting?" Lasgol asked Egil.

"Of course there are. This great city has many good taverns; there are some in the higher part of town where only the rich and influential go."

"Then why did you choose this cesspool of criminals?" Astrid wanted to know.

"Precisely because no one of good breeding would come to this dump. Them or most of the citizens. It's a perfect place to do certain business... with people who don't want to be seen or recognized..."

"I see..." Lasgol said, realizing Egil had come here to speak to one of his clandestine contacts.

"The man you were talking to is some kind of informant?" Astrid asked him.

"I see you took a peek."

"Only to make sure you were okay," she winked at him.

"He's an undercover agent who does certain tasks for me," Egil told her, winking as well.

"Oh I see, okay," she nodded.

"Let's get going, I don't want anyone to see us around here. I don't want to compromise this location."

They headed north along a street that looked dangerous. There were several groups of two or three people posted at the ends and in the middle of the street. Astrid took out her knives ostentatiously, showing that if anyone was looking for trouble they would find it.

"Did you find out any information that might serve us?" Lasgol wanted to know as he also took his weapons out and carried them visibly in his hands.

278

"I got some information, but not about the matter at hand."

"Oh, then about what?"

The ghost of a smile appeared on Egil's face. "About something that I carry on my back for being who I am, or rather, whose son I am."

Lasgol understood—Egil had received news of the league of the Western Nobles.

"Good news?" Astrid asked.

"Some good, those referring to the West. Others not so much. The alliance between Norghana and Irinel troubles my allies of the Western League."

"I see you keep informed and in touch," Astrid told him with a slight smile.

"I keep in touch. The well-being of the West and all of Norghana is what drives my actions. That hasn't changed and never will. That events have turned out as they did and that I might be waiting for the right moment for my interests and those of my allies doesn't mean I've forgotten or neglected them. Not by a long shot," Egil stated.

"I guessed as much," Astrid said. "You aren't one to neglect matters, and least of all one to forget them," she smiled.

Lasgol saw the gleam of intelligence and the hardness of past experiences in Egil's eyes. He was never going to forget what had happened to his family, and that was a heavy load to carry on his young shoulders. And it was even heavier because he owed his loyalty to the Rangers, and although they served him as cover for his clandestine movements with the Western League, Lasgol knew that Egil loved being a Ranger. Most likely Egil would be happier being simply that, a Ranger.

They went down a street on the right, which was also not one of the safest in the city. So far no one had bothered them. The fact that they were armed and showing that they would not back out of a confrontation also helped.

"Why should the alliance with Irinel concern them? Isn't it good for everyone?" Lasgol asked as he went over the matter in his head.

Egil nodded. "From a global point of view, it is. It's good for Norghana because we need allies, especially now that we're weak and don't have any. But from an internal point of view, it strengthens Thoran. That means it strengthens the Nobles of the East. As you can imagine, that's not exactly good for the interests of the West."

279

"If you look at it that way…" Lasgol admitted.

"Situations change according to the prism you look through. We all want a strong Norghana, economically and militarily, leading the continent, respected by the other kingdoms. Unfortunately, who rules Norghana and how, is something that must be weighed carefully to see alternatives and consider actions to be taken."

"I see you keep abreast of everything that happens around the throne and Norghana," Astrid said. "The fact that you're alert and vigilant eases my mind."

"I'm not so sure it eases mine…" said Lasgol, who was afraid his friend might be plotting against Thoran and his brother.

"Don't worry, for the time being I'm only watching the evolution of the different political plots. There's no risk of myself getting too involved." He smiled and put his hand on Lasgol's shoulder so he would feel better, as if he knew what his friend was afraid of and wanted to reassure him.

"As long as you're watching the kingdom's development from the shadows, I'm easy," Astrid said, showing him her support.

"I am, and I always will," Egil promised, and this time his gaze and his tone were firm.

They turned left to go down another street. They were already leaving the unfriendly quarter. Egil led them through streets and finally into a commercial area where several guilds had workshops and shops.

"Are we going shopping?" Astrid joked.

"Yup, shopping for the most valuable item: information," Egil whispered with a mischievous grin.

Lasgol had the impression that his friend delighted in everything to do with this world of undercover agents, spying, secrets, and obtaining precious information. Yes, he definitely loved it—he guessed as much by the happy look on Egil's face.

They arrived in front of an oil lamp workshop and Egil stopped.

"Wait for me here, I'm going to buy something," he told them before going into the workshop.

"I doubt it'll be a lamp," Astrid joked.

"I guess not," Lasgol replied in the same tone.

Egil was in there for quite a while, and when he came out at last Astrid and Lasgol looked at him questioningly. Egil shook his head and they left the place, going toward the west down a narrow street.

"It seems that our mysterious character knows how to hide his trail very well," Egil commented.

"Who do you mean?" Astrid asked him.

"Drugan Volskerian, the warlock who attacked Lasgol," Egil said as he kept going up the street without stopping.

"Oh, are you asking about him?" Lasgol asked, surprised,

"Of course. Before we went on the mission I ordered several trustworthy agents to search for him since I couldn't. One must use all the means at his or her disposal to obtain the desired success. Luckily, I have the means and contacts."

"Rather than fortune, I'd say effort and intelligence," Astrid said.

Lasgol smiled, because even though it was true that some of Egil's contacts and allies were because of who his family was, most of them he had obtained by himself with the sweat of his brow and his brilliant mind.

They kept wandering the streets while Egil led them from one neighborhood to another. Lasgol was already lost with so many turns and twists along the streets they had wandered. Egil took some detours, and on some turns he went a lot faster, as if he was afraid they were being followed and wanted to lose their possible pursuers. Lasgol was no longer sure where they were; in fact, he could have sworn they had already passed the square with the fountain in the shape of an eagle they were passing through now.

"I don't think anyone's following us," said Astrid, who must have reached the same conclusion as Lasgol.

"Better to be sure. Not only in case someone related to my family's name is following us, but in case it's someone related to yours," he told Astrid.

"Oh…" Astrid glanced over her shoulder. "You think my uncle's men might be following us?"

"It's a likely guess."

"And why do you think they'd be following us?" she asked him as she looked around unobtrusively.

"For the same reason I've been following them," he replied.

"You've had my uncle and his men followed?"

"Most certainly."

Astrid looked at Lasgol and he shrugged.

"Don't ask me…" he said in a whisper.

"Don't stop, we're almost there," Egil said as he pointed at a narrow street on the left.

"Why did you have my uncle followed?"

"For two reasons. One, because he must be seeking the same man we are, Drugan Volskerian."

"To recover the orb," Lasgol guessed.

"Of course, my dear friend."

"That makes sense," Lasgol said to Astrid. "Your uncle stole the orb from me and the warlock stole it from him. He must be searching for it."

Astrid nodded. "And the second reason?"

Egil replied without stopping. "Because both you and I want to speak to him."

"That's true," she agreed.

"Add me to that wish," said Lasgol and reached for his head where he had received the blow.

"We're here," Egil said and stopped his almost-race.

Astrid and Lasgol looked back to see if they were being followed. They could not detect anyone but they were not comfortable.

"I'm going in," Egil said, and Lasgol realized their friend had led them to a brewery.

"Are you thinking of buying beer?" Lasgol asked him as a joke.

"Yes, but it's only to pretend," his friend smiled. "There's someone I want to talk to here."

"We'll wait for you and make sure we haven't been followed," said Astrid.

Egil nodded and entered the premises.

Lasgol and Astrid separated and each went along the street in opposite directions, looking for anyone following them. They went around the houses that surrounded the brewery but did not see anything suspicious. They stood one on each corner and waited for Egil to come back out. It took him a while, but he finally appeared and signaled them to come closer. They did not speak in front of the brewery but headed to the center of town at a quick pace. Egil was silent, thinking.

When they arrived in the vicinity of the main square, "The Invincibles Square," Egil stopped.

"I'm afraid that all my inquiries and search for the mysterious warlock and his minions have turned out empty. He covers his trail well. He's not known here or in any nearby kingdom. I paid well to

282

be given information but without any result."

"What do you think?" Lasgol asked him.

"We find ourselves before an intelligent, grim, mysterious, and powerful adversary. It's not usual that those with power, like this warlock has proven to have, should hide in the shadows. They usually like to show how powerful they are and make a name for themselves. The fact that this warlock doesn't do that gives me a bad feeling and a lot to think about. He has strong motives, an important goal to reach, and because of this he keeps to the shadows and doesn't let himself be seen. He's neither attracted to fame, glory, or gold, otherwise he would be known and would serve someone important..."

"That's good reasoning," said Astrid.

"Thanks, but I wish I wasn't right, because this makes things a lot more difficult. Finding him isn't going to be easy, as we're already finding out."

"You think he's still here?" Lasgol asked.

"I can't say for sure. In order to know where to find him we must first find out what he's looking for. If we find that out, we'll know where he's going and we'll be able to find him."

"We know he wanted the Dragon Orb," said Astrid.

"Yes, but for what?"

"To gain more power? The orb has Drakonian magic, and Camu believes it's powerful," said Lasgol.

"That's the hypothesis I'm focusing on, but there might be something else he's looking for that we haven't discovered yet," Egil said.

"My uncle might know what he wants. They might even be looking for the same thing," said Astrid.

"Very true. Your uncle might know."

"Let's go find him then," she said.

"At his estate?" Lasgol asked.

"Yes. He'll have taken shelter there. I sent a letter to his valet asking him whether my uncle was home—I should receive an answer soon."

"You don't need to wait for a response. Your uncle isn't at his estate," Egil confirmed to her.

"Have your contacts told you that?"

"That's right. I have the estate under surveillance. He hasn't returned since we went on the mission."

"Then we have to find him," Astrid said, making a fist.

"First, my dear Assassin, we'll pay a religious visit."

Astrid and Lasgol stared at Egil with wide eyes.

"Religious?"

"That's right, and then we'll play cat and mouse," Egil told them enigmatically.

Chapter 35

The following day they woke up well-rested, and after breakfast Egil suggested visiting the capital's Ice Temple.

"I have no intention of setting foot in a religious temple," Viggo refused. "Besides, I have more important things to do."

"Like visiting bards?" Nilsa asked mockingly.

"Precisely. My epic stories aren't going to tell themselves. I'm going to go downtown to visit several spots where I'll find out who the most popular troubadours and bards are and speak to them."

"Wasn't it enough torturing the royal bard?" Ingrid said.

"I didn't torture him at all. On the contrary, I explained my glorious adventures and he was so impressed that he's already writing two odes which he'll present before the King and the Court."

"You're joking, aren't you?" Nilsa said.

"Not at all," Viggo replied and resumed that silly pose with his hands on his hips, stomach in, puffing up his muscles and walking as if he were sashaying his feet forward. It was weird, but for some reason Viggo was sure he looked impressive.

"Do you have a stomach cramp?" Ingrid asked him when she saw him begin strutting.

"You can say what you want, but soon I'll be famous in all Norghana and you'll be grateful to walk beside me."

"For one thing, I doubt that very much, and for another, it'll never happen," Nilsa said, looking convinced.

"Besides, you can't go telling your adventures to bards and troubadours. They're secret since they're part of our missions," Ingrid told him.

"Don't worry, my beautiful blonde with eyes the color of the ocean. I switch one kingdom for another, one goal for another. No one's ever going to realize where I was, or what happened in the telling."

"Oh sure, since you're the slyest person in all Tremia," Astrid intervened, who did not believe Viggo could disguise his feats properly.

"I don't know why you say that, I'm very sly. My doings are

devious and secret. No one knows them."

"No one will know about them if they don't come out of your mouth," Ingrid told him. "The moment you open it, everyone will know them and it'll reach the ears of those who will consider you a traitor to the kingdom for blabbering."

"I doubt it very much, my Archer goddess of the sea," Viggo replied, pretending to release an arrow at her heart.

"You should be careful what you say out there, especially to those who will spread it through squares and taverns," Egil warned him. "Being a Ranger involves not revealing our missions, and being Royal Eagles even more. King Thoran won't appreciate the least reference to the missions he's entrusted us with."

Viggo was thoughtful.

"I don't think I've told anyone anything that might be used against me."

"You don't *think* so?" Ingrid asked him with a look of horror on her face.

"I'm sure. You worry too much about everything. You're not living life to the fullest. We must enjoy the moment. That said, I'm going to the city to speak with those bards."

"It's like talking to a door..." Nilsa said, shaking her head.

Ingrid snorted hard while she watched Viggo head into the city with his peacock strut.

"I'm going to talk to the royal bard to see what that numbskull has told him," said Ingrid.

"It would also be a good idea for you to watch what he shares in the city," Astrid advised her.

"Yeah, as soon as I see the bard I'll follow my little numbskull to see what messes he gets into."

"And to make sure he doesn't drink all the beer in the city..." Nilsa said.

"Yeah, that too," Ingrid said, rolling her eyes as she left.

"Are you coming to the temple with us, Nilsa?" Astrid asked.

"If you don't mind me not coming with you, I have several things to deal with here."

"Things to do with handsome boys of the Rangers, or the Royal Guard?" Astrid asked with a mischievous smile.

Nilsa blushed. "I won't say no to that... but Gondabar has asked me to help him with a couple things I used to handle and which apparently my substitute isn't doing very well. I'm obliged to see to them."

"Oh, in that case, go," Astrid told her.

"Besides, I want to hear all the gossip and tattle circulating through the court, and I can only do so if I wander around and speak to everyone, handsome boys included," she said with a naughty smile.

Lasgol and Egil chuckled.

"Nilsa is better than you at getting information," Astrid said to Egil, joking.

"I'll say she is. I'm going to hire her as an agent," Egil said, also joking.

Nilsa shook her hands in refusal.

"I have enough duties, thank you, I don't need any more. All the gossiping and finding out what's cooking I do as a hobby. I've always liked that."

"In that case I won't hire you, because when a hobby becomes a job you lose interest," Egil replied with a smile.

"Exactly," Nilsa said as she raced off as if she were going to run out of time for all the things she had to find out.

Lasgol looked at Astrid, who smiled at him sweetly.

"Astrid and I will come with you to the temple," Lasgol said, and Astrid smiled.

"Great. I'm not expecting complications, so we don't need the whole group," Egil explained. "We're only going to have a friendly chat with an Ice Cleric."

"I don't trust anyone anymore, and the fact that he's a Cleric doesn't give me any confidence either," Astrid said, taking out one of her knives and studying it carefully to make sure it was in perfect condition.

"I only know that trouble always finds us, whether we want it or not. So I'm also going to come prepared," Lasgol said as he slung his composite bow over his shoulder and picked a quiver filled with arrows of several types, some Elemental ones among them.

Egil smiled. "Caution is always the best strategy, even when we're going to visit a temple and in it are only men of faith."

They left the Royal Castle and headed downtown. The castle guards let them through without even stopping them. Everyone knew who they were and respected them so much that they did not dare bother them. It was a feeling Lasgol was not used to and it surprised him. The admiration and respect they inspired had him mystified. During most of his life he had been either hated or ignored, or held in suspicion. This new chapter of his life seemed strange, although he had to admit he liked it. Seeing looks of appreciation was different from the looks of hatred he had been so used to. It was a change he was thankful for.

Egil led them to the center of the great capital beside the main square. As they walked they remained alert to anyone who might be following them or to any possible problem they might encounter. Lasgol had the feeling he was going to be attacked from behind again and could not shake it off. He kept glancing back every now and then. Egil's investigations had made him nervous, and he now saw shadows following them everywhere. The day before he had been more at ease, but knowing that Egil had agents throughout the city and that it was possible that other agents or the like were watching them had him restless.

When they arrived at the square, Egil led them along a wide street north of the square to another plaza which only had one entrance. In the middle was a building which they immediately recognized as the Great Ice Temple of the city.

"Wow… what a curious building," Lasgol commented as he looked at the temple with great curiosity. It was unmistakable, a completely white construction built to imitate the shape of a tall, rectangular glacier. It looked like it was really made of ice. Lasgol had the impression of being back on the Frozen Continent, looking at the glaciers he had seen there. The only difference was, that instead of having a blue or dark shade like the ones they had seen there, the building was pure snow-white, and when the sun hit it, it hurt his eyes.

"Hadn't you seen it before?" Astrid asked him.

"No, I've never come to this square…" Lasgol admitted.

"That's natural. There's only the temple here, and only those who want to pray to the Ice Gods come here," Egil explained. "Although in Norghana almost everyone believes in the Ice Gods, in one way or another, not many come to pray."

"Praying or paying homage to the Gods doesn't really suit the Norghanian mentality…" Astrid said. "Well, except for funerals, then yes, so the deceased may enter the Realm of the Ice Gods and live there the rest of their new life with the Gods."

Egil nodded. "That's why there are only a few Ice Temples located throughout Norghana. To be exact, there's one at each of the four corners besides this one, which is the main and most important one."

"It's so Norghanians can find them easily," Astrid joked. "There are many morons, but at least they know where north, south, east, and west are."

"I wouldn't be so sure," Lasgol said, chuckling.

"Let's go in," Egil said and headed to the entrance door, which seemed to be dug out of a glacier's icy wall.

They went it and found themselves in a curious place. The interior of the temple was mostly hollow and with walls imitating a glacier's rose in different areas, forming chambers. In the center of the great building there was a fountain crowned with somewhat abstract representations of the Ice Gods. They had no definite shape.

They saw two Ice Priests who appeared to be praying to some sculptures that had to represent the Ice Gods, only they had no definite shape either. They looked like strong Norghanian warriors but without recognizable features. The priests were wearing long white robes. Their hair and beards were long and white too. They looked like the Ice Magi, but in their hands they carried primitive staves of white cedar instead of the elaborate white ones with gems of power at their tips that the Magi used. From what Egil had told them, the clerics lived in the temples and rarely left them. They spent their days praying to their gods and tending to those who visited the temple. The Norghanians believed the gods listened to the pleas of those who came to the temples and prayed with the Ice Priests.

They toured the temple in silence, gazing at its construction, and they saw a few locals praying on their knees beside a couple of clerics. They were asking for health, money, and fortitude to face the days to come.

In a separate chamber at the end, bigger than the rest, an ancient cleric was resting on what looked like a throne of ice. For a moment Lasgol wondered whether it was an Ice God descended to earth. They went over to him slowly without making any noise, since he seemed to be sleeping.

But he suddenly opened his eyes.

"Welcome to the temple," he said with a smile.

"Thank you, we come humbly seeking the blessing of the Ice

Gods," Egil said in a low voice.

"Humility is always necessary when you seek the blessing of the gods," the cleric replied.

"Do we stand before the Principal Cleric of the Temple?" Egil asked.

"That is so. I am Helge, and I'm the person responsible for the order and the temple."

"We are grateful to be tended to in the temple."

"Everyone who seeks to pray to the Ice Gods is welcome in this temple."

"We also come seeking wisdom and guidance," Egil said in a tone of great respect, bowing his head to the priest.

"Are you believers?" he asked, looking each of them in the eyes.

"We are," Egil replied before anyone could say anything.

Lasgol did not believe much in the gods, ice or any other, but he did believe that a little help was always welcome, whether human or divine. Astrid was not a believer either, but like any good Norghanian she had grown up believing in the Ice Gods and she respected them. The only one in the group who did not believe in the Ice Gods and admitted it openly was Viggo—according to him, if they had never come to help him, why should he believe in them.

"I am glad to hear it," the cleric said, nodding heavily. "In what area are you looking for wisdom and guidance? How can this servant of the Ice Gods help you?"

"We are here because of the preachers who are roaming Norghana with a message of death and destruction," Egil explained.

The cleric nodded heavily again.

"There have always been those who believe that salvation is in destruction. Their view cannot be more erroneous, and those who follow them will end their days doomed to the lie they have believed in and divulged."

"That's precisely what troubles us—the message those preachers are spreading about the new order and which people are listening to. It's a message they're using to fool the people by using fear as their means. That's not the message of the Ice Gods," Egil explained in a calm tone marked with concern.

"It's not indeed. The Ice Gods love their people, the Norghanians. They will never let anything happen to us since we are their people and we serve and worship them. They protect and guide us, and when we fall they carry us to their realm of infinite ice."

"Do you know the preachers I'm talking about and their message?" Egil asked him, trying to make sure the cleric knew what he was referring to.

"I have also heard talk about those preachers who proclaim the end of the era of men and the beginning of a new order ruled by the all-powerful lords," Helge said saddened.

"That's them, yes, and that's their message," said Egil.

"Their blasphemy has reached me. You are not the first to come and ask me about them. The faithful inform me and keep me up to date about what goes on in Norghana. It might seem that I am no longer in possession of all my faculties, but I assure you that I am, by the grace of the Ice Gods."

"If you know about these preachers of fire and destruction, you'll be able to tell us about their leader..." Egil said.

The cleric remained thoughtful.

"Why do you want to know who leads them? What's in it for you?"

Astrid and Lasgol exchanged glances. The cleric wanted to know their reasons. He was not going to give them information without a reason, and it would have to be a good one. Egil's mind must be thinking the same thing.

"We are guided by our good will and respect for the Ice Gods," Egil explained. "We have come across several of these preachers and their message has troubled us. They put fear in the people... this might create despair, anguish, panic even. We want to protect the people."

"That's why I asked the King to throw them out of Norghana," the cleric said.

"And he's doing so. But new preachers keep appearing. That's why we want to get to the root of the matter and pull it out."

"That's the only way to get rid of all the weeds, true," the old cleric agreed with him.

"Then will you help us find their leader?"

"I'll try, since it's for the good of all Norghanians. The Ice Gods hear your concern. There are more like you; I listen to all and try to help all."

"We're thankful for it," Egil bowed his head in respect.

"A repentant preacher came to us. We found him one morning at the door of the temple. He was dying, badly wounded. We looked after him, called several healers who treated him. In the deliriousness caused by the fever he spoke about his lord, he who had made him see the light of the morrow."

"That's who we're seeking," Egil said. "Did he mention his name or alias, anything?"

The cleric shook his head.

"No, he did not mention any name."

"Pity, that doesn't help us much…" Egil said ruefully.

"What he did mention, and I found it very surprising, was the head of a giant snake. That I remember well, since it caused a great impression in me."

"The head of a giant snake?" Egil asked. This detail must have seemed very significant, because he interrupted the cleric's explanation.

"Yes, he spoke about the giant snake head that made him see the future of fire and destruction. Take into consideration that he was delirious. It's likely that the vision occurred only in his mind, forced by the high fever."

"That is highly likely. What did he say about the leader? You said he didn't give his name?"

"No, but he said he carried two swords with snake heads on them."

"He said snake? Not dragon?"

"He said snake, that I remember because I thought that only an evil man would carry swords with snakes on them."

"Did he say where he was? How to reach him?"

"No, he did not," he shook his head.

"Could we speak to the repentant?" Egil asked.

"I'm afraid that's not possible. The poor wretch died a few days later."

"And has no one else like him come?" Egil asked.

"No, no one has."

"Has the temple received any information that might help us locate this leader?" Egil insisted.

"I'd like to help you, because you're good Norghanians and servants of the Ice Gods, but I do not have the information you seek. If I had it I would have given it to the Royal Guard so they could apprehend him."

"I understand. Thank you for your time," Egil said resignedly. They were not going to get any more information.

"Time is all I have, until the Ice Gods claim me to their side."

Astrid, Lasgol, and Egil took their leave of the cleric.

"Thank you for listening to us."

"Go and honor the gods," Helge said.

They left the temple down-spirited. The answers seemed to be hiding from them, avoiding them. Once outside in the square, they shared opinions.

"Well, we didn't have much luck in there," Lasgol admitted disappointedly.

"I wouldn't say that," Egil said.

"Did you learn something?" Astrid asked him.

"A couple of important things, in my opinion."

"Tell us then," Lasgol said.

"The swords with a pommel in the shape of a snake's head are very likely the same ones you saw, Lasgol."

"The ones I saw had dragon pommels..." Lasgol recalled, narrowing his eyes to think.

"True. But to the uninitiated, to someone affected by something external, the head, whether snake or dragon, might appear one and the same. They're both reptiles."

"Which leads us to the conclusion that the leader we're looking for is none other than Drugan Volskerian," Astrid reasoned.

"Exactly. Drugan Volskerian is the one creating these preachers and sending them out into the world with that message of destruction."

"That means... it's not my uncle..." said Astrid. "For a moment I thought it might be him and his sect... or whatever they are..."

"Yeah, I also considered that, but this clears him. It's not your uncle who's creating these preachers."

"Then what is my uncle searching for? Why is he involved in this?"

Lasgol scratched his temple. "More so... what is it they both want, your uncle and Drugan Volskerian? Is it the same thing, or are they after different goals?"

Egil nodded repeatedly.

"I said I had some answers, not all of them. We have to keep searching. Those are good questions we must find answers to. We'll get to the bottom of this, it's simply a question of digging. It might take us time, but we'll get to it."

"Let's hope it's before anything horrible happens. I have a terrible feeling in the pit of my stomach and I can't get rid of it," Lasgol admitted.

"You're not the only one," Astrid said.

Chapter 36

For several days Egil continued searching for information about Drugan Volskerian and Astrid tried to find out where her uncle might be. Neither was making much progress, although they were determined to find them both, no matter the cost. They both left the castle in the morning and did not come back until late in the evening, once they had exhausted all possibilities for any clues or hypothesis they were following. It would take time and effort, but they were determined to succeed.

Lasgol used the time when Astrid and Egil were busy with their search to take Trotter and go out to visit Ona and Camu. After a few days with them, Lasgol had to move them to a deeper forest further from the city. Camu was working on improving his flight and needed a lake or deep pond to practice at, particularly the descent and definitely the landing. He took them to the Green Ogre Forest. This was a little frequented place because an ogre had once been found there and no one went near for fear there were more or that another would appear. In the middle of the forest was a large blue pond deep enough to cushion Camu's bumps when landing.

Eicewald joined them in the forest as well and helped Camu improve his flying on top of developing a new skill. The creature wanted to develop a powerful blow with his tail, since he had heard that dragons used their claws and tails as weapons. Camu had no claws but he did have a long tail, so he insisted on developing a skill that would allow him to deliver a tremendous tail lash to defeat his enemies. Camu's long tail was already powerful enough that he could knock down a man, but Camu wanted something more powerful.

Lasgol enjoyed Eicewald's lessons and Camu's progress. The creature was gradually improving his flight, although he crashed into the pond water every now and then. Eicewald assured him it was only a matter of time and practice for Camu to master flying. The powerful tail lash, on the other hand, resisted him, but since he was so stubborn, he did not give up and kept trying. Lasgol hoped he would end up succeeding, more than anything else because he was so stubborn. He would not stop trying.

At the same time, Lasgol used the days off to work with Eicewald, both to fix his inner bridge and improve his skills. He followed the Ice Mage's advice, and although he still had not managed to improve his skills significantly, he did feel like he was making progress. He felt like he was improving and was closer to achieving his goal. Unlike when he tried to improve a skill on his own and nothing happened, in the Mage's presence and with his help, Lasgol could feel the skill beginning to improve inside him, even if he did not have complete control of it.

Eicewald told him that he spent his nights studying the silver pearl. So far he had not managed to decipher what it was or what it was for, but its inner source of power was so distinct that he had to hide it in a special box. The box was another object of power with a special skill: masking power. It had been created to hold bewitched weapons, and although it could not disguise all the pearl's power, it disguised it a little. It was enough for now, but Eicewald was already planning to take the powerful object somewhere else. The Ice Magi of the Tower had noticed that Eicewald had a powerful object with him and were asking what it was and what power it treasured. Considering his bad experience with the Star of Sea and Life, Eicewald did not want to take any risks. He planned to hide the silver pearl some place where no Mage would find it. Meanwhile, he had created two powerful ice traps that protected the object. If anyone tried to grab it, the traps would deal with the thief.

Lasgol realized that Eicewald did not trust the other Ice Magi in the Tower, something Lasgol found strange, since several were his own pupils who he had prepared and guided to become Ice Magi. Eicewald had told him that power corrupted the souls of the weak-spirited and that one always had to be careful not to show off that power because envy and greed were dangerous, treacherous enemies. Lasgol appreciated all the Mage's lessons and advice.

One morning several days later, the Royal Castle woke up in the middle of a loud disturbance. Warning horns sounded and everyone jumped out of bed. The Panthers got dressed and ready as fast as they could. They grabbed their bows, arrows, and other weapons and prepared to face whatever was happening.

"Everyone, with me!" Ingrid cried, already at the door.

"Are we being attacked?" Nilsa asked.

"I don't think so. That's a call to line up, not of alarm," Astrid said as she listened with tilted head.

"True, it's not an attack, but something's going on because they're calling everyone," said Lasgol.

"I can make out four different horns… it's true, they're calling everyone to line up," Egil said, also listening carefully.

"So let's go then," Viggo said. "I want to know what the racket's all about. Maybe it'll be something fun."

They left their room and found all the Rangers running downstairs to line up before the Tower. The Panthers quickly followed them and entered the courtyard. They stood in the first line to better see what was happening and also due to rank, since being Royal Eagles they outranked their veteran comrades. The Rangers finished lining up and Gondabar appeared with his personal assistants and stood in front of the Panthers.

"What's going on, sir?" Ingrid asked Gondabar.

"You'll soon find out. Line up and wait for orders," he told them without a hint of whether it was a serious matter or not.

"Yes, sir," Ingrid replied.

To his left, Lasgol could see the castle soldiers running to line up in the bailey while several officers shouted orders at the top of their lungs. For a moment he thought something bad was happening, although there was no movement on the battlements and the call was to "line up," not "alarm" or "to arms." Something that also puzzled him was that the soldiers were carrying Norghanian flags and banners, which only happened when they went to war or foreign dignitaries came to visit. The officers lined up in front of their men in arms.

Something similar was going on with the Ice Magi. They saw Eicewald leading   the other four magi in their snow-white robes with their ice staves. They lined up in front of their tower, powerful and undaunted.

Another group that caught everyone's attention was the Invincibles of the Ice, who lined up in their white cloaks and white standards, with winged helmets, swords, and round shields. The best infantry of the continent were lined up beside the Ice Magi. Seeing them all together in their white attire, Lasgol could not help but appreciate the power they represented and the fear they instilled in the enemies of Norghana.

Once they finished lining up, all the soldiers of the guard, the

Rangers, the Invincibles of the Ice, and the Ice Magi stood in position, forming four compact blocks.

"Even the Invincibles are lined up," whispered Nilsa, "This must be big."

"Yeah, because they don't like to waste time," Ingrid whispered back.

"I find it strange that even the Ice Magi are lined up," Astrid commented in a barely audible whisper. "Something important must be afoot."

"Definitely." Egil said.

"D'you know what's going on?" Lasgol asked him.

"I can make an educated guess."

"And that is?" Nilsa was eager to know.

"We have an important visitor," Egil replied

Suddenly the doors of the palace opened and the Royal Guard came out, followed by the Royal Rangers. After them came several members of the court in dress armor, cloaks, and fancy clothes in red and white, the colors of the kingdom. They were mostly nobles of the east, who made way for the two final figures. In their best regal finery came King Thoran and his brother, Duke Orten. They were wearing fancy armor in silver and gold and the King was wearing the royal crown.

The Royal Guard stood in two blocks before the entrance to the palace on both sides of the door. The Royal Rangers stood in front of them, barring access. The members of the court were behind, and then the King and his brother stood in the middle of the corridor the Royal Rangers were guarding.

They waited.

"Definitely, someone important is coming," Ingrid whispered.

"How exciting! No one warned us of any important visitor," Nilsa whispered.

"I don't feel like having visitors," Viggo said, wrinkling his nose.

"Behave. Don't say a word and everything will be fine," Ingrid warned him.

Suddenly, a warning horn sounded. The officers ordered everyone to stand firm.

The gates of the Royal Castle opened wide.

The Panthers saw a retinue begin to cross under the portcullis and enter the Royal Castle's bailey. First they made out a dozen light cavalry soldiers that led a column of about fifty infantry men. They looked at them carefully.

"Don't you think those soldiers look familiar?" Viggo asked.

"Of course they look familiar. The tear-shaped shield, javelin in hand and more on their backs, the green and white colors green, the embroidered white flower with six heads worn as a badge on their chests…"

"They're Irinel soldiers," Nilsa said.

"They are," Astrid confirmed as she watched them with narrowed eyes.

In the center of the infantry column was an elegant carriage with elaborate carvings and details of gold and silver. The carriage was drawn by four magnificent white horses, as beautiful as the carriage.

"That's a royal carriage…" Lasgol guessed.

"I was going to say a carriage worthy of my level," Viggo commented, smiling.

"Who would be traveling in the royal carriage? Has King Kendryk come to sign the treaty?" Lasgol asked.

"He did say he would fulfill his part of the deal, which confused me at the time," Astrid said. "I wondered what he meant by that."

"Yeah, I was also surprised by the King's comment," said Lasgol.

"Well, whatever he's come to do, he's here today," Ingrid said.

"I'm afraid it's not the King of Irinel traveling in that carriage," Egil ventured.

They all looked at him.

"It's not? Then who is it?" Ingrid asked.

Egil nodded for them to keep watching. "We'll soon find out."

The retinue stopped before the Royal Rangers. At an order from King Thoran, the Royal Rangers split in two and formed a corridor of honor. Two officers of the retinue stood by the carriage door and opened it.

Before the expectant gaze of all present, a figure exited the carriage.

The Panthers recognized her at once and their jaws dropped.

It was the Royal Princess Heulyn of Irinel.

"It can't be her," Ingrid shook her head.

A second figure leapt out of the carriage, dressed like a Ranger but wearing the green and white colors of Irinel and carrying a bow on her back. She took off her hood and they all saw who it was.

"That's Valeria," Astrid said, annoyed.

"Then it is indeed Princess Heulyn," said Ingrid.

"What are they doing here?" Nilsa said blankly.

"I don't understand…" Viggo said, scratching his head.

Lasgol looked over at Egil. He had a bad feeling about the reason behind the Princess's visit and this royal welcome.

"You'll soon understand," Egil told them with a mischievous grin.

From among the nobles and courtesans came Ambassador Larsen, who hastened to welcome the Princess with elaborate bows and sweet words. The Princess listened haughtily without deigning to glance at him and allowed him to make way for her to the King and his brother. Valeria followed behind. A dozen of the Princess' guards escorted them along the corridor the Norghanian Royal Rangers and Guards had formed.

Princess Heulyn was well aware that everyone was looking at her and that this welcome was in her honor. She walked stiffly, with her chin high and a condescending gaze. Her expression was so haughty that she looked like a goddess whom everyone must pay homage to at every step or suffer the consequences of her wrath.

As she arrived before the nobles they parted to let her pass, amid elaborate bows and greetings, so she could get to the King. The Princess did not deign to return any of the greetings she received. She went on as if neither soldiers, guards, or courtiers deserved a single glance from her. She walked as if all of them were so beneath her that they did not even exist. That was likely the case in her mind.

Heulyn reached King Thoran and stopped. Her retinue did so as well. Ambassador Larsen made the introductions.

"My liege, allow me to introduce Princess Heulyn of the Kingdom of Irinel. Princess, may I introduce you to his Majesty King Thoran of Norghana."

King Thoran bowed to the Princess.

"Welcome to the Kingdom of Norghana, Royal Princess of Irinel," the King said.

There was a pause, and everyone wondered how the Princess would react. Especially the Snow Panthers, who already knew her and her character. The situation could get awkward quickly, depending on how the Princess reacted, since King Thoran would not tolerate any rudeness before his combined forces. And everyone knew the King's temper.

"Thank you for this royal welcome. I am happy to be in the Kingdom of Norghana," the Princess replied with a courtesy.

"A Royal Princess deserves a royal welcome. I wish to express my most sincere appreciation and respect, and that of the Kingdom of Norghana," Thoran said, extremely courteous.

"The feeling is mutual, and I can assure you that you have the respect of the Kingdom of Irinel," Heulyn replied.

King Thoran bowed in acknowledgment.

"I believe you have not met my brother, Duke Orten," Thoran said with a gesture to his brother.

"I have not had the pleasure," Heulyn said.

"The pleasure is all mine," the Duke replied. "You are indeed a true beauty of Irinel," Orten said with an elaborate bow.

"I appreciate the compliment, Duke," the Princess said, looking as if everyone knew that.

This left the Panthers mystified. Lasgol did not know what to think. The Princess was not behaving as he had expected her to. Why was she here? Had her father sent her to ratify the deal? Why was she not behaving in her usual rebellious manner? Why was she being so respectful and contained?

"If you will do me the honor," Thoran said and indicated the great door that accessed the interior of the castle.

"By all means, my liege," the Princess replied.

"I will lead the way," Ambassador Larsen said, moving ahead.

The Princess turned to her escort and signaled that it was not necessary for them to accompany her inside.

King Thoran and Princess Heulyn went inside the Castle between the Royal Guard, following Ambassador Larsen. Duke Orten followed them a moment later, and the court nobles went in behind.

Lasgol watched the scene blankly; he looked at his friends, who gave him the same blank look. No one seemed to understand what was going on. No one, except for Egil.

"What's happening?" Lasgol asked his friend, looking for an answer to what they had just witnessed.

"I'm afraid this is the prelude to a great event."

"What great event?" Ingrid asked, puzzled.

"One that unites kingdoms and lineages," Egil said with a big smile.

"What unites kingdoms and lineages? Gold?" Viggo asked.

"That too, but I don't think that's what's happening here," said Astrid.

"It's a royal wedding," Nilsa guessed. "What's going to happen is there's going to be a royal wedding!" she guessed with eyes wide open.

Lasgol threw his head back when he realized Nilsa was absolutely right.

"Irrefutable, my dear friends. We're in for a royal wedding," Egil beamed.

Chapter 37

By sundown the news of the royal wedding between King Thoran of Norghana and Princess Heulyn of the Kingdom of Irinel had spread throughout the realm like a hurricane wind coming down from the Eternal Mountains. The Panthers had already guessed as much when they witnessed the welcome, but just in case they asked Gondabar, who confirmed it.

"Indeed, King Thoran will marry the Princess of Irinel, and with that the kingdoms of Norghana and Irinel will be united in a blood alliance," The leader of the Rangers explained.

"Is this then the last part of the deal King Kendryk meant?" Ingrid asked.

"It all makes sense," Astrid said.

"King Thoran and King Kendryk agreed on the wedding for the union of the kingdoms and lineages," explained Gondabar.

"And for that they needed to rescue the Princess from the Druids first," Nilsa reasoned.

"Yes, that's true," Gondabar confirmed.

"So there could be no deal if there was no Princess," Viggo reasoned.

"There can't be a wedding without a bride," Ingrid said.

"That's right," Gondabar confirmed again. "You have done an excellent job, and as a result we have a royal wedding which will unite both our kingdoms in a blood alliance. Norghana will be stronger as a result of this union. It's an achievement you can be proud of."

"We are, sir," Egil said in a kind tone, although not very happily.

"When will the wedding be, sir?" Nilsa asked.

"No date has been set for the great event yet. The wedding will not be announced until there is one. There are still some loose ends to tie up," their leader told them and then left to continue his duties.

The Panthers left the Tower and continued watching the group of Irinel soldiers, who waited stoically for word from the Princess.

"Don't you have the feeling we've been used to kidnap a bride? Or is it only me?" Astrid said, frowning.

"Yeah… I was thinking exactly the same thing," Ingrid agreed.

"Do you think her father is making her marry Thoran?" Nilsa asked with a look of disgust on her face.

"But she doesn't seem to oppose it..." Lasgol commented.

"Sometimes duty is a heavy burden that makes you do things you would never do if you were free from the responsibility," Egil said, looking like he was speaking from personal experience.

"What the know-it-all means is that she's doing what she must for the kingdom of Irinel," Viggo said.

"And for her parents, the King and Queen of Irinel," Egil added.

"Well, that doesn't leave me more at ease," said Astrid. "Duty or not, the Princess was hiding, and we kidnapped her to deliver her to her father."

"Who in turn is delivering her to our wonderful King," Nilsa said with a look of horror.

"It's not dignified or honorable," Ingrid said, folding her arms.

"I think they're made for one another," Viggo commented. He did not care at all what happened to either of them.

"The fact that we don't like her or him isn't a good enough reason to not feel responsible," said Lasgol.

"On the other hand, we followed orders from two kings," Ingrid said. "We can't be held accountable. We did as we were ordered. Our duty is to obey the throne."

"Following orders doesn't free us from certain personal responsibilities..." Astrid said. "In the end, we're the ones who carried out the orders..."

"I'm not proud of what we've done, to be honest..." Nilsa admitted. "Just thinking that she's going to marry Thoran makes my stomach turn."

"It could've been worse—it could've been Orten," Viggo said humorously.

"Don't be a smartass," Ingrid chided.

"What? It's the truth," he replied defensively.

"I don't feel comfortable with this situation either," Lasgol admitted. "I have a bad feeling in the pit of my stomach..."

"Only kings and queens know the reasons behind their designs. Commoners don't question them, they comply with them," Egil recited.

"Let me translate: be quiet and obey, or become a king or queen," Viggo told them.

"Something like that, yes," Egil smiled at him. "We don't know the true reasons behind this wedding—the Kings', the queen's, or the Princess's. We can only guess and arrive at conclusions that might be wrong."

"You mean to say that the Princess might *want* to marry Thoran?" Nilsa asked, astonished.

"Power is a great motivator, and aphrodisiac," Egil replied with his head to one side.

"So the charming Princess is marrying for power," Viggo clarified.

"I don't think so," Astrid shook her head.

"Egil is right. We don't know Princess Heulyn's reasons. Until we do, we can't arrive at a conclusion," Ingrid said firmly.

"If you think so, but I don't believe she's getting married for power," Astrid insisted.

Lasgol was undecided. The Princess was haughty and spoiled—she might be doing it for power. Becoming the Queen of Norghana would allow her to compete with her own father's power. But it seemed more likely she was being forced to marry out of duty to the realm and crown. They would have to find out which of the two it was, or whether there was a third option they were not considering.

They saw a figure coming out of the palace accompanied by two officers of the Royal Guard—it was Valeria. She headed to where the Irinel soldiers were lining up, exchanging a few words with the soldiers and the two officers of the Royal Guard. A moment later the Irinel soldiers followed the Norghanian officers to the barracks.

Valeria turned and saw the Panthers in front of the Ranger's Tower. She came over nonchalantly.

"It seems we meet again," said the Princess's blonde bodyguard with a friendly smile.

"Thank you for speaking well of us to the King and Queen of Irinel," Nilsa said, voicing the same thing Lasgol wanted to say but dare not, so as not to have an argument with Astrid. Lasgol recognized the hatred Astrid felt for Valeria, and although in part it was because of the betrayal, part of it was her interest in him, and that made him nervous.

"I had a debt of gratitude to you. I wasn't going to let the princess drag you to the gallows without a reason."

"Why not? I bet you'd love to see us dead," Ingrid said.

"That's not true. That's never been my wish, to see you dead," Valeria replied,

"Oh no? Even though we found you out and sentenced you to exile?" Viggo said.

"I've never wished any of you ill. In fact, I owe you my life. You pardoned me, and I haven't forgotten that. I owe you my life, and because of that I'll try to repay my debt to each one of you."

"Well, it's going to take you quite a while, because there's a few of us," Viggo said sarcastically.

"Let's say that my words in your favor to the King and Queen of Irinel to prevent the Princess from hanging you are worth the life of one of you. I'm going to choose the person I most appreciate in this sublime group," she said, looking at Lasgol with bright eyes. "Lasgol, we're even now."

"That's not necessary..." Lasgol began to say. He did not think Valeria owed him her life for having her banished instead of executed for her betrayal.

"Don't bother repaying me for anything. If it'd been up to me you'd be dead, and my opinion hasn't changed," Astrid said with a glare full of rage.

Valeria shrugged. "As you wish. But life takes many turns, I'm living proof of that, and you never know when you'll need a friendly hand, even one like mine."

"I'm never going to need your help, nor would I accept it," Astrid said, convinced.

"We'll see..." Valeria said, shrugging.

"There's something I don't understand though.... You're freely walking around the palace... why haven't you been sent to prison for being a Dark Ranger?" Nilsa asked her.

"That's true. You're on the list of Dark Rangers and there's a conviction over your head," said Ingrid.

Valeria shrugged and smiled.

"Politics..."

"What do you mean by 'politics?'" Astrid wanted to know since she was not convinced by the answer.

"They can't touch her because she's under the protection of the Royal House of Irinel," Egil explained. "She has diplomatic immunity."

"Even though she's a traitor to the realm?" Astrid asked with a look of disbelief on her face.

"Even though she's a traitor, yes. It's a crime to this kingdom. If the King of Irinel gives her his protection we can't try her or imprison her. It's the same with the rest of his official retinue or the Princess herself. They all enjoy immunity," Egil explained. "Otherwise no member of any royal house would ever visit another kingdom."

"I can't believe it!" Astrid cried.

"Yeah, now that I remember, ambassadors and the like have the same protection," Nilsa said.

"Yes they do. It is necessary or they would expire prematurely." "I also had my doubts, but my lady, Princess Heulyn, assured me no one would lay a finger on me as long as I'm under her protection. And from what I've seen… it's true. It looks like King Thoran won't convict me," Valeria said.

"Perhaps he won't, but we will," Astrid said with a look of hatred. "You've violated your sentence. You're back in Norghana. You know what's waiting for you. We warned you when we banished you."

"I serve Princess Heulyn. I go wherever she goes, it's my duty. I didn't decide to come here. My duty has brought me back to Norghana."

"Don't talk like that, you traitor, we all remember very well what you did and why your life was spared. You came back, and you knew it would cost you your life," Astrid said, pointing her finger as if it were one of her knives.

"Not coming would also have cost me my life. I couldn't fail at my post, my duty, Princess Heulyn wouldn't have accepted it."

"So death by the Princess or death by the Panthers—you're in a tight fit," Viggo said ironically.

"Yes, I realize that. It wasn't pleasant to receive King Kendryk's order to accompany and protect the Princess. But I had no choice."

"Circumstances change, but you knew your punishment if you returned," Ingrid said.

"I agree with Astrid and Ingrid on this. It doesn't matter if you're here on orders. You knew what awaited you and you came back anyway," Viggo said to Valeria with a lethal gleam in his eyes.

"We're not going to kill her," Lasgol said firmly, emphasizing it with a gesture of his hands.

"Oh, we're not?" Astrid raised an eyebrow and reached for her knives.

"Of course not," Egil supported Lasgol. "We can't kill her... before the wedding that is."

They all looked at Egil blankly.

"Before the wedding?" Nilsa said, frowning.

"If we kill her *before* the wedding, Princess Heulyn will demand King Thoran to deliver our heads on a pike for taking the life of her confidant who has immunity. King Thoran can't risk the wedding for an incident, so he would be forced to grant the Princess's request and we'd end up decapitated or hanged."

"Oops, well right now's not a good time for me," said Viggo. "I haven't yet lived my greatest and most heroic adventures."

"I'd prefer not being hanged either, I have a lot to live for," said Nilsa.

"They don't need to know it was us..." said Astrid. "I can do it without leaving a trace."

"You do realize I'm right here in front of you listening, don't you?" Valeria said in a tone of disbelief at how ridiculous they sounded.

"We don't care whether you listen or if you're right here," Ingrid said. "The result will be the same, whatever we decide to do. You won't be able to avoid it."

"I'm not saying I won't, but if you kill me, even if you don't leave a trail," Valeria said, looking at Astrid, "the Princess will know it was you and will ask the King for your heads."

"And how's that?" Nilsa asked her.

"I've told her our personal history and what happened," Valeria said. "I've also told her that if I came back to Norghana you'd kill me."

"And does she fancy having a traitor as her bodyguard?" Ingrid asked her, frowning.

"She understood. Unlike others, Princess Heulyn is an intelligent person who knows how to appreciate certain values and skills in people."

"I'd never trust anyone who already betrayed others," Ingrid said.

"That's because you're a strict and dignified person. Let's say that the Princess isn't as much—her morals are a little more flexible than yours. Her vision and values are a lot more malleable than yours."

"You mean she's quite the viper," Viggo said and made the sign of a snake with his arm.

"My lady is a survivor, and very intelligent,"

"Is she really going to marry Thoran?" Nilsa asked, as if she found it preposterous.

"It's her parents' wish and her duty to her kingdom," Valeria replied seriously.

"Does she have any idea who she's marrying? The kind of person she's marrying?" Ingrid asked.

"She knows she's marrying the King of Norghana to become the Queen and unite the kingdoms of Irinel and Norghana by blood. She is also aware of the kind of person King Thoran is. His reputation precedes him—he is well known in Irinel."

"Up close and personal he's much worse," Viggo said. "You'd better tell your Princess. If I were her I'd run in the opposite direction."

"The Princess has decided to follow her parents' desires and get married. That's all I can tell you," Valeria said, spreading her hands.

"No matter how much I might want to be a Queen I'd never marry like this, and least of all to that man," Nilsa said with a look of repulsion on her face.

"Yeah, I would also feel an insurmountable aversion," Ingrid said, "but I also understand that duty is duty."

"Marrying a heartless swine isn't acceptable, no matter how much it might be your duty," said Viggo.

Lasgol looked around in case anyone was listening. Speaking like this openly about the King was dangerous. Those words constituted treason, even coming from a Ranger.

Egil was nodding as he listened. "Many people want to be kings or queens but they forget the sacrifices and obligations that entails. This is a clear example. If you wish to be Queen of Norghana, you must accept marrying the King, no matter how abject and not honorable he might be."

"So, the viper of Irinel is going to marry the boar of Norghana—it's going to be an interesting match to see," Viggo said humorously.

"Be careful what you say," Ingrid scolded him as she also looked around to see whether anyone was listening.

"We'll have to wait for the events to unfold and see how this royal wedding develops," Egil said. "I understand there's still not a date for the nuptials."

Valeria shook her head.

"Not yet. It must be agreed upon, as well as some other details that are still being negotiated."

"Gold, no doubt," said Egil.

Valeria shrugged.

"I don't know the details, only that certain parts of the deal still need to be addressed."

"Now that the traitor's given us enough information, I think the best thing is to carry out the sentence. You don't all need to pay for it, I'll do it myself," Astrid said, taking out one of her knives,

"Astrid, no!" Lasgol cried as with a swift movement, he stood in front of her and grasped her hand with the knife by the wrist.

Viggo was watching Valeria with his hand on his chin, wondering.

"I think we can let her live until the wedding. Then things will change since the Princess will be Queen of Norghana and I understand she'll lose her immunity just like her escort. Isn't that so, Egil?"

Egil thought for a moment.

"Most likely, yes. I can't guarantee it, but yes, I think so."

"So, no immunity equals..." Viggo passed his finger along his neck from side to side.

"We're not going to kill Valeria, not now or later," Lasgol insisted.

"Speak for yourself, weirdo," said Viggo.

Lasgol, who was still holding Astrid's wrist firmly, looked into her eyes. He saw she would never yield.

"We'll wait for the royal wedding to take place. Then we'll decide what to do with the traitor," said Ingrid, closing the subject.

"That's for the best," Nilsa said.

Astrid relaxed and Lasgol let go of her wrist.

"I love you, Lasgol, but never try stopping me if I decide to act."

"Even if it's a terrible mistake?"

"You'll have to trust me. I don't make mistakes."

"I trust you. But killing Valeria is a huge mistake."

"Let's not argue because of her."

Lasgol nodded and let the matter be, although he had a knot in his stomach.

"Well it seems I'll live a little longer, at least until the royal wedding," Valeria said with absolute nonchalance, as if she did not mind too much.

"Enjoy what's left," Viggo told her.

"Thank you, I'm planning on it," she replied. She gave a small nod and walked away seductively.

Lasgol had a bad feeling, not only about Valeria's fate but about his relationship with Astrid. It was going to be tested, and it would be very difficult.

Chapter 38

The arrival of Heulyn and Valeria, besides the future royal wedding, had unsettled the group. It took them a couple days to come to terms with the new situation and resume their searches. Egil continued looking for the Warlock Drugan Volskerian and Astrid went on searching for her uncle Viggen Norling. Tired of not getting any answers, Astrid decided to visit her uncle's estate and see if she could find out any information about his whereabouts one way or another. Since it was not a good idea for anyone to search for answers alone and Lasgol was busy with Camu and his flying lessons, Viggo offered to act as bodyguard for Egil while Ingrid and Nilsa went with Astrid to her uncle's home. Seeing what had happened to Lasgol and considering they were going to stick their noses where they had no business, it was best to take every possible precaution.

With the first light of day, the three Rangers left the city at full gallop. Egil and Viggo also left early; they had to visit several of Egil's contacts and see whether they had any new, useful information. Egil was sure that soon they would find the clue they needed. Viggo was not so sure, but he did not oppose his friend because he wanted to check with the bards about the heroic odes about himself he had ordered from them. Lasgol and Eicewald arrived at the Green Ogre Forest and went to the blue pond, where they found Camu and Ona playing near the edge. As soon as they saw them coming the two creatures ran to welcome them. Lasgol received them with hugs and petting, Eicewald with friendly smiles.

The weather was a little off, Lasgol looked up at the sky and realized a storm was approaching and the winds were beginning to blow hard.

"I'm not sure it's a good idea to fly today…" he told Camu and pointed at the black clouds running toward the forest.

I fly, I not fear.

"I know you have no fear. You don't have much common sense either…" Lasgol told him.

Me much sense.

"Yeah, yeah… tons of it…"

"I think it would be wiser if we don't spend too much time on the flying exercise," Eicewald intervened to help Lasgol, "the wind is going to blow hard…"

I can fly with wind.

"I know, but although you can cope with the wind in the air, gliding, it will make it hard for you to land," Eicewald explained.

Maybe no good… Camu had to admit.

Ona chirped once in agreement.

"Very well. Let's hurry then. Do three take-offs and landings before the storm arrives," the Mage told Camu.

Okay, the creature messaged, and at once he called on his Drakonian Flight skill.

Lasgol watched Camu glow with strong silver flashes and suddenly those amazing wings appeared on his back, as magnificent as they were ethereal. Lasgol went over to Camu and tried to touch his right wing. His hand went through it, and as it did all the hairs on his hand, arm, and back of his head stood on end.

Wing of magic, the creature messaged him.

"I know, but it looks so real you can't help but want to touch it. I know it's not physical, that your magic creates it, but I couldn't help myself."

I handsome. With wings more.

Lasgol put his hand to his forehead and shook his head.

"You're a beauty," he said in a tone filled with irony.

Right? Camu messaged back. As usual, he had not picked up on the sarcasm of Lasgol's comment.

Ona growled twice.

Eicewald laughed. "Come on, Camu, fly until you're a hundred paces high, do three complete turns around the pond following its edge, and then land carefully right where we're standing."

Okay.

Camu started to beat his wings hard, raising a breeze Lasgol noticed was getting stronger with every practice they had. With a big leap, Camu soared and began to fly. He no longer rose vertically like he used to, but at an angle, coursing through the air and rising fast while he beat his splendid, ethereal, silver wings.

As Eicewald had told him, he rose until he was a hundred paces high. Lasgol noticed that Camu was now capable of controlling the distance that separated him from the ground. Eicewald had taught him to do it through a curious system. When Camu wanted to determine the height he was at, he called on a pulse of pure energy and directed it at the ground. Once the pulse of energy hit the ground it disintegrated and Camu could feel the distance the pulse had traveled.

"That's a good trick, using a measuring pulse," Lasgol congratulated Eicewald.

"I can't take all the credit. It's a frequently used spell you learn when you start practicing magic. I used to do it with a water sphere. I called it the great measuring drop. It's what Water Magi use. Since I don't know anything about Camu's magic and he's unable to make measuring spheres, we opted for pulses of pure energy, which he is capable of creating. His magic must be Drakonian Magic indeed, like he says, because I do find it quite distinct. The thing is, and it puts me in a tight spot, there's no record of this type of magic in our tomes of knowledge. If it were some known magic, I could get access to a tome that could help him. On the other hand, magic is universal, as are its principles, regardless of the school you follow. Therefore, Camu should be capable of creating a measuring spell, and as we see, after many failures, he did it."

"And in my case?" Lasgol asked Eicewald.

"In your case Magic of Nature will help you, and I believe there are other types of magic in you we've yet to discover. For instance, the skills you've developed for your bow remind me of Martial Magic."

"I've never heard of it..."

"It's not very common around here, but there are warrior magi—warrior warlocks to be precise, since that's how they're known—who use it. They're capable of improving their fighting skills or weapon wielding thanks to this type of magic. I believe that in your case there's some of that magic in you."

"You mean I'm a warlock?" Lasgol asked, upset.

"I mean to say that you use Martial Magic like the warrior warlocks, which isn't the same," Eicewald explained with a kind smile.

"I don't know if that eases my mind..."

"Don't let yourself be driven by your prejudices. Warlocks have a bad name because they devote themselves to war and conquest. But their magic, Martial Magic, is powerful and can be used to defend, not only to conquer."

"I hadn't thought of it that way…. The thing is, there are terrible stories about powerful warlocks…"

"Yes, like Haidar the Relentless, who almost conquered Rogdon with his Desert Scorpions, or Giles the Untouchable, who almost reigned in Zangria thanks to his incredible capacity to fight with spear and shield. They weren't pleasant. At least, that's what Egil has told me…"

"Yes, I'm referring to them, and others like them," Lasgol nodded.

"Remember the universal law: the same magic can be used for good or evil. You can use it to heal or to kill. It's the decision of whoever uses it."

"I know. I know the law, but sometimes it's hard to see."

"Whenever you use your magic for good, you're doing the right thing," Eicewald said, putting a hand on Lasgol's shoulder.

"I try to do so…"

"You must consider another universal law, not only of Nature: people make mistakes and don't always see that what they're doing is wrong."

"Meaning that even though I believe I'm doing the right thing, that might not be the case. I might be choosing wrong and doing evil," Lasgol said.

"It's a pleasure to be your tutor and instruct you, you understand concepts at once."

Lasgol blushed. "Thank you, I try to understand everything you explain to me."

"You do. You're intelligent. Make sure you have someone in your life to talk about these concepts—good and evil, right and wrong. Someone to tell you whether what you believe is right or not."

Lasgol nodded. "I have a whole group who will always do that: the Snow Panthers. They'll let me know whether I'm making a mistake or if my view is incorrect. I have no doubt."

"Then you're very fortunate. Don't you ever lose the Panthers' friendship."

"I never will," Lasgol said confidently.

"What I find interesting is that you use Magic of Nature and Martial Magic without ever having been instructed in them. That means you're a natural, which is also uncommon. Most people with the Gift, if they're not discovered and instructed, don't manage to develop it by themselves. With the passing of time the Gift becomes dormant and finally dies within the person. They never manage to do any magic. It's sad, but that's what happens. The fact that you, ever since you were little, already showed the Talent and were capable of developing it is quite significant."

"Not really... my father helped me. When I developed my first skill and he realized I had the Gift he brought me tomes from the Royal Library and helped me work on it. Well, with the little knowledge he had and my lack of knowledge. But he tried."

"Well, your father did a great job, you owe him your Talent. Because if he hadn't helped you begin to develop the Gift, it's likely that now it would be buried somewhere within you and you couldn't use it."

"I didn't know that... I'd never thought of it that way. I owe my father so much..."

"Right now there must be half a dozen people in Norghana born with the Gift who don't know it. Very likely they never will, since no one will discover them and help them. The Gift will be lost in most of them," the Mage explained.

"Wow... that's a pity..."

"It is," Eicewald nodded.

"Shouldn't someone find and help them so they can develop their talent?" Lasgol suggested.

"Every now and then we, the Ice Magi, set forth to seek people born with the Gift who might join our ranks."

"That enables you to find some of those who otherwise would lose their Talent," Lasgol said more cheerfully.

"Indeed. In any case, even if we find someone with the Gift, it doesn't guarantee they will enter our ranks. Not everyone is able to become an Ice Mage. Their Gift must be aligned with the Water Magic or be very powerful. That's not usually the case."

"I see. And those who don't fulfill the requirements?"

"We open their eyes to their Gift. We explain what it is and what they must do. We suggest they look for a school of magic that will accept them, or a tutor."

"I see..."

Lasgol and Eicewald watched Camu do his flying exercises while they continued chatting. The flight in itself went quite well each time, but the landings were quite disastrous. In his last attempt Camu landed beside them. He couldn't control his wings, blowing up a great cloud of dust and leaving long marks in the ground in his effort to brake and not fall headlong into the pond.

"That landing was a little accelerated," Eicewald told him with a look that meant it had not been good at all.

I try reduce speed. Not do, Camu apologized as he looked at the palms of his four legs.

"You have to reduce your speed a lot more before landing," Eicewald told him.

Easy say, difficult do.

"Yeah, we see that," Lasgol said with a smile.

"Rest a little, Camu," Eicewald told him.

I not tired.

"I know, but if you consume all your inner energy to maintain the Drakonian Flight skill, you won't be able to learn other things I want to teach you," Eicewald explained patiently.

Learn? New things? Camu asked, excited.

"Today I'm going to show you how to create a new skill."

Lasgol and Camu looked at one another—they were both intrigued. Ona moaned twice and moved away a little.

"It'll be useful. It's one of the things we both struggle to do and find more frustrating," Lasgol admitted to Eicewald.

"That's only natural. Trying to develop a new skill without training is like banging your head against a wall."

"That's how I feel at times."

I not. I angry.

"What you're going to teach us I understand works on humans, but will it work on Camu?" Lasgol asked.

"I don't know. I have no experience with magical creatures from the Frozen Continent, but we have nothing to lose if he practices this with us."

"That's true, we lose nothing by trying," he admitted.

I want learn.

"Then let's get started," Eicewald said.

They both nodded.

"Sit down beside me," the Mage indicated with his finger. The three sat down on the ground, forming a triangle. Camu lay down, since he could not sit.

"I'm going to teach you one of the first spells we Magi learn. You two are more advanced and have developed your own skills thanks to your experiences, but you've skipped the basic principles."

We smart, Camu messaged them.

"Yes, you are, but if you learn things in the correct order it'll be easier to improve and then do them better."

We learn.

"Yes, and this will help you learn more easily."

I want learn more.

"Yes, we both want to learn more skills," Lasgol agreed.

"Every person who is aware that they have the Gift wants to have more skills," Eicewald smiled. "In order to develop new skills, which as you know from experience is quite difficult, you need to master the basic principle of magical creation. It's an easy concept to understand but difficult to carry out."

"I'd guessed as much," Lasgol smiled.

Eicewald smiled too and took a candle out of his satchel. He lit the candle with tinder and a stone and placed it in the middle of the three of them on the ground.

"The principle of magical creation states that, to use a skill, you first have to create it by yourself. Skills can't be copied or passed from one person to another, or inherited, or transmitted in any way."

"Wow, I didn't know that..." Lasgol said.

I not know either.

"I'll lend you the tome explaining the principles of magic so you can study it. It's the Norghanian version. Every region has its own tome of principles, but these are quite accepted both in the north and west of Tremia. In other regions they might vary, but the basic principles are universal," Eicewald explained and took a thick tome out of his satchel with gold covers and a silver spine.

"Thank you, Eicewald," Lasgol said gratefully.

"You can begin studying it, although without help interpreting the principles it will be difficult to understand them and put them into practice. I'll try to find time to help you."

"And we'll find the time to study and practice them," Lasgol said, although he doubted they would have much time to do so.

Eicewald nodded. "Look at the candle and the flame burning at its end. I want you to put it out without touching it."

Lasgol and Camu looked at once another. Camu blinked hard.

Blow?

"No, you can't blow. You must use your inner energy, your magic, to put out the candle, and only that."

"We can't use anything else, or move or anything," Lasgol asked to clarify.

"Exactly. You must use your inner energy exclusively."

Lasgol looked at the flame thoughtfully.

"The candle is something physical, external… our energy is internal…"

"You're on the right track," Eicewald encouraged him.

Create skill with energy. Put out candle.

"That's it. That's what you have to do."

"I see…"

"It's a simple exercise," Eicewald pointed at the candle. A small sphere of water issued from his index finger, a perfect drop that remained levitating. The Mage moved his finger and the sphere settled onto the flame. Fire and water touched. The sphere burst and the water put out the candle.

"I don't find that so simple…" Lasgol said with a look on his face that said he could not do that even in his dreams.

Not simple, Camu joined him, blinking hard, which indicated he was not convinced either.

"What I've demonstrated is an example. You have to find the way to do it with your magic. It might be as simple as blowing. The only rule you have to follow is that it has to be with your magic and using a skill you don't already have."

Not can be with tail? Camu messaged as he moved his tail right and left, ready to lash at the candle.

"No, that would be cheating," Eicewald stopped him as he put another dry candle on the ground and lit it.

"We'll try," said Lasgol.

"The goal is simple: put the candle out. The means, the skill you use, is what you have to create. Focus on the small flame, locate it in your mind. Search your inner pools of energy, your power, and try to create a skill that helps you put it out."

Lasgol crossed his legs and got as comfortable as he could to focus on the flame. It truly seemed like an easy exercise, but he knew it was not. Even so, he concentrated and struggled to create a skill that could put out the candle. His mind was focused on the small flame before him. The candle was small and the flame was tiny. Putting it out did not require any effort—a simple blow, pinching it with moist fingertips, nothing. The problem was that they had to create a new skill, and that was not simple at all. Lasgol tried with all his might for a long time and did not succeed. His inner pool of energy remained completely still: no skill had activated. And worse than that, the possibility of it happening did not seem even remotely possible.

No can yet. I try more, Camu messaged them as he looked at the candle fixedly with eyes wide, as if he wanted to pierce it with his gaze, or power. He was not having any success either.

All afternoon and well into the night, both pupils tried to make their tutor happy, but unfortunately neither managed to extinguish the candle.

"I think that's enough for today," Eicewald told them when night was already upon them.

I want go on, Camu messaged them.

"It annoys me to have to stop trying," said Lasgol.

"Don't worry. It's natural you find it hard. Best to rest and continue at dawn with renewed energy," Eicewald told them.

Lasgol had to admit the Mage was right. He felt exhausted, and it was strange because he had not done anything; he had spent the whole day sitting and looking at a candle. Several candles, to be exact, because each had slowly burnt down. He found it odd to feel as exhausted as he did. It had to be mental, although his whole body ached.

"Yeah, we'd better rest a little. I'm exhausted."

Eicewald nodded. "Magic is hard and takes its toll on the body, not just the mind."

Lasgol understood. All his mental effort was affecting his body too: that was why he was feeling so tired. Camu pretended to be okay, and of course he would never admit he was tired, but his eyes were closing.

The following morning they resumed the exercise. They started without losing courage, filled with optimism and strength. They tried all morning without success. But they did not give up and continued in the afternoon after eating something and drinking half a water-skin each. For some reason their mouths were very dry.

"The spontaneous creation of a skill is a rare occurrence. You

320

must be as specific as possible about the skill you want to create," Eicewald explained to help them.

"And what happens if you still can't do it?" Lasgol asked.

"What skill are you trying to create?"

"Wind, a breath of wind."

Me rain.

"I think those two skills aren't really well aligned with your own powers. Creating wind—whirlwinds, hurricanes, and the like—belongs to Air Magic. It's not Magic of Nature or Martial Magic, which are the areas you're most inclined to, Lasgol. In your case, Camu, I don't know what you can achieve with Drakonian Magic, but I doubt it'll be rain. That's a skill that belongs to Water Magic, what I practice and the one I've specialized in."

"Then what should we do?" Lasgol asked.

"You must think of a skill aligned with your magic first and then try to create it."

"Well, that's complicated…" Lasgol made a face.

I not know how.

"I can't give you the answers, you must look within to find them," Eicewald said. "That's the base of the exercise and the principle you have to understand."

I try. I do. Camu got down to it at once with his usual stubbornness and perseverance.

Lasgol thought about it. It could be a weapon-focused skill using Martial Magic, like an arrow shot so precise it grazed the candle and put out the flame. Yes, that might work. *Grazing Shot* came to his mind. On the side of Magic of Nature he thought of *Forest Breeze*, which was a variant of the potential wind skill, and he thought it might work since it was based in nature. He decided to try both ideas and see if one worked.

By nightfall Lasgol was aiming his bow at the candle. Eicewald had moved to the side since he had been directly in front of him. Lasgol was concentrating on the flame and trying to create *Grazing Shot*. He could see it in his mind—the arrow would graze the top of the candle without touching it, skimming the surface, and the flame would go out.

Camu, on the other hand, was staring at the tip of his long tail and then at the flame of the candle. He was coming up with some scheme that involved his tail.

"You can't use your tail, nothing physical," Eicewald reminded him.

No physical. Tail like wings.

"Oh, I see. That might work, yes. A magic tail."

Whiplash, magic tail.

"Yes, I see what you mean. That's fine, as long as you put out the candle and don't destroy it…"

I put out, not destroy. Magic Whiplash.

Camu was obsessed with learning skills that would allow him to use his tail, and this could be one of them.

Night came and neither Lasgol nor Camu had achieved their purposes, although they had chosen their skills.

"Another day has passed and I don't see any progress. I'm beginning to worry. Maybe you don't have the potential I thought you had. Perhaps I've made a mistake. It happens to even the most experienced of Magi," Eicewald told them.

"It's very frustrating…" Lasgol muttered.

Much frustrating, Camu's message reached them with a feeling of exhaustion and rage at the same time.

"It is indeed. Let's rest tonight. We'll continue tomorrow," Eicewald told them.

They started the third day filled with energy and optimism. They were going to do it. Both Camu and Lasgol were sure they were going to succeed. Eicewald was not so sure. His pupils were not doing so well.

By mid-afternoon Lasgol had abandoned *Grazing Shot.* No matter how much he tried, it had been impossible to create the skill. He could visualize it perfectly in his mind, but his inner energy did not become activated. The pool remained perfectly still. This annoyed him—he felt frustrated, even a little of a failure.

Camu, on the other hand, was as stubborn as always and kept trying to create a Magic Whiplash with his tail. When something got into his head, nothing and no one could get it out. He would try until he failed or triumphed, but he would not change his mind.

By nightfall things had not changed. They could not manage to create either the *Forest Breeze* or the Magic Whiplash. They were both exhausted after three days of attempts and their heads were about to burst from the tremendous effort of so many hours of concentration. They did not want to give up, but it was becoming impossible to continue.

"I don't want to mention the number of novice magi, beginners with the Gift, and students with talent, who have succeeded in this exercise throughout history. There must've been thousands. Don't tell me that you two, who aren't beginners and with all the natural talent and potential you both have, can't do it," Eicewald told them in a disappointed tone.

I do, Camu messaged at once. He was not going to be less than others under any circumstance. *I more than dragon, I do,* he messaged, filled with frustration.

At that moment Camu's tail flashed with an intense silver glow. A swift, powerful lash followed, only it was not his tail but an immaterial tail identical to Camu's. The tip of the tail brushed over the tip of the candle without touching it and the flame went out.

"Exercise conquered!" Eicewald told Camu.

I do! Camu burst in delight.

"You've done it indeed. Congratulations," the Mage said.

Camu was looking at his tail. *I Magic Whiplash!* he cried joyfully and began to do his happy dance. Ona joined him immediately—the poor panther was bored to death.

Lasgol was distraught. Camu had done it but he had not. He was deeply happy for the creature, of course, but unfortunately he had not succeeded. He was about to give up, but seeing Camu so happy he decided to try one last time. He concentrated on the flame and saw in his mind what he wanted to have happen. A light forest breeze had to form and pass over the candle, putting out the flame. He could imagine it perfectly, the breeze stirring the fallen leaves, a light breath of the forest to extinguish the candle. He concentrated on his inner pool of energy, which remained still. He sought to activate the pool with all his might, a stone falling in the middle of the pool to create a wave when the stone penetrated the water. And as he was wishing for it with his whole being, a small part of his energy in the pool was consumed and there was a green flash that ran along his arm. With a movement of his arm Lasgol led the breeze toward the candle and put it out.

"Yes! I did it!" he cried excitedly.

"Well done, Lasgol, you did it," Eicewald congratulated him with a satisfied smile.

"Thank goodness! I was convinced I wasn't going to make it."

Happy dance, Camu messaged, and Lasgol had no choice but to join Ona and the creature in their dance. Their success deserved celebration.

"And with this, my dear pupils, we finish the first lesson in the basic principles of magic," Eicewald announced.

Lasgol stopped dancing and snorted.

"This is going to be a long and winding path…"

Much long, much, Camu agreed as he stopped dancing too.

"No one said the path of magic would be an easy one," Eicewald smiled at them.

Chapter 39

Nilsa, Ingrid, and Astrid were riding toward the home of Viggen Norling, Astrid's uncle. They had been traveling for two days and were close to their destination. They rode up a hill, and when they reached the top, Astrid told them to stop.

"This is where my family's land begins," she told them.

"Is that huge keep we see in the distance the lord's house?" Ingrid asked.

"It is," Astrid confirmed.

"It looks like a fortified army keep or the fortress house of some noble," Ingrid said, looking at the large house in the distance.

"That's because it is. It was a fortress back in the day. My uncle keeps it in good condition."

"Do you think we'll find your uncle in the house?" Ingrid asked while she patted her horse's neck.

"I don't know. Egil has the estate under watch by his contacts and my uncle hasn't appeared so far," Astrid admitted.

"Then… why have we come all this way if you knew your uncle wasn't at home?" Nilsa asked her with a look of surprise.

"I want to speak with old Alvis, my uncle's valet, and find out if it's really true. I also want to see what I can get out of good Alvis. He's always had a weakness for me. He might know something Egil's agents haven't been able to find out."

"Don't you trust the information Egil receives?" Ingrid was surprised. "It's usually spot on, and his sources are trustworthy."

"I fully trust Egil and his sources. But we haven't made much progress and sometimes it's better to grab the bull by the horns," Astrid said, frowning.

"It's never a good thing to grab a bull by the horns," Nilsa said, surprised by the expression.

"We'll see," Astrid said doubtfully. "What I can tell you is that I want to get answers and I'm not waiting any longer. I'll find them on my own."

"I've always found the direct approach to be the most adequate course of action," Ingrid agreed.

"Careful, some of Viggo's character is rubbing off on you," Nilsa warned her.

Ingrid made a horrified face but did not contradict her.

"I'll go to the keep," Astrid said.

"Alone?" Nilsa asked.

"Yes. There's no reason I can't visit my home and ask for my uncle. If anything goes wrong, it'll mean something's going on inside."

"So, we are expecting trouble?" Ingrid asked.

"Perhaps," Astrid replied. "Keep a safe distance but stay within shooting range, in case I need you or you see danger approaching once I'm inside."

Ingrid nodded.

"Be careful and good luck," both Ingrid and Nilsa said.

"I'll be careful, don't worry. The fact that this is my old home won't distract me from what's going on in there with my uncle and his strange order, brotherhood, or whatever it is."

Nilsa and Ingrid dismounted, and after tethering their horses to a tree they began to approach the keep through the fields, one on each side of the road. At the same time Astrid rode to the fortified keep along the road, escorted by the two lines of elm trees leading to the entrance. She remained alert to the terrain around her, not only in case she was attacked but for the tracks she might find on it. This was not a busy road, only those entering or exiting the estate used it, and any footprint or strange trail could indicate her uncle's presence.

As she got closer and was able to see the large house properly and the surrounding lands, nostalgia washed over her. She saw the well and remembered how she used to take water out of it with Alvis's help when she was a little girl. The stables and the barn behind it were her favorite places, since she loved horses and playing hide-and-seek in the barn. She also saw a small hill to the east with a stone bunkhouse and a small adjacent tower, which was where her uncle's men lodged.

She dismissed all the memories that came to her mind and focused on the mission at hand, which was none other than finding her uncle Viggen and having him answer her questions. Rage overcame her at the thought of the cowardly attack on Lasgol by her uncle's men. All other feelings vanished.

She reached the keep's entrance and, instead of dismounting and waiting for anyone to come out and welcome her, she headed to the stables. She wanted to see whether her uncle's horse was there. Her uncle liked Rogdonian horses, black and about sixteen hands tall. If there was one like that, it would mean her uncle was hiding there. She also wanted to give Nilsa and Ingrid time to position themselves, just in case.

She saw a dozen well-kept horses in the stable, but unfortunately none were Rogdonian. Most of them were Norghanian. She counted three Nocean ones and one most likely from Erenal. She did not find what she was looking for and was slightly disappointed.

Two of her uncle's men appeared and came to meet her. They were clearly Norghanian. They were wearing the long gray robes with the embroidered two silver circles, one inside the other on the chest. Once again she had the strange feeling she had seen that symbol before. She could not remember when or where, in her childhood most likely. When she saw the weapons they were carrying, a short broad sword and long knife in the Erenal style, she stopped trying to remember and focused on them. She recognized them. They were Albon and Bestand.

"Welcome, Miss Astrid," Albon greeted her, and his tone was courteous, but not as kind as the last time she had visited.

"Thank you, Albon, it's good to be back home."

"Your uncle isn't at home. He's away looking after important business," Albon said hastily.

"Is that so? Well…" Astrid pretended to be sorry to hear that.

Albon looked at her in silence, and there was a tense moment. He did not seem to want her to stay. He had not invited her to dismount or come inside. The other man, Bestand, was waiting a little further back, silent. Astrid decided not to pussyfoot around and dismounted nimbly.

"Are you staying, Miss Astrid?" Albon asked.

"Yes, I'm staying. I want to see Alvis," she replied and looked at him sternly.

"Alvis is feeling a little under the weather, he mustn't be disturbed. That's what the healer who came to see him told us."

"He's ill? Then I want to see him and make sure he's okay."

The two men exchanged glances. There was a moment of silence, and the tension rose. Astrid stared fixedly into Albon's eyes, letting him know she would not budge.

"Of course, Miss Astrid, I'll take you myself," Albon said at last.

"I'll look after your horse," Bestand said, who like Albon maintained a tone of courtesy but was not exactly welcoming; he exchanged an unobtrusive look with Albon which indicated they were not at ease with her being there.

"Come inside with me please," Albon said to Astrid. He opened the heavy reinforced door and went inside.

Astrid noticed there were two men on guard duty, the same ones she had seen during her previous visit. They were in their thirties, tall, thin, with short dark hair and slightly darker skin than was usual in the north. Astrid guessed they were from Erenal, although they were dressed like all her uncle's other men so they likely belonged to his brotherhood.

They went inside the large keep and Albon led Astrid to the great main hall.

"Wait here, please. I'll go and tell Alvis."

"Can he get up?" Astrid asked. She did not know whether to believe Alvis was sick. It sounded like an excuse for her not to see him.

"That's what I'm going to find out," Albon said.

Albon left and Astrid noticed there were two more guards in the great hall, one beside the bookshelves as if he were guarding them, and the other at the foot of the stairs that led to the upper floors. She also made out another guard at the end of the corridor toward the kitchens. She had the feeling there were too many guards for the lord not to be at home.

She had to wait a while for Albon to come back. To her surprise, he did so with Alvis. For a moment she had thought they would not let her speak to the old valet either.

"Alvis! I'm so happy to see you!"

"My young Miss Astrid, it's this old servant who's so happy to see you!" he said with a smile.

Astrid went to Alvis and hugged him affectionately.

"They told me you were sick."

"Indisposed, rather. It must have been something I ate that didn't agree with me."

"Let's sit on the couch and talk," Astrid said.

They sat down and Astrid smiled fondly at the old man. He looked tired and he certainly looked his seventy years of age, but he did not look ill. That put her at ease. The fact that Albon had not lied to her also comforted her. She looked over her shoulder and saw that Albon was standing beside the door.

"Your uncle Viggen isn't at home, my dear Astrid," Alvis told her. "I already told you by pigeon, there was no need for you to come. I would've sent you another one if your uncle had returned."

Astrid nodded. "Do you know where he is?"

Alvis shook his head. "Your uncle is always traveling. I never know his exact whereabouts. He only tells me once he's back, and sometimes not even then."

"I must speak to him, it's urgent, Alvis," Astrid said gravely.

"Is milady in any trouble? Can I help in any way?"

"The only one who can help me is Uncle Viggen. I need to know where he is and speak to him. It's important. Some things have happened that I need him to explain."

"I'm afraid I can't help you with that. I don't know where he is, he hasn't told me where he was going."

"Do you know what he's involved in? What he's doing?"

Alvis shook his head. "I'm afraid your uncle doesn't share his plans with me, or his intentions. I'm only his valet."

"You're family, you've spent your whole life here."

"Thank you, milady, I really appreciate that."

"Then you don't know where my uncle is or what he's doing," Astrid said, beginning to doubt she was going to gain anything positive from her visit.

"I'd like to help you, but I can't. I don't know."

"Do you know, Albon?" Astrid asked, turning toward him.

"No, milady, the lord's business is his own," Albon replied.

Astrid looked at him fixedly. She did not believe that answer.

"What does my uncle do when he needs you?" she asked.

Albon stiffened.

"Milord sends a pigeon or a personal messenger."

"A messenger? Someone he trusts?"

"Of course. Someone he trusts, one of us."

"And he hasn't sent anyone recently," Astrid said, staring into his eyes.

"No, milady, no one," Albon replied, lowering his gaze.

"You're a bad liar, Albon."

"Milady... I'd never dare to... lie to you..."

"You're lying right now. I saw the horse from Erenal in the stable. He arrived this morning. There are tracks on the road, and his animal was still sweating. I want to speak with the person who was riding it."

"Milady, no..." Albon raised his hands in denial.

"Alvis, has anyone arrived at the fortress today?"

"I couldn't say, milady. I've been lying in my bed all day, indisposed. Albon would know, he's in charge of receiving visitors. If he says no..."

"No problem, I'll search for him myself. I know every inch of this keep," Astrid said and stood up.

"I assure you it's unnecessary..." said Albon.

At that instant Astrid saw someone running down the corridor toward the kitchens at the back. She narrowed her eyes and watched him run. When he was about to turn to head toward the stairs that led to the cellar, he glanced toward the hall where they were. That was a mistake. Astrid recognized the man. It was one of the six men who had gathered with her uncle at the library, one of his trusted men who probably knew where her uncle was. It was the rider who had arrived that morning.

"Stay where you are!" Astrid shouted at him.

The man looked at Astrid for a moment longer and then ran down the stairs.

Astrid leapt and started to go after him.

Albon got in her way with his weapons drawn.

"You can't go after him," he said with determination.

"I'll go wherever I please, more so in this house, which is my family's."

"Our duty is sacred. No one can interfere, not even a member of the family," said Albon.

The other two guards in the hall came to stand beside him, barring her way to the corridor where the man had fled.

"Don't you dare touch her!" Alvis warned them. "Milord won't tolerate that or forgive anyone who hurts her. You're risking your lives."

"Milord owes himself to the cause, like us. No-one can get in the way. No-one. Our lives are not important, the new order is. The new all-powerful lords are," Albon said.

"I don't want to kill you, so tell me where my uncle is at once."

"If milord wanted to be found, you'd know where he was," Albon replied.

"Bad answer. Get out of my way right now, or you'll regret it," Astrid threatened, looking lethal.

"Sound the alarm!" Albon shouted.

At once cries of alarm were heard from the entrance. One of the men who were barring her way went outside and started shouting to the men in the bunkhouse at the top of his lungs.

"That was a mistake," Astrid said.

"It's a mistake to get in the way of the new lords' destiny and the new order they're bringing," Albon replied and showed Astrid his sword and dagger.

"You asked for this," Astrid said. She reached for her long knives and lunged into attack.

Albon launched the first stroke to her torso, followed by a slash to the neck with his dagger. Astrid diverted the first attack and blocked the second with her knives. He attacked again, changing his combination. Astrid blocked and deflected. She noticed that Albon knew how to fight—he was skilled. Astrid launched a kick which caught her rival in the chest and forced him to back up a few paces. At once the other two guards lunged at her with similar combined attacks. Astrid dodged, moved, blocked, and dodged again. These men were either soldiers or mercenaries. They fought well. Much better than what was expected of guards, not to mention a sect or apocalyptic religious order.

Outside, the guard who had given the alarm at a run received an arrow full in the chest—an Earth Arrow from Nilsa, which exploded against his chest and left him stunned and blinded. A dozen men came out of the bunkhouse and ran toward the keep, weapons in hand.

Ingrid aimed at the one in the lead and released. She hit him in the leg and made him trip and fall. Nilsa hit the one coming next with an Air Arrow. The shock it produced reached him and the one running beside him. They both fell down amid strong convulsions.

The rest of the guards were alerted to the presence of the two archers. They divided and charged against them. That was exactly what Ingrid and Nilsa had intended, to distract them so Astrid would have the chance to solve her situation inside. The first two that ran toward them received arrows in the leg and fell down.

Inside Astrid had knocked down two of the guards with blows to the temple and nose with the butt of her knives. Albon and another guard were trying to stop her advance toward the corridor but were having serious trouble. Astrid blocked Albon's sword stroke with a knife and the other guard's sword with her other knife. Moving like lightning, she spun toward the other guard and hit his support leg, unbalancing him. Before he could recover, Astrid kicked him in the face. The guard fell backward, unconscious.

"You won't be able to stop the new order," Albon told her as he delivered two strokes with his sword and dagger.

Astrid threw her body back and dodged both attacks.

"We'll see about that," she said.

"No one can stand up to the supreme lords."

"They're not here yet, are they? Well, we'll see whether they come or not," Astrid said to see if she could get something out of him.

"The Sleeper has awakened. The day is close."

"Who's the Sleeper?"

Albon realized Astrid was trying to making him talk and his face changed.

"I'll tell you nothing, you're not one of us. You don't believe in the new future, in the new gods, in the new tomorrow."

"That's a lot to believe in, I'm not convinced," Astrid said and launched a combined attack. She attacked with both knives in a thrust and then opened her arms to deliver two oblique slashes followed by a spinning kick, all in the blink of an eye. Albon was unable to block them or dodge the attack, and he was left unconscious on the floor with a broken nose and two cuts on his torso.

Astrid raced down the corridor, chasing after the man who had fled.

Outside the keep, Nilsa was releasing against the last of the running guards. This time it was a Water Arrow, and she left the guard half frozen on the ground. She lifted her gaze and watched Ingrid burying two arrows in the legs of the last of the guards trying to reach them.

"All clear," Ingrid said.

"All clear," Nilsa replied.

"I'm going to the bunkhouse, you go inside the keep," Ingrid told

Nilsa.

Nilsa nodded and ran to the entrance.

Astrid was going down the wide stone steps that went to the cellars, taking them three at a time. She could not let the messenger escape. Messenger, or whatever he was, he had to know where her uncle was. She arrived at the first cellar and searched it from top to bottom without wasting a moment. He was not there. All she found were supplies of different kinds, well organized and stored. She ran out and checked the second cellar. She remembered playing hide-and-seek in those cellars when she was little, and that her tutors did not like it at all. There were a couple of torches lit in the corridor. She took one to help her see in the dark, since the cellars were so gloomy.

She continued forward, her ears alert to any sound. The messenger outdistanced her but he must have hidden somewhere in the cellar, because he had not gone back up the stairs.

She stayed still and listened. She was calm—he was not going to get away. There was no way out. But then she remembered the sewer trapdoor.

"How could I have forgotten!" she muttered angrily under her breath.

There was one way out, one few would use: the keep's sewers. She ran back to the third cellar, the farthest one which she reached by taking another set of stairs. She arrived and saw the messenger moving the stone slab trapdoor, which must have weighed a ton. Astrid remembered three men were needed to move it. The messenger had managed to slide it to the side just a little, it was his way out.

"Stop, I want to talk to you," she said.

The man looked at her. He was one of those at the secret meeting, without a doubt. He paid no heed to Astrid's words and kept pushing. The slab moved a little more.

"Stop doing that. Where's my uncle?"

The man looked at her and continued pushing the slab.

"I told you to stop that."

The man ignored her and went on with his attempted escape. He managed to move the slab enough to create a crack he could slip through. He went in feet first. He was going to let himself down into the sewers and escape that way.

Astrid dropped the torch and lunged at the man the moment he vanished through the opening. She grabbed the messenger's shoulders with both hands.

"Stop!" she cried, closing her fists tightly on the man's robe.

The messenger slipped and dropped into the pit. Astrid was left holding the man's robe. She heard his plunge as he started swimming.

"He's getting away!" Astrid thought of lunging in after him. She threw the robe to one side and heard a metallic jingle. She stopped and looked, wondering what the object might be. It had not sounded like a weapon—swords and daggers sounded more solid. She picked up the torch and looked around. In a corner she saw a metallic rod. She bent down to look at it.

It was one of the Quills of the True Blood.

Chapter 40

Egil and Viggo were walking through the center of town. Egil had business to attend to and information to collect, and Viggo was acting as his bodyguard in case anyone had bad intentions. Viggo was almost hoping someone would try something, because he soon got tired and bored with inactivity. Searching for information was not turning out to be at all exciting, especially because of Egil's secrecy. He would barely tell him anything.

The city was more alive than ever. The news of the arrival of the Princess of Irinel had caused all kind of speculations. On the lips of everyone in every square, market, tavern, fountain, and any other corner where people gathered, was that there was going to be a royal wedding. There had been no official announcement yet, but even so, the citizens were already preparing for the possible event. Traders in particular, of nearly every guild, were preparing possible sales and gathering supplies like crazy. Once the event was announced, and everyone was betting it would happen shortly, it would be difficult to find goods and the price would double or triple.

"Will you please tell me where we're going?" Viggo asked as he glanced around, looking surly while they dodged people. "Every day you take me to weirder places."

"You'll know soon," Egil smiled as he made his way, slipping through the passersby.

"I hope it's a more interesting place than the places we've gone to the last two days, because I've been quite disappointed with your secret contacts."

"That's why they're secret contacts," Egil replied, smiling.

"I hope we go to a good tavern this time, or an inn. Yes, an inn would be better."

"You'll see when we get there."

"There you go with your third-rate mysteries. We'll finish sooner if you tell me."

"That would spoil the surprise and the fun," Egil said with a mischievous grin.

"And that matters?"

"It matters."

"And they say I'm the most twisted one of the group—hah! I'm laughing my head off."

Egil laughed out loud.

"You're right. I don't fall far behind when it comes to being twisted."

"And dark," Viggo added as he pushed away the people who hurried past them.

They arrived at the market area, and there were so many people coming and going in such a hurry that Egil had to stop.

"They're like chickens with their heads cut off running hither and thither," Viggo commented.

"The news of the possible royal wedding has everyone very busy."

"And happy," said Viggo, pointing at a group singing beside a fountain.

"These are good times for the kingdom, and that always cheers the peoples' spirits."

"We'll see whether they're good or bad..." said Viggo distrustfully.

They decided to make a detour along a couple of streets more to the east to avoid being trapped by the crowd. Then they went down a street that went south and arrived in front of an establishment that made them stop in their tracks.

"Tell me it's here," Viggo said with wide eyes.

"It is," Egil confirmed with a broad smile.

"Wonderful! 'The Blue Parrot'! I've heard about this place. They say pirates and mercenaries frequent it. That's a place with a good atmosphere."

"That's what they say indeed, haven't you ever been here?" Egil asked, surprised.

"I've tried a couple times, but Ingrid was always close by and I haven't been able to. Apparently the waitresses here are very attractive, although I don't know why my fierce Norghanian warrior would worry. My heart is hers—no pretty face is going to wrap me around her little finger."

"Higher towers have fallen..." Egil said in a tone of warning.

"I don't fall. I have a lot up here," he replied, pointing at his temple with his finger.

"Oh yes, tons," Egil agreed and looked the other way so Viggo would not see his smile.

"It's great that we're coming here, I've really wanted to see this place!" Viggo said, studying the front of the building, which was shaped like a large Norghanian war ship.

"Then today's your lucky day," said Egil.

"Wonderful!" Viggo punched the air with his fist in triumph.

"We'll go in separately. You go first and then I'll come in," Egil told him. "When we're inside we'll pretend we don't know each other, okay?"

"Understood," Viggo nodded.

"You go to the counter and I'll take a table."

"Good, I like that plan. I'll pretend at the counter."

"Very well, but don't pretend too hard or it'll go to your head," Egil warned him and raised his arm as if he were drinking.

"Don't worry, I'm becoming immune. Like with poisons," Viggo winked at him.

"That requires drinking small amounts, tiny ones, of poison—not drinking five mugs of beer."

"Beer is a mild poison," Viggo said nonchalantly.

Egil shook his head. "Stay sober, I need you ready for action."

"I was born for action," Viggo replied, putting his hand to his waist where his knives were.

"Don't forget it," Egil winked at him and motioned him to go in.

Viggo went into the tavern and at once had a most pleasant surprise. The interior was also decorated with nautical motifs, and it was huge. Larger than any tavern or inn he had ever been to before, and he had been to many. The counter had sculptures of mermaids on the front and it was the longest he had ever seen. Five people were attending it. The place was crowded, both the counter and the tables where people were playing dice, cards, and anything else that people might bet on. There was a terrible cacophony of noise inside and a dozen waitresses navigated among the multitude of tables serving food and drink to the customers. The waitresses were very attractive indeed, and most of the customers looked like they employed themselves in illicit deeds, although there were also soldiers sitting at a couple of tables. In all likelihood, they would be losing their pay to cheating professionals.

A big smile appeared on Viggo's face. This was his kind of place.

A waitress came over smiling.

"Looking for something, handsome?" she asked him with an insinuating smile.

"Only beer," Viggo smiled back. "My heart is already taken."

"Well, that's a pity," she smiled and winked.

Viggo did not heed the compliment and walked up to the middle of the counter, eyeing the tables to make sure there was no danger. He saw nothing to worry about. Everyone sitting at the tables looked bad, so danger could come from any of them. Indeed, there were pirates, mercenaries, scoundrels, thieves, cheaters, and the like. The crowd had tough, surly faces, and many were marked with scars. There were some who had lost an eye, an arm, or even half a leg. Those who had not, were probably unscathed because they were good with a knife. Viggo and Egil would have to be wary. For the time being, he ordered a mug of beer to watch unobtrusively from the counter what was going on.

Egil came into the tavern after a while, and without a glance at Viggo he headed to the left side of the far end. There were three relatively full tables, and another one where there was only one person. Egil approached the mostly empty table and sat down in front of the customer who was drinking wine. They nodded to one another and started chatting as if they were friends.

Viggo took a sip of his beer and watched the person Egil was talking to. The truth was he had not noticed him, he looked quite ordinary. He was not very tall or short, with an average built and an insipid-looking face. In the midst of all those tough men of sea and land he did not stand out at all—on the contrary. Viggo realized that, precisely because of that, he would be one of Egil's clandestine contacts. The more unobtrusive, the better an agent he must be.

A tough guy came up to the counter and shoved a customer who was ordering. He started to protest, but the other one hit the man in the nose before he could say, "these teeth aren't even mine."

"No fighting!" a muscular man shouted from where he was sitting at one of the corners of the establishment.

Viggo had already located four large individuals, one at each corner of the premises. They were in charge of keeping the peace. By their looks and that of the customers, many days likely ended in conflict.

"He's only letting me through!" the tough guy replied and

gestured for the man he had hit to stay quiet for his own good.

"Well, he can let you through without you hitting him."

The tough guy arrived at the counter, just beside Viggo.

"And what are you looking at?" he asked Viggo roughly.

"At how ugly you are and how much I'm looking forward to fixing your face with my knives," Viggo replied without batting an eye.

The tough guy threw his head back as if Viggo had hit him with his comment. He did not seem used to anyone standing up to him.

"You're going to swallow those words!" he said and pulled his arm back to punch him.

In a movement so swift no one saw it, Viggo broke the mug of beer on the tough guy's head with one hand and with the other hit the man's head against the counter.

The tough guy fell to one side, unconscious.

The man he had punched seized the chance and kicked his attacker in the privates. Then he stood beside Viggo at the counter and greeted him with respect.

"What's going on here?" one of the tavern's bouncers asked.

"He slipped and hit the counter," the man beside Viggo replied. His nose was still bleeding.

The bouncer snorted and came closer. He grabbed the legs of the unconscious thug and dragged him out of the premises.

"Another beer, please," Viggo ordered as if nothing had happened.

Egil chatted with his contact for a good while, and Viggo waited, watching the customers in case one of them did anything suspicious. Most were minding their own business, drinking, arguing, or betting at cards or dice. But there were two or three who were sitting at tables and drinking quietly. This caught Viggo's attention. In a place like this, practically everyone was talking. Those who were not must have a reason, one which might be conflictive.

At last, Egil rose from the table. He nodded at his contact as he had done when first arriving and left. He crossed the tavern nonchalantly, without looking at anyone and avoiding tables, and stepped outside. His contact did not leave but stayed at his table. Viggo was about to go out after Egil when he noticed that two people from one of the tables where no one was talking had got up. They were thin and wore gray cloaks. They did not look bad like most of the customers, but something about them gave him a bad feeling.

Viggo went out after them. He was expecting to see Egil waiting outside in front of the establishment, but he was in for a surprise. Egil was not there. Viggo was concerned. Where was his friend? What had happened? He looked down both sides of the street and glimpsed Egil walking away south down the street.

"What the heck…?" he muttered under his breath. Why had Egil not waited for him? Why was he leaving without him?

And then he realized that the two men who had come out of the tavern were going after Egil.

Viggo flattened himself against the left-side wall and waited for a moment. He did not want them to notice he was going to follow them. It was a pity it was broad daylight. He would not be able to use all his Assassin's arts, too much light. He watched the long street and saw the two men glancing back. He flattened himself even more. A house corner blocked him from the two men, but if he came out, even with his Assassin's arts, with so much light they would see him following them.

He decided to opt for a 'higher' following method. He watched the structure of the house he was leaning against and nodded.

"Piece of cake," he muttered to himself.

While Egil was walking down the street, the two strangers following behind him, Viggo climbed the wall of the house to the roof with agility worthy of the best Assassin. Once on the roof, he moved carefully and with stealth until he reached the end. With a nimble leap he passed onto the roof of the next house. He went along one side and then jumped to the next one. It did not take him long to catch up with the two men in the street, only at a much higher level.

Egil turned right, which was bad for Viggo because now he would have to cross the street.

"Egil… left, not right…" he muttered under his breath.

His friend disappeared down the new street he had taken. The two men following him disappeared after Egil. Viggo had to think fast. He was on the wrong side of the street. He got to the last building and calculated the distance.

"I can do it, the street isn't so wide," he told himself.

He took a good run and leapt with all his might. He flew over the street and landed on the roof of the house in front.

"Watch and learn, Camu," he muttered and continued running along the roofs.

Egil reached the end of the street and found himself in the Square of the Lost Ones. It was called that because it was a square without exits and everyone who ended up there was precisely because they were lost. It had no exits, so they had to turn around and go back down the same street they had arrived from.

"How silly of me, I seem to have gotten lost," Egil muttered as he took out the city plan and began to consult it. What he did not notice while he checked his map were the two men quickly approaching him from behind.

He heard footsteps rapidly approaching and turned with the map in his hands.

The two strangers who were following him stopped and unsheathed swords with dragon heads on the pommels.

"Funny swords," Egil said, indicating the weapons with a nod.

The two men stopped two paces away from Egil and looked him up and down.

"You've been asking a lot about our lord," said one with blond hair and blue eyes. He looked Norghanian, southern by his accent. "For what purpose?"

"What lord is that?" Egil asked in the tone of someone who had no clue what they were talking about.

"Don't play the fool with us. You know perfectly well what lord we mean," the other one with dark hair replied. This one was not Norghanian. From his accent Egil guessed he was from the Kingdom of Rogdon to the west. He found it significant that people from such different kingdoms should work for the same leader.

"You can believe me when I say I have a slight suspicion, but to be honest, I've been asking about two lords, and I don't know which one you mean."

"You do know, and you shouldn't have asked about him," the blond one said, upset.

"By the clothes you're wearing, I don't think you serve Lord Viggen Norling."

"We don't serve him," the dark one said angrily, as if that name

341

was not unknown to him and it grieved him.

"But you do know him, don't you?" Egil asked, trying to elicit information.

"There's only one true Visionary, and he's not the true one," the blond one said, narrowing his eyes.

"Am I to understand that Viggen Norling is a Visionary?"

"He and his people say he is. But that's not true. The only true Visionary is our lord," the darker-haired one said, clenching his teeth with rage.

"I understand that both of them have the same vision, the same goal, and because of that they're considered Visionaries..." Egil said as if trying to understand, to see if they would give him more information.

"Only the vision of our lord is the true one. The All-Powerful Lords are about to arrive. The new order will soon begin. Those who are on the side of the new supreme lords will survive and prevail. They will rule beside them. The rest will perish," the blond said as if reciting a message.

"Funny, you two aren't preachers, but you recite the same message they do."

"We are the Visionaries, those who follow the great Visionary. His vision, his truth will come. The world will change. Man will perish and the supreme gods will rule the world," the dark-haired one said, also as if he were reciting a message.

"I see. The preachers are spreading the message of the end of the era of men, and with it fear and anguish. You, the Visionaries, are in charge of making the great plan of the Visionary come true. Correct?" Egil said.

"You ask too many questions instead of answering the one you've been asked," the blond one said, threatening him with his sword.

"Don't worry, I'll answer politely," Egil said, raising his hands. In his right was the map.

"Why are you asking about our lord?" the dark-haired one asked, his eyes shining dangerously.

"Well, you see, your lord, Drugan Volskerian, stole an Object of Power that belongs to us and which we want to recuperate. We're prepared to offer a large amount of gold for the orb," Egil offered.

The two Visionaries exchanged glances.

"That object is sacred and belongs to our lord," the blond one said.

"It can't belong to him since we're the ones who found it," Egil replied.

"The object belongs to the Visionaries. You and your people are sacrilegious," the dark-haired one said rudely.

"I want to arrange a meeting with your lord and offer the exchange," Egil said.

"Our lord will never accept," the dark-haired one said.

"Tell him my offer. We can meet here tomorrow to talk," Egil said.

The two Visionaries exchanged glances again.

"Our lord isn't interested. He wants to know why you're asking so many questions about him," the dark-haired man insisted.

"I'll tell him in person tomorrow, here," Egil said adamantly.

"That's not possible," the blond one said.

"The day after tomorrow then?"

"Never. Because we're going to finish you," the dark-haired one said.

Egil leapt backward to get out of range of the two Visionaries' swords. Before they could step forward to attack Egil, a shadow fell on top of them from the roof of the last building at their backs.

The two Visionaries received a tremendous blow on their backs and fell on their faces. Viggo rolled off them and stood beside Egil.

"I need them alive," Egil told Viggo.

"Killjoy," Viggo replied as he faced them with his knives in his hands.

The two Visionaries had received a good blow. The dark-haired one could not get up and the blond one did so with difficulty. Viggo came at him fast—the Visionary lunged a sword stroke at Viggo's torso, which he diverted with one of his knives. With the other knife he cut the Visionary deeply in the sword hand so he had to drop the weapon. Viggo kicked the sword away.

The dark-haired man had already recovered and tried to attack Viggo, but the blow to his back had been too hard and he fell again. Viggo hit him in the arm and he lost his sword too.

"Well, now that you're disarmed, I think we can speak calmly," Egil said.

"Are you sure I can't kill them?" Viggo asked.

"No, we need information," Egil told him. He patted Viggo's

shoulder.

"As you wish..." Viggo said resignedly.

Egil took a step forward and something unexpected happened. The two men reached for containers hanging around their necks on silver chains.

"Don't let them take it!" Egil cried, reaching toward them.

Viggo also took a step forward to try and stop them, but he was an instant too late. Both men drank the liquid in the container.

"What are these lunatics doing!" Viggo cried, already suspecting what was happening.

The two men started to convulse uncontrollably. After a moment white foam spilled from their mouths. An instant later they were dead.

"They've taken a potent poison," Egil said.

"What a pair of fools!" Viggo said, unable to believe they had taken their own lives.

Egil examined them. They were dead.

"I don't know this poison, I'm not familiar with it," he said, smelling the container. "There are still a couple drops left. I'll take this to study it." Then he checked to see whether they were carrying anything else. Nothing. He only found some coins and the weapons they had wielded.

"Let's get away from here before the city guard arrives," said Viggo. "Otherwise there's going to be much explaining.

"Yes, that would be for the best. We don't want to have to explain anything."

They left the square and headed to the center of town at a quick pace. As they walked they looked back in case anyone was following them. After making sure no one else was coming after them, they stopped beside a fountain.

"How did you know those two were going to follow you at the Blue Parrot?" Viggo asked his friend.

"I didn't. I was expecting something. These past few days I've been trying to provoke a reaction, a movement. It's been terribly hard. You see, I've been rocking the boat a lot. The warlock knows we're looking for him and I've put a lot of money on his head with several bounty hunters and information dealers."

"He can't have liked that at all," Viggo guessed.

"That was the idea," Egil smiled.

"You've inconvenienced him on purpose."

"I have indeed."

"So he would come out of his hiding place and take a wrong step."

"And that's what's happened." Egil said with a gleam of triumph in his eyes.

"A risky plan…"

"Didn't you like the plan?"

"The truth is, I did. I'd rather be attacked than having to seek them out from filthy lairs."

"I knew you would approve."

"That's why you asked me to come with you."

"Irrefutable, my dear friend."

"This is going to be material for another ode, I can see it coming. I'll have to speak to the troubadours again. Enemies taking their own lives rather than standing up to me from the fear I instill."

"Sounds fantastic."

Chapter 41

It was mid-morning by the time Nilsa, Ingrid, and Astrid arrived at the Rangers' Tower in the Royal Castle. They left their mounts at the stables and hurried inside. They went to the room they shared with the group and found Viggo and Egil inside. Viggo was resting on his bunk and Egil was writing in his notebooks.

"My beautiful Nordic blonde beauty with the iron spirit! I'm so happy you're back!" Viggo greeted Ingrid, jumping up from his bed.

"All this about bards, poetry, and odes is going to your head," she said, jabbing her finger at him.

"Isn't there a comeback kiss for your beloved Assassin?" Viggo said with a lovelorn look.

"Will you shut up?"

"Like a door."

Ingrid went over to Viggo and, hugging him tight, kissed him passionately.

"That's what I call a good welcome!" Nilsa said, laughing.

"We've missed you," Egil said cheerfully.

"And we've missed you too," Astrid replied, smiling.

"What a beautiful day it is when you burst in with your beauty..." Viggo started to recite as if it were a song.

"Silence, you numbskull troubadour," Ingrid kissed him again so he would stay quiet.

"He's surely not going to say a word that way," Nilsa laughed.

"What happened at your uncle's?" Egil asked Astrid. "Did you find out where he is?"

"Not exactly, but it was interesting... we saw some action," she replied.

"That sounds interesting, do tell," said Egil.

So Astrid told Egil and Viggo what had happened at the estate with as much detail as she could remember. When Astrid finished, Egil was thoughtful.

"I understand that the rod you found in the man's cloak is one of the Quills of the True Blood, am I right?"

"I think so, yes," said Astrid, and she took the rod out of her satchel and handed it to Egil.

"Fascinating…" Egil said as he examined it carefully.

"Is this rod supposed to have any purpose?" Viggo asked.

"It's not a weapon," Ingrid said. "Neither the tip or the edges are sharp."

"I think it's some kind of enchanted object, from what Astrid told us of what she saw at her uncle's meeting," said Nilsa. "And from what Lasgol told us he witnessed when he was attacked."

"That's what I think too," said Astrid. "It's supposed to vibrate when it detects what it's looking for. But I'm not too clear about what it's supposed to be looking for…. According to what I heard, the quills will always point to the pure of blood…"

"All that about the true blood sounds a bit twisted and discriminatory," Viggo said. "I have slum blood, and it's as good as the purest blood that rod can point at."

"I doubt that's the meaning of 'true blood'…" Ingrid commented.

"What we do know is that it vibrates when it's near the Dragon Orb. That's how they knew Lasgol was carrying it, and then they stole it," Astrid said.

"We find ourselves before a very singular object, enchanted with a powerful magic. If I'm not mistaken, this quill is actually a seeker."

"A seeker? What do you mean?" Ingrid asked.

Egil studied the rod a little more, lost in thought.

"Yes… I think its function is to seek out people or objects."

"Please explain," Astrid said, intrigued.

"We know the quill or enchanted rod vibrated in the presence of the Dragon Orb, which is what your uncle's men used to locate it. It's reasonable to assume it can somehow locate the orb, most likely from the type of magic it emits."

"That makes sense, yes. That's how they must have found out Lasgol had the Orb," said Ingrid.

"So then, that thing has the type of power the bug has, since it's what the Orb emanates," Viggo said, making a face.

"It's possible, yes," Ingrid nodded.

"And what about people?" Astrid asked.

"I'm guessing that from what your uncle called it: the Quill of the True Blood, and from what he said: 'it will always point at those pure of blood.' If we're speaking of blood, it can't be an object, it has to be a person," Egil said.

"Or a creature," Nilsa added.

"Exactly, it could be a creature. That's a good thought. A person, animal, or creature that has blood," Egil said.

"True blood," Viggo added. "Whatever that means."

"Yeah, we still have to decipher that part. I'm not sure what they mean by that," Egil admitted.

"Did you find out anything about the warlock?" Ingrid asked.

"We made some progress, yes." Egil replied and told them what had happened calmly, including every detail.

"So the Blue Parrot?" Ingrid said in an accusing tone, looking at Viggo severely as soon as Egil finished telling them everything.

"Is that all you heard of everything he said?" Viggo raised his arms in disbelief.

"Did they take the poison so they wouldn't talk?" Nilsa asked, horrified.

"Yes, they seem pretty loyal to their leader and his secrets," Egil said.

"I'd say loyal to the death," said Astrid.

"Well, that doesn't help us," said Ingrid. "We still don't know where that warlock is, or Astrid's uncle."

Egil was thoughtful again and then smiled.

"Perhaps we can find out where they are…"

"I don't see how," Viggo said.

"That's because you're blind and have no brain," Nilsa could not help herself.

"What have you thought of, Egil?" Ingrid asked.

"It has to do with the rod, doesn't it? Astrid guessed.

"The rod will lead us to them," Egil stated.

About mid-afternoon Egil led the rest of the group into the Green Ogre Forest. They arrived at the pond and there found Lasgol, Eicewald, Camu, and Ona, who were practicing flying and magic.

"You're back!" Lasgol welcomed them happily as he came to greet them.

I happy we all here, Camu messaged.

"Me not so much," Viggo said, looking up at the sky and then at

Camu. "If you fall on me in one of those crazy flights of yours, I'll give you something to remember me by," he threatened Camu.

Ona chirped happily.

I fly much better, Camu messaged.

"Sure, yeah, and I'm an enchanted prince."

"I think I'm going to kiss you and see whether you turn into a frog," Nilsa said seriously.

"Don't even think about it! Those are meaningless fables! And you'll poison me!"

"It's you who'll get poisoned one day, from biting your own tongue," Nilsa snapped back.

"Everyone all right?" Eicewald asked with a smile.

"Looks that way," Ingrid replied.

"Everyone's fine," Astrid confirmed after giving Lasgol a long kiss they both enjoyed intensely.

"I'm sorry to have to leave you, but I must go back to the castle," Eicewald said. "I've already been away too long today with our magic lessons."

"Before you leave, I'd like to ask you about something," Egil asked him.

"Go ahead. You can count on me to help you with anything I can."

Egil took out the rod from the satchel he kept it in. The moment he took it out it started vibrating hard. Egil looked at it, surprised. He had not been expecting that.

He was not the only one. All the Panthers were staring at the Quill, puzzled.

"What's that rod? Why is it vibrating?" Eicewald asked, surprised.

Egil noticed that the Quill of the True Blood was vibrating and at the same time it began to whistle shrilly. The vibration increased, as did the whistle, and an unknown force made Egil point the rod toward one of them: Camu.

"I wasn't expecting it to do that," said Egil. "I wanted to ask you, Eicewald, whether you could tell me if it's enchanted or charmed."

I can tell. It has Drakonian Magic, Camu messaged to them.

They all turned to look at him.

"How do you know, Camu?" Astrid asked him.

I feel the magic.

"I believe that answers your question, Egil," Eicewald said as he looked at the object with great interest. "What's it for? Why is it vibrating and whistling?"

"We believe it's a seeker," Egil said. "It vibrates in the vicinity of certain objects or people—or in this case, creatures."

"Interesting," said Eicewald as he closed his eyes and passed his hand over the rod, which continued vibrating and pointing in Camu's direction. The Mage was intoning words of power. They all waited for the Mage to finish his analysis.

"What do you think?" Egil asked when the Mage stopped his incantation and opened his eyes.

"Yes, it's definitely enchanted. As Camu says, the magic is most likely Drakonian because it's alien to me, distant. It would take me a long time of study and research to find out the use of this rod."

"That's not necessary," Egil told him.

"Besides, we've already taken up too much of your time as it is," Lasgol said, who did not want to give too many explanations to Eicewald about the rod and the sects they were involved with.

"In any case, I would like to study this strange object further. It's really interesting," Eicewald added interestedly.

"I think Camu can give us information, after all he seems to be able to sense the magic of the spike," Egil said. Eicewald, I'll bring you the rod when we've seen what Camu can learn from it so you can analyze and study it as you wish.

"You promise to bring the item to me when you're done?" Eicewald hesitated.

"We promise," said Egil confidently.

"Well, great then. If you need me you know where to find me," Eicewald said, smiling, and he left after saying goodbye to all.

Egil put the Quill back in his satchel and the vibration and whistling stopped.

"Thank goodness," Viggo said. "It was giving me a headache."

They waited until the Mage had left the forest and then Egil started explaining what had happened to Lasgol and Camu.

"I see you've been busy…" Lasgol said when he finished.

"Exactly. Not like others, who've been playing with Magi and hiding in the forest," Viggo said.

Not play, learn, Camu messaged proudly.

"It sounds like we haven't been able to find either Viggen Norling or Drugan Volskerian," Lasgol said regretfully.

"Right, but Egil has an idea," Astrid announced, winking at Egil.

"That's always hopeful," Lasgol smiled.

"It's only a theory that might help us find them," Egil said.

"Go ahead, explain your plan, we're listening," Lasgol said, interested. He, more than anyone else, wanted to find the two individuals who had attacked and robbed him. He wanted to understand why. He also wanted to know why they were spreading the message of the end of the era of men and a new order to the people of Tremia. He wanted to make sure no catastrophe was going to happen.

"I believe we can use this rod to find Drugan Volskerian or Viggen Norling. I'm not sure who to look for first, but I'm convinced that once we've found one, the other won't stay away for long," Egil explained.

"Explain your plan a little more please," Ingrid said, frowning.

"If I'm not mistaken, and everything indicates I'm not, it's a seeker. What I suggest is that we use it to seek Drugan Volskerian the same way Viggen Norling's men used it to find Lasgol," he said.

"Whoever attacked me was seeking the Dragon Orb…" Lasgol said, trying to understand what Egil wanted to get at.

"And those who finally took it were too," Ingrid said.

"We can assume they were both seeking the Orb and that's why they attacked you," said Egil. "Viggen's men found you with this rod," Egil said, showing it to him. "This seeker will take us to the Orb."

"Which the Warlock Drugan has, right?" Nilsa guessed.

"That's what we think. But we can't be sure because Viggen will likely try to take it away from him, if he hasn't already," Egil speculated.

"In any case, if the rod leads us to the Orb, it will also lead us to one of them," said Ingrid.

"That's the idea," Egil nodded.

"I like the plan," said Viggo. "Now, how do we do it?"

"We need the rod to find the Orb," Egil said, and lifted the satchel where he kept it safe.

"Then we have to get closer to the Orb so the rod vibrates and tells us where it is?" Ingrid asked.

"But it could be anywhere in Norghana…" said Nilsa.

"Or even outside Norghana…" Astrid said pessimistically.

"I don't think so," said Egil. "The Visionaries who attacked us were in the capital and had received orders from Drugan, the man I was looking for. This makes me think he's not far, since he received the information that I was looking for him insistently and with means. He might even be hiding somewhere in the capital, or nearby. It's only a guess, but I think it makes sense."

"He might be, yes, but how are we going to find him?" Ingrid asked. "Are we going to comb the city with the rod to see if it vibrates?"

"And if it doesn't vibrate, move to another city? Travel through all of Norghana?" Nilsa asked blankly.

"That's what Viggen's men were doing, and they found me," Lasgol said.

"Yeah, but you weren't hiding like the warlock. You were taking a stroll, minding your own business in the middle of the city," Viggo told him.

"Yes, that's true, and that's why they found me," Lasgol realized.

"What's your idea, Egil?" Astrid asked.

"I think we can get the Quill to indicate the way if we increase its radius power. Right now it won't indicate anything because it doesn't pick up the Orb. That's because the Orb is far away. But the Quill is constantly listening, so to speak. It doesn't hear the Orb because its range doesn't reach that far. My idea is to amplify the range of its hearing."

"I like how you've explained it," said Viggo, "but how are we going to amplify that hearing range?"

Lasgol understood how.

"Using magic, power," he said. "It's like my skills—the more power they have, the farther they reach."

"Fine, but the Quill, or rod, doesn't seem to have more power than what it has right now," Nilsa said.

"Then we'll provide the extra power," Egil said.

"How?" Ingrid asked.

I give power, Camu messaged.

They all turned toward him.

"That's the idea," Egil beamed. "The Quill and Camu use the same type of power, Drakonian Magic. If Camu imbues the Quill with his power, it'll amplify its reach. It can work, in theory."

"Yeah, in theory I'd be a magnanimous king…" said Viggo. "The truth is something else entirely."

"I didn't say it *will* work, I said it might work."

I make work, Camu said.

"Camu, you might not be able to…" Lasgol said.

I do. I more than dragon.

"Let's try at least," said Lasgol. "We won't lose anything by trying."

"Go ahead," Astrid encouraged Camu.

"I'll hold the Quill," Lasgol offered. "After all, I have magic and I might be able to help."

Egil nodded and handed Lasgol the satchel, and he took out the rod. As soon as he did so it started to vibrate and whistle. Lasgol let the Quill aim at Camu.

"Very well, Camu. Let's see what you can do," Lasgol said.

Ona moaned and stepped back.

I try, he messaged and shut his eyes. Suddenly a powerful silver flash issued from Camu's body.

"He's using his power," Lasgol explained.

"Well, nothing new seems to be happening, the rod's still just as shrill," Viggo commented.

"Don't be a killjoy, wait a little," Ingrid told him.

Camu gave a second silver flash. This was followed by a pulse from the Quill. It stopped vibrating and whistling. It was no longer aiming at Camu but straightened itself vertically.

"Camu seems to have made it stop pointing at him," said Lasgol.

"Fascinating," Egil commented.

"Let's see whether he can make any further progress," Astrid said cheerfully.

All of a sudden, a beam of pure energy issued from Camu's body and went to the Quill. Lasgol held it tight, half-afraid Camu's energy would make it fly out of his hands when it hit the rod. But nothing of the sort happened. The Quill seemed to be absorbing the energy Camu was sending it. It was remarkable, because the amount of energy Camu was sending was great and yet it seemed as though the rod could easily absorb it.

They all watched what was unfolding with great interest and also concern about what might happen.

Camu flashed again and directed more energy toward the Quill, which remained static, without giving any sign that anything might be affecting it.

"It seems to me like this isn't working…" Viggo said.

At that moment, as soon as he said it, as if wanting to gainsay the Assassin, a powerful, bright silver pulse issued from the rod at lightning speed. The pulse spread in a circle with its center in the rod and left them at amazing speed, sweeping everything that surrounded them as it moved away, making the circle wider and wider.

"You were saying, numbskull?" Ingrid told Viggo.

Camu stopped the flow of energy and opened his eyes.

Done, he messaged.

"Great work, Camu," Lasgol congratulated him as he continued holding the Quill with both hands.

"Watch how it moves away," said Egil.

"And it's not stopping, it's spreading and moving further away," Nilsa said.

"Do you think that if it finds the Orb it will send some sort of signal?" Lasgol asked Egil.

"That's what I'm hoping for, although I can't be sure," Egil replied.

They waited a moment and the wave was lost in the distance. It vanished in the distant horizon.

"Let's wait," said Egil.

The others nodded, waiting to see if anything happened.

Nothing did. They waited a little longer, but nothing happened.

"I don't think it worked," Nilsa said.

"Good try, know-it-all, but you failed this time," Viggo said.

At that moment the Quill started to vibrate and whistle again. Surprised, Lasgol held it tight. The rod made him turn left and went on vibrating and whistling.

"I think it's telling us where the orb is—it must have found it," Egil said, smiling.

"Where is it?" Ingrid asked.

Egil looked at Lasgol.

"From the direction Lasgol's indicating, it's west of here."

"Far west? or near west?" said Viggo.

"That, my dear Assassin, is what we must find out," Egil said with a grin.

"Let's find out," said Astrid.

Okay, Camu said.

"So let's get a move on," Ingrid ordered, pointing west. "We'll find the Orb and whoever has it in his power."

Chapter 42

The group marched slowly to the west, following the indications of the Quill of the True Blood. They had soon found out it was the far west and not the near west. They had left the capital behind after using the Quill again, and it had indicated a southwest direction. Thinking it could be far and that likely there would be some fighting, they had taken horses, supplies, and weapons.

They were now entering a great plain that opened to the southwest.

"Are you sure we're on the right course? If I remember correctly, there are no cities in this area," said Nilsa.

"The weirdo should know that, because we're on the western side of the kingdom," Viggo said.

"You're not wrong, Nilsa, there's no city here," Lasgol confirmed.

"We're taking for granted that the warlock is hiding in a city, but it doesn't have to be that way," Astrid said.

"He could be hiding anywhere," Egil said, "although I believe his hiding place won't be too far from the capital, since he seems to be aware of whatever happens and probably visits the capital every now and then."

"How do you know that?" Viggo asked.

"I don't, it's a guess," he replied. "The Visionaries need orders to follow and they were in the capital. Someone had to give them orders."

They watched the great plain, and at the far end against the horizon they glimpsed some ruins.

"What's that place?" Ingrid asked as she put her hand to her eyes to try and see better.

"Back in the day it was a city, but now there are only ruins," Lasgol said. "I don't remember what battle it was destroyed in."

"It's the old city of Osluren," Egil said. "It was razed by the Rogdonian troops in the last great battle between the Rogdonians and Norghanians."

"The Rogdonians came this far west?" Nilsa asked, surprised.

"They did, on their majestic coursers, the best in the continent,"

Egil explained. "Their mounted lancers destroyed our infantry after crossing the river Utla. The troops regrouped and took shelter in the city. There was a great battle and the Rogdonians set fire to the whole city to get the infantry out of the houses. They didn't want to fight between houses because their superiority was in open terrain, where they could use their horses."

"They were no fools," said Viggo.

"The fire razed the city and our troops took shelter in Norghania. Shortly after, a peace agreement was reached and the lancers returned to their kingdom," Egil finished the history lesson.

"And now only ruins remain of Osluren," Lasgol said.

"It was never rebuilt?" Nilsa asked.

"It was so destroyed they didn't think it was worth it," said Egil.

"Well, that's where we're going," Astrid said.

"At this pace we'll cross the river Utla and reach Rogdon, you'll see," said Viggo.

They went on, crossing the great green plain and arrived at the ruined city. They stopped and looked at what had been a great city and was now a pile of ruins scattered everywhere. Grass covered the rocks and the half-crumbled walls of the old buildings. They could make out the houses, even the bigger dwellings of nobles, and a fortress, of which remained part of one wall. Another part of the protecting wall was still visible.

"Let's cross the ruins," said Egil.

Ingrid nodded, and they entered the remains of the destroyed buildings.

"Being here gives me the willies," said Nilsa as she looked at the ruins covered with grass, moss, and ivy.

"I find it quiet and serene," Viggo said as if the place emanated peace.

They arrived at what was approximately the center of the city, in front of which was the fortress that had protected it back in the day.

"Lasgol, let's see what the Quill says," Egil asked him.

"Right. Camu, get ready to send energy into the Quill," Lasgol said.

Okay.

Ona moaned twice and moved back a little. The others watched in silence from their saddles.

Lasgol took the rod out of the satchel and at once, without Camu needing to do anything, it began to vibrate.

"We seem to have arrived," Egil said, beaming.

"Here? But there's not a soul!" Viggo said, looking everywhere. "Here there's only rocks and more rocks, covered with grass and plants!"

The Quill began to whistle shrilly while it vibrated.

"There's no doubt, it indicates here," Lasgol said, pointing at the old fortress.

"And it indicates right here because Camu hasn't had to intervene," Astrid said.

"It looks that way," Ingrid said, readying her bow. Nilsa quickly followed suit.

"Everyone, be alert," Astrid said as she poured poison on her knives from a container.

"Lasgol, put away the Quill. It's making too much noise," Ingrid said.

Lasgol put the Quill back inside the satchel. The vibration and noise stopped.

"The workings of this Quill are curious…" Lasgol commented.

"It's brought us here, and accurately I believe," said Egil.

"Camu, do you pick up anything?" Lasgol asked him.

Not pick up.

"But he should, shouldn't he?" Viggo said.

"Not necessarily," Egil replied, "it depends on whether the Dragon Orb wants to communicate or not."

No communication.

"Then it might not be here," said Nilsa.

"There's something here, or else the Quill wouldn't have brought us here," said Astrid.

"I bet it's Camu's long-lost brother!" said Viggo.

"Don't talk nonsense, numbskull!" Ingrid scolded him.

"Whatever it is, let's find it," Lasgol said, dismounting. He stroked Trotter and sent him a mental message: *Retreat a little, to the outskirts of the ruins.* The good pony obeyed at once and went away. *If anyone arrives, come and get me,* Lasgol transmitted to him, in case they were surprised from behind.

"The best thing will be to search the area carefully," said Ingrid. "Let's form groups of two and search the ruins and surroundings."

They all dismounted quickly and reached for their weapons.

"Viggo, with me," Ingrid told him.

"Always," he smiled at her.

"Focus…" she said and pointed to the east of the fortress.

Astrid looked at Lasgol, who signaled that he was staying with Camu. She nodded and made a sign to Nilsa for them to go together. The redhead joined her at once. They headed to the west of the ruined fortress.

"It appears I'm staying with you," Egil said to Lasgol.

"And with these two," Lasgol said, indicating Ona and Camu.

"I couldn't ask for better company."

"We'll go straight to the center of the fortress," Lasgol said. "I have the feeling that's where the key to this matter is."

"A straight approach is often the winner," Egil said.

We ready, Camu messaged.

Ona growled once.

"Perfect, then let's follow a straight line like the Quill marked," Lasgol said, and they started moving toward the interior of what remained of the great fortress.

Camu made himself invisible and Ona stalked forward with all her feline instincts alert. Lasgol and Egil, with composite bows in hand, advanced cautiously. There were only rocks and moss around them, but they were wary. If the Quill had indicated the fortress it meant something was there, even if they could not see it yet. Egil and Lasgol looked everywhere as they advanced. Visibility was not good because the crumbled walls and granite blocks everywhere prevented them from seeing two steps ahead.

The ground was covered with grass, plants, and moss, so that did not help much either. So Lasgol decided to use his tracking skills since the fact that no one was around did not mean there had not been someone before. He bent down and inspected the whole central part of the old fortress for any trails. Egil and Camu watched him a few paces behind. Ona was with Lasgol and tracked with him. They looked to see whether they could see their comrades, but the half-fallen walls prevented it.

Lasgol raised a hand. He had found something. Egil came over stealthily.

"A trail, recent," Lasgol whispered, pointing at the ground.

"I can't see it…" Egil had to admit.

"It's here, believe me. Let's follow it."

Egil nodded.

Lasgol followed the trail at a crouch, reading the terrain. They passed a broken wall that bordered what must be the remains of one of the huge fortress towers which must have fallen to the ground during the attack. They continued carefully until they arrived at what must have been the main square of the fortress. Lasgol stopped a moment to check for more tracks. He raised his gaze and saw another trail coming from the east.

"I see two… no, three trails converging here," he whispered to Egil.

"Interesting. Where do they lead?"

"To those large blocks ahead."

Egil nodded. "Let's investigate," he told his friend.

Lasgol led them through the ruins to the two large blocks of granite that seemed to have fallen one on top of the other. They approached carefully, and when they went in between the two blocks they found a large wooden trapdoor on the ground hidden since it was surrounded by stone.

"Surprise, surprise…" murmured Egil.

"We've found the entrance," Lasgol confirmed, noting the footprints ended there.

Lasgol put his ear to the wooden trapdoor and listened for a moment.

"D'you hear anything?" Egil asked him.

"Nope. We'll have to open it and see what's below."

"Let's go," said Egil.

Lasgol opened the trapdoor carefully to not make any noise. Ona put her head in and sniffed. She chirped twice. She sensed no danger. Lasgol motioned his friends to follow and then went down warily. Ona followed at once, then Egil, and finally Camu, who fit in the trapdoor by a hair's breadth.

They went down the secret trapdoor and found themselves in the cellar of the old fortress. To their surprise, it was pretty well kept in comparison with the ruins above ground. The fire had not damaged the foundations enough, at least here, and this part of the fortress was still holding up. Egil checked the wall to his right and signaled to Lasgol that it was solid.

They followed a stone stairway and found themselves in a wide hall, dark and grim. Lasgol bent down again and inspected the floor in the dark. He had to use all his knowledge as Tireless Tracker in order to make out the trail in the shadows. He indicated to Egil that the trail turned left and they followed it. They arrived at another stairway and went further down into a second level under the fortress.

The place seemed to be enormous, and if Lasgol did not follow the trail correctly it was likely they would get lost. On the other hand Lasgol did not want to use any light in case they were found out, so following the trail became complicated. They turned three times to the left and then saw light at the end of the corridor they were in. Lasgol made a sign to go carefully.

They arrived at the source of the light and stopped. Lasgol put his head around the corner in a swift move to see into the hall. What he saw puzzled him greatly. There were a dozen guards who, by the swords in their hands, Lasgol identified as Visionaries. He thought he had seen three men gagged and tied with ropes to wooden chairs. A dragon's head floating before them was threatening them.

Lasgol hid and shook his head. He had to have seen it wrong. It had to have been some strange optical effect. He looked again to see what was really going on. To his surprise, he saw the same thing again.

"You look," he whispered to Egil.

Egil nodded and put his head out quickly to take a look.

"There's something weird going on in there," he told Lasgol.

"Did you see the dragon head?"

"Yeah, and it seemed to be doing something to those prisoners."

"Something very bad," Lasgol said.

He looked in again and now made out a barely visible figure holding the dragon head. That made more sense, since at first he had thought the head was levitating on its own. The figure must be using some camouflage spell or of semi-invisibility, or perhaps it was the dragon's head magic, because he was barely discernible.

Egil also poked his head out and they both watched. All the Visionaries were absorbed in what was happening and did not seem like they would discover the Rangers.

"Open your mind! The past doesn't exist, only tomorrow! The past life has no value, it doesn't deserve to be remembered!" the dragon head said suddenly, and a silver light came out of the head and bathed the prisoner in the middle. The poor wretch was staring at the source of the light with eyes like saucers. It was undoubtedly an Object of Power, as they had suspected. The voice of the message came out distorted, making it monstrous, as if the dragon head were real and that was its true voice.

"That's how they do it..." Egil whispered.

"This is the message of the supreme lords!" the voice continued, seeming to come from the dragon's head. "The message is unique and clear! The deserts of the south and the mountains of the north, everything will burn with true fire that will consume the impure! Only those who embrace the new order will be saved!"

The silver light bathed the prisoner, who seemed incapable of closing his eyes or looking anywhere else but the dragon head.

"It's not the dragon that's speaking. It's the figure holding it. They're casting some kind of spell to insert the message in the minds of those poor men," Lasgol guessed.

Egil agreed.

The figure holding the head went on.

"The end of days is near! The great awakening is happening! The new order, a new era, is approaching, and the time of men is coming to an end!"

Lasgol and Egil withdrew and stopped watching to avoid being discovered. They already knew what the Visionaries were doing.

"We must stop this and free those wretches," said Lasgol.

"Yes, they're erasing their memories and corrupting their minds."

"I've counted a dozen Visionaries, and I think the one speaking must be some kind of warlock or something."

"I wonder if he'll have the Dragon Orb," Egil said.

Lasgol looked behind him, at Camu.

"Do you feel it?"

I not feel orb, Camu messaged to them.

"Hmmmm... the Quill pointed in this direction... but we can't take it out now, because if it starts vibrating they'll find us out," said Lasgol.

"We can't lose the surprise factor," Egil said in a warning tone.

"We have to bring the others, it'll be risky if we try it on our own."

Ona, go get the others and bring them here.

The Snow Panther moaned and turned her head to indicate Camu as if to say, "I'll help here."

Camu stays. Ona, go bring the others here.

The Panther moaned again but obeyed and left stealthily.

The translucent warlock continued with the process of erasing the person's memory and installing the supreme message into the next prisoner.

Lasgol called on his *Cat-like Reflexes* and *Improved Agility* skills, as well as *Hawk's Eye* and *Owl Hearing*. Then he called on *Animal Presence* to make sure he had all the Visionaries located.

"There are twelve Visionaries and the warlock," Lasgol said. "I've made sure."

"I'm thinking of something while we wait for reinforcements," Egil said and whispered the plan to Lasgol and Camu.

"I think it's a good plan," Lasgol nodded.

I camouflage, Camu messaged and became invisible.

The warlock was already working on the third prisoner. The silver light the dragon head emitted bathed him from head to toe. The prisoner looked like he was in a trance with his eyes wide open. The warlock began to erase his memory, using the object and his own magic.

All of a sudden the light emanating from the dragon head went out. The prisoner closed his eyes and the warlock became entirely visible.

"What's going on?" he asked when he realized the spells were failing. He looked at himself and then at the dragon head which, it was now clear, he was holding in his hands. The Object of Power was silver and the portrayal of the dragon head was impressively realistic.

The Visionaries began to come over to the warlock they could now see well. It was not Drugan Volskerian or the one accompanying him when they robbed Lasgol and took the Orb, but he was also a warlock. That meant there was a third one. He was athletically built and tall. His long, dark hair fell in tight curls over his shoulders. Seeing that something odd was going on with the dragon head, he left it on a pedestal to his right and looked around with narrowed dark eyes, trying to find someone or something.

"My lord?" one of the Visionaries said.

"Something's going on. Go to the entrance to look and come back to report immediately," he said in an urgent, angry tone.

The man nodded and sent two other Visionaries to investigate.

The two men arrived where Lasgol and Egil ought to be and went past. The other Visionaries were restless.

"No one must interrupt our sacred duty," the warlock told them.

"No one will," the Visionary, who must be the highest in rank, said.

The warlock looked at the dragon head, scratching his chin. He could not understand what was happening. He picked it up with both hands and tried to activate it again. He could not. He was absolutely flabbergasted.

"Where are those watchmen I sent? Why aren't they back yet?" he asked as he put the dragon head back on the pedestal and unsheathed a long sword, Rogdonian-looking but with a dragon pommel.

"I don't know, my lord. You three, go and see what's happening, quick!"

The three men left at a run. They vanished through the entrance to the hall and suddenly they heard blows and muffled screams.

"Someone's coming in! Finish whoever it is!" the warlock shouted.

Four other Visionaries raced out to face the attack. Ingrid and Viggo appeared at the entrance. The four Visionaries running toward them raised their swords to finish them.

Ingrid released twice before the Visionaries could reach them. The two men fell down with arrows in their hearts. Viggo gave a tremendous leap and with his legs, hit the Visionaries attacking him. They flew backward, and Viggo lunged at them and killed them before they could get back to their feet.

"Get them!" the warlock yelled.

The Visionaries attacked Ingrid and Viggo as they were already preparing to face them.

"You're going to pay with your lives, as my name is Vingar Ronanef!"

"I don't think so," Viggo told him in a condescending tone.

Suddenly, out of nowhere Egil and Lasgol appeared beside the warlock. When he saw them he opened his eyes wide in surprise; he tried to attack with his sword but Lasgol did not give him time, he delivered two right punches while holding his knife and axe and knocked him down senseless.

Egil released at the one organizing the Visionaries' attack and got him in the abdomen. He fell to the floor, writhing in pain.

Ingrid released, slid to one side, and released again, sliding to the other as if she were skating on the rock floor. Viggo blocked with his knives, dodged a sword attack, blocked again, and with his other knife killed two of the Visionaries in the blink of an eye.

Egil nocked another arrow and aimed. There was no one left to shoot at.

"This is much better," Viggo said, stretching his arms. "A bit of action is good for body and spirit."

"Where are Astrid and Nilsa?" Lasgol asked.

"Ona went to fetch them, I think," Ingrid replied. "She led us here and then left."

"Yeah, she must have done that." Lasgol nodded; he knew the good panther would obey his orders.

Vingar Ronanef, half-stunned on the floor, tried to get up. Viggo ran to put his knife to his neck.

"Don't even think about it, little warlock."

All of a sudden, there was a noise of rocks grinding against rocks at the bottom of the hall. They all turned.

One wall had slid to one side.

Seven figures appeared in the shadows, coming into the hall.

"What do you think you're doing?" Drugan Volskerian demanded.

Chapter 43

On the surface, Ona reached Astrid and Nilsa, who were at the back of the crumbled fortress inspecting some recent footprints.

"Ona, beautiful, what's up?" Astrid asked the panther as she bent down to welcome her.

Ona moaned and pointed her head toward the trapdoor in the center of the fortress ruins.

"You want to tell us something?" Nilsa asked Ona as she also got down beside the panther.

Ona moaned again and turned her head toward the center of the ruins, then back at the two Rangers.

"I think she wants us to go to where she's pointing," Astrid said.

"That means they've found something," Nilsa guessed.

Ona growled once.

"That's a clear yes," Astrid said.

"Well, let's hurry then."

They stood and saw a dozen men coming out of the last ruins. The men saw them and ran toward them.

"Watch out. Enemies!" Astrid warned and lunged behind a half-crumbled wall. Nilsa did the same, and Ona went after them with a growl.

"How many did you count?" Nilsa asked Astrid.

"At least a dozen."

"Do you think they'll come after us?" Nilsa asked as she nocked an arrow.

"I'm sure of it," Astrid replied.

"So sure?"

"Yes, absolutely sure," Astrid said as she poured poison on her knives. "In fact, they've followed us."

"How do you know that?" Nilsa took a peep over the wall that hid them.

"You'll soon understand."

"Those robes with the two circles symbols... those are Viggen Norling's men, your uncle's..."

"Exactly," Astrid said with resignation.

"Why are they coming after us?" Nilsa asked.

"I think they're really here for the Orb. I'm afraid we've found it for them."

"Oh great…" Nilsa said, annoyed.

"Yes, Egil told us we were going to be playing cat and mouse, and he wasn't wrong. I went to get information out of my beloved uncle, and it turns out he used me to get here."

"We can't let him get his hands on the Orb again,"

"No, we won't let him. We'll deal with his men. They won't get to the Orb," Astrid said firmly.

"Well, then let's get down to it," Nilsa got up like lightning, aimed at one of the attackers, calculated the trajectory between the rocks, and released. The arrow brushed a broken wall and a large rock and ended buried in the right shoulder of the attacker, who fell to the ground.

Astrid came out from behind the wall and ran to fight three of the attackers who were approaching on her right.

"You should never have followed us," she told them in a deadly tone.

Under the fortress, Lasgol watched Drugan Volskerian as he threatened them with his two short swords with dragon pommels. He was wearing a bright silver robe with a long hood, and they could only make out a sharp face and gray eyes under the hood.

"Let my warlock Vingar go at once if you want to stay alive," he ordered them with the authority of someone who would carry out his threats.

"We can also stay where we are and dice you up," Viggo replied, absolutely undaunted.

"Shall I kill him, my lord?" the man beside Drugan who was wielding a large two-handed sword asked. Lasgol recognized him at once. He was in his thirties with short brown hair and brown eyes and had been with Drugan when he was attacked. He noticed that the silver bracelets on his wrists flashed in the torchlight.

"Easy, Xoltran, I'm sure they'll reconsider and let him go."

Viggo was about to reply, but Ingrid put her hand on his shoulder so he would not say anything else.

"We're here for the Dragon Orb," Lasgol told him.

"I know why you're here," Drugan said. "I also know that you have no idea what is happening and least of all what's about to come. You do not accept the vision, and of course you will also not accept that I am the Visionary and my vision is the true one."

"Why don't you explain that vision? We'd like to understand," Lasgol asked, trying to get him to say more.

Drugan looked at Lasgol and smiled.

"Why should I? You are nothing but some heathens who do not want to accept the sacred message, who do not want to be enlightened with the true vision."

"Is the vision that message your preachers are spreading among the people?" Lasgol asked him, noticing that the leader of the Visionaries seemed to light up as he spoke of his vision.

"The people, all of Tremia, must understand the message, accept the vision."

"Why do you want them to hear the message?"

"Because they must know that the era of men is coming to an end. They must accept it and join the cause, become Visionaries. My duty is to make this happen."

"To have all the people in fear? Under control?" Egil asked as he began to understand what was happening.

"The people must be enlightened. Those who become Visionaries will be saved. You should understand," he told Lasgol, pointing his right-hand sword at him.

"Me? Why should I understand it?" Lasgol asked.

"Because you are of the blood," Drugan said. "I can feel it in your magic."

Lasgol was puzzled. This man could feel his magic? What did it all mean?

"What do I or my magic have to do with all this?" he asked, not seeing the connection.

"Your ignorance is an affront to our lord," Drugan said, shaking his head and looking offended.

"Lord? Aren't you the leader of this sect?" Ingrid asked.

"Sect? We are no sect. We are here to serve our lord, and I am nothing but his most humble servant."

"Who is your lord then?" Lasgol asked.

"His lord, as is mine, is he who has awoken and is waiting to reincarnate," a voice said at Lasgol's back.

They turned and saw Viggen Norling and his six trusted men at the entrance. They were wearing the gray robes with the two rings on their chest and were armed with swords and daggers in the Erenal style. They all carried a round silver shield with the same symbol as their robes.

"You should not have come here, Viggen, or your congregation of Defenders of the True Blood," Drugan told him, pointing his sword at him.

Lasgol realized the warlock leader of the Visionaries knew Astrid's uncle and his group. Not only that, he had mentioned their name, one the Panthers had not known until now.

"I have come to recover what you stole and which belongs to us," Viggen said without flinching. He did not seem to fear the warlock and his men.

"You're a fool if you think I'm going to return the Sleeper. Today you and all your people will lose your lives," Drugan said.

Lasgol looked at Egil, who in turn looked at Ingrid. The situation was complicated, to say the least. And a three-sided confrontation was about to take place which might end in a blood bath.

"As for you, Lasgol," Viggen went on, "it has to do with you, because you are of the true blood."

Lasgol frowned.

"I have no idea what you mean by that. What are you two insinuating?"

"That's because the message hasn't sunk in you yet. You reject it, and in so doing you doom yourselves because the time of men is ending and the new supreme gods will rule the world," Drugan told him.

"Give me back the Sleeper!" Viggen ordered Drugan as he pointed his sword at him and covered his own body with his silver shield.

"The Sleeper stays with me," Drugan said and looked back. The Dragon Orb appeared hovering beside Drugan's head.

Family, Camu messaged Lasgol.

Stay camouflaged and alert. This is going to get very ugly very quickly, he transmitted to Camu.

Lasgol barely had time to finish transmitting his message to his friend before chaos ensued.

"Kill them all!" Drugan ordered his minions.

"Recover the Sleeper and end the search!" Viggen ordered his men.

The six Visionaries accompanying Drugan launched the attack with their dragon pommel swords. At the same time, the six Defenders of the True Blood launched their attack as well. The Panthers watched how the twelve lunged into battle, ignoring them. For a moment Lasgol thought they were going to remain out of the conflict, that the followers of both leaders would kill each other without them having to intervene. That would be great.

The delusion was short-lived. Xoltran lifted his big sword, cast a spell under his breath, and attacked. Viggo saw the warlock coming at him and prepared himself to receive the attack. Ingrid, who was beside him, saw it and released at Xoltran with Punisher. The arrow went straight at the warlock's torso as Xoltran raised his sword to decapitate Viggo with one stroke. The arrow hit the torso and something odd happened. The two silver bracelets the man wore on his wrists flashed and there was some kind of roar; at the same time an explosion of energy came out of the bracelets. The arrow was diverted to one side when the roar of energy reached it.

"What on earth?" Ingrid was puzzled.

The sword slashed down to decapitate Viggo, who had to leap aside so the huge weapon would not reach him. As he leapt, the warlock Vingar who had been knocked to the floor was free, and he got to his feet with great speed. An instant later he drew a long sword with a dragon pommel.

Xoltran attacked Ingrid with a huge stroke at waist level. The blonde Archer had to leap back to get out of the weapon's range while she nocked another arrow and prepared to counterattack.

Viggo lunged at Vingar swiftly before he had time to cast a spell on him. To the Assassin's great surprise, the warlock knew how to use the long sword and defended himself with great skill. He delivered a back-handed stroke that forced Viggo to move to one side in order to avoid it. These warlocks were good with a sword, besides using magic.

In the center of the hall the Visionaries and the Defenders were fighting with all their might. They were not using magic, so assumedly they did not have the Gift, but they did know how to use a sword well. The fight soon became brutal. The Visionaries seemed to have entered a frantic state, as if they were delirious, fighting as they recited the message. The Defenders were using their shields to protect themselves from the wrathful attacks and counterattacked with their own swords.

Egil and Lasgol stepped aside to avoid being in the middle of the fray and nocked arrows to help their comrades. The problem was that Ingrid and Viggo were fighting the warlocks at the other end of the hall. The middle was taken up by the Visionaries and the Defenders, and they could not release through them.

"I'm going to use *True Shot*," Lasgol told Egil. "Cover me while it activates, it takes a moment."

Egil nodded. He had his bow ready and was aiming without a fixed target.

Drugan began to conjure while Viggen came at him fast, crossing the hall, determined to complete his search.

"You're going to die a death of purifying fire," the warlock threatened.

"Your fire can't finish a Defender of the True Blood," Viggen replied, convinced.

From Drugan's swords came a jet of fire intended to roast the leader of the Defenders. Viggen raised his silver shield and put it in front of the jet of fire, hiding behind it. Something singular happened—the fire did not touch the shield. It was headed toward it, but when it reached it, it was diverted upward, to the ceiling of the hall.

"This is a true shield. It protects me from your magic," Viggen said.

Drugan looked surprised. He had not been expecting that. He sent fire from his swords again, but the shield diverted it upward to the ceiling and it did not touch Viggen, who was shielded from the attack.

"Fool. You might be able to divert my magic, but not my steel," he said and attacked with his two swords, striking at great speed.

"We'll see." Viggen defended himself with his shield, blocking the strokes using his defense in a martial manner.

Lasgol felt *True Shot* activating and his arm flashed the usual green. The arrow left his bow and crossed the hall from end to end. It grazed the head of one of the Visionaries, the ear of a Defender, Ingrid's shoulder, and finally headed to Xoltran's torso. But the warlock's silver bracelets flashed, there was the roar of energy, and the arrow was diverted at the last instant.

"It's some kind of defensive spell," Egil guessed as he followed the arrow with his gaze.

"Let me think of what to do," Lasgol said while his eyes swept the hall.

Viggo was attacking the warlock Vingar, forcing him back. The warlock defended himself well with the sword, but all he could manage to do was defend himself. Viggo did not give him time to attack, immediately lunging at the warlock with combinations of slashes and knife thrusts. Vingar decided to flee and ran away.

"Where are you going, you coward?" Viggo asked, amazed by his escape.

But the warlock stopped and turned. He was four paces away from Viggo. He opened his mouth and a deep, beastly roar came out of him. He had not fled, he had retreated to be able to cast a spell. Viggo lunged at him. He felt something hammering his head with tremendous force. He stumbled and fell on his face, stunned.

"At last I could cast a spell," the warlock said with a smile. "I must admit it was difficult. But you know what they say—when the warlock conjures, the warrior dies," he told Viggo, grinning, and he raised his sword for the final blow.

Lasgol's arrow caught Vingar in the side and buried in deep. The warlock let his sword arm drop and reached for his side. He realized he was badly wounded and looked toward his leader, who was fighting Viggen. Holding his side, he withdrew to the back chamber they had come through.

I protect Viggo, Camu messaged, and he ran to his side, dodging the fight. Everyone was so focused on the fray and fighting for their lives that they did not notice that suddenly Viggo disappeared; he vanished from the scene as if he had been swallowed by the shadows.

Xoltran was fighting Ingrid and saw his comrade retreat badly wounded. He delivered a tremendous slash at her, but she slid to one side, avoiding it. The warlock could not manage to hit the Archer, whose movements were exceptional. Ingrid could not reach the warlock because his defensive magic diverted her arrows. Xoltran launched two more attacks with his big sword, which Ingrid dodged. Then he opened his mouth and roared loud. Ingrid felt a terrible blow of energy that threw her backward.

"I've got you," the warlock grinned.

At that instant an arrow reached his torso. The defensive magic of his bracelets activated and the arrow was diverted. The warlock turned to the Archer at the entrance of the hall. It was Nilsa, and with her were Astrid and Ona. They had just arrived from the surface.

"Let's help Ingrid!" Astrid cried.

The three attacked Warlock Xoltran, who prepared to face them.

At the far end of the hall, Viggen and Drugan were fighting to the death. The Orb had withdrawn a few paces and was hovering at the entrance of the secret chamber, as if it were watching which of the three parties would win the fight—the Visionaries, the Defenders, or the Panthers. Drugan conjured over Viggen, this time using a spell similar to those used by Vingar and Xoltran. He opened his mouth and a beastly roar attacked Viggen with a tremendous force that negatively impacted body and mind equally. Viggen placed his shield in front of his face and stood behind it. The shield protected him from the spell, which did not touch him.

"You cannot hide behind that shield forever," Drugan said as, with a feint, he was able to wound Viggen in the right leg. The leader of the Defenders was bleeding from three cuts which Drugan had given him, while Viggen had been unable to hit the warlock a single time.

"Let's all release against Warlock Xoltran," Egil proposed to Lasgol. "Let's see whether his defense is capable of diverting all our attacks."

Lasgol nodded in agreement and signaled to Ingrid and Nilsa to release against Xoltran, who was fighting Astrid and having trouble defending himself from the Assassin. Ona was crouched behind Astrid, ready to jump on the warlock.

Xoltran used his roar the moment Ona jumped at him and caught her in mid-air, she was thrown backward with tremendous force. Astrid managed to move sideways so the roar did not reach her. Immediately she launched a combined attack Xoltran could not manage to defend himself from completely with his great sword, and Astrid managed to cut him in the arm.

"Well, this is the beginning of your end," Astrid told him.

"You will not defeat me," Xoltran assured her.

"I think I will. My knives are poisoned—you'll feel the effects in a moment," she said.

Xoltran looked down at the cut. Four arrows sought his torso right at that moment. The silver bracelets flashed and three of the arrows were diverted. The fourth one hit its target, burying itself in Xoltran's right shoulder. The warlock cried out in pain. He looked at the four Archers and then at the Assassin and began to retreat. He roared twice more, diverting Nilsa's next arrow and making Astrid step back again.

"We have him," Lasgol said to Egil, and they both released again at the warlock as he retreated without turning his back on them. He got to where his leader was fighting Viggen.

"Retreat, sir?" Xoltran asked.

Drugan considered the situation and saw four arrows flying toward them. The two warlocks roared with great force in unison and the pure energy behind the roar stopped the four arrows before they reached them.

Powerful magic, watch out, Camu messaged in warning.

Lasgol thought the creature was warning them about the warlocks, that they were going to conjure again. He was wrong. At that instant, the Dragon Orb emitted a powerful silver pulse from within that spread throughout the hall. To the Panthers' surprise, the pulse went through the Visionaries, the Defenders who were still standing, and their leaders without harming them. But it did catch the Panthers by surprise. It hit Egil, Lasgol, Astrid, Nilsa, and Ona with tremendous force and they fell to the floor, stunned. It was as if some energy had burst against their bodies and minds.

"We have to protect ourselves..." Lasgol said as he tried to stand but could not.

Watch out! More magic!

A second silver pulse of energy came from the Orb, this one even more powerful. It flew through the hall and hit the Panthers with such force that it knocked them out. All except Camu and Viggo who, protected by Camu's skills which kept them invisible and cancelled the magic, were not affected. Viggo, who had managed to recover, stayed still with his knives ready to defend his friends. Only he remained standing, and he knew it.

Better not speak, not do anything. They not see, Camu messaged him.

Viggo touched Camu's right leg as a yes.

All fighting stopped immediately in the hall. Viggen and the

Defenders of the True Blood who had survived regrouped in the middle of the hall without turning their backs on their rivals. Drugan, his two warlocks, and a couple of the surviving Visionaries were in front of them.

They stared at one another uncertainly. Almost all of them were wounded and bleeding.

"Let's finish this now that there are no interferences," Drugan said, pointing his swords at Viggen.

Viggen nodded and raised his shield and sword.

Neither was going to yield.

The Orb hovered until it was between the two men.

Kneel before your lord, a powerful, deep voice came out of the Dragon Orb, a voice that left no doubt about his order.

The Visionaries and Defenders, together with their leaders, knelt at once.

"We serve our lord," Drugan said.

"We obey his plans," said Viggen.

Who is your lord? the voice asked—it was not a question but a demand.

"Dergha-Sho-Blaska is our lord," they both replied in unison.

I am Dergha-Sho-Blaska, the Immortal Dragon, he who sleeps when he should have died.

"Our lord is king among the dragons," said Drugan.

"The Dragon King whom death can't reach," said Viggen.

You will join forces and serve me. Both of you, the voice ordered so powerfully and with such truth that it was practically impossible to refuse.

Viggen and Drugan looked at one another.

"So it shall be," they both said and bowed their heads humbly.

I have awakened and I must reincarnate.

"You will, my lord," the two leaders said at once.

Take me to a body in which my spirit might revive.

"Lead us to it, our powerful lord," Drugan begged.

"Our lord will reign again," Viggen promised.

I will reign over the whole earth. Now let us depart.

The two groups rose and followed the Dragon Orb which vanished, hovering, at the far end of the hall.

Viggo exhaled. As soon as he was sure they were alone, he ran to help his friends.

Chapter 44

A few days later, the Panthers were lying on the cool grass by the peaceful pond in the Green Ogre Forest, recovering from their latest escapade. They were becoming attached to this place—it was far enough from the capital to lose themselves in it, leaving the large city behind, and at the same time not so far that they could not get back in the same day. Egil's only complaint was that the great forest was not far enough west for his taste.

It was a gorgeous day with a bright sun which was only shadowed by Camu's figure as he circled above them.

"Will you please stop covering the sun! A clear day is a rare thing here!" Viggo shouted at him.

Camu looked down.

Not shout. I good ear.

"And terrible flying skills!" Viggo snapped.

I fly spectacular, you see, Camu replied as he dived to soar again under the afternoon sky.

"Let him practice his Drakonian Flight. It's awesome, honestly," Ingrid told him. "He looks like a god up there with his silver wings."

"We've told him over and over not to fly too high so no one sees him from afar, that's why he's diving over us," Lasgol explained as he lay on his back.

"The trees are tall and the forest is deep—as long as he doesn't soar too much I don't think there'll be any trouble," Astrid said as she lay beside Lasgol with her head resting on his stomach.

"You'll see when he tries to land and runs us over. Then you won't find him so divine," Viggo warned.

Ona moaned twice and looked up to see where her brother was flying.

Nilsa put her hand to her eyes to protect them from the sun while she watched Camu's flight.

"I hope he lands on you, see if that takes some of the wind out of your sails. You're hopeless," she told Viggo.

"Me? My sails? I've no idea what you're talking about," Viggo made a surprised face.

"About your dealings with bards and troubadours and your stupid strutting around the castle."

"I see we're in a good mood today," Egil said, reaching for his satchel to take out a couple potions and his Healer's notebook. "Time for the potions," he told his friends.

"Do we really have to keep taking them? They taste horrible," Viggo protested.

"I have to agree with Viggo on that," said Nilsa. "They taste like damp soil with worms,"

Ingrid made a disgusted face.

"Better drink it and shut up," she told her comrades.

"We have to drink them for a couple more days. The Orb's attack has marked us all…" said Egil.

Ona, you too Lasgol asked her.

Ona growled once.

"You gave me a scare," said Viggo. "I thought it had killed you all."

"One more pulse and it would have," Egil assured them as he handed them the potions to drink.

"Not me. I'm indestructible," said Viggo, pummeling his chest with his fists and smiling from ear to ear.

"You too. It was Camu's protection that saved you."

I cancel magic, the creature said as he dived past them once again.

"I wonder why the Orb didn't finish us off…" said Lasgol, who had been thinking about this while his comrades were talking.

"Maybe it thought we were already dead," Nilsa guessed. "It nearly killed us. It might have thought it had."

Ingrid nodded.

"True, but it could also be that it didn't want to waste more energy, or time on us," Egil ventured.

"Why not?" Astrid asked.

"Because we're insignificant to it?" Lasgol said.

"I'm quite significant, and that Orb, spirit, or whatever that thing is will have a chance to remember me," Viggo said, making a fist.

"Maybe we are not a threat to that thing, ¿what was its strange name again?" Ingrid asked.

"Dergha-Sho-Blaska" Viggo said slowly, remembering the name and pronouncing it as he had heard it.

"Very weird name," Nilsa said.

"We can only assume we found ourselves before a powerful being or the spirit of one," said Egil. "There's no doubt about that."

"A being who wants to reincarnate and come back to life, according to what we heard," said Lasgol.

"Worse than that, he's a king among dragons, according to Drugan," Ingrid said.

"The Dragon King death can't touch, according to my uncle," Astrid stated.

"Well, if we're to believe him, we have a small gigantic problem," Viggo said gloomily.

"Do you really think we're dealing with an immortal dragon king who's going to come back to life?" Lasgol asked.

There was a long silence while they all thought about it.

Dragon king powerful. Family. I feel, Camu confirmed as he dived over them again.

Ona gave a long, pathetic moan.

"We should assume that as a possibility. In fact, the most prudent thing to do, considering what we've seen, is to believe that's exactly what we're dealing with," said Egil. "That way we'll be prepared and able to face it in case the threat becomes a reality."

"I sort of find it hard to believe it's possible..." Ingrid admitted with a dismissive wave of her hand.

"I don't. My uncle has turned out to be the leader of a secret society of defenders of that being, but he's an intelligent and educated man. If he believes in it, that's because it's very possibly true. Furthermore, this is the famous Quest he's devoted his whole life to. He already has his Sleeper, who's awakened and now wants to live again and rule over Tremia. He's about to achieve what he spent his entire life searching for without pause. I think there's a lot of truth in all this."

"On the other hand, the Visionaries with their preachers predict a new order, one born of flames and the destruction of man, where an all-powerful supreme being is going to reign. It might well be what's coming," Lasgol said meditatively.

"I'm not afraid of that immortal dragon," Viggo said, unimpressed. "If he wants to return, let him. I'll deal with it. What I do believe is that if the weirdo and the bug are involved, we're likely to have a big mess on our hands. Therefore, I bet it's true."

"What do you think, Egil?" Nilsa asked, upset.

"I've been pondering this for many days while we recuperated, and I have to say that the more I think of it, the more I believe we're about to face an unimaginable tragedy. I believe that the spirit of Dergha-Sho-Blaska is in that Orb, and that he is a powerful dragon king who, once he reincarnates, will not only destroy Norghana but half of Tremia," he admitted with a troubled look on his face.

"So to summarize, we have two groups of lunatics trying to rescue a dragon, who's supposedly immortal, so he can reign over Tremia."

"They're not lunatics…" Ingrid said.

"They're freaking loons!" Viggo replied.

"Some are visionaries and others, defenders. Both with a terrifying vision of the future," said Nilsa.

"I'm surprised they're both after the same goal and yet fought amongst themselves to reach it," Lasgol commented.

"They most likely arrived at the same conclusion following very different paths and using different methods. The dragon has been asleep, hibernating for a thousand years frozen in the ice. Now he's woken up and his followers were already on the lookout for him. I wonder how they got the clues to determine that the dragon would wake up from his eternal slumber in the ice," Lasgol said.

"I told you repeatedly that there was a blasted dragon in that block of ice and you didn't believe me," Viggo told them. "And what's happened in the end? There was a bloody dragon in the ice just like I told you! I told you so!" Viggo cried up to the sky.

Not shout so, scare birds, Camu chided from above.

Viggo threw a stone at him and missed by a long shot.

"You were somewhat right in the end…" Ingrid admitted.

"If we confirm it's a dragon," said Nilsa.

"Of course we'll confirm it," Viggo said.

"Seeing that both groups, Drugan's and Viggen's, arrived at the same conclusion by different paths…. If you think about it again, the threat becomes even more real and worrisome," said Egil.

"And besides, as a rule, sect leaders aren't usually the most cooperative and enlightening," said Astrid.

"A pity they didn't kill each other. They were close though," Astrid said.

"That's why the Orb intervened, to stop them. It must need them," Egil said.

"To find a body to reincarnate in," Astrid said.

"Irrefutable, I'm afraid," Egil replied.

"Well, if they bring him back, I insist we kill the dragon—problem solved, I don't see why we should worry so much," Viggo said.

"Except that dragons are supposed to be mythical creatures, colossal beings with immense power that can't be hurt by human weapons. Besides the fact that they breathe scorching fire," Egil explained.

"Oops. Well, if you put it that way... I guess we do have a small problem..." Viggo admitted.

Dragon very powerful. You not kill, Camu messaged as he dived again.

Viggo looked up and cursed under his breath.

"What I think we need to do is keep the dragon from reincarnating. That's our best asset," said Lasgol. "Once he does, he'll be unstoppable. We need to focus all our efforts on keeping that from happening."

"I absolutely agree with you," Egil said.

"Easy. Then we stop it and don't have to kill the dragon," Viggo simplified.

"And how do you propose we do that?" Ingrid asked Viggo,

"Oh, I'll leave that to the know-it-all. Let him think up one of his twisted plans that always turn out so well."

"Yeah, because your plans..." Nilsa said.

"They're spectacular, but since you don't like them, I'll leave it to the know-it-all," he said with a shrug.

"Thank you, I'll do everything in my power," Egil replied with a small bow and a wide smile.

"Well, let's not lose hope, not everything's bad news," Nilsa said in a sudden attempt to cheer them up.

"It isn't?" Ingrid asked, raising an eyebrow.

"No, not at all. We'll soon be celebrating a Royal Wedding!" she said and bounced up and down.

"That's right, I don't think they'll wait too long before they announce it," said Egil.

"And afterward the execution of a traitor," Astrid said in a cold tone with a lethal gleam in her eyes.

"That's what I call a good party, a wedding plus an execution—perfect!" Viggo smiled from ear to ear.

"We'd better focus on the immortal dragon problem and leave executions for a quieter time," Lasgol suggested, glaring at Astrid out of the corner of his eye. The brunette took no notice.

"I want to enjoy a Royal Wedding. It'll be spectacular and we'll have a great time," Nilsa said, clapping her hands.

"Not a bad idea, considering what we'll have to face later," Egil said.

Lasgol nodded. "Yeah, we could really do with some partying and joy!"

"As long as no one tries to murder the future queen, and we know that sort of thing is prone to happen in royal weddings..." Viggo commented.

"Don't be a killjoy," Nilsa told him.

"In the end it's you who brings us the bad luck, you scatterbrain," Ingrid chided.

"So be it, as you wish. Everything's going to be fantastic, right, Egil?" Viggo asked him with an ironic look.

"Fantastic and fascinating," Egil grinned mischievously.

"Well then, let's all go and celebrate!" Viggo cried and clapped his hands like Nilsa.

"Yay! Let's have some fun!" Nilsa joined him.

I want party too, Camu messaged as he came down to land.

Lasgol tried to let their enthusiasm and optimism infect him, but knowing what was ahead of them, he found it difficult.

At that moment Camu landed, and he did it pretty well but not quite perfect. He ran Viggo over and they both ended up in the pond headfirst.

"Brainless bug! Look where you're going!" Viggo exploded with water up to his waist.

Camu looked at him and blinked hard twice.

Viggo very soft, he messaged them.

They all laughed heartily while Viggo muttered curses and waved his arms at the sky. For a moment, they were all happy. They knew it will go fast. For that reason, they enjoyed it fully. New adventures and epic trials awaited them, but for that moment, they decided to rest and be happy.

They would save the kingdom a little later.

The adventure continues in the next book of the saga:

Note from the author:
I really hope you enjoyed my book. If you did, I would appreciate it if you could write a quick review. It helps me tremendously as it is one of the main factors readers consider when buying a book. As an Indie author I really need of your support.
Just go to Amazon end enter a review
Thank you so very much.
Pedro.

Author

Pedro Urvi

I would love to hear from you.
You can find me at:
Mail: pedrourvi@hotmail.com
Twitter: https://twitter.com/PedroUrvi
Facebook: https://www.facebook.com/PedroUrviAuthor/
My Website: http://pedrourvi.com

Join my mailing list to receive the latest news about my books:

Mailing List:
http://pedrourvi.com/mailing-list/

Thank you for reading my books!

Other Series by Pedro Urvi

THE ILENIAN ENIGMA

This series takes place several years after the Path of the Ranger Series. It has different protagonists. Lasgol joins the adventure in the second book of the series. He is a secondary character in this one, but he plays an important role, and he is alone…

THE SECRET OF THE GOLDEN GODS

This series takes place three thousand years before the Path of the Ranger Series

Different protagonists, same world, one destiny.

You can find all my books at Amazon.
Enjoy the adventure!

See you in:

PEDRO URVI

RISE OF THE INMMORTAL

PATH OF THE RANGER BOOK 15

Made in United States
Troutdale, OR
09/01/2023

12529703R00219